By

Beaufort 1849

a novel of antebellum South Carolina

by Karen Lynn Allen

Cabbages and Kings Press

San Francisco, CA

Cabbages and Kings Press
San Francisco, California
www.cabbage-king.com

Printed in the United States of America.

ISBN 978-0-9671784-1-7
Library of Congress Control Number: 2010919210

Categories:
Fiction/literature
United States—Beaufort, South Carolina—Fiction
United States History—Civil War—Secession Movement—Fiction
United States History—Antebellum plantations—Fiction
United States History—Slavery—Fiction

for Peter, Spencer, Veronica and Abigail

Note: John Calhoun, Barnwell Rhett (the "Father of Secession"), William Aiken, and Richard Fuller were all real people. Some of their writing and dialogue in this story is taken from their actual writings. The rest of the characters in this novel are fictitious, and any resemblance to persons living or dead is coincidental. The Garden of Eden story in Chapter Eight is adapted from *Charity Moore, Born in Slavery: Slave Narratives from the Federal Writers' Project, 1936-1938.*

Chapter One

Though Jasper Wainwright had once lived in Beaufort, a score of years had passed since then, years he'd mostly spent drifting from Canton to Bengal to Paris like a ghost ship borne by the currents. Despite his long absence, on this mild April day Jasper could still navigate with ease the part of town known as the Point, his route taking him along sandy streets strewn with crushed oyster shells and lined with stands of cabbage palmettos and gardens of forsythia and quince. After all as boys he and Henry had explored every inch of this district flanked on three sides by the Beaufort River. A few new houses here and there made little difference. Yet, like a clever mistress, Beaufort could still surprise him. On rounding a corner, Jasper chanced upon a tableau so striking he had to rein in his horse in order to savor it fully.

It was a pretty picture to be sure. In the middle distance, framed by an alley of oaks, a girl—a young lady, actually—strolled down a lane holding a parasol while her slave girl followed a step behind, basket in hand. Their progression was leisurely, meditative. The fair-skinned girl was clearly lost in her thoughts as her parasol spun slowly behind her head. Her dusky maid cooperated with the silence.

Jasper unexpectedly found such matter-of-fact evidence of owner and owned in his native land unsettling. Still he lingered where he was, admiring the scene before him. He told himself he should wait in any case as a courtesy to allow Mercer, his Yankee companion, to catch up.

It turned out Mercer wasn't much of a horseman, and the stallion he'd been loaned was beyond his faculty. The Bostonian must have made a wrong turn a few streets back because he was nowhere to be seen.

The girls had not yet noticed Jasper. As he watched, they passed under a canopy of live oak branches that hosted colonies of Spanish moss and Resurrection ferns. The shade was gentle. Flecks of spring light mottled the girls' arms and shoulders, while a few languid fingers of silvery-green moss draped low enough to skim the blue silk of the parasol.

As the two drew closer, he could see that the dark-skinned girl was similar in age to her mistress but shorter and stockier. Though her head was bare and her dress made from practical brown calico, a glimpse of shoe tip beyond her hem showed her to be highly valued by her masters. His gaze traveled to the young woman whose auburn curls peeped from beneath a rice straw bonnet. Her dress of gauzy silken yellow had a narrow waist and wide pagoda sleeves that had been all the rage in Paris the year before. At her throat a jabot of lace made a delicate white froth. She must be a wealthy planter's daughter, he deduced, to go out for a walk in so fine an outfit.

Beaufort still grew its girls pretty, Jasper acknowledged with a smile remembering girls from another age who had worn fashions now long outdated. Even though this land resisted change like it was a disease—neither the marvels of the telegraph nor the railroad had reached this part of South Carolina yet—in this instance he couldn't deny it was to everyone's benefit.

The young lady was bound to spot him soon and wonder at his stares. Jasper was about to direct his horse down an intersecting street when scampering in a tree branch caught his eye. A squirrel above the girls' heads was admiring the fringe on the parasol, scolding and chattering like a fishmonger in a Cantonese market. The rodent was so admiring, in fact, that it reached out a paw and caught hold of the fringe. Objecting to this larceny, the girl pulled her parasol away, though not vigorously, fearing to damage the sunshade. The short slave waved her arms and basket; still the squirrel persisted in its tug of war from the low-hanging branch.

The situation was irresistible. With a laugh Jasper urged his horse forward.

As he approached, his horse must have upped the ante beyond rodent caution because the squirrel scampered off. In the struggle, however, the parasol had become caught on the branch itself. The chestnut-haired girl in the straw bonnet stood on tiptoe, trying to disengage the fabric from the tree with her outstretched gloved fingertips.

"Allow me, Miss," Jasper said. The girl was even prettier at close distance. Perhaps it was fortunate that his stay in Beaufort would be short, he thought. He'd forgotten how potent the Lowcountry's attractions could be.

Accepting his assistance, the girl stepped back to make room for the horse. It was the work of a moment for Jasper to free the parasol from a twig and hand it to her. Both her smile and curtsy in response were charming.

"I'm much obliged. Thank you, sir."

The gentleman, for he was clearly that, had dark, waving brown hair and a generous moustache that drooped slightly at the ends. He tipped his hat and was off. Cara watched him go with interest since unknown gentlemen seldom appeared in the town of her birth. At the junction with the next street he was joined by a younger man who trotted up on a stallion that he had some trouble reining in. Catching sight of her, the younger man raised his hat well off his head and did his best to bow from the top of his fidgety horse. Though Cara declined to acknowledge the salutation, she did look on attentively as the two men disappeared from view.

"Who are those two, Minnie? I didn't think anyone in town had guests visiting this week. Have you heard anything?"

"No, Mis Cara. Jus dat Marse Henry's trabble cuzin due sumtime nex munt."

"Well, neither of them could be Uncle Henry's traveling cousin. He's ever so old." Cara narrowed her eyes. "The one who helped me with my parasol had a dissolute look to him, didn't he? Like a riverboat gambler."

"When yuh see no rivuhbo gambluh?" Minerva asked in her grumbling way.

Cara didn't answer. It was often best not to hear things from slaves that were inconvenient, and besides, even if she'd never seen a riverboat gambler, she'd certainly read about them. It was hardly her fault she had to rely on the written word. "You know, I could swear one of those horses was the roan Henry bought in Charleston in February. But how could they have company today? Mary and the boys aren't back from Silver Oaks until tomorrow."

"Ebbenso, dem two bin head down de road tuh Villuhdessie."

Cara brightened. "Let's get home. It's only just noon. If Mary's come back early and they have gentlemen guests at Villa d'Este, I expect they'll invite me and Papa to dinner." And the young woman, Beaufort's prettiest girl in a generation, who had just visited her mother's grave in St. Helena's churchyard to perform her weekly caretaking duty, picked up her pace and might have run home if it hadn't been for her stays and her desire not to leave any unpleasant markings in the underarm areas of her dress.

Still in their riding clothes, Jasper Wainwright sat with Mercer Kingsford on the bottom level of the two-story piazza that stretched the entire south-facing front of Villa d'Este. Both men gazed out over the tidal plains of the Beaufort River towards the marsh grasses and woods of Lady's Island in the distance. Mercer, a young man with sand-colored hair, a thin, prominent nose, and slightly protruding eyes ringed by pale lashes, was enjoying his first ever julep served in a silver cup that had acquired a layer of frost on the outside, courtesy of Couts's expert preparation. Jasper looked down at the glass in his hand that held water. While Adam's ale, as men jokingly called it, might have been the drink of choice in the Garden of Eden, it was not a libation Jasper had been known for when he'd called South Carolina home.

Mercer frowned earnestly. "Villa d'Este—you said that was the name of this place. Isn't that some old estate in Rome?"

A fond smile played beneath Jasper's moustache. "The story is, when Henry went to build this house, he told his wife, Mary, that it would be the Villa d'Este of Beaufort. I guess it stuck."

Mercer's frown didn't ease. "So it's some kind of joke? People don't jest like that in Massachusetts. The name of a place, it's important."

Jasper shrugged, though it did seem to him that towns such as Braintree, Sandwich, and Woonsocket might be an occasional source of levity. "Southern humor can be peculiar I suppose."

"The South seems to relish its peculiarities, institutional and otherwise," Mercer said darkly. "I don't understand. I know your sympathies are with the anti-slavery movement, but you don't seem to disapprove of this opulent and indulgent way of life that slavery makes—"

Jasper raised a hand, silencing the Yankee as Henry Birch strode out from the house onto the porch with his customary energy. Henry had a head full of black hair, bright blue eyes, and a physique trim enough he could ride twelve hours, dance a reel, and then still outrassle any one of his boys, though he admittedly was likely to lose when all three took him on at once.

"Jasper, Mr. Kingsford, back from your ride, I see. You toured the highlights of our great metropolis, I take it? Excellent. Looks like you're ahead of me with a drink, Mr. Kingsford. No, don't apologize. I'd be furious if Couts had done any less. Couts, Couts, where are you? Get me a whiskey." Henry eased down into a chair next to them. "What's that in your hand, Jasper—water?"

"Water," Jasper confirmed.

"Good God Almighty, what kind of savage customs did you acquire during your travels? Don't they drink wine in Europe anymore?"

"They drink plenty of wine," Jasper assured him and then sipped his water.

Henry's sharp eyes evaluated him before turning to his other guest. "Now, where did you say you were from, Mr. Kingsford—Framingham?"

Mercer cleared his throat. He'd only conversed with his host for five minutes when he first arrived that morning and was still intimidated by the man's obvious wealth and position, even if he disapproved of the means used to acquire them. "No, sir, Framingham. It's a town twenty miles west of Boston, though I live in Boston now."

"Ah, yes, Boston. The shining city on the hill. And that's where you met up with Jasper?"

Mercer leaned forward, his enthusiasm tempering his bashfulness. "Yes, we were both attending a lecture on Buddhism's influence on the West given by Professor Horace Flaxberg. Have you heard of Mr. Flaxberg's theories on the Four Noble Treatises?" When Henry shook his head, the earnest Yankee actually looked disappointed. "Well, afterwards I elicited from Mr. Wainwright—" Mercer gestured appreciatively to Jasper. "—who happened to be sitting next to me, the tales of his journeys through the Orient. He's seen things rare for a Westerner, most rare indeed. When he indicated that his next destination was Beaufort, I was astonished at the coincidence. You see, I'd been intending for the last year to visit your fair town in order to consult with Professor Randall who wrote the illuminating monograph on Emperor Qin Shi Huangdi in *The North American Quarterly of Oriental Study*. I'm sure you've read it. No? And that's when Mr. Wainwright kindly invited me to travel with him. Naturally I never dreamt of imposing on hospitality as gracious as your own."

As genial as he was, this was as much academic zealotry as Henry could stand without a drink in his hand. "Couts, where are you?" he called out crossly.

A black man with grizzled grey hair walked softly onto the porch. In his white-gloved hands he carried a silver tray that held a glass of whiskey and a cup of green tea. "Ders no sugah in der, Marse Jaspuh, suh. Spit Jim say dats da way yuh like it."

Jasper took the cup from the tray. "It's perfect, Couts. Thank you."

With an impassive face Couts offered the tray to his master.

"At last," Henry said testily. He took a large swallow from his glass as his servant left the porch and was instantly in a better mood. "All right, where were we? Oh yes, old Qin Shi Huangdi. Just fascinating." Henry glanced at Jasper who seemed to be repressing a smile as he enjoyed the sunlight playing on the Beaufort River bounded by its shores of undulating cordgrass. "I'm sure the good professor will be overjoyed to discuss every aspect of the old geezer with you for hours at a time. In fact, you'll be delighted to know I've invited him—Professor Randall, I mean, not Emperor Qin—to dine with us this very afternoon."

"This afternoon? But I didn't realize Mr. Wainwright had told you of my interest in Chinese history. In fact, I thought you were unaware I was accompanying him."

"You're correct, I didn't know. I thought clever Jasper, here, would be traveling alone three weeks from now. You were lucky to find us returned to Villa d'Este ahead of schedule. Of course, since the telegraph hasn't reached Beaufort yet, communication can be slow. They do say letters still work, though, if people trouble themselves to write them." He gave Jasper a sideways reproving look. "Anyway, as it turns out, Professor Randall is a kinsman of mine, my brother-in-law, in fact, though his wife died long ago. He and his daughter dine with us often."

A heron near the shore stretched out its great wings like two silken fans in a ceremonial dance. "Professor Randall," Jasper repeated thoughtfully. "I don't think I ever knew your brother-in-law had a reputation as a Chinese scholar. I take it his daughter is your little niece who was so fascinated with the Orient that I was obliged to send postal cards and remembrances from my travels. Did they amuse her when she got them? I've always wondered."

"Oh, they amused her," Henry said. "But that wasn't the reason I put in the request. You're a rotten correspondent. It was our way of keeping tabs on you, or you'd never have written at all. But as you'll soon see, our niece is not so . . . Ah, here's Mary." The gentlemen all rose as a dark-haired woman in a dress of myrtle green joined them on the porch.

"Mary, my dear, may I present Mr. Mercer Kingsford?"

Though Henry's wife of seventeen years was in her mid-thirties, her dimpled smile hadn't lost its ability to warm the hearts of gentlemen of a certain age from three counties around. Willowy in her youth, she hadn't grown stout as many women did who had born five children and buried two of them. Henry was proudly aware her figure still received its share of admiring glances, and as long as the looks remained only glances, he didn't mind.

Home only an hour, Mary had already made sure her boys were settled and would be fed soon in the back parlor. In addition she'd given nearly a score of instructions to various slaves concerning the comfort of her unexpected guests and the quickly approaching dinner, not to mention she still had to attend to her toilette and change out of her travelling clothes into a gown that she hoped Nettie was busy pressing the wrinkles out of with a hot iron at the moment. In spite of these demands, her good manners were easily equal to the challenges presented by a surprise Yankee from Boston. "Mr. Kingsford," Mary said, holding out her hand, "any friend of Jasper's is a friend of ours."

"Mrs. Birch, it's an honor," Mercer said, bowing clumsily but still touchingly over her hand.

To Jasper she went so far as to embrace him as she would a brother. "At last," she said, her eyes misting as she took his two hands in hers. "At last you've returned after so many years. I can't tell you how much this means to us."

Though Jasper's answering smile was fond, he couldn't help look at her quizzically. "You can't possibly have missed my wretched company, Mary, but in any event, I'm delighted to be here, meet your fine passel of boys, and see what you and Henry have created here in Beaufort. From the day you were married, I knew the two of you would make an unbeatable team." He gestured at the grand structure around him. "And look what you've produced. A palace on the Beaufort River befitting a woman who was always meant to be a queen. You know you don't look a day older than when I left."

Mary positively beamed at him. Henry laughed. "All right, enough gallantry, or I'll suspect you of having designs on my wife. Besides, you two gentlemen had better get busy and change out of your riding clothes. Have a bath if you'd like, just tell Couts and he'll get it going for you. Dinner's at two."

At half past one the gentlemen were assembled in the formal parlor in frock coats and silk waistcoats, their black cravats tied in elegant knots under the pointed tips of their snow-white collars. With a rustle of skirts, Mary joined them accompanied by an elderly man and a young woman. Mary's dress, a plum silk with long, full sleeves, sloped shoulders, and a scooped neckline, showed off to advantage an intricately carved coral necklace against the background of her fair skin. The young lady at her side wore lavender silk cut in a similar fashion, but this dress exposed a delicate neck that had seen only twenty years instead of thirty-five. It was an advantage lost on none of the men in the room, however handsome a woman Mary still was, and however fond of her they might be.

"Ah, our guests have arrived to make us a fashionable party," Henry said buoyantly. "Gentleman, this is, my niece, Miss Cara Randall." Cara curtsied to the men. "Cara, this is my peripatetic cousin, Jasper Wainwright, whom you've heard so much about over the years. And this is his recently acquired friend, Mercer Kingsford."

The girl's hair had been freshly arranged into a coil in the back interwoven with a ribbon rather than the ringlet curls she'd sported earlier. To be sure, Jasper recognized the pretty girl accosted by the squirrel, but as he bowed he couldn't entirely hide his surprise at her identity. Interestingly, he noted that consternation was also evident on her face. Mercer, on the other hand, showed no ambivalence in his certainty of the felicity of the moment.

"Delighted to meet you, Miss Randall," he said, pumping her hand that had only been hesitantly extended as an accommodation of un-usual Northern customs. "We saw you in the street earlier. I must say you were a vision of loveliness under those grand oaks."

"You're too kind," Cara murmured, gently extricating her fingers.

Having a Yankee fall at his niece's feet was entertaining to Henry, homage to Cara being due course with young men, but he felt the need to move the conversation along. "Professor, these two gentlemen are both so deeply interested in all things Oriental that I'm sure our table will be laden with Chinese verbiage the entire meal. We must make sure the three of you sit together so the rest of us can converse in English."

In his early sixties, Professor Randall looked older than his years. A faded, graying man with a small goatee, he gave the impression of attending to ordinary conversation with only half of his attention, as if the call of history had dibs on the rest. "Oh, I don't speak Chinese," the Professor said with a vague laugh.

"Nor do I," Mercer said with matching jocularity.

Henry knowingly looked at Jasper for what now had to be admitted.

"Badly," Jasper said. "I speak it badly. I would pain the ears of any Chinaman within earshot, I assure you. Jim's the one who really picked it up. He turned out to be quite the linguist on our travels."

"Who's Jim?" Mercer asked, brightening at the possibility of yet another Chinese expert in residence.

Mary darted a glance at her husband. The subject was a difficult one. "His servant," Henry said brightly.

Mercer's face fell in disappointment and confusion. He'd already met Jim on the trip south, and while it might be admirable for a Negro to learn Chinese, it wasn't as if he could discuss the experience with him over dinner.

The group settled into pairs under the high ceiling of the front parlor as they awaited their meal. The first five feet of the walls were wainscoted with wood that had been painted pale green. Above the wainscoting, silver and green wallpaper extended all the way to the elaborate cornice that demarcated the ceiling. The room itself was richly furnished with settees, chairs and elegant side tables, some dating from the Federal Period, though most had been acquired after the Jackson presidency. Gracing the wall at the far end of the room hung a full-length portrait of Mary painted two years before by a Dutch artist fashionable in Charleston. Jasper thought the likeness quite good, capturing both her humor and tenderness in the carefully applied layers of paint.

With the women deep in conversation, and Mercer exploring the joys of Emperor Qin Shi Huangdi with the Professor, Jasper and Henry had a chance to talk in armchairs at one end of the room.

"I can't tell you how good it is to see you, Jasper. First we thought we'd lost you with the Dengue fever, and then there was that month in a Nabob's prison over what, a gambling debt?"

As Jasper crossed one elegant leg over the other, Henry couldn't help admire the French tailoring of his trousers. "Not exactly," Jasper countered placidly. "It had to do with a borrowed elephant. And it was only three days, not a month."

Henry cocked his head. "Elephant? No, don't tell me; spin the yarn at dinner sometime, when we have a passel of guests to entertain. Anyway, even though you survived fever and prison, when I heard about the siren charms of Paris, I was certain you were gone from us forever."

Jasper smiled. "The siren songs were temporary. There was a time when I didn't expect to return to the South, but as you can see," he waved a hand, indicating the present, "I changed my mind."

"As I can see," Henry repeated. "And you brought a Yankee with you, trailing along like a lost puppy, not that I mind in the least. It's good for Northerners to see the real South in person. Maybe it'll counter the cock and bull stories those newspapers up in Beantown like to fob off as journalism. Well, Jasper, now that you've made it all the way back to Beaufort, I hope you'll honor us with a long and proper visit." Henry nodded toward the women. "So, what do you think of my little niece?"

Jasper gave him an arch look. "You told me she was a child. You had me traipsing through Chinese toy shops."

"She was a child . . . twelve years ago. She grew up."

"Oh." Jasper glanced at the women again uncomfortably. "I suppose I lost track of time." He took his pocket watch from his waistcoat and eyed it. "I brought her a doll from Paris."

"I'm sure she'll love it," Henry said with a laugh.

Cara and Mary were murmuring by the fireplace in the way women do when, for reasons of privacy, they want to be seen but not heard by their menfolk. If they had a mind to, women could plot entire revolutions, all within sight of their unsuspecting kin. "Surely he's not old enough," Cara was saying. "I thought he's been traveling for decades."

"Twelve years," Mary said. "It's not all that long."

"Over half my life," Cara insisted.

Mary smiled. "You're young. So I see he's not what you expected. What did you envision all those years you were tracking his expeditions in the atlas and plotting his ports of call?"

"I don't know, someone . . . august. A scar on his face, a limp, a lion's mane of white hair, maybe?"

"Oh dear," Mary said with a laugh. "An ancient warrior with one foot in the grave. Well, I'm afraid he's fallen off the lofty pedestal you had him on. Let's hope it's a soft landing."

Cara glanced over at the mustached man who oddly seemed both comfortable and ill at ease while Henry described his latest project for improving the drainage at Silver Oaks. That there was an unusual air about him was certain.

"Aunt Winnie said he nearly killed himself with drink," Cara noted.

Mary looked down at the rings on her left hand. "He did. After his wife and son died."

"Aunt Winnie said he nearly killed himself with drink before that, too. And that there were duels."

Mary frowned. "Aunt Winnie says a great many things she should keep to herself. Jasper was always a good man deep down, and during his travels, he brought that good man to the surface. You know Henry thinks the world of him, and when it comes to people, Henry's always right."

Cara glanced at her mother's sister a touch maliciously. "Aunt Winnie says Mr. Jasper Wainwright is a known abolitionist."

Mary pursed her lips. "Don't say such things, Cara, not even in jest."

Henry nodded at his niece by marriage. "Don't you think she's a pretty little thing?"

Jasper coughed slightly into his fist. "Lovely. You going to marry her off?"

"I'm trying. You know she's had fifteen offers of marriage? Fifteen. The young bucks of the county practically line up to throw themselves at her. She's turned them all down."

"Why?" Jasper said with amusement. "I'm told girls in Boston only decline the first half-dozen. Gets too risky after that."

"She's a stubborn cuss, that's why. Says she'll never marry. Why, she's twenty already. She'll be an old maid soon if we're not careful. It's a pity my boys are too young for her. If Billy were sixteen instead of twelve, I'd lock her up in a room and make her wait for him."

Jasper folded his hands across his waistcoat fashioned out of bright blue Chinese silk. "Women in Europe often don't marry until their late twenties."

Henry snorted. "Well, we're not Europe, are we, thank God. We'd be having revolutions and rebellions like fleas on a hog if we were. I don't know what got into those people there last year. It's not like it did them any good. Now they have a Napoleon in charge of France again, for heaven's sake. These people don't understand democracy even when it slaps them in the face. Oh, I grant you, Zachary Taylor may not be the finest product of our three-quarters of a century experiment, but at least we don't have rioting in the streets. What's that, Couts? Dinner?" And the host led his guests into the dining room that was designed to show that after five generations in South Carolina, the Birch family had finally arrived in the world.

After a leisurely meal, when the ladies left the gentlemen to their brandy in the dining room, Jasper excused himself and stepped out onto the verandah with a cup of green tea. The sun was beginning to drop in the sky, creating long shadows in the front garden. Maintained with meticulous care, the area between the front of the house and Villa d'Este's dock on the river was a paradise of flowers, blooming trees and a stretch of lawn that no doubt kept Mary's gardener and yard boy well occupied. With the benefit of the early Southern spring, a pair of camellias by the stairs were in full bloom, and out next to the front gate an orange tree scented the mild Sea Island breeze with its blossoms. In the distance, a crescent moon hung low over Lady's Island hours ahead of when any stars might join it. The idyllic panorama caused Jasper to think back to other Aprils and other moons so long ago. Through all the years and all the continents, the beauty of Beaufort had endured in his imagination. Now the reality—this halcyon blend of river, sky and graceful culture—did not let him down.

In the midst of his reverie, Cara stepped out on the porch for the air as well. "Pardon me," she said with surprise when she found she wasn't alone. "I thought the gentlemen were still in the dining room." She moved to head back inside.

"It's a fine afternoon," Jasper observed. Something caught his eye. "Look, the dolphins agree." He nodded at several gleaming bodies that arched and splashed their way through the river in front of them.

Cara glanced at the animals briefly. "They're often here at high tide," she acknowledged and turned to leave, her eyes averted.

"May I observe, Miss Randall, that you seem somewhat . . . unsure of me?" Jasper said, trying to be as kindly, even fatherly as he knew how. After all, he must be some sort of absent uncle figure to her, mustn't he? "Whatever stories you've heard," he joked, "I promise I'm less dangerous than that squirrel this morning."

She glanced away. "You'll have to excuse me, sir. You're just not . . . what I expected." With an uncomfortable curtsy, she escaped back into the house.

In spite of himself, Jasper was offended. "Not what she expected?" he said to Mary when she found him fuming on the porch a short time later. "I go to the trouble of sending her trinkets from around the world, and she's disappointed in me?"

"Those trinkets meant the world to her, Jasper," Mary assured him. "The combs, the fans, that precious little tea set. She played with them for hours on end, and the stories she created around them—why, you've never heard such tales. In her mind, you were a hero more glorious than Ivanhoe, impossible for any mortal to live up to. Don't be offended. She'll come to know and like the real you very soon."

Jasper frowned as he considered the advice. "She really liked the fans?"

Mary smiled. "She still uses them."

He shrugged. "I suppose being confronted with me when you were expecting Ivanhoe would be a cruel blow to anyone."

"She'll recover," Mary assured him.

The next morning Jim carefully scraped a razor along Jasper's neck in the upstairs bedroom at Villa d'Este. "So, what time are we leaving for Sleety Pines tomorrow?"

Jasper laughed as well as a man might laugh with a sharp piece of steel pressed against his throat. "We've been gone a dozen years, Jim. I've got to stay at least a fortnight."

"So you can drink sweet tea and talk nonsense with these pampered lords and ladies of slavery." Jim snorted as he wiped the razor on the rag he was holding. "This place hasn't changed one damn bit."

"You've no fondness for the years we spent here?" Jasper asked whimsically.

Jim glowered as he straightened up. Half a decade older than Jasper, he was taller as well, with skin as black as ebon that testified no hodgepodge mulatto blood ran in those veins. His mother had been pregnant with him when she was captured at the end of the slave trade years. She'd lived through the horrific passage only to be brought to

South Carolina, the last U.S. state to receive such cargo, and sold as chattel. The child she gave birth to had been her sole connection to the husband, children and life she left behind. Language and stories were lovingly taught; medicine, crafts and religion transmitted; hopes and dreams passed down. Though neither born nor bred on the Dark Continent, Jim had felt its reach through all the strange twists and turns of his life. A life he'd mostly spent somehow connected to Jasper Wainwright. "Please explain how nostalgia grows from blood and servitude."

Jasper considered the point. "My years in Beaufort were the best ones of my childhood. In fact, they're the only good memories I have of the entire South."

Jim tilted Jasper's jaw to access the other side of his neck. "Don't know why you need to spend time cherishing anything here. Beaufort may look pretty, but its foundation ain't tabby. It's suffering." Jasper made no effort to disagree. "With all this nostalgia," Jim said, carefully shaving around the mustache, "you ain't perhaps fixing to change your mind?"

Jasper caught Jim hard by the wrist. Jim stood still as their eyes met. "How could you possibly ask that?" Jasper said, his expression fierce.

Jim stared back a long tense moment. "I'm sorry," he said finally. "That was uncalled for."

Jasper let Jim's hand go as he eyed his former slave narrowly. "A few weeks, Jim, that's all. They've waited twelve years; they can wait a few more weeks. Sleety Pines will still be there."

Jim shook his head. "Being here again is like someone walking over my grave. It does things to me. Bad things. Forget I said anything."

Jasper wiped his face with a towel. "We've been vagabonds for over a decade. No roots, no family, hardly even any memory. Facing this was inevitable."

Jim snorted. "Fine. Face it and get out already."

Standing in front of an oval mirror hanging on the wall, Jasper pinned a collar onto his shirt, then slipped a cravat around his neck and began to tie it.

"Here," Jim said impatiently. "Let me do it. You always mess it up and then people think I can't tie no stupid knot. It's humiliating."

Jasper put his hands down and let his valet do his work.

Up at dawn as usual, Henry had already been out for his morning ride and now awaited a hearty breakfast in the dining room. For family breakfasts, they usually used the back parlor, but with guests in the house, especially a Yankee guest, the impressive dining room was pressed into service as often as possible. Henry's three boys, Billy, Hugh and little Robert, were already tucking into their shortcakes and slices of ham before they left to attend to their studies. The lads were quieter than usual this morning, all three still cowed by the arrival of their mythic and long-awaited Uncle Jasper.

"Ha," Henry said, striking his paper with delight. "Eustace Woods has struck again."

"What does he say this time, dear?" Mary inquired as she poured Jasper tea. She'd ascertained that he took one cup of black tea at breakfast. The rest of the day it was all green.

"This time it's crop rotation, and he says just like I do that you can't be putting cotton in every year just to squeeze out every dollar you can. You'll destroy the soil that way until there's nothing left. That's why you see all these crackers packing up and going west—their soil's exhausted and won't be good again for years. Every third year you've got to rotate your cotton with corn underplanted with cowpeas, and after the harvest, let the pigs graze on the leftovers and do their business. Of course, every seventh year you've got to let the field rest completely with just a cover crop, and that takes a mighty amount of discipline, let me tell you, but it has to be done. The health of the soil is everything. Now, with these rotations of crops and fallow, I might have a few less fields planted in cotton than some people, but I get double the yield of most Sea Islands planters, and it's not like I can't use the corn and cowpeas, too. Plus I get fat pigs. I must say, Mr. Woods is exceedingly sensible when it comes to the science of agronomy. I'm proud to see his letters in a Southern paper."

"Is Mr. Woods a Beaufort man?" Jasper asked.

"No one knows where he's from," Mary said. "He signs letters to the editor of *The Charleston Courier* with just his name. But Henry admires him. In fact, I think they may be twins, separated at birth."

"I take it he rarely writes about politics then, knowing your distaste for the subject, Henry."

"Only to lambast the idiots in Columbia, again exactly to my liking," Henry said, folding his paper shut.

"What I find pleasant about him is his turn of phrase," Mary said. "He uses words so eloquently, it makes me wonder if he isn't a literary man."

Henry looked skeptical. "There's too much science and industry in him for that. Why would Eustace Woods waste his time on literary matters when there's the whole Southern economy to reform?" He turned to Jasper. "We've been a backwater for industry far too long. Why send our cotton to mills in Massachusetts or Manchester to be made into cloth when we can do it right here? I'm hankering to start a mill myself, but I don't have a proper creek. I'd have to do it with steam power."

"You're not content with your agricultural paradise at Silver Oaks?" Jasper asked with a smile. "I thought mechanical pursuits were outside the realm of a gentleman."

Henry shook his head. "I'll never understand why dirt and manure are considered acceptable for a gentleman while the steam engine is not."

Mary patted his hand. "You do very well with dirt and manure, dear. And remember our last steam engine exploded. Luckily no one was killed."

"You have to experiment," Henry countered. "That's how progress happens."

The boys were ready to depart for the activities of their day. They each received a kiss from their mother and a quick pat on the back from their father before bravely setting off to decipher the mysteries of the alphabet, the victory at Yorktown, or the opening lines of *The Aeneid*, depending upon their age. After they left, Mary received a letter carried by a small black girl with braids sticking out every which way on her head. She took the paper and waved the girl away with a flick of her fingers. "Oh, lovely," she said as she read it. "Professor Randall has invited us all to supper."

"You mean Cara has invited us all to supper," Henry said. "She probably wants to show off."

"Well, let her," Mary said. "It's how she prepares for when she's really running her own household."

"She's not running it now?" Jasper asked, curious because he knew Cara's mother, Mary's sister, had died nearly two decades before.

"She likes to think so," Mary said fondly, "but Ceres does most of it, truth be told."

"Ceres?" Jasper said. "Like the goddess?"

Henry looked up from his latest copy of *Scientific American*. "Didn't I ever tell you that story? When the good Professor married Annabelle all those years ago, he got it into his head to rename the slaves after Chinese dynasties, but the house staff wouldn't have it. No Shang, Qin, or Ming for them, no sir. So the Professor compromised with Roman gods and goddesses. They've got a Neptune and a Saturn over there, as well as a Minerva and a Pomona. It's delightful."

Mary glanced at her husband. "I'm afraid not everyone shares Henry's sense of humor."

"More fool them, not to enjoy the eccentricities of life when they trot across your path," Henry said, perusing his magazine again. "I don't need to visit the Pantheon; I can have the gods serve me right here in Beaufort."

Mary frowned. "Dear, that borders on blasphemy."

"There's no one here but Jasper, and I know for a fact he's more sacrilegious than I am."

Jasper smiled. "I'll no doubt be *persona non grata* to Reverend Smith far into the afterlife, God rest his soul. I'm sure he never forgave me."

"Forgave you for what?" Mercer said, wanting to share in the good humor as he joined them at the grand table. His face was freshly shaven by Piper, the valet that Henry had generously shared that morning since Mercer had not traveled with a servant.

Neither Mary nor Jasper was inclined to acquaint Mercer with Jasper's youthful run-in with Reverend Smith, but they couldn't stop Henry. "Well, Mercer," Henry drawled, "years back, when he first came to us to drink from the scholarly fountain of Beaufort College, our Jasper was a regular hellion. Liquor and guns were all he cared about, that and every dangerous, crazy stunt he could come up with. On dares he climbed across ridgepoles, swam during storms; he even tried to trap an alligator. You've still got the scar from that one, don't you, Jasper? If my boys pulled any one of those harebrained stunts, I'd whip their behinds and wonder if they were suicidal, but in those days, Jasper had nine lives. One night, under the influence, he went out for target practice with his rifle and shot a hole right through the cross on top of St. Helena's steeple. Reverend Smith's response was decidedly unchristian."

Mercer looked at Jasper oddly. "I thought you attended Harvard."

Henry waived a hand. "That was later, after he got expelled from South Carolina College."

"Beaufort College is a preparatory school," Mary told a confused Mercer. "Our oldest son, Billy, attends there when we're in town."

"By the way," Henry said to Jasper, "we're planning on a new building for the college on that empty lot on Carteret at Duke Street. Something larger, more substantial. In fact we're raising funds for the project right now. And seeing as how I'm a trustee—"

Jasper smiled. "You're soliciting alumni to contribute? I'd be glad to."

Henry nodded in approval. "Much obliged. I knew you wouldn't let the alma mater down. We'll settle the details later. By the way, they're also looking to fix up the old Arsenal—"

"Which I will decidedly not contribute to," Jasper replied before eating his last piece of biscuit. Henry just laughed. After the target practice incident, Jasper's rifle had been confiscated and kept in the Arsenal for three long months, a punishment he'd felt to be grossly unjust at the time.

Mercer, however, wasn't prepared to let the subject go. "How old were you when you got drunk and shot the cross?" he asked Jasper.

Jasper shrugged. "Must've been thirteen."

Mercer stared, uncertain whether to be impressed or horrified.

"After that, he reformed," Henry assured him. "His father wanted to flay him alive, but instead my father persuaded him to send Spit Jim to Beaufort. Calmed Jasper right down, Spit Jim did. Magic touch. Our Jasper laid off the liquor and was nearly a model student the rest of his time in our fair burg."

"Has this become local lore?" Mercer asked in his quaint, clipped accent that reminded his Southern hosts of a barking dog. "When people in Beaufort see Mr. Wainwright, do they say, 'That's the boy who shot the cross'?"

"We'll soon see," Henry said, amused by the young man's goody two-shoes incredulity. "But I expect so. No one ever forgets anything in the South."

How very agreeable this stay in Beaufort was going to be, Jasper thought as he sipped his tea resignedly. He mentally made plans to leave this land of backwater and gossip as soon as he could gracefully do so without offending Mary. Though his mother's lineage allowed him to lay claim to a string of Sea Island ancestors as long as Henry's, he was sure Beaufort didn't reciprocate any feeling of kinship and would shed few tears over his departure.

Chapter Two

Cara looked as lovely as an illustration from *Godey's Lady's Book* as she greeted her guests in her front parlor. Her auburn ringlets and dove gray silk dress were at the height of American fashion, although admittedly that fashion was a year or two behind the European vogue.

"Father will be down shortly. He was just resting," Cara said as the three men and Mary seated themselves on settees and sofas. As required by their stays, the women's backs were straight as rulers, while the men were a degree or two more relaxed. "Mr. Wainwright, I hope you don't mind, but Ceres has asked Spit Jim to give her a lesson on how to make your green tea."

"That's very kind of her, Miss Randall, but it really isn't so different from black tea."

"Then she'll master it quickly," Cara said with a toss of her chin. "It must be very good that you've become so fond of it."

"It's palatable," Jasper acknowledged.

"It looks like boiled grass," Henry said, "and smells worse. Now that you've returned to the South, we've got to acclimate you back to whiskey. Speaking of which . . ."

"Oh, yes," Cara said with a start. "Neptune," she called. "Bring the gentlemen their drinks."

The Randall house, comfortable enough for a widowed man and his daughter, was modest compared to Villa d'Este. Like most residences in Beaufort, it faced south and had the obligatory porch stretching across both the upper and lower stories. Also similar to most Beaufort homes, its front and back doors could be opened wide to catch the breezes that the town was famous for, allowing the cooler evening air to sweep down the main hallway and out the back.

From the street visitors were welcomed by a charming if compact garden of azaleas and camellias shaded by a massive live oak so ancient it had undoubtedly witnessed the massacre of early Beaufort residents by the Yemassee Indians in the beginning of the eighteenth century. Back of the house, out of view of visitors, were the dependencies, smaller buildings that included a kitchen, laundry and quarters for the house slaves. There was also a patch for vegetables and a coop for chickens.

Inside, the front parlor was generous and graceful in its proportions. The greatest prize of the room was stationed in a place of honor near the front windows: a gleaming grand piano recently imported from London, with sheets of music on its rack attesting to its use. Adjoining the parlor, the dining room was adequate for their party, while the back parlor and Professor Randall's study, unseen by the guests on this occasion, were positively cozy in size, although well furnished with an eye to the Professor's taste for all things oriental. Upstairs, the house had three bedrooms, and of course no ballroom to speak of. Still, for Cara and her father, it was nearly perfect.

Professor Randall didn't appear until it was nearly time to eat, and then only after Cara sent Neptune to inquire after him. He seemed to be in a sleepy daze throughout the meal, preventing Mercer from delving more into Chinese minutia. Instead the conversation was general and remained so even after the men rejoined the ladies in the parlor. Conversation again touched on Eustace Woods.

"You know, it's remarkable how often the enlightened Eustace mentions the very topics on my mind," Henry said. "Sending messages over telegraph wires is remarkable enough, but some ideas must be in the very air."

"I read that letter about crop rotation in *The Charleston Courier* today, too," Mercer said enthusiastically. "It's heartening to find such forward-thinking thoughts in a Southern paper."

Henry frowned. It was one thing for him to call Mr. Woods enlightened, quite another for a Yankee. "The South is always forward-thinking. Why, I was just reading some of those new German philosophers tearing apart Yankee capitalism in—what was it called, *The Manifesto of the Communist Party* or some such nonsense. Herr Marx and Herr Engels. And you know what? They're wasting their time. We've already got the ideal society right here in Beaufort. Everyone contributes according to his ability, everyone's provided for according to his needs. No one goes hungry; no one is without work or shelter. The sick are taken care of, and so are the elderly. In short, a perfect society."

Jasper thought Mercer's eyes were going to bulge out of his head. After trying to catch the younger man's glance and failing, he cursed silently. He'd warned the Yankee on the way down what he'd find in Beaufort. Yes, Henry's misinterpretation of Communism was nothing short of demented, but really, none of this should come as a surprise. It was South Carolina, after all. What was surprising was that Henry had bothered to read the manifesto at all. As far as Jasper knew, it hadn't even been translated from the German into English.

"Sir," Mercer said earnestly. "I beg to differ. A society based on slavery can never be perfect. In addition, I believe Herr Marx in his manifesto is prescribing a society that is the antithesis of slavery, not the thesis."

Cara glanced at Mary who in turn looked beseechingly at her husband.

"Miss Randall," Jasper said a touch hurriedly, "would you give us the pleasure of playing for us?"

Cara looked relieved. "I'd be delighted." And she sat down at the stool in front of her elegant, powerful instrument. She started off with a Haydn sonata and then continued with a mazurka by Chopin, playing each with much more facility than Jasper had anticipated. Perhaps he'd become jaded after being subjected to sparsely talented young ladies in the drawing rooms of Europe, but he couldn't deny that he'd never known anyone to play that well without consistent practice for several hours a day. He was impressed.

As the last notes of the mazurka trailed off, her audience clapped appreciatively.

"Have you started learning that new waltz Maestro Pavini sent you last week?" Mary asked. "Cara takes lessons when she can from Maestro Pavini in Charleston," she informed Jasper. "They say he's world-renowned. Have you heard of him?"

"No," Jasper said good-naturedly, "but that doesn't mean his reputation isn't deserved."

"Play the new one, Cara," Henry urged. "I want to hear what the Maestro was raving about."

Cara got out the music, settled herself, and then started off the preliminary diaphanous notes. In those first measures, there was a delicate balance between harmony and disharmony, a longing, a sadness of something glimpsed that could never be attained.

She stopped abruptly. "No, it's not ready. I'm sorry, I don't know what I was thinking. I don't even have the rhythm of the first line right yet."

"You're not far off," Jasper assured her.

"How do you know?" Cara asked a little sharply. "Do you play?"

"No," Jasper answered slowly, "but I heard him play that piece last year. I'm glad you're learning it. It's one of my favorites."

"Him—you mean Chopin?" Her eyes widened. "You heard Monsieur Chopin himself perform it?" She looked as if a wisp of smoke would knock her off her seat.

"Oh dear," Henry said. "Now we'll never hear the end of it. From Cara, it'll be Chopin this, Chopin that, and then we'll have Aunt Winnie carping about the immorality of Chopin and George Sand all spring. Jasper, please don't tell me you've met Madame Sand too. The world might collapse into pieces."

"I have met her," Jasper said, trying to restrain a smile. "Her real name's Baroness Dudevant, and she's a charming woman. But she and Chopin are no longer . . . together, shall we say, so that should help quench any censure. Actually, I hear he's taken a fancy to Jenny Lind."

Cara looked shocked. "That silly little Swedish soprano? Why would a great man like him form an attachment like that?"

"Why do men do anything?" Mary said crossly. "Besides, I don't know if this subject is appropriate for Cara."

"Talk about it now and get it out of your system," Henry advised, "because starting tomorrow, all interesting conversation will be verboten. Winnie and the Senator are coming home from Columbia. Worse,

I bet Barnwell Rhett and his shenanigans won't be far behind. If only they'd all stay in Columbia permanently."

"Your uncle is a senator from South Carolina?" Mercer asked Henry, always willing to be impressed by money and status.

"He's Mary's uncle, and he was a senator," Henry told him stretching his arm lazily along the back of the sofa towards his wife. "He fell out of favor with the Governor and wasn't re-elected by the state senate, so he's in retirement for the time being. Well, we've had two days by ourselves before the dragons return. It's been pleasant. Next spring, Mary, we should come back to Beaufort even earlier and get a good dose of dragon-free time."

Mary pursed her lips. "Our guests are going to think you shockingly rude. Starting tomorrow, I do hope you'll behave."

"I will, my dear. I always do. Don't I, Cara?"

But Cara was still looking at Jasper as if she'd just been told people in France played the piano with their teeth. "You truly got to hear him play?"

"It's Cara's dream to go to France and hear Chopin," Mary told Jasper and Mercer. "Maybe when the boys are a little older we'll take her with the family on a grand tour."

Cara didn't seem to register the prospect of a Grand Tour, too busy instead enduring the keen injustice of Jasper experiencing the great master when she had not.

Mercer decided this was a good time to gain favor with his pretty hostess. Joining her at the piano, he cajoled the opportunity to be allowed to turn pages of music for her while she played a Mozart rondo. Not long afterwards he was sitting with her near the small fire in the fireplace, telling her of Boston where he had recently joined a law practice as a very junior partner. The senior partners, one of whom was his uncle, had graciously allowed him to travel south for his scholarly pursuits—his vocation, he might say—but he would soon need to return north and pursue his worldly, and soon-to-be (he hoped) remunerative, career. Still, this had been a wonderful journey for him, and he would be all the better for his adventure after meeting such clever, lively people he never dreamed existed in South Carolina.

His hostess, while only mildly affected by the flattery, began to grasp the opportunity presented to her. This was a young man who, though perhaps of little sense, had a substantial amount of information. He was worth talking to.

From a distance Jasper noticed as Cara grew quite interested in Boston, asking questions that went beyond courtesy and extended into true inquiry. With one ear, he listened to Mary converse politely with Professor Randall while Henry snoozed on the couch. With the other he overheard a Southern girl inexplicably want to know if the streets of Boston were laid out in grid formation, how many parks and public spaces were there and of what size, and was there a communal fire brigade? She followed these questions with inquiries into the religious inclinations of the people, their cultural activities, was there a public library, and how many volumes did it contain? But when she asked if there was a freed slave population and in what part of town it could be found, Henry opened an eye and inserted himself in the conversation.

"Did you know, Mr. Kingsford, that Beaufort has one of the greatest libraries in America? We are a people dedicated to culture, and our classical collection, purchased in Europe, rivals even Harvard's." (Though both Jasper and Mercer raised their eyebrows at this dubious claim, they politely didn't contradict it.) "The Beaufort Library Society," Henry went on, "has over 3000 volumes, and any resident of Beaufort can borrow them. Why, Cara, here, goes there nearly every week. I think by now she's read every blessed book in the collection."

"I'm sure she has not," Mary disagreed serenely.

"All right, we'll cross off the volumes in Greek, but to be fair no one reads those."

Cara frowned. "I often go to get books for Father—isn't that right, Papa?"

Professor Randall looked up vaguely. "Yes, dear. I'm sure you're correct."

Henry decided to turn the conversation in yet another direction. "Jasper, don't you think it's uncanny how much Cara takes after her mother?"

Glancing at the girl in the grey silk dress, Jasper remembered another young woman, in a blue dress, laughing and surrounded by beaux at an outdoor summer party. "Yes, she does resemble her," he admitted.

The Professor patted his daughter's arm. "Cara is a great comfort to me. Sometimes it's as if Annabelle is still in the room with us. Like she never left."

Mary smiled fondly at her niece. "Having my sister's memory live on through her child is one of the greatest blessings of my life."

Though Cara looked faintly embarrassed by these accolades, she was used to serving as the focal point of her relatives' nostalgia for her mother and bore the attention well enough.

"Annabelle Smullen was the great beauty of her day," Henry told Mercer. "Young bucks throughout the Lowcountry were sweet on her. Why, even Jasper here, at age fourteen, thought she was a goddess. Not that he ever got up the nerve to speak to her. He was content to worship from afar."

Shifting in his chair, Jasper gave his cousin an annoyed look. For her part, Cara looked nearly as peeved by her uncle's turn of conversation as her guest did.

"If her daughter resembles her, I can certainly see why," Mercer said enthusiastically, although it hadn't been Mercer's enthusiasm that Henry had been trying to provoke.

Jasper's eyes traveled to a cabinet that displayed various curiosities. On one shelf, next to a blue and white vase that might be Chinese, was a small, delicate tea set. This he knew with certainty had come from the other side of the world because he himself had sent it. He glanced at Cara, but she was studiously not looking in his direction.

The carriage ride home was short. After all, the Professor's house was a mere four blocks from Villa d'Este, a distance that could easily be walked if riding in the carriage wasn't so plainly required by people of the Birch's stature. Indeed, gentlemen in South Carolina would rather wait twenty minutes for a horse to be saddled than walk two stone's throws.

"Henry, I think you delighted in saying things tonight that tomorrow would make Aunt Winnie's head spin," Mary admonished her husband as the carriage rattled along, its interior faintly lit by two lanterns attached to the outside of the vehicle. She turned to Mercer and Jasper. "Aunt Winnie doesn't believe women should read anything beyond *Godey's Lady's Magazine*, and she'd give Cara undue grief if her Library Society habits were exposed. So please be kind and not repeat any of Henry's exaggerations."

"Cara has a good, strong mind," Henry said, yawning in the corner. "I helped develop it, and I'm proud of it. I refuse to pretend she's a ninny like most of the girls in this town."

"Her faculties for logic and reason are quite developed," Mercer agreed eagerly. "I was exceedingly impressed with the questions she posed about the city of Boston. I know less than half a dozen women who even think about matters such as public sewage."

"Oh, tell me she didn't," Mary said with a wince. "That girl. Public sewage, indeed."

"You want her talking about grosgrain ribbons, I suppose," Henry said with a sleepy smile. "The girl wants the gritty details of underground drainage structures, and you want her to talk frippery. Are we sure Cara's related to you and not me?"

"She's well able to talk frippery when she needs to," Mary said.

"When she has to please Winnie, you mean," Henry replied. "Poor thing. A life spent humoring Mary's aunt would be a fate worse than cholera in my book. Thank God I wasn't born a woman. Tell me, Mercer, if you were to choose, would you be born male or female?"

Though the question was obviously provoked by Henry's habitual high spirits rather than any desire for moral analysis, Mercer gave the question due consideration. "While the intellect of some women are highly developed, as evidenced by our female companions tonight—" He bowed to Mary, who graciously nodded back. "I believe that the moral and intellectual achievements of women are generally inferior to that of men, and so I must choose the male sex."

"All right, that makes two. What about you, Jasper, if you had to choose, which one would it be?"

"In my observation, being female is far more difficult than being male," Jasper said. "So since I'm lazy, I'm afraid I'd choose male."

"And you, Mary?" Henry asked. "Which would you select?"

As the carriage rolled through Villa d'Este's back gate and came to a stop in front of the stable, Mary looked displeased with their game. "You silly men. Women are the ones who make everything in the world possible, and you don't even know it."

A servant opened the carriage door. With a laugh Henry jumped out. "Fair enough, my dear. I'll agree that women are the most important sex because if it weren't for women, I wouldn't want to be in this world. So there, you and your sex win for the evening." Mary was somewhat mollified as her husband handed her down from the carriage, though she knew Henry was just being strategic. After all, he was the last man to continue an argument in the bedroom, which was where they were shortly headed.

As Henry predicted, the dragons arrived in Beaufort the next day and promptly came to Villa d'Este for dinner in order to inspect the two newcomers that Beaufort had already been spreading rumors about. Seconds after entering the room Winifred cornered her niece for details, so it was left for her husband, Senator Gideon Pickens, to pounce upon the nephew-in-law.

While John Calhoun had been the senior senator from South Carolina from time immemorial, the junior senator slot from the Palmetto state had a habit of seeing a fair amount of turnover. As Henry had related the night before, Mary's uncle was no longer in office, but the honorific title of Senator would proudly remain with him until it was eventually inscribed on a headstone in St. Helena's churchyard. The Senator's bushy eyebrows now met together on his forehead, and his double chin, framed by whiskers, became more pronounced as he tried to fathom the wisdom of letting that bloodthirsty youth, Jasper Wainwright, back within his well-mannered town's city limits. "Wasn't he an unruly renegade when he went to school here?" the Senator asked in the stentorian voice that had filled the chamber of the U.S. Senate more than amply for a little under two years.

"That was twenty-five years ago, Senator. I assure you, he rarely even carries a gun anymore," Henry joked.

"Why not?" the Senator barked. "Every Southern gentlemen should be able to shoot, ride, and dance a reel with a lady. Is there something wrong with the man?"

"Nothing at all, sir. Not a thing. Can I get you a whiskey?"

The Senator glanced at his wife who was occupied interrogating their hostess. He nodded at the wide open doors and the porch beyond. "If you're having one, it'd be unsociable not to join you. Out on the piazza, if you don't mind. Could use a breath of fresh air."

Henry smiled. "Certainly, Senator. Couts, Couts, where are you?" And the two men went out of view of their wives.

"You say he brought a Yankee with him?" Winifred said in a voice not conspiratorial or hushed in the least. Both tall and on the stout side, she had iron gray hair and a force of will to match. In her youth she'd been known to be a fashion plate with a taste, even a flamboyancy for color. But the last two decades, ever since her niece's death, she'd dressed entirely in black.

Mary looked around her, glad to see her houseguests were still upstairs and, she hoped, out of earshot. "The Yankee is really very pleasant. Perfectly well behaved. His name is Mercer, by the way. Mercer Kingsford. He's quite complimentary of South Carolina, and I desire it to stay that way."

Aunt Winnie pursed her lips disapprovingly. Many women in Beaufort marveled how Winifred, with such severe facial expressions, managed to achieve so few wrinkles in her complexion. "So demon-boy Jasper Wainwright has returned to us. I hope you're keeping him away from Cara."

Mary was genuinely surprised. "Why on earth would we do that? He's Henry's cousin. Why, he and Cara are almost related."

"They certainly are not, and it wouldn't matter if they were. That man is no good. From the second he stepped foot in this town, I didn't like him, his drinking and his duels. And then he sent that poor child to her death, and followed it up with her brother. Elizabeth was the goddaughter of Honoria, you know, who is the second cousin by marriage of my cousin Verbena. I will never forgive him. Never."

Mary placed a hand on her aunt's arm. "He didn't send her to her death, Auntie, childbirth did that. And he's suffered for it, believe me. There is such a thing as redemption."

"That's decided by our savior, Jesus, not by us," Winifred said sharply.

"And we must leave the judgment of our fellow sinners to Christ as well," Mary answered gently.

Winifred sniffed. "Is he even Christian after all those years among pagans and Hindoos? Not that he ever was a good one here."

"Jasper and Mr. Kingsford," Mary exclaimed with more than a little relief. "Aunt Winifred, may I present Mercer Kingsford and Jasper Wainwright."

Jasper gave a bow twice as low any other he'd given in the South. "It's a pleasure to see you again, Mrs. Pickens."

"Hmpf. Mrs. Gideon Pickens," Winifred corrected austerely, wishing there were a way she could slip the word "senator" into her name. Then she stared so pointedly at the hand Mercer held out that, after a second, the young man let it fall by his side. Though Mercer might be slow, he wasn't entirely hopeless, and belatedly he followed Jasper's lead and bowed to the older lady. "Ma'am, it's an honor."

"Indeed, Mr. Kingsford."

Mary smiled weakly. "Gentlemen, I'm sure you'd like to meet the Senator, too."

Winifred looked around. "Where did they go? Oh, heavens, Henry is plying the Senator with drink on the porch. I turn my back for one minute . . ."

Thanks to Henry, the Senator was quite affable by the time he made acquaintance with Mercer and re-acquaintance with the black sheep of the Wainwright family. He found the Yankee less priggish than reported and Wainwright completely transformed. "A cultured Southern gentlemen who's traveled the globe," he told his group of friends later as he drew on a cigar that his wife was powerless to prohibit even though she loathed the smell. "I think he does us credit as to what a Beaufort education can accomplish."

That night, in the privacy of their bedroom, his opinion was not shared by his wife, but the Senator would not be shaken on this one. On no uncertain terms Jasper Wainwright would be accepted into Beaufort society, and his wife had not only better get used to the idea, he expected her to facilitate it. Though Mrs. Gideon Pickens in no way like the Senator's tone, she had long ago learned that a wife was obliged from time to time (though certainly not often) to bend her will and judgment to that of her lord and master. To say that her compliance was grudging, however, would be an understatement.

"Best drink of whiskey I ever served," Henry quipped that evening after the Senator and his wife had left and the four of them remaining enjoyed the sunset on the piazza in the spring evening twilight.

"I think you got three down him before we got out to the porch," Mary observed.

"Then they were the best three drinks of whiskey I ever served," Henry said. "Of course it helped that Jasper presented the good Senator with a bottle of French brandy and a box of Havana cigars."

"I apologize I didn't have a present for him," Mercer said, abashed. "I didn't know I'd be meeting him."

"You didn't need one," Mary assured him warmly. "You are our guest, and it wasn't expected at all."

"It's Jasper who needed the bribe, and in a significant way," Henry laughed.

"The bigger the crime, the bigger the penance," Jasper said with a quiet smile. "I'm not sure the French lace went over too well with Mrs. Pickens though."

Mary's dimples flashed. "She may never wear it, but it had its effect. She was about ready to forbid you from seeing Cara. Now she'll have to make do with just cutting you whenever possible."

Jasper frowned, nonplussed. "Forbid me from seeing her? Why?"

"You don't understand, Jasper," Henry said. "Winifred never had any children, so Cara's the greatest treasure she has. To allow you access to the jewel in her family tiara—well, that's really something."

"Was she going to deny me access, too?" Mercer said, alarmed.

Henry suppressed a smile as he sipped his fourth whiskey of the day. "Oh, I don't think she saw you as a threat. Killed any men lately, Mercer?"

Jasper rose, walked to the edge of the porch, and looked out over the river that had turned shades of persimmon and magenta as it reflected the glowing sky.

"Henry," Mary said in a sharp undertone to her husband.

"But you know," Henry said directly to Jasper's back, "it's not the duels and the drinking that gave Jasper his reputation. In the South, duels and drinking are time-honored traditions. It's that he left. That's the clincher."

Thumbs in his waistcoat pockets, Jasper turned on his heel to look at Henry in the gathering dusk.

"But you've come back. The prodigal son has returned to us." Henry raised his glass to his cousin and friend. "All will be forgiven. You'll see."

The fact that Henry had loaned his uncle-by-marriage five hundred dollars in February after the Senator lost a sizeable amount at the Jockey Club races no doubt had something to do with the Senator's willingness to accept Henry's cousin back into the fold. That financial transaction, however, was not mentioned at the present time.

Cara and her father were invited to dinner at Villa d'Este the next two afternoons. At each gathering she sought Mercer's company to inquire more about the city of Boston and even New England as a whole. When Mercer's resources in that category stretched thin, her questions turned to the subject of his education and family relations. The young man answered her questions warmly. He'd never encountered a girl so beautiful, so inquisitive, and such a good listener. He was beginning to positively regret his imminent departure and actually wrote to his uncle for an extension of his visit. The uncle very promptly, via telegraphic message to Charleston that was then conveyed to Beaufort by steamer, directed his nephew to return home on the double. The looming end of his visit prompted Mercer to look forward to his daily chats with Cara even more longingly. Jasper noticed that for all Cara's interest in Boston, she asked him not one word about China, India, or even France. He began to wonder if she'd ever even read the postal cards he'd sent.

However, when Henry and Mary's three boys figured out that Uncle Jasper was good for stories about snakes and Chinamen and exotic places like Canton and Bangalore, they began to settle into a routine where they pestered him for stories during supper each evening in the back parlor. Jasper, amused by the boys' jokes and antics, would sip his tea and tell them about the Renegade Elephant, the Snake Who Slept in His Trousers, and the Camel Who Would Not Obey. Henry and Mary enjoyed the stories as much as their boys and made sure to join the suppertime powwow in the back parlor even if they were going out for the evening. They were finding it wasn't easy to elicit tales of Jasper's travels at any other time. Their guest was usually quiet at dinner, content to let Henry regale them with idyllic tales of Silver Oaks pontificated mostly for Mercer's benefit and for the edification of the entire Yankee race.

Cara often walked over to Villa d'Este in the afternoons for one reason or another, but once evening story hour instituted itself as a custom, her visits grew oddly later, or she made two in a single day. One time she returned a copy of Henry's *Scientific American* that had been loaned to her father ("Why, Cara, you didn't have to make a separate trip," Mary said), and another she brought an armful of yellow roses that were especially fragrant. ("Cara, they're lovely, but Minnie could have walked them over.")

Cara wouldn't actually go in the back parlor during these visits but instead listened just outside the door while nonchalantly examining her gloves for loose buttons or fraying seams. The servants had no little trouble getting past her wide skirts as they travelled back and forth between the back parlor and the kitchen. As with most Southern houses, the kitchen building was located in the backyard to reduce risk of fire as well as add less oven heat to the main house.

"We tried everything," Jasper told the boys one evening. "Pushing and prodding, bribing and scolding. Our guide cursed that camel a blue streak. It's probably a good thing I don't know much Arabic because I would have blushed to hear such language. But despite our best efforts, the beast absolutely refused to get up. In the end, we had to make camp and spend the night."

"Did he get up the next day, Uncle Jasper?" Billy asked.

"Yes, he was right as rain, first thing the next morning."

"Was he just being stubborn?" Hugh said. "Mama says I'm stubborn."

"Undoubtedly. Camels are some of the most stubborn creatures alive. But probably not as stubborn as you are, Hugh."

"I'd like to ride a camel," Robert, the youngest, lisped. "Right between its humps."

"Well, this camel only had one hump, but it got me across the Sinai, so one must have been enough. Jim's camel, needless to say, was a cooperative dream of animal. It didn't slow us down ten minutes the whole trip."

"Show us where the Sinai is Uncle Jasper," Billy said, and they referred to the family's atlas yet again.

"Why don't you come in and sit with us at the table, Cara?" Henry called out. "You're just in Mitty and Bets' way there."

Cara excused herself and went home.

The next day at dinner, with Cara's yellow roses on the table, Henry had a brainstorm. Mercer, who would be leaving soon, absolutely could not be allowed to head north without first attending a proper Southern party. There should be good music, good food, good drink, pretty girls, and dancing. "Lots of dancing," Henry said. They would have it at Villa d'Este Saturday evening, though there wouldn't be any of that newfangled foolishness of festivities lasting until dawn. A naturally early riser, Henry had no tolerance for the nocturnal habits fashionable in Beaufort or anywhere else. One in the morning was late enough for any party, and that was when Henry's guests better take it into their heads to go home, or he'd personally escort them to the door.

"But Uncle Henry," Cara said, "that's just three days away. Can you plan a party so quickly?"

"We'll bring supplies from Silver Oaks," Henry said confidently. "Thomas and Paul can row there tomorrow and bring Tremmy and whatever else we need back with them the next day. Hock, my coachman, and Tremmy are the best fiddlers in the Sea Islands," Henry told Mercer, "if I say so myself. We can do it, can't we, Mary?"

"If you say so, dear," Mary agreed demurely.

"I think it's a capital idea," Senator Pickens said from the other side of the dinner table. "We'll be off to an excellent season in Beaufort. With this as a start, there'll be a dozen parties every month." Since parties, fêtes, balls and even barbecues were chances to drink away from the eyes of his wife, the Senator had become quite a champion of a busy social calendar in Beaufort.

Mary turned to the dragon she was responsible for. "What do you think, Aunt Winnie? I suppose it'll give Cara a chance to wear the new watered silk we had made in Charleston."

At this, Aunt Winnie, who was on the verge of vetoing the entire affair, visibly softened. Cara did look so lovely in that light green silk, and they'd taken such pains with the dressmaker to get it right. It would be something to show this Yankee and Henry's infidel cousin just how lovely a Southern girl could look. "Hmm," she said unenthusiastically even though she was warming to the idea. "Well, don't blame me if the weather doesn't hold until Saturday. That's what you get if you throw early parties. By the way, I hear the Patterson family is returning to Marshview this week."

Cara looked up briefly from cutting the chicken on her plate but said nothing. Henry and Mary glanced at each other.

"Excellent," Henry said jovially. "That means we can count on at least Johnny to do some dancing. Couldn't keep that young man still if you nailed his feet to the floor."

"Johnny is a beau of Cara's," Winifred informed Jasper and Mercer with a touch of severity. "His father is one of the largest landowners in the county, and all the girls in town consider him a dashing gentleman of the highest caliber."

"She's turned him down twice already," Henry said mischievously. "But yes, he's the favored horse in this race."

"Henry," Mary reproached.

"What was that?" Professor Randall asked vaguely. "Johnny Patterson is back in town? I always liked Johnny."

Cara continued cutting her chicken as if she'd heard none of the conversation. As he drank his water, Jasper eyed the young woman across the table from him thoughtfully. In any event, the party had now been officially sanctioned, and knowing Henry, it would happen come hell or high water, which was a good thing given that both conditions visited Beaufort with some regularity.

Cara glanced up from her plate. "Are you a dancing man, Mr. Wainwright?"

"I can't say that I am, Miss Randall," Jasper responded.

"I dance," Mercer said.

"Good for you," intoned Aunt Winnie.

Though Mercer made his share of missteps throughout the dinner, it wasn't until dessert, when the Senator started on a political diatribe that the others knew to keep rhetorical, that the young man waded into quicksand.

"I believe the reason South Carolina has less representation in Congress than a state like New York is entirely a matter of population, not Yankee scheming," Mercer explained earnestly after Senator Pickens complained of the current state of affairs.

"Tarnation," the Senator roared. "I'm a senator, for Heaven's sake, don't you think I know that? But it's not for other states to meddle in

South Carolina's sovereign matters. We may have agreed to the Constitution, but we didn't agree to other folks sticking us with tariffs and meddling in our trade."

"But aren't tariffs part and parcel of being a nation in the nineteenth century?" Mercer inquired tentatively. "How could we have financed the Erie Canal or fought the Mexican army without the tariff monies to pay for it?"

The Senator's fist crashed on the table, causing the women to start in their chairs. Though Henry compressed his lips at this lapse of manners, he decided to ride this one out. "You Northerners like passing tariffs that protect your commerce and not ours, and then you spend the money on infernal improvements that benefit your states and not ours. Didn't South Carolina do more than our share for our sacred revolution against King George? Didn't we fight more battles on our soil, lose more men and spill more of our blood than any other state in the Union? I've read the Constitution forwards and backwards, and let me tell you, that document specifically protects states' rights in every area beyond the powers explicitly given to the federal government. And nowhere does it say the federal government can impose tariffs to protect industries from foreign competition. Now, if a federal power isn't listed in the Constitution, then it can't just be passed into law on a Congressional whim. It takes an amendment, I tell you, and there's no way South Carolina will ratify amendments that are against her interests, however much the Northern states try to obfuscate and flummox us. We know what our forefathers agreed to when they signed the Constitution. A deal is a deal, a contract is a contract, and we will not be cheated." The fist came down again, causing cutlery to jump.

With a frown, Mercer appealed to Jasper. "Surely Massachusetts lost the most men in the Revolution?"

Jasper shook his head. "South Carolina." This was a fact every child in the Palmetto State learned before they lost their first milk tooth.

"The fighting here was quite vicious," Henry said breezily. "My grandfather lost his two younger brothers. In fact, Beaufort was occupied by British troops for four years. Luckily, they didn't burn us down like they did so many other towns." He turned to his wife. "My dear, I think the gentlemen are ready for their brandy." It was with relief that the ladies followed Mary to the parlor. Even Winifred hoped Henry got a brandy down the Senator in short order. Mixing the Senator, politics, and a Yankee was just asking for trouble, and all of them knew it.

Henry did work his magic with the brandy, and when the men joined the ladies in the parlor, they were ready for pleasanter conversation. Soon the health-giving properties of the town of Beaufort was the topic at hand, and since the beauty and perfection of Beaufort was a chorus to which Mercer could happily add his voice, it was a conversation destined to please everyone.

"It's the breezes," Winifred said of Beaufort's secret charm. "It keeps us cool here all summer."

"Relatively cool, anyway," Henry said.

"We also don't have the insects that the other islands do," Cara added. "And the fevers almost always seem to skip us."

"Charleston had a terrible spell of Yellow Jack last year," Mary said with a sad shake of her head. "I would hate to raise children there." All the other Beaufort residents nodded in agreement.

"Darned unhealthy place, Charleston," the Senator said. "Amusing to visit for a time, but I don't know why anyone lives there. They should all move to Beaufort. Maybe you've heard—Beaufort's now called the Newport of the South."

"Newport?" Mercer said with some enthusiasm. "I was just there last summer. I'd say that while there certainly are similarities, Newport is probably twice the size and—"

"Mercer," Jasper gently interrupted, seeing the faces of his fellow South Carolinians turn stony. Mercer turned to him, perplexed. "Say after me," Jasper said. "Beaufort is the Newport of the South."

It took the earnest Bostonian a moment to accede to the request. "Beaufort is the Newport of the South," he repeated, confusion evident on his face.

"Good. Now we're all in agreement."

There was a pause in the conversation as the indelicacy of preferring the real Newport to its Southern image was papered over.

Mary was the first to come to her social senses. "Of course, even though Beaufort has everything we need, we always go to Charleston in February for the Jockey Club races and the St. Cecilia Society ball," she assured Mercer.

"Naturally," Mercer agreed, although he had no idea why this might be important. "But I wonder, how do the planters effectively see to the workings of their land if they're absent all summer and here instead?"

"Some effectively don't," Henry said dryly. "And some of us do a great deal of traveling in the summer while leaving our families to enjoy the pleasant climes in town."

"Pshaw, Henry," the Senator said. "All it takes is hiring a competent overseer. You just never trust anyone to do as good a job as you."

"That's entirely true, Senator."

"My boy, that kind of attitude will put you in an early grave. You've got to relax and enjoy life more, Henry."

"I enjoy my life very well, Senator, believe me." Though no one in the entire of state of South Carolina would dream of accusing Henry Birch of being anything less than a complete gentleman, some voices might delicately observe that his zeal for his plantations bore an uncomfortable resemblance to ambition rather than the nonchalance fitting a Southern squire. Henry's relatives by marriage were always trying to get him to take up an academic passion or even drink and gamble rather than show so obvious a relish for farming and profits. Henry was of the opinion that they could stuff it.

Mercer's eyes had found Cara, her hair and face illuminated by the slanting afternoon sun like a Botticelli angel. "I can definitely see why Beaufort deserves its fine reputation," he enthused, the brandy going to his head. "It's full of elegant homes, cultured citizens, and some of the most beautiful women in the land. Everyone here is so educated and refined, and leads a life of such grace and ease, I don't know why anyone would ever leave."

Though this sentiment was received with appreciation by most of the party at hand, Jasper could only conclude that Mercer had contracted amnesia about the subject he had sermonized so long and volubly about the entire journey from Boston to Beaufort. It struck Jasper as remarkable how easily Northerners, after just a few weeks in the South, cottoned to the lifestyle of having slaves wait on them hand and foot.

Mercer made two solo visits to Professor Randall to consult with him on matters of Chinese scholarship. Although he found the time spent with the professor in his study edifying, he'd hoped to find Cara at home as well. Unfortunately, on both occasions she'd been out, a coincidence he lamented when he happened to meet up with her in front of the shops on Bay Street Friday afternoon. It had rained briefly earlier in the day, vindicating Mrs. Pickens's concerns about planning a party too early in the season. By the next day, however, the weather had turned, leaving one to wonder if even the elements were obliged to obey Henry's plans.

Indeed, on Saturday evening a warm, wisteria-scented breeze wafted through town to create a Southern approximation of paradise. Upstairs in the second floor ballroom of Villa d'Este, the young people of Beaufort danced with gusto to the cotillion, polka and reel music supplied by the dueling fiddles of Hock and Tremmy. Throughout the ballroom candlelight was reflected and amplified by a splendid array of gilded mirrors inlaid in the decorated paneling underneath the fourteen-foot high ceilings. When Henry had first shown Jasper around Villa d'Este, he'd grumbled about the expense of the ballroom, the waste of space, and how, despite the extravagance, he couldn't deny Mary what all the fashionable houses in Charleston possessed. Jasper had just smiled at his cousin's obvious pride in this expensive, glittering space that enabled him to entertain such a large portion of the town in style. The colonial house that the Birch family had occupied for three generations until Henry sold it to raise funds for Villa d'Este had been a shanty in comparison.

And tonight, some sparkling style it was. The older guests sat at the sides of the ballroom or enjoyed the breeze outside on the adjoining piazza. They tapped their toes and nodded their heads in time with the music as they looked on at the merriment, often while being liberally supplied with punch by a near army of dark-skinned, white-gloved servants. The young Birch boys peeked through doors to see the adults, and those slaves not involved in serving still managed to have a look at the gaiety.

Johnny Patterson, Cara's implied beau, lived up to Aunt Winnie's claims. An athletic, devil-may-care young man with sun-kissed blond hair and sideburns, he was clearly popular with the young ladies and young gentleman of the party alike. In the milieu of his home turf he moved about like a young lord, confident of both his personal and familial merit. Delighted to see Cara, he claimed the first two dances with her.

As Henry stood next to Jasper on one side of the ballroom, both of them in the formal tails, white waistcoat, and white cravat expected at such an event, he nodded at the young couple. "Johnny and Cara grew up together here in Beaufort. He's been infatuated with her since they were knee high to a mosquito. She used to run and climb trees right alongside him until it was time for her skirts to go down and her hair to go up. Johnny's always been a bit wild, like you were in some ways, of course not to that extreme. No one could be that extreme. Everyone thinks Cara'll accept him eventually, when he's had time to settle down."

That Johnny was in love with Cara was clear from the way he laughed and teased and commanded her attention when she was with him, and from the way he gazed at her broodingly when she wasn't. That Cara enjoyed his company was also unmistakable. Still, she was careful not to dance too many dances with him and switched partners often to some of the other young men, including Mercer. Mercer seemed to be having the time of his life at the party, clapping with the fiddle and letting Hetty, Johnny's seventeen-year-old sister, teach him the Virginia Reel. But his favorite partner was obviously Miss Randall.

After the first eight or nine dances, it grew warm inside the house, and Mercer became anxious that Miss Randall should obtain a breath of fresh air. Since the upstairs piazza was crowded, he suggested downstairs as a better venue for tranquility. Though Cara gave him a sharp look, she agreed to accompany him.

The first floor verandah held more shadow than light, only a few candles scattered about in hurricane glass, but Cara's loveliness shone even in the semi-darkness. Her off-the-shoulder gown had been flounced with lace to highlight her elegant neck and shoulders; then it drew in sharply to emphasize the feminine narrowness of her waist. As she sat perched on a chair, her gloved hands demurely folded on top of the gathers of her bell-shaped skirt, Mercer pulled another chair up close to her.

"Miss Randall, I must tell you, the last fortnight has been one of the most pleasant of my life," he began.

"I'm glad Beaufort agrees with you," Cara said cautiously, as if she sensed this was only an opening passage to a much trickier cadenza ahead.

"Oh, more than Beaufort agrees with me. Miss Randall, I must tell you how great a role you've played in my happiness here."

Cara didn't flinch at this sentiment, and she didn't look for an avenue of escape. "You're too kind, Mr. Kingsford."

"Miss Randall, you've been so interested in Boston. Have you ever thought about what it would be like to live there?"

"Thoughts, yes, but no true desire, Mr. Kingsford. I'm a Southerner, through and through." She glanced down at her gloved hands. "I don't expect I'll ever leave the South."

"But Miss Randall, perhaps if the right person were to show the North to you, you might find you could be happy there. If the right person were to ask you to . . . be his wife?"

Cara looked at him steadily, gravely, waiting for him to continue in the flickering light. The gaiety upstairs seemed a universe away. Mercer leaned forward in his chair.

"Miss Randall, I adore you. You are the gentlest, prettiest, most perfect girl in the world. Will you marry me?"

Cara shut her eyes for just a second before she opened them again, quite composed. "Mr. Kingsford, you do me a great honor, and I hope you'll believe me when I say that any girl would be more than grateful for an offer from such an amiable, hard-working, virtuous man who has a future ahead of him as bright as yours."

Mercer looked flattered but somewhat wary. This wasn't immediately going in the direction it was supposed to.

"But Mr. Kingsford," Cara continued, "you know you've made this offer to the wrong girl. There's someone else who has your love and your allegiance."

"No, Miss Randall," Mercer exclaimed, startled. "There's no one else."

She gave him a long deep look. "You mean to tell me there's no girl back in Boston who brightens every time you walk into the room? Whose eyes follow your every movement? Who makes sure she's invited to the gatherings you're invited to, who does you services when she can, who comforts you when little afflictions arise?"

Mercer frowned and began to look confused.

"She may not always be the prettiest in the room, but she is true and loyal and will make you a wonderful wife."

"Wait," Mercer said. "You mean Betsy? How could you know about her? Mr. Wainwright doesn't even know about her."

"By this time next year," Cara said, "you'll have married her and be rejoicing in your good fortune. All your friends and family will think you were so clever to pick such an adoring, practical wife because she'll be the making of you."

Mercer seemed hesitant. "She *is* very practical and economical, a good thing, I suppose, for the wife of a lawyer just starting out."

"And she's always concerned for your comfort."

"Yes, that's true," Mercer agreed slowly.

Cara tilted her head. "And she's healthy and strong. She'll make an excellent mother."

Mercer nodded, bemused as he stared off into space. "She never twists her ankle like some girls, and she can walk up a set of stairs without getting out of breath."

"And she's devoted to you," Cara suggested gently. "She's loved you for a long, long time."

"Why, why—you're right," Mercer said. "She does love me. Why didn't I see it before?" He rose. "Miss Randall, you're astonishing. I can't express my gratitude enough. Please excuse me, I — I – I need to pack and write a letter. I want to get the first steamer out tomorrow. "

"Certainly," Cara said graciously. When he had gone, she sank into her chair and leaned her head back with uncharacteristic fatigue.

"I must say, Miss Randall, you handled that like a professional."

Cara sat up with a start to see Jasper leaning against a porch post. "Mr. Wainwright. You should've made your presence known."

"You're right, I should have." Jasper folded his arms lazily across his chest. "I was worried Mr. Kingsford had lured you down here in order to importune you, and since I brought him to Beaufort, I felt obliged to intercede if necessary. But as it turns out, I needn't have bothered. I am in the presence of a master. I take it dear Betsy was just a very good guess?"

Cara turned and gave him a look in the half-light that Jasper was to remember the rest of his life. It reminded him of something both terrible and sublime, something he'd seen on his travels, but he couldn't quite put his finger on it. In any event, it wasn't a look that conveyed pleasure in his company.

"There's always a long-ignored Betsy waiting in the background for men like him," Cara said grimly.

"So was poor Mercer number sixteen? Tell me, if Johnny Patterson up there asked you twice, does he count for one or two?"

Cara rose, contemptuously gathered her watered silk dress around her, and went inside without another word.

That night as Jasper undressed in the early hours, he thought about the look Cara had given him but came to no conclusion. As he lay in bed in the quiet darkness of his room, he wondered if it'd been somewhere in the Guangdong province that he'd run across it. Or maybe in one of those dark, fetid alleyways off the ivory market in Macao? But that had been full of opium addicts. Did he really equate Cara with an opium addict?

He was still puzzled when he went for his morning ride with Henry. The men conveniently used the ride as an excuse to avoid going to church with Mary and the boys, although they got back in plenty of time and could have managed to go if they'd so chosen. Jasper thought about that look as he saw Mercer off on the steamer to Charleston, as he wrote a letter to his brother at Sleety Pines, as he stood on Villa d'Este's piazza overlooking the river, drinking his green tea in the afternoon. It wasn't until he set his cup and saucer aside, leaned both hands against the railing, and looked down for a moment that it came to him.

In northern India, outside a nabob's palace, he'd come across a mammoth pit dug into the bare ground. Peering down into it, he found a tiger pacing as best as it could in its tight constraints. For the amusement of both the nabob and the public, the tiger had been captured and placed in this putrid hole that was too deep for even its great leaps to allow escape. The powerful animal's muscles rippled as it paced, and every once in a while, when it was thrown a chicken, it was able to show a flash of its true strength. Jasper had gazed with pity at the animal in its captivity. Eventually the nabob would grow tired of the novelty and the tiger would be shot or, worse, starved to death. The tiger at that moment had glanced skyward at Jasper with a look of longing, bitter fury, and hopelessness. That was what he'd seen in Cara's eyes the night before. Jasper looked off at the river, stunned.

Chapter Three

One of Henry's proudest recent achievements was the addition of a bath room to the second floor of Villa d'Este. A water closet already existed on the first floor, but the previous autumn, after he'd learned that water closets were no longer the pinnacle in plumbing comfort, Henry had installed a water tank in the attic that fed to a porcelain bathtub encased in wood paneling. He'd brought in a plumbing expert all the way from Philadelphia to do it, driving the technician nearly mad by watching over his shoulder and commenting during the installation. The hot water entered the room via a pipe that coiled down the chimney, gathering heat if a fire was burning in the room below. If it was too hot for a fire, the servants could always bring up hot water from the kitchen. As might be expected, the slaves preferred to light a fire, so the bath room was usually on the warm side until the heat of summer made cool bathing welcome. The attic tank was not effortless, however. It was necessary for the water to be conveyed up three stories by a suction pump, similar to a ship's bilge pump, powered by slave muscle. Still, the arrangement was as fine as anything Jasper had seen in Paris, and he was ready to give Henry credit for an almost Yankee level of ingenuity.

After a long, nostalgic horseback ride with Henry devoted to visiting some of the sites of their youthful capers, Jasper had a good soak in the bath before dressing for dinner. Then, in the privacy of his room, Jim gave him a shave.

"So now that Mercer's had the good sense to return north," Jim said, "are we going to be leaving, too?" He seemed fondest of pressing his case for removal when he had a razor at Jasper's throat.

"We'll have to delay a while longer," Jasper said. "I've had a letter from my brother. He's taking his wife and daughters on a tour of the hot springs of Virginia next week."

Jim snorted. "Whatever for?"

Jasper shrugged. "Sleety Pines can be a dull place."

"It can be a dull place for lots of people, people who don't get to tour spa country," Jim observed.

Jasper lifted a palm. "If my brother's not there, I can't transact the matter. We'll get to Sleety Pines soon enough. Look, Jim, give me a little more time. Once we leave Beaufort, I'm never coming back, so this is my last chance to get to know Henry and Mary's boys. Your problem is you've got nothing to do, so you're bored. Why don't you drum up a few patients, get a little practice going?"

"As if that would be appreciated by the medical community here."

"You mean Dr. Goode? Why do you say that? He always liked you. Anyway, he doesn't need to know. If you help a few slaves here and there with home remedies, well, root doctors do that all the time and it's tolerated. As least you won't be putting hexes on people."

"And if I cure something real? Something that Dr. Goode can't?"

"Then everyone should be grateful," Jasper replied.

The Senator and Mrs. Pickens sat in the parlor with Mary, Henry, and Jasper as they awaited the arrival of Cara and her father for dinner. Henry had sent his coachman, Hock, in the carriage to pick them up so they were sure to materialize momentarily. No one could ever say that Henry wasn't solicitous about the comfort of his brother-in-law and niece.

Winifred frowned as she sat in her chair with a ramrod straight back. It had not been an easy day. That morning at the planning meeting for the church bazaar Mrs. Steven had definitely undervalued Winifred's idea of selling embroidered suspender straps. She didn't know why. The senator would no doubt love a pair.

"By the way," she said crossly to Mary, "on Saturday I could see that Cara's watered silk was made with too large a waist. I thought I told that seamstress in Charleston to be exact."

Mary didn't look up from the pillowcase she was embroidering with fine, even stitches. "It's twenty-two inches, just as usual."

"Next time I see her in it, I'm going to measure. Must be twenty-four, sure as day. She looked as big as a rain barrel."

"I thought she looked lovely at the party," Henry put in as he skimmed a magazine while the Senator perused yesterday's *Charleston Courier.* "How about you, Jasper?"

Jasper sipped his green tea. "I can't say I noticed the size of her waist."

"Every other girl in Beaufort has a waist of eighteen inches," Aunt Winnie said indignantly. "Why, Dorthea Howard told me Rebecca's this season is sixteen and a half."

"Becky Howard's going to end up with a broken rib, just like that silly Herman girl in Port Royal," Henry said with an edge of annoyance. "If Cara's waist hasn't prevented her from receiving fifteen marriage proposals, it can't possibly be a problem. And you know Dr. Goode says tight stays aren't good for the lungs, not to mentioned the kidneys."

Winifred snorted indelicately. Of course, her waist was forty, if it was an inch, but when she was twenty it hadn't been. "If Dr. Goode had his way, women wouldn't wear stays at all. When you look at the latest fashions from Europe, you can just see the waists getting more and more wasp-like. If Cara isn't careful, she'll soon be démodé."

Henry barely refrained from rolling his eyes. "Are women so keen to have their internal organs crushed in Europe as they are here?" he asked Jasper.

"I'm afraid so," Jasper responded. "It's an international menace. In China, waists aren't the issue: it's the feet they bind and deform. A man there can't imagine marrying a woman with feet longer than four inches."

"Mr. Wainwright," Winifred said sharply. "I'm sure you like to look at a trim waist as well as any man."

"That I do, ma'am," Jasper admitted with a lazy smile behind his moustache.

Winifred looked at Henry victoriously.

"Cara's waist is fine," Henry said with finality. When Cara was sixteen, she'd fought a series of skirmishes with her great aunt over the tightness of her stays. Mary hadn't known which side to take, but when Cara appealed to Henry for assistance, he had personally approved twenty-two inches, and he was damned if he'd let Winifred budge him now. In addition, he'd already caught Jasper looking at Cara's waist plenty often, however démodé it might be.

The arrival of the lady in question imposed a merciful cessation of all waist circumference talk. The men politely rose from their seats at her entrance. Cara had come alone. Her father was indisposed, she said, and Dr. Goode thought it best for him to rest. Their party was made even smaller when, soon after dinner, the Senator developed indigestion severe enough that Mrs. Pickens decided to take him home and send for Dr. Goode. Too much alcohol, she diagnosed with a disapproving glance at Henry.

"Couts, get Cara's wrap," Winifred ordered. "Cara, we'll drop you off on our way."

"No need for that," Henry said, cancelling his in-law's order to his servant with a gesture. Couts, who hadn't become major-domo of Villa d'Este without wits quicker than a cricket in a chicken coop, thought it prudent to evaporate from the room. Even though he'd worked diligently for many years to be on good terms with Miz Pickens, he knew who buttered his bread with various privileges and even pocket money that put him among the most elite of Beaufort slaves. The wrap stayed put. "I'll take her home in an hour or so," Henry assured Winifred. "You go get Dr. Goode to take a look at the Senator. You know, he looks a little green around the edges. Maybe he's bilious."

Alarmed, Winifred got her husband in the carriage in haste as Mary and Henry waved them off. Clouds were gathering, darkening the sky like heavy curtains and causing twilight to set in early. It would rain soon.

"Too much alcohol my foot," Henry grumbled to his wife as they returned inside. "It was too much duck. He must've had six slices and a leg. How I'm supposed to keep my guests from overeating, I'll never know."

Back in the parlor, Jasper and Cara were waiting for their hosts separately and silently, Jasper appearing to examine the oil portrait of Mary at one end of the room while Cara looked out a window on the other. Henry gave Mary a glance.

"Cara, dear," Mary said, settling herself with her embroidery on the sofa, "will you play for us, please?"

Cara looked glad of the request. It'd been a tense five minutes of refusing to look at or speak to Mr. Wainwright while her aunt and uncle were absent.

Henry put a hand on his wife's shoulder. "Mary, I need to check with Couts a minute." His wife nodded. "Excuse me," he said to Jasper and his niece.

Eyeing his cousin narrowly, Jasper noticed something familiar and not a little suspicious in Henry's eye. Still, he relaxed back in his chair and prepared to enjoy the sonata Cara had begun. She did play beautifully. He noticed she never sang to accompany her instrument. Jasper thought he might like to hear her sing.

After a minute, Mary quietly got up, causing Jasper to rise from his seat. "Sit back down," she whispered, a light hand on his arm. "I need to check on the boys. I'll be back." Now Jasper definitely suspected a plot afoot. His misgivings were confirmed when Mary, before leaving the room, lit a single lamp near the piano as rain began to pour beyond the porch. The lone light created a glowing circle around Cara, leaving the rest of the room in a murky dusk. Jasper frowned at her, but Mary just flicked her fingers at him, indicating he should move closer to the piano. Jasper chose to remain where he was in the semidarkness.

Looking up, Cara realized two-thirds of her audience had deserted her. "Shall I continue?" she said crisply after a moment. The question appeared to be to the room rather than to Jasper in particular.

"If you please," Jasper said. "Just forget I'm here."

"I'll do that," Cara answered. And to make sure he was aware she wasn't playing for him, she turned the recital into a practice session devoted to tackling the new waltz in C sharp minor by Chopin. Though she'd mastered the rudiments, she was still unsatisfied with the way many of the passages rippled under her fingers. She played the opening chords two or three dozen times until they met with her satisfaction; then the opening arpeggio received almost a score of repetitions until gradually it became more fluid. After that she contended with the fleeting, ephemeral refrain, repeating it again and again as she tried to increase the speed and precision of her fingertips.

At first Jasper was amused at her disregard for him; then he was intrigued to witness just how her craft was put together. He was sitting motionless enough and far enough out of her range of vision that perhaps she did forget about him as he watched her in the lamplight.

"What are they doing?" Mary whispered, trying to peer over the shoulder of her husband as he took in the scene.

"He's just sitting there like a toad in the dark," Henry said with some disgust as the rain outside tapered off. "Here we give him an opportunity most men would give their right arm for, and he sits there like a big lump. Time for step two."

Henry strode into the room. "Looks like I've got a problem with my water pump. Jasper, do you mind taking Cara home in the buggy? It's hitched up and ready to go."

Cara looked more than a little startled by this request. "Surely Hock can take me, Uncle Henry."

"I'm afraid not. He's my best mechanic, and I need him at the moment. Only Jasper here is available."

Jasper evaluated his cousin sourly. "Certainly," he agreed, but with a lack of enthusiasm that paid a young lady no compliment. Cara raised her chin, received her wrap, and headed out the back door where the buggy was waiting.

Though Jasper could have asked why Henry he had gone to the trouble of having the buggy hitched when the carriage had already been out once that day, he didn't bother. Henry's fashionable Clarence carriage was large and roomy and could hold four, plus a driver up front. His buggy, a Studebaker Stanhope, barely held two on a good day, and necessitated the driver almost sit on the wide skirts of his passenger if female. If she'd known, Aunt Winifred would never have permitted her great niece to sit in a buggy with an unmarried man without a plank of wood wedged between the two. Why, just last fall hadn't a boy from Beaufort been tossed out of The Citadel in Charleston for taking a buggy ride with a girl?

After pulling on his gloves, Jasper was ready to hand Cara into the buggy but found she'd already coerced the favor from her uncle. Instead he climbed in beside her, took the reins, and they drove off without speaking a word to each other.

Mary looked after them with concern. "I don't think it's working, dear."

"They're both as contrary as blue crabs," Henry said confidently. "Give it time."

Since in matters such as these her husband was invariably right, Mary nodded her head and went inside.

Pockets of the sky had cleared, allowing a last glimpse of golden rays and indigo clouds as the sun set for the night. There was no one else on the road between Villa d'Este and the Randall house, in part because the Harmon family who lived between the two had gone north for the summer to visit the real Newport in Rhode Island, leaving the whole block dim and quiet in the lee of the ancient oaks. Even so, the lanterns attached to the fore corners of the buggy meant the gloom did not impede their way. Jasper urged the horse on at a steady, unhurried pace while Cara, her hands primly folded in her lap, squished herself as far to the right of the bench seat as space allowed. After the rain, the air was fresh and gentle with crickets all around serenading in their mesmeric fashion. Fireflies had appeared on the scene, winking chartreuse as they flew by like Chinese sky lanterns. With a smile Jasper thought back to a buggy ride on a spring evening a year ago down a country lane on the outskirts of Paris. His companion then had been a little more interested in his company.

At the Professor's house, Jasper climbed down, crossed around the buggy and extended his hand to help Cara off. Her gloved fingers touched his for the briefest of seconds as she artfully avoided an awaiting puddle. Once on the ground, she nodded and gave a slight curtsy. "Mr. Wainwright."

He bowed back. "Miss Randall." With a swish of her skirts she went up the stairs into the house and didn't look back. Well, that made thirteen words she'd spoken to him that evening. The ice from that girl could freeze the Sahara, he thought. With a laugh, he shook the reins over the horse's back and returned to Villa d'Este in the gathering darkness.

The next day, Henry decided to take Jasper with him on a visit to Silver Oaks. The crops had been sown but fast-growing weeds needed proper hoeing, there were some accounts that needed addressing, and Jasper should have a chance to become acquainted with twelve years of improvements at the plantation. Though Henry had overseers at his two other plantations, Three Reeds and Birch Hill, at Silver Oaks he preferred to operate with only Negro drivers and a Negro headman under his own personal supervision. This arrangement, however, required frequent visits throughout the summer as a matter of practicality and as a matter of South Carolina law.

"I suppose, dear," Mary said resignedly when informed of the plan at the breakfast table. "If you must."

Henry leaned over her and kissed the side of her face, even in front of Jasper. "We'll be back on Thursday, well in time for the Saddler's party Friday evening," he assured her. But worry about missing the party didn't seem to be the source of Mary's melancholy.

"Why does he wear that moustache?" Winifred said crossly later that day as the women had tea in Mary's parlor. "Is it some new European style? Whiskers ought to be enough facial hair for any man."

"I think it looks perfectly nice," Mary said, pulling her needle through her pillowcase. "Don't you agree, Cara?"

Cara, dutifully embroidering a handkerchief, evaded her aunt's question with a non-committal murmur.

"Jasper was always a handsome man," Mary continued. "But now I'd say he looks . . . distinguished. Back in the day, he had half a dozen girls in Beaufort swooning after him, though he didn't much care."

"Too busy drinking and shooting things he wasn't supposed to shoot," Aunt Winnie said with a sniff.

Jasper enjoyed the tour up Broomfield Creek, a good-sized stream that stretched from the Beaufort River to the Coosaw. Slicing all the way through Lady's Island, the creek provided a useful waterway directly to Henry's property if approached and timed correctly. Fed and then starved by the swelling sea, the first half of the saline creek could be navigated as the high tide came in from the Beaufort River, pushing the boat along. Then, if tables had been consulted and the tide read perfectly, the second half of the journey was equally as effortless as the ebbing water pulled the boat towards the Coosaw. To be sure, two powerful slaves were along to row as well, speeding things up considerably. In less than two hours they'd reached nearly the far side of Lady's Island and disembarked at a sturdy landing a short distance from the big house at Silver Oaks. A boy was there biding his time with horses for the gentlemen. Though he'd been waiting for who knows how long, he seemed content enough to lie on the bank of the creek and soak in the sun, a worn straw hat covering his eyes.

As they rode to the house, Jasper noticed two small boys wearing only long shirts playing together on the branches of an enormous oak. Their skin was noticeably lighter than the other slaves, identifying them as mulattos. Henry took some candies out of his coat pocket and tossed them to the boys on the branch. In response they clapped and called out merry thanks. As Henry gave them a wave, Jasper couldn't help notice there was something familiar about these two children. On closer scrutiny, he recognized they had the same brow and the same eyes as someone familiar, though in a darker hue. They had the same brow and eyes as the man riding next to him.

After a quick stop for sustenance at the house, Henry proudly showed Jasper around the estate that Jasper had visited only once before, on the occasion of Henry and Mary's wedding. If the plantation had been large and profitable then, it was doubly so now. Henry had substantially extended its holdings by draining many of its marshes and by buying bits of neighbors' adjoining lands during low cotton-price years when his neighbors had been interested in raising cash.

First on the men's comprehensive tour was the street of slave cabins. There, they actually dismounted and went inside a few of the well-maintained buildings constructed with white oak boards, brick chimneys, glass windows and wood plank floors. Each building consisted of two cabins, a slave family in each. Each cabin had a fireplace, two rooms, and a loft, and was furnished with a table and chairs, a sideboard, and at least one real bed covered by a colorful slave-made quilt. Behind the cabins were vegetable gardens in which slave families were allowed to grow food for themselves in addition to the rations of rice, hominy, lard, cornmeal, flour, molasses, milk, and butter they were given. Why, the slaves even had a ration of coffee.

After that Jasper was shown the gin house used for processing the silky Sea Island cotton. Long staple cotton was too delicate to go through a regular gin with its brushes and wire teeth, but since the seeds of Sea Island cotton were fuzz-free, a gin of non-destructive rollers was all that was needed to separate the pips from the long staple lint. Sea Island cotton only grew within forty miles of the sea, so Jasper had limited direct experience with it. At Sleety Pines, the cheaper, sturdier, more stubborn upland cotton had been the varietal cultivated. As they went on, Jasper saw spinning and weaving rooms where half a dozen women worked to make the fabric that would provide each slave with two sets of clothes—cotton for summer, wool for winter. Further on, well-removed from the living quarters due to its stink, lay the tanning yard where hides were turned into the leather that would be made into the shoes for slave feet. Tucked away in a shed behind one of the barns was even Henry's very own still that produced the rations of whiskey given out at Christmas holidays. If there was a whipping post, Jasper didn't see it.

Silver Oaks had a small blacksmith shop, a woodworking shop and a cobbler's shop. At the end of the row of slave cabins was a praise house for Sunday and Wednesday services. While the servants in Beaufort went with Mary to St. Helena's Church every Sunday and sat upstairs in the gallery that overlooked the main floor (more slaves generally attended than masters), here at Silver Oaks the slaves had their own services led by a Negro elder. Though Henry wasn't enthusiastic about the time the slaves spent at the praise house, Mary was adamant about their weekly attendance. Ring shouts, however—worship in the form of a shuffling dance joined by call and response singing—Henry considered too tribal and wouldn't abide. Plus, the shouts lasted half the night and left the slaves worthless for work the next morning.

In pastures scattered throughout Silver Oaks, a dozen horses, half a dozen mules, a hundred and fifty head of sheep and an equal number of cattle grazed. The dozens of cows Henry owned were kept closer at hand to be rounded up each evening for milking. Henry was proud to say his smoke house was still half full of meat even in early May, and he accomplished this feat without having to raise hardly any pigs and chickens himself. Instead, he let his slaves raise them and then bought eggs and meat from them for the big house as it suited him. In theory such transactions were illegal but in application it was a practice widely tolerated. In order to keep his slaves from spending their earnings on drink, he kept a small store of items that appealed to their fancy on the plantation for them to buy.

During the winter, under Mary's watchful eye, all the soap and candles for all three of Henry's plantations were made at Silver Oaks. In the late fall and early spring, provisions were transferred to the other locations, with Mary, two seamstresses, and Ike, the cobbler, along to turn leather and fabric into shoes and clothing. The self-sufficiency of Henry's enterprises was so complete that the hard cash that cotton brought in could be nearly entirely spent on the finer luxuries that the family enjoyed.

Throughout his tour Jasper nodded, smiled and gently praised. He admired the smell of rich earth and complimented the geometric symmetry of the newly planted fields. He agreed without reserve that Henry's slaves were fed, clothed and housed in a manner on par with, if not better than any plantation he'd ever seen. In fact, they were better fed, clothed and housed than most the peasants he'd observed in Europe. He even had to concur that Henry's Negroes all looked docile and content with the rhythm and pattern of their lives at Silver Oaks. Yes, each was expected to complete his or her daily task unless truly ill, but in general if they started at sun up and worked steadily, they could finish their work by three or four in the afternoon with the rest of the day theirs to attend to their own interests. On Saturdays, the abbreviated tasks could be accomplished by noon, and at Christmas there was a near week of festivities with few duties. As lives of servitude went, Jasper had to agree that these slaves had it good. Though Jasper's brief tenure at Sleety Pines had been an improvement over his father's, his part of the plantation had never been half so profitable, half so liberal, or half so well run as Silver Oaks. From the outset he'd had neither Henry's boundless energy nor his abundant enthusiasm for the task. Then, as the siren call of drink had commandeered ever-increasing portions of his life, his efficacy had plummeted further still.

As they rode through the handsome fields and tranquil stands of woods, Jasper and Henry reminisced about Birch Hill, the ancestral home, actually a simple farmhouse on St. Helena Island. Because the generations of Birch men before Henry had been more interested in politics than farming, the Birch Hill plantation had been a modest enterprise that rarely supported its family members in the style of their peers. It was one of the reasons that Henry, believing his state and his country to be far enough along in their political evolution to prosper without him, had eschewed politics and had instead concentrated on lifting the fortunes of the Birch family from the merely adequate to the positively flourishing. Since Birch Hill held happy memories for Jasper, he was glad to hear Henry had been keeping it up, and it was fine with him that the Birch Hill overseer and his family were occupying the house. He was glad to think of children playing there again.

At sunset, near the end of the extensive tour, Jasper and Henry emerged from a copse of oaks out onto an outlook point with a view of the broad estuary basin of the Coosaw River just before it widened into the Saint Helena Sound. Behind them in the distance was a two-story farmhouse that looked, if not neglected, at least forgotten. Jasper wondered if its owner was an absentee, living permanently away from the Sea Islands as a number did.

"Have you ever seen Smullen Point before?" Henry asked.

Jasper looked again at the farmhouse. That was where they were? He shook his head. The week of Henry's marriage to Mary had been a wild one, and much of his memory of it was lost in a haze fueled by alcohol. "Who owns it these days?"

"In theory, the good Professor Randall," Henry said.

Jasper raised his eyebrows in surprise. "He actually runs a plantation?"

"No," Henry said. "I run it. He and Cara reap the profits in the form of silk dresses and new pianos. Not that it's been easy," he confided. "Prices for cotton the last five or six years have been abysmal, but last year was finally decent. I think things are looking up."

Though Jasper knew some of the Smullen story, he wanted to know more, and Henry enjoyed telling it. Mary's father, Horace Smullen, had been a prosperous planter with two sons and two daughters. Soon after his youngest child, Mary, had entered the world, his wife had left it, leaving him a widower. Already in his fifties at that point, he hadn't had the taste for remarrying and instead looked to Winifred, his late wife's sister, for support in raising his offspring. Childless, she'd been happy to oblige, but the years that followed had not been easy. A yellow fever epidemic killed off one son; another drowned as a youth swimming. This pair of tragedies obliged Horace Smullen to pin his hopes for continued family prosperity on acquiring sons-in-law of substance. Since his daughters were both beauties, he calculated the odds were in his favor.

When forty-year-old bachelor Aristotle Randall came to town for a visit, Smullen hadn't given him much thought, viewing him as too old for fair Annabelle. Up until then, his oldest daughter had refused all marriage offers, aggravating her father and foreshadowing her daughter's fastidious ways. Annabelle, however, unaccountably fell in love with the Professor's patrician good looks and refined manners. Indulgent father that he was, Smullen had been loath to disappoint her. Randall had been on the faculty of the University of Virginia but had taken an extended leave due to unspecified health ailments. On further investigation the "health ailments" proved to be a nervous malaise caused by trying to instruct wild young men who could care less about classical Rome, much less ancient Chinese dynasties. Smullen knew Randall was a gentleman from a good family in Virginia with an inheritance due to him. Supposing any Virginian, even one with an agitated malaise, was capable of running a farm with some instruction, he consented to his daughter's wishes. After all, being out in the healthy Sea Island air would cure even the worst of nerves in short order. Randall, however, proved more inept at the task of farm management than Smullen had thought possible, and after only a single winter of attempted apprenticeship, the father-in-law waved a white flag and gave up. He built the pair a house in town, wished them well, and with increased anxiety looked to a second son-in-law to carry on his endeavors.

In this he was more fortunate, though the appearance of the prospective suitor had not been immediate. During their Beaufort College days, both Henry and Jasper had ignored Mary when, in pigtails, she'd tagged along to watch as they rigged sailboats or shot squirrels or set off in homemade canoes. But when Henry had returned home following his graduation from South Carolina College and attended a party that Smullen had thrown for his youngest on her seventeenth birthday, Mary had caught his attention profoundly.

Unfortunately, Mary's sister, Annabelle, died a year after the birth of her only child, casting a long shadow on the beginning of Mary and Henry's courtship. Smullen, growing old and ill himself, realized he needed to work effectively and fast. With only the modest acres of Birch Hill behind him, Henry couldn't offer the wealth of Professor Randall, but he came from an old Sea Island family with a good name, and, as Smullen shrewdly discerned, had drive and ambition enough for half a dozen sons-in-law. Moreover, Henry successfully wooed the tender heart of Smullen's youngest until she would have immolated herself on a pyre like a Raja's widow had her choice not been approved. The relieved father sanctioned Henry's suit, and after the conclusion of a year of mourning for his first daughter, gave his second one away. During his final days, it was no small consolation to Smullen to watch Henry take over his property and run it with an élan that assured him the Smullen fortunes were secure.

In his will, Smullen divided his property into two unequal parts, Silver Oaks for Mary, and the somewhat smaller Smullen Point for Annabelle's husband and baby. (After all, Horace Smullen had given his daughter and son-in-law a house in town, and Randall did have some money of his own, even if it had to be obtained by selling slaves and land in Virginia.) When his father-in-law died, Henry continued with the management of both properties, using the proceeds from Smullen Point to maintain Professor Randall and his daughter in the style the Smullen's were accustomed to.

"And what have you gotten out of all this, Henry," Jasper asked fondly. "Except double the work and half the money?"

Henry laughed. "It's been no sacrifice. I couldn't love Cara more if she were my own daughter. You know Mary and I more or less raised her because her father wasn't capable of managing a child. As far as I can tell, the Professor has run through most of his own fortune on books and ancient Chinese scrolls, so I've been caretaker for Cara's birthright that some day I'll hand over to her husband. I've improved the land here with the same techniques I used on my own, and through good management and healthy living, the number of slaves on Smullen Point has nearly doubled the past fifteen years. I've made a science of fertility, I'd say. Now the Smullen Point house—" Both men looked back to the plain farm house and the street of slave cottages behind it. "—is certainly modest, but it can be improved, or torn down and a new one built."

Jasper turned back to the last gleaming rays of sun playing on the tidal waters in front of him. "Do Cara and the Professor spend their winters here?"

Henry shook his head. "They live in town year-round, although Cara pays visits to Silver Oaks. They have their books there, and Cara has her piano and other amusements. No point them sitting here amidst crops they couldn't care less about." Then Henry remembered himself. "Of course, Cara's been instructed by Mary so that she knows how to be mistress of a plantation when the time comes."

Jasper smiled. "You're a good man, Henry, doing all you have for them with no reward for yourself. Maybe you should lock Cara away for Billy. That way you could keep this all in the family."

"There are easier ways to keep this in the family," Henry said.

So there it was. Jasper slowly turned to his cousin. "I thought that's what you had up your sleeve last night. The answer is no."

"Jasper," Henry said, "let me lay my cards on the table for you."

Jasper laughed. "Henry, you are physiologically incapable of laying all your cards on the table. You're a schemer through and through."

"Well, then, let me lay most of my cards on the table for you. Cara would be perfect for you. You should marry her, settle down on one of the most beautiful pieces of land next to what is arguably the most beautiful, cultured town in America and live the life you were meant to lead. Flitting around the world is all well and good, but you're a

Southerner, man, this earth is in your blood, and it's time for you to do something real with your life. Your marrying Cara and taking over Smullen Point would more than pay me back for all my years of hard work. Just think, Jasper, you and me together again. The last thing I want is for her to marry some idiot I can't stand and watch him run this place into the ground."

"The offer is kind," Jasper said dryly, "though I can't quite see how you can make it without Cara being involved. But the answer is still no."

"You don't find her attractive?" Henry asked.

"Henry, she's lovely, but that's the least that matters. First of all, I've been married before, remember? And I was an abject failure at it."

"Not at an abject failure."

"Abject."

"You were young, Jasper. It was a long time ago. You need to forgive yourself and move on."

"Secondly, I have no intention of staying in the South. I'm just passing through." He held up a hand when Henry tried to counter this. "Thirdly, Cara doesn't like me; in fact, she's not even speaking to me at the moment. So you see, it may be a nice idea in fantasy, but in reality you're just going to have to accommodate whomever Cara does eventually set her cap on, someone who's younger and less jaded and less weary than me. Truly, Henry, let this idea go." He kicked his horse and started back for Silver Oaks where it would soon be time for supper.

"Is there someone else?" Henry asked, catching up to him.

"No," Jasper said.

"But there was," Henry suggested.

"There was, but not now."

Henry was quiet the rest of the ride home in the twilight. After supper, he showed Jasper to his room.

"Do you want me to send up a slave girl?"

Jasper looked at him oddly. "I can undress myself."

Henry rolled his eyes. "As if I meant that. I have a girl I traded for last month who's nearly a quadroon. Do you want to see her?"

Jasper scrutinized his cousin. "I'm fine. Thank you."

Henry shrugged. "Suit yourself. You won't find any public women in Beaufort, as you well know, so tell me if you change your mind."

As Jasper lay in bed, he couldn't believe that Henry had asked him to marry his niece in the afternoon and then offered him a slave girl for his bed in the evening. The thumping noise and muted laughter coming from Henry's room made it clear Henry had a Negro concubine, and Jasper wondered if Mary knew. Of course, how could she see those mulatto boys every day that bore such a resemblance to her own sons and not know?

Then again, intimately familiar with Henry's predilection for scheming, Jasper thought it possible Henry had fully expected him to turn down the slave girl. Maybe the offer had just been to remind him of the pleasures of female company, to evoke the gratifications he was missing. If so, he'd succeeded, because now Jasper was thinking about female company, and not in terms of some quadroon slave either. It was Cara who was floating through his thoughts and what her charms might be on closer acquaintance. No, that prettiness was the worm dangling on the hook. He would not take the bait. Damn Henry anyway, he thought, punching his pillow and turning over on his side. For the slave girl's sake, he hoped she wasn't being offered to every man who visited Silver Oaks. If she was, he uncomfortably realized there was nothing he could do about it.

"Why isn't Cara speaking to you?" Henry asked over breakfast the next day. He'd been up at dawn, ridden over half his property and attended to business while Jasper slept in.

Jasper wiped his moustache with his napkin. "I happened to witness Mercer proposing to her Saturday night and couldn't resist making an inappropriate comment that she was right to take offense at."

"Mercer proposed? Ha," Henry exclaimed with delight. "Good old Mercer, came through in the end. That makes sixteen. So did you apologize?"

"To Cara?" Jasper had to think about. "No, I guess I didn't."

"Well then," Henry said, buttering his toast. "That's obviously your next step."

"There is no 'next', Henry. There's no future."

Henry sipped his coffee. "There's always a 'next.'"

"Cara's an unusual girl," Henry observed that evening as he swirled the French wine in his glass under a candlelit chandelier. They'd spent most of the day riding out of doors with just a short break for dinner, and now they were contentedly sunburnt and tired as they supped. "There's not one man in a thousand who could really appreciate her."

Jasper looked up cautiously from his turtle soup. Mary kept her main cook with her at whichever house she was residing, but this secondary cook at Silver Oaks wasn't bad. They'd already had a fine dish of baked oysters that Jasper had found quite tasty. He had to admit over the years, he'd missed the cuisine of his homeland no small amount. "I'm sure Cara will find a suitable husband in time."

"No, really," Henry insisted. "She's been right to turn down all the boys who've asked so far. Well, and one old widower, I don't know what he was thinking proposing. All of them, including Johnny, would've made her miserable. She's sensitive, astute. And subtle, very subtle, that one. She's like a thoroughbred: she can go the distance but she has to have the right man in the saddle."

Jasper sipped his tea. "Save her for Billy then. The boy's smart—I think he's going to follow in his father's footsteps."

Though Henry was pleased by this evaluation of his son, he was not to be deterred. "Get to know her. Talk to her. She actually knows more about the Orient than the Professor."

Jasper raised a skeptical eyebrow.

"It's true," Henry said. "And all of those magazines of mine she borrows? Her father doesn't read them, she does."

"Better not let that get out," Jasper observed. "If it gets around she reads *Scientific American*, she'll never dance a quadrille again."

"You joke, but do you see what I'm up against? She needs someone exceptional. Someone like you."

Jasper tilted his head. "Henry, do the words 'My wife died because I made her so miserable' mean anything to you? Is that what you want for Cara?"

"That wasn't you. You were out of your head with drink. You've redeemed yourself, Jasper. You've learned; you've changed."

Jasper was ready to counter this, too, but then he just sighed. "You're a good man, Henry, you really are. I know you want the best for Cara, and I'm flattered you've included me as part of that. But some things aren't meant to be."

Henry just swirled his wine. "You don't know how good it is to have you here, Jasper. There are so few people I can really talk to. Most of the men in this county have their heads so wrapped up in politics they can hardly string two sensible words together. You know you always spoke sense, even when you were three sheets to the wind."

"And now that I'm sober?" Jasper asked.

"Now that you're sober," Henry said, "you're capable of more than just talking sense. You're capable of doing it."

On returning to Villa d'Este, Henry brought Mary up-to-date on events.

"You straight out told him you want him to marry Cara?" Mary said with alarm. "Why? Now he'll resist everything we try to do."

"Maybe," Henry said. "But the idea will worm its way into him, and the more he tries not to think about it, the more he will. Even better, the more he tries not to admire Cara, the more he'll see her as the epitome of grace and beauty. It's perfect. If we can just keep him in Beaufort for the summer, we'll have a betrothal by autumn as sure as you're Mrs. Henry Birch. Why didn't Cara tell you about, Mercer, do you think?"

"I don't know," Mary said. "Maybe there are others she hasn't told me about."

"Others?" Henry said, brightening. "You mean the count might be even higher?"

The count grew to seventeen on Friday evening in the Saddler garden with Thomas Purcell. After Cara encouraged Thomas to follow his dream and join all the others rushing pell-mell to golden California, she stood a minute alone among the azaleas enjoying the solitude. Hugging her arms to herself, she couldn't imagine the world offered many places more enchanting than a Beaufort garden on a warm spring night. Her contentment lasted until she spotted someone on a bench tucked behind an oleander bush. Someone sitting quite still except for the occasional motion to sip his green tea.

"Mr. Wainwright," she said severely. "Your manners are . . . are . . ."

"Appalling?" he answered for her. "Actually not, Miss Randall. I've been sitting here, completely minding my own business, and it's hardly my fault that the fervid youth of Beaufort choose this spot for their liaisons. You all could go down to the river, you know." He didn't mention that he sometimes sought out quiet spots because he found it difficult to watch other men drink, and drinking was the predominant male pastime at Beaufort gatherings.

"There've been others out here?" Cara asked in surprise.

Jasper pulled his watch from his waistcoat that he could just see in the moonlight. "Let's see . . . three couples in twenty-five minutes. This place is like a train station."

Not appreciative of her affairs being compared to steam engines, Miss Randall gathered her skirts and went inside.

After a sumptuous dinner Sunday afternoon, Henry proposed they take a walk by the river to allow the ladies some exercise. Since Henry rarely walked anywhere, it was a more than unusual suggestion, but the warmth of the late afternoon did beckon one out of doors, and Henry was a firm believer that physical activity was necessary for good health, even for the females in his clan.

The Senator and the Professor were not enticed, preferring a snooze on the couch and in the armchair, respectively. So just five of them set out: Henry, Jasper, Winifred, Mary, and Cara. The men wore wide-brimmed panama hats while each woman had a bonnet firmly tied under her chin. But after only a few minutes Henry remembered a task calling him back to the house and told them to go on without him. Soon after that, Mary had something of strong import to relay to Winifred, (something bordering on gossip, a vice Mary seldom indulged in, but a desperate ploy was a desperate ploy) slowing the older women's pace. The result was that quickly Jasper was left strolling silently with Cara who wouldn't look at him.

Jasper couldn't help himself. "Tell me, Miss Randall, do you plan to ever accept any of the lovelorn men who throw their hearts at your feet?"

Cara pursed her lips, her pretty nose well shaded by the protective expanse of straw and silk that made up her hat. "No, Mr. Wainwright, I do not."

"Why is that?" he asked, genuinely curious.

She looked away, as if the barefoot boy on the other side of the road carrying a note for his master was entirely engrossing to her. "Because I prefer my life as it is."

"Without a husband, children, or home of your own? I thought that's what all women wanted."

"I'm unacquainted with all women, Mr. Wainwright. However, I have a home of my own, a loving father, and no husband to tell me what to do. This allows me to spend most of my time as I please. I see not the faintest advantage to giving that up."

Walking cane in hand, Jasper strolled along thoughtfully, admiring the unfurled velvety blooms of a graceful magnolia. "Well, that's reasonable enough. I've long thought marriage akin to indentured servitude for women, so I can see why you might not leap at the chance for its fetters."

Cara glanced at him suspiciously.

"But then," Jasper said, "if you don't want to marry, why do you go to so much effort to appear so . . . comely, shall we say. Yes, you have natural attractions, but they could be diminished with a pince-nez, dowdy clothing, and a sour expression. Why, you could throw out your corset and make your waist as big as a rain barrel, if you so chose. It seems to me with your curls and ribbons and charming smiles, you'll constantly attract precisely the attention you don't desire."

Cara looked down, more than a little perturbed at such an observation. "My ability to do as I please depends on my . . . looking comely, as you say."

Jasper made a guess. "It's Aunt Winnie, isn't it? You've got to be up to her standards, or she's all over you."

"Or I have to live with her," Cara admitted in a small voice.

"Oh dear," Jasper said. "If I had that threat hanging over me, I'd wear a corset and curl my hair, too."

Cara gave him a small smile before looking behind her to make sure Aunt Winnie was out of earshot. "My great-aunt was the belle of her day, and her love of fashion has never waned. Only now it's me that gets dressed up and goes to dances. So you see my predicament, Mr. Wainwright."

"All too clearly, Miss Randall. You desire freedom, or at least more sovereignty than the average Southern female is allowed. And the price is eternal beauty."

"And eternal proposals," Cara said a bit sadly. "I try not to encourage them, you know. I don't like turning them all down."

"Which is why you reject them with such compassion. Although I can't say it's a kindness to encourage someone to risk their life around Cape Horn."

"It's what Thomas wants to do," Cara said defensively. "He'll regret it to the end of his days if he never sees California."

"Maybe," Jasper said with good humor. "But you don't think he's right about gold nuggets waiting for him on the beach, do you?"

"I think he'll find much on his journey beyond gold," Cara said.

Jasper glanced at her as they walked along. "Miss Randall, since you've been good enough to take me in your confidence, I'll be so bold as to take you into mine. As you may know, I was married once. It was a difficult experience for both my wife, God rest her soul, and me, mostly due to reprehensible actions on my part. I've no wish to repeat the episode. In addition, I've no plans to stay in the South. I'm truly just passing through."

"I see, Mr. Wainwright," Cara said slowly.

Jasper squinted as he looked off at the river. "It's never pleasant to reveal one's transgressions, especially not ones as large as mine, and I don't do it idly. I assume this past week you've noticed that you and I have been thrown together with some regularity."

Cara inspected the button at the base of her glove. "I have, Mr. Wainwright."

"And you have your suspicions why this might be the case?"

It took Cara a moment to answer. "Their intentions are good. We must keep that in mind."

"Be that as it may, Miss Randall, we don't have to accept it passively."

Cara frowned. "What do you propose?"

"A deal between us. A mutual independence pact. I work to preserve your independence while you work to preserve mine. That way neither of us has anything to fear for the duration of my stay in Beaufort no matter how often we're thrown together."

Cara smiled slightly. "You're saying we'll meet Henry and Mary's stratagems with the weapons of lucidity and logic. But we'll not lose our fondness and respect for them."

Jasper glanced at her keenly. "Not for one minute. Henry and Mary are precious to me."

"Then we have an understanding, Mr. Wainwright. Should we shake hands on it, do you think?"

"I don't know, are your aunts watching?"

Cara surreptitiously snuck a glance at them. "They are."

"Then let's not. I know your word's good."

They'd walked far enough along the shell-lined street to reach the steamer landing and the scattering of shops along Bay Street that had been closed all day, naturally, for the Sabbath. "Mr. Wainwright," Cara said hesitantly, "you said in your travels you learned some of the Chinese language. I wonder if you also learned to read any Chinese calligraphy?"

"A little," Jasper answered. "Enough that I had the temerity to translate a classic Chinese text as an exercise."

"Which Chinese text would that be, Mr. Wainwright?"

He looked at her curiously. "*The Tao Te Ching*. It's a work of philosophy."

"*The Tao Te Ching*?" Cara said. "All of it? I've only seen a few passages rendered into English. Is it long?"

"Only five thousand characters," Jasper said. "Brevity was one of Lao-Tzu's strong points."

"Have you considered publishing your translation, Mr. Wainwright? I'm sure readers of *The North American Quarterly of Oriental Study* would find it engrossing."

He laughed. "All ten of them. I assure you, Miss Randall, what I've done is the work of an amateur. I'll leave it to a real scholar to do it justice."

Cara considered the information. "I have a text at home that has passages in both English and Chinese," she ventured. "I wonder if you might be willing to decipher the Chinese part?"

"I'd be delighted to make an attempt," Jasper said with good humor. "And if I fail completely, which is likely, we can appeal to Jim." Before long, Cara was asking him questions about the Portuguese colony of Macao, about China's conflict with Britain over opium importation, and about the life foreigners led in the acutely restricted environment of Canton. For never having travelled beyond boundaries of the southern United States, she had a surprising knowledge of the world.

Their conversation continued with animation even back at Villa d'Este. She had a thirst for information that, in spite of himself, Jasper found very pleasant to slake. Oh, yes, he could see why Mercer fell for her. As Henry and Mary exchanged pleased, knowing looks and Aunt Winnie glowered in the background, Jasper realized he would have to be so careful. To have such a beautiful young woman engrossed in his every word and offering insights more discerning than nine-tenths of the men he ran across was a dangerous thing, independence pact agreed to or not.

Chapter Four

J asper tossed Jim the previous day's edition of *The Charleston Courier* that had been delivered on the early steamer and then brought to the house by one of Henry's servants assigned to meet the boat. After Henry perused the paper each day, Jasper generally brought it up to his room so Jim could have a turn with it. Since it made white men nervous to see a black man reading, especially something as topical as a newspaper, Jim could hardly read it anywhere else. A newspaper found in a slave cabin such as the one Jim shared at present with Hock would be incendiary.

"Look at the letter to the editor in there," Jasper said. "I think this man, Eustace Woods, has potential."

"What do you mean 'potential?' " Jim asked, arching an eyebrow.

"Potential for creating change," Jasper said seriously. "If men like Henry think he's sensible, he's developing a real audience."

"Don't hold your breath," Jim advised. "No one gives away wealth and power just because someone writes something sensible in a newspaper once in a while." Jim opened the paper to the editorial page. There was yet another letter in the long running feud between Vernon Hoffman and Joseph Cook that was likely to get one of them called out eventually. Then came the missive from Mr. Woods:

To the Editor of The Charleston Courier:

Dear Sir,

I would like to congratulate The Charleston Courier *on its equanimous reporting of the controversy regarding the proper nourishment and maintenance of slaves. Such composure is requisite when delving into a subject so near and dear to both our economy and our morality. As every upstanding planter knows, the slaves of our great state are our Christian burden to provide for, just as our gracious Lord provides for all his children. With this burden, we who possess slaves have a duty to ensure the physical and moral welfare of those within our dominion. We all know that no true Southern gentleman would deny a slave the sustenance and raiment necessary for physical health, especially since the Bible itself permits Christians to own slaves only on the condition that those slaves are well treated.*

For over a hundred years it has been the law of this great state to require every slave owner to provide his servants with adequate food, clothing and shelter. Enforcing this regulation with an occasional inspection would not serve to injure the honorable among us. Only the ignominious need fear it. Furthermore, collectively protecting the welfare of our slave population would have the happy practical result of increasing our workforce—and hence our wealth—statewide.

I need not remind you that since the importation of slaves is no longer possible, this is the sole method at our disposal to increase the numbers available to labor either on plantations or in future industrial capacity. Those who argue that masters should be unrestrained to starve or freeze their slaves if they so wish are grievously myopic. We must never forget the burden that we, the educated and the privileged, must bear on behalf of our less elevated brethren. Moreover, it's patent hogwash to think that stinting an asset near term could ever bring about a profitable long-term result.

Sincere regards,
Eustace Woods

"What's so great about that?" Jim said in disgust. "So he thinks that cold, starving people make bad laborers—which is obviously true, but that's beside the point. He still backs slavery one hundred percent. In fact, he wants to breed slaves in the state as fast as he damn well can."

"No, no, you've got to see beyond that. Look at the details: he's recommending legislation that would require inspectors to ensure slaves receive adequate food, clothing and shelter. Don't you see? The government would methodically intervene to regulate slave welfare. It's monumental."

Jim snorted a little. "Well, the legislature will never do it, that's for sure."

"But someone's at least talking about it."

Jim shook his head. "Jasper, the South ain't going to change without God himself coming to smite the blow. It just ain't."

Jasper picked up the page and read the article again. "It could. One minuscule step at a time. It could."

"And gold could start spurting out of the ground any day now."

"They say it happens in California," Jasper said wryly. "By the way, I saw you in and out of the neighborhood dependencies yesterday evening. Scare up any patients?"

Jim shrugged. "Two running noses, one whooping cough, and a kidney ailment."

"Cure them?"

Jim looked surprised. "Of course."

Jasper was set for a morning ride with Jim headed west towards the Broad River, but he wanted to make a stop at Professor Randall's before they started off.

Jim shook his head. "You going to let some pretty curls mess with twelve years of good sense?"

"I've no taste for giddy ingénues, as you well know," Jasper said, which was a fair assertion since he'd artfully evaded at least half a dozen in London and Paris over the course of the previous two years. "It's just that cloaked inside this particular set of petticoats and bonnets, there's a mind I feel some compassion for, that's all."

"Hmmf," Jim snorted, but it didn't dissuade Jasper from his object. At the Randall house, he dismounted and handed his reins to Mercury, the yard boy, before climbing the stairs to Cara's front door. Allowed in by a surprised Neptune, he was led to the parlor where the door was partly open. Through the gap he could see Cara, standing with her back to the door, speaking to Minnie. Curiously, the slave girl sat at a desk near the far wall, dipping a steel nib pen into a pewter inkwell.

"End it by saying something about the fine weather we're having, and how I hope to see her again in Charleston next February. Something like that. You know what I mean."

Neptune cleared his throat nervously. "Miz Cara? Marse Wainwright heyuh da see yuh."

Cara spun around. "Neptune, tell him I'll—" But now she could see Jasper was just beyond her slave's shoulder.

Jasper noticed Minnie quickly place her writing instruments in the desk's main drawer.

"Mr. Wainwright," Cara said, lifting her chin as Minnie hurriedly left the room. "This is a surprise."

Jasper held out a book to her. "Pardon my intrusion, Miss Randall. I've heard you're a voracious reader, and I suspect even with your great town library, material may sometimes be lacking in Beaufort. A friend gave me this novel to read on my trip across the Atlantic, and I thought you might find it amusing. It's about a girl with a strong will and mind of her own. I assure you it's quite fashionable right now in London."

Cara looked down at the cover that proclaimed, *Jane Eyre*, by Currer Bell, in gold lettering. Her eyes widened slightly. "I've heard of this book. Yes, I believe I would indeed like to read it." She took the volume from him and curtsied. "Thank you, Mr. Wainwright."

Jasper bowed. "You're welcome, Miss Randall."

"Compassion for her mind," Jim muttered as he and Jasper made their way out of town. "What a load of hooey."

Jasper ignored the comment. "Do you know what I found Miss Randall doing in her parlor?"

"Sewing a ribbon on her bonnet to cover her intelligent mind?" Jim asked sarcastically, giving his horse a prod with his heels to pick up the pace.

"No, dictating a letter to her slave girl, who was writing with an elegant pen on an elegant piece of paper."

Jim seemed impressed by the news. "Does the girl write in her mistress's hand?"

"Interesting question," Jasper said as they passed the last house on the western edge of town. The street that they were on, which before could accommodate two carriages in passing, had narrowed into a lane with just enough width for a single vehicle. Wider spots could always be found if necessary, and there was plenty of room for two abreast on horseback. "I'd think she must write in the same hand, or the correspondents would notice. See, Jim, all sorts of unusual things are happening in Beaufort, once you scratch the surface. This town could truly be ready for change."

"Jasper, this place is full of the most pro-nullification, pro-slavery, pro-secession hotheads in the South. It's going in the reverse direction of any kind of freedom, and here you think it's ready to burst from its slavery cocoon and become some kind of abolitionist butterfly. If I didn't know better, I'd think you got an opium pipe tucked away in your luggage somewhere."

"They're on the wrong side of history," Jasper said thoughtfully, "and they've got to be feeling it. They've got to be. It's fascinating, really, observing how a civilization prepares to reinvent itself."

Jim shook his head as he ducked under a low handing branch. "You've been smoking a whole chest of opium. Never seen someone so delusional."

That evening, the Senator and Mrs. Pickens came to supper as well as Professor Randall, which meant the host and hostess could not conveniently leave Cara and Jasper together again. They did induce Cara to play a few pieces on the piano for them all, however.

"You play very well, Miss Randall," Jasper said when she was finished.

She flushed slightly as she rose from the piano stool and made her way to a vacant chair. "Given the virtuosity you've witnessed in the capitals of Europe, you must not make light of my abilities, sir."

"I don't make light at all. I'm wholly sincere." He ignored the suspicious look Mrs. Pickens was giving him. "Were you aware that some women in Europe make careers out of their artistic talents? It can even be a path to financial independence." Cara looked at him sharply before averting her eyes to her hands that were demurely folded in her lap.

"What women would these be?" Winifred Pickens asked. "One could hardly call them ladies."

"Clara Schumann, wife of the composer Robert Schumann, is unquestionably a lady," Jasper observed mildly. "And she's considered one of the greatest pianists of our time. She performs concertos throughout Europe."

"Europeans," the Senator said from the depths of his armchair. "Never did trust any of them."

"Public exposure can do nothing but bring a woman shame and notoriety," Aunt Winifred said.

"I don't know," Henry said, looking to stir the pot a bit more. "Look at Jenny Lind. Everyone seems to consider her the nearest thing to an angel on earth. There's virtue for you."

Cara's face, which had brightened on considering Clara Schumann, now darkened. "I hardly see how she can be an angel. They say she has a nose like a potato."

"Cara," Mary remonstrated.

Jasper smiled. "It's not far off the truth. But when she sings, her face transforms, and she becomes almost ethereal. It's uncanny really."

"Probably why Chopin's enamored with her," Henry observed with a sly glance at Cara. "The man's a bit unearthly himself."

Cara frowned, not liking her idol to be in any way impugned.

"I don't care if that Swedish singer grows wings and flies around on stage," Aunt Winnie said crossly. "No true Southern lady would ever make a public display of herself. Just imagine it. Disgraceful."

"No one has proposed that a Southern lady perform in public," Mary said, attempting to calm roiled waters.

Aunt Winnie glanced irritably at Jasper. "Some people seem to have suggested it. The proper business of a lady is her husband and her children, if she has the good fortune to have any."

The Senator cleared his throat. "Henry, forgot to tell you. Heywood heard it from Barnard who heard it from Harrington that the editor of *The Courier* is confirming that Eustace Woods is definitely a Beaufort man. Or at least that they've traced the letters to the Beaufort packet."

Henry's face lit up. "Truly? What fun. Now we can speculate endlessly on Woods's true identity within a finite range of candidates we actually know. To think that living among us is someone far more sensible than I supposed is much more than I hoped for. I confess I'm delighted."

"Hmphf," the Senator grumbled. "I go with Woods to a point, but this last letter about sending around inspectors to every plantation—it's too much."

"If it wasn't done in a high-handed way, I wouldn't mind," Henry said with a small shrug. "I've nothing to hide in the treatment of my slaves, and neither does any true gentleman, so it'd really affect only the lowest class of slaveholder. And after all, if you can't afford to feed and clothe your slaves, you probably shouldn't have them."

"If the problem's so small, then why bother to regulate it?" the Senator grumbled. "Just ties the hands of those who are running their properties well."

"Surely," Cara said slowly, "it might substantiate the South's claim of responsible treatment of its slaves and reduce the North's criticism of our institutions if we verified the vast majority look after their slaves well and then penalized the few involved in mistreatment?"

Aunt Winifred glanced at the Senator. "You men shouldn't be talking politics amongst us ladies. You know it's a toxic influence on some people."

"Cara has a better mind for politics than most of the men in this town," Henry stated. "I'll take sense wherever I can get it." He turned to Cara. "The problem is, if we legislate in response to Northern criticism, it'll never end. They want slavery done away with, simple as that. All intermediary steps would be a steep slope to their ultimate goal."

"Most of the civilized world has outlawed slavery at this point," Jasper observed. "Do you think a hundred years from now the South will still have slaves?"

Henry sat back in his chair and crossed his legs. "As you well know, I'm a great believer in science, and the rate of technological progress we're experiencing right now is nothing short of astonishing. My grandfather in his wildest dreams couldn't have imagined the steamboat, the telegraph, or the railroads. If you'd told him someday he'd get his news the day after it happened, that ships would cross from New York to Liverpool in eleven days, and steamers would make it from Beaufort to Charleston in three and a half hours, he'd never have believed it. So when I think of the lives my grandchildren and great-grandchildren might lead, I can entertain that there might be ingenious machines doing things that human brawn does now. Yes, it's possible we'll be able to replace slaves with mechanical power. But not within my lifetime, I wouldn't say."

"Henry," Aunt Winifred said severely, "you should be careful with your sentiments. How could machines ever take care of children or wash clothes or prepare food?"

"Aunt Winnie, just because I can't answer you today doesn't mean someday somebody won't."

The Senator rose from his chair, more than ready to expound on a topic he'd argued before with great majesty in the Senate chamber. "If we even admit a future without slavery, we're doomed," the Senator said, his hands behind his back as he began to pace. "Slavery is a fact of human existence. It's justified in the Bible from the very beginning, when Noah curses Canaan to be the slave of Shem."

"I always thought that was a little unfair of Noah," Henry reflected. "After all, he was cursing his own grandson for an act he hadn't even committed."

With a glare at Henry, the Senator went on. "Slavery was part of every great ancient civilization. The splendors of Greece, Rome, and Egypt would've been impossible without slavery, and no one apologized for it then. No, we admire the architecture, literature and refinements that slavery made possible. In addition, let's not forget that the Africans themselves own slaves and to this day are glad to sell their brothers any chance they get.

"Now," he continued, "how can anyone argue that slavery isn't a positive good for the Negroes? Because of it, they're not blighted by famine or drought, nor do they suffer the ravages of war. Instead they're blessed with food, shelter, and clothing, as well as God, the Bible, and civil order. You think running around with voodoo and nakedness and no knowledge of the Bible is what God wants for them? Not in the least. God wants the inhabitants of the earth to know and love him, and let me tell you, they can't do that banging away on drums in the middle of the jungle. No sir. And another thing, even though our Northern brethren don't like to acknowledge it, slavery has been good for our country. Indigo and rice picked by slaves paid for our revolution against Britain and produced our independence as a nation. For the past fifty years, slave cotton has fed our Northern mills, driven our industrial engine and paid for more than our fair share of the Mexican war and all the infernal internal improvements in the North. America suckled on slavery from its infancy: there were slaves from the first settlement at Jamestown. It's deep in our blood and our heritage, and if we yield one inch to the northern abolitionists, we'll betray the sacrifices our forefathers made to bequeath us this way of life. So, no, I don't care how clever you make your machines, Henry, slavery is here to stay."

"Nearly everything you say was also true for Britain and her colonies," Jasper observed, "and yet the British abolished slavery fifteen years ago."

The Senator turned and faced him directly, bellowing like a bull enraged by a matador's sword. "Jasper Wainwright, are you telling me you side with the abolitionists?"

Winnie fixed her eye on Jasper with displeasure while Mary twisted her hands together anxiously. Cara looked back and forth between the two men as if she wished she could say something but didn't dare.

Jasper looked the Senator over calmly. "I mean merely to engage in friendly discussion while attempting to comprehend your point of view."

"In your learned opinion, Senator," Henry cut in, "who could be the true writer of Mr. Woods's letters? Anyone you'd place odds on? It's certainly not Jasper here, since the letters began while he was still in Europe. How about Robert Barnwell?"

The Senator shook his head. "Woods sounds like a younger man to me. Someone more familiar with all the scientific gibberish you like to talk about, Henry. Maybe Comstock?"

Henry considered. "If it is, he hides it well. Comstock has never struck me as particularly thoughtful a day in his life."

Aunt Winnie rose. "Senator, it's late. Professor, may we offer you and Cara a ride home?" The Professor, who had been dozing in an armchair, woke up at this forceful query, but Aunt Winnie didn't wait for an answer. "Cara, get your wrap," she directed.

Since there was no way to sidestep the dictate, all parties yielded to Aunt Winnie's compelling will. But as the carriage was brought around the half moon entrance drive, Cara hung back on the front porch. "Mr. Wainwright," she said in low tones, "I am enjoying your book. However, I can't believe it was written by a man. The voice of the main character seems so particularly feminine."

"I agree with your appraisal, Miss Randall. But you know sometimes women in Europe write under male pseudonyms. Surely you're familiar with the works of George Sand?"

Cara looked down, her face illuminated by a lantern placed on the porch newel post to aid the guests in their descent of the stairs. "I'm not allowed to read Monsieur, or I should say, Madame Sand."

Jasper smiled. "In any event, I shouldn't be surprised to find Mr. Currer Bell revealed to be a different person altogether."

"Cara, come," Aunt Winnie directed with a wave of her arm from the door of the carriage. With a curtsy, Cara left. "Where is the Senator?" he heard Winifred bark crossly.

As Jasper headed up the interior stairs towards his room, he caught a glimpse of the wayward husband. He was still in the parlor in conference with Henry.

"He's certainly not an abolitionist," Henry was saying. "He freed Jim because of heroic personal service on their travels, that's all. He still owns two score slaves back in Sleety Pines."

"Then what was all that hundred year talk about?" the Senator grumbled.

"Just an interesting mental exercise," Henry assured him.

So that was the story Henry was giving out, Jasper thought as he quietly climbed the grand staircase. Well, he supposed he didn't blame him. Henry had to keep his cousin from being run out of town on a rail somehow.

The next afternoon when Cara visited, she found a private moment to slip the copy of *Jane Eyre* back into Jasper's hands. He had to admire how well she'd hid the four-hundred-page novel in the voluminous undersleeve of her dress.

"You're done?" Jasper said with surprise.

"I finished it this morning," Cara answered.

"By daylight or candlelight?" he asked with amusement, noticing there were faint shadows under her eyes.

"Both," she admitted with a guilty smile. "I found the moral trajectory of the conflict quite engrossing. That Mr. Rochester could be so thorough a villain and still a hero is remarkable. I don't believe I've ever run across such a conflicted, disconcerting character before."

Jasper had to smile as he turned the book over in his hand. "He's a hero in the Lord Byron tradition —'mad, bad and dangerous to know.' It makes him terribly attractive, I fear. Luckily, Jane's the strong one, and she puts everything to right."

"Cara, what are you and Mr. Wainwright talking about? Mr. Wainwright, what's that I see in your hand?" In deference to the indomitable Aunt, Cara and Jasper reluctantly drifted from the entryway to the parlor.

Jasper held up the item. "It's just a book I thought Miss Randall might find amusing."

"May I see it?" Aunt Winifred held out her hand imperiously, leaving Jasper no recourse but to hand it over. She raised an eyebrow. "*Jane Eyre*," she hissed with a significant look at Mary.

"Oh dear," Mary said, a bit shocked.

"I'm sorry, Cara, I can't allow it," Aunt Winnie opined.

"Really?" Jasper said. "It's quite popular in Europe, even among unmarried girls. I've read it myself, and while it has its dramatic moments, I can assure you it's in no way immoral."

Winifred gave him a look indicating that his assurances and eleven cents would buy her a yard of cheap calico at Ensler's Dry Goods.

Mary, however, was more uncertain. "Aunt Winnie, I know your cousin Verbena disapproves of it, but you say yourself she can be a bit stodgy. Maybe we should look it over and just make sure it's as inappropriate as she says."

Winnie drew herself up even more stiffly on her straight back. "Very well, Mary, you and I will peruse it. Mr. Wainwright, I must request to be allowed to remain in possession of this book."

Jasper nodded, glancing slightly at Cara. "Of course, Mrs. Pickens."

"I hope this isn't too disappointing, Cara," Mary said solicitously.

"Oh, I understand," Cara answered as she sat down demurely next to her aunt. She didn't so much as sneak a look at Jasper.

How good she was at deceiving her aunts, Jasper thought as he eyed the young woman coolly. He suspected even Mary had little idea of Cara's depths.

"What have you done to my wife?" Henry asked Jasper crossly the next day in the back parlor. "She's got her nose so deep in that novel you gave her she'll barely speak to me. It's a good thing we have slaves, or we wouldn't get more than bread and butter for supper."

"Mama just loves that Mr. Rochester," said Billy, the oldest, who'd wandered into the room in preparation for supper and story hour soon to come.

"Don't be saucy," Henry reproved. "How do you know the names of the characters anyway?"

"I already read the good parts," Billy said, pulling a chair up to the table. "The mad women setting the fires, the fortune teller, Rochester going blind. Rusty Drysdale has a copy."

"It's that lurid?" Henry said, looking at Jasper.

"Just a little dramatic," Jasper said. "Not that I ever expected a twelve-year-old boy to find it entertaining."

"Rusty's mom wouldn't let his sister read it up in Richmond, so that's when Rusty got a copy and underlined all the good parts."

Henry pointed a finger at his son. "Do not tell your mother. She'll have a fit, and then Aunt Winnie will go around burning half the books in Beaufort. You understand me?"

"Yes, sir," Billy said, abashed by his father's warning but also proud of having gotten his hands on the forbidden fruit when he'd had the chance. Just wait until he told Rusty about his cousin being banned from reading it and his mother tearing through the pages like there was no tomorrow.

Henry looked at Jasper. "See what you've done?"

"Me?" Jasper said. "Rusty Drysdale had all the good parts underlined before I got here."

Mary was in a dreadful mood the next day as she searched the front parlor. "Aunt Winnie took it, I just know she did. It was right here next to this chair when she stopped by this morning. She saw it and took it with her when she left. And just when Mr. Rochester had proposed."

"What damn fool book is your wife giving my wife to read?" the Senator asked Henry over juleps on the porch before dinner that afternoon. "She stayed home so she could keep at it. Says she has a headache. Headache, my right eye. And while she has her head full of some English moor, I have to leave my own house to get a decent meal. You've got to keep those European books out of Beaufort, Henry. European culture is becoming more depraved by the day."

"That does it," Henry said. "I'm going to Three Reeds tomorrow until this *Jane Eyre* mania is over. One of the sluice gates failed, and I've got a whole field of rice flooded out at exactly the wrong time anyway. I'd invite you to come, Jasper, but we don't have much in the way of accommodations on the New River yet. Besides, it's a long day of travel to get there, not to mention the mosquitoes can be savage even this early. I don't think you'd enjoy it."

"How long will you be gone?" Mary inquired worriedly. "You know I hate you subjecting yourself to the miasma there."

"Now, Mary, have I ever got the ague from Three Reeds? No, not once, not even the first summer when I had to spend two weeks in

July. I'm healthy as an ox. I'll be away four, maybe five days this time, but there's no help for it. I've got to make sure Turner takes care of this right." He put a conciliatory arm around his wife. "Tell you what, my love, let's have something to look forward to. Since it's obvious this town needs some excitement beyond an idiotic book, I propose a fete the week after next at Silver Oaks. We'll invite the whole town to come out for a barbecue, how about that? We'll have ice cream, lots of punch, and I'll even set up a shooting range out over the Coosaw. You know how much the young bucks loved hitting those targets over the water last time. What do you say, Mary, are you ready to host a party Beaufort will talk about for years?"

"Are you sure, Henry? Maybe we should hold it here at Villa d'Este. I know it'd be cramped, but it'll take ever so long for everyone just to get to Silver Oaks."

Henry looked extremely pleased with himself. "No, it won't. You and I and the boys will go out ahead of time to prepare, but everyone else can come on *The Beaufort Heron*. I've arranged to hire it for the day. It'll leave Beaufort at ten in the morning, return at midnight and can fit nearly a hundred people with no luggage when the tide's high and there's enough water for the draw. What do you say to the wonders of the nineteenth century, my dear?"

Mary stared at her husband. "We can hire the whole steamer just for our party?"

"Just for our party. Isn't it decadent? We'll put those old Romans to shame."

So it was settled. The festivities sounded just fine to the Senator, and Mrs. Pickens, intent as she was on the woes of Thornfield Manor, wasn't there to object.

However, the Senator did have a small discussion with Henry over brandy after Jasper had excused himself from the room. "That Negro of Wainwright's—"

"My understanding is he doesn't actually belong to Jasper any more, Senator," Henry observed evenly.

"Slave or servant, Wainwright brought him here, so he's responsible for him," the Senator answered crossly.

Henry nodded. "I agree with you there. What's the problem?"

The Senator sniffed a pinch of snuff. "Nothing exactly. Just some grumbling. From Rhett."

"About what?" Henry asked, frowning.

"About . . . about the way Wainwright's Negro looks at people. He doesn't show the proper respect."

Henry tilted his head as he considered. "Well, Spit Jim's a free man now, but being a free Negro in the South is a different matter than being one in Europe. Since he grew up here, you'd think he'd know, but maybe he needs reminding. I'll talk to Jasper." Satisfied, the Senator accepted another drink and the two men toasted *The Beaufort Heron.* "What do you think about that fellow, Garibaldi, defeating the French in defense of Rome?" Henry said heartily. "He seems to stir up trouble wherever he goes."

The Senator shook his head. "Those Europeans. With all their so-called revolutions, they don't know if they're coming or going. All they've accomplished is pandemonium, if you ask me. Don't know how Jasper stood that nonsense there last year."

Though Jasper had taken the revolutions of 1848 in stride, he received the warning about Jim later that evening less philosophically than Henry had hoped. He said little, however, just sipped his green tea on the porch and looked off over the dark river.

"Take it as friendly advice," Henry said. "Nothing to be alarmed about. It's just better not to get Rhett's dander up."

"Rhett?" Jasper questioned. "Which one?"

Henry shook his head. "I forgot, you don't know. This Rhett is a newly minted one. You knew him as Smith—Robert Barnwell Smith. Just after you left, his uncle, childless on his deathbed, cut him and his brothers a deal—you change your name to Rhett, I'll leave you money in my will. I suppose if their name had been something less pedestrian than Smith, they might've had scruples, but as it was, reminding everyone that William Rhett, the pirate catcher, was their ancestor—and getting money in the bargain—must've been hard to resist. So now we refer to him as Congressman Barnwell Rhett, the wild-eyed fire-eater who's done his best to start a conflagration in Washington these last twelve years over nullification, tariffs and whatever else he can get his hands on. He decided not to run for re-election last fall because he's angling for a Senate seat, but any way you cut it, the Rhetts are power-ful and ornery. They own *The Charleston Mercury* you know. Best not to cross them."

Jasper stared off at the water. "I knew there was a risk bringing Jim here. It just makes it obvious we can't stay too long."

Henry waved a hand. "You're too indulgent, Jasper. You allow him to be so familiar with you, he forgets how to behave with everyone else."

"How to be subservient, you mean," Jasper said quietly. "Yes, he's forgotten that."

Henry was silent a moment. "Free blacks get along here; we have a good dozen in Beaufort. Let them guide Spit Jim, be his model."

"So he can relearn the rules, you mean. Only speak when spoken to, enter through the back door, always let whites pass first, never con-tradict, never look a white man in the eye. Basically be as invisible and subservient as possible," Jasper said, still gazing at the tidal river that lapped quietly against the marsh grass.

"Well, yes, that would help," Henry agreed.

Jasper smiled, or maybe winced, sadly.

"You'll talk to him?" Henry asked.

"Yes, I'll talk to him," Jasper answered.

"What do you expect me to do?" Jim asked when he heard the news later in the privacy of Jasper's room.

Jasper glanced at his friend. "I don't expect anything. What I want is to keep you safe."

"Then let's leave. That's the answer, not me turning into some kind of misfit that makes everyone edgy because servile isn't part of his vo-cabulary anymore."

Jasper closed his eyes. "Can't you just lie low?"

"As if I haven't been trying. You know what this is about? I was down at the dock, minding my own business waiting for the afternoon mail packet, and I hear Rhett strolling along, shooting his mouth off to the Senator, some twaddle that ended with the usual bunkum about the Southern way of life being nonnegotiable. I gave him a look—one look—and he happened to catch it. He turned so purple, I thought his head was going to explode. The Senator grabbed his arm and dragged him into the feed store, or he probably would've had me whipped right then and there."

It was worse than Jasper feared. "Rhett's the loudest voice for secession in the South. You don't want to take him on."

"I didn't take him on," Jim protested. "I just looked at him."

Jasper gave a short laugh. "Same thing." He shook his head. "Lie low a couple more weeks? Please?"

Jim snorted. "I'd go on ahead of you, except you wouldn't follow, and then I'd just have to come back. I wish a certain set of petticoats wasn't so captivating."

Jasper gave Jim a sour look. "Give me some credit. That girl comes wrapped in a plantation tied with a big, fat slavery bow. I'm not that big a fool. Jim, up till now we've always assumed there was no way the South would give one inch on slavery. What if we were wrong—what if the South could change?"

"Not a chance."

"Isn't there always hope? Shouldn't we attempt to prevent the catastrophe ahead if we can?"

"And just how is this miracle supposed to take place?"

"How about through the entity known as Eustace Woods?"

Jim held up a hand. "Wait a minute. Eustace Woods hardly seems interested in ending slavery; plus, you don't even know who he is. How are you going to do anything through him?"

"Eustace Woods is credible and popular. He has an audience and influence through *The Charleston Courier* that can fight Rhett and his crazy secessionist rhetoric in *The Mercury*. Now, what if Eustace Woods is Henry? No, give me a chance here. Henry has the education and intelligence to write like that; moreover, his opinions and Eustace's are always in uncanny agreement. I think there's real potential here. If we can move Henry, we can just possibly move public opinion."

"By 'we', you mean 'you.' I ain't going to convince Henry or 'Eustace' of anything."

"You will through me. You'll feed me the arguments and persuasion I'll need."

Jim looked darkly at Jasper. "Hope is the most dangerous narcotic of all."

Once Henry departed for Three Reeds on the New River, Aunt Winnie essentially moved into Villa d'Este for the duration, making life difficult—or at least a great deal duller—for Jasper. Jasper sensed that were it not for Henry's express orders, Winnie's presence at Villa d'Este would be a common state of affairs. When he alluded as much to Mary, she explained that the Senator and Winnie's house was just a bit old, a bit dark and a bit small. After all, the Senator had focused on politics the last two decades, not his plantation, resulting in income not as high as some, so she tried to oblige her aunt with time in Villa d'Este's more luxurious surroundings when opportunity availed. Just as Mary had helped raise Cara, Winnie had been a substitute mother to Mary, and the bond of affection still held. Jasper wondered how the Senator viewed his wife's absence from home. Maybe he approved because this way he didn't have to hear his wife's constant clucking like a dyspeptic hen over the pages of her book that Jasper was now subjected to. A slow reader, Winnie hardly got through a page in five minutes. At this rate *Jane Eyre* would last until Christmas.

"This Mr. Rochester—my, my. So intemperate. Cara certainly shouldn't be reading this. And the heroine, Jane—far too headstrong. It'd just give Cara ideas. We had a hard enough time keeping her from running off to be a schoolteacher. I shudder to think of the episode this might provoke."

"Was Cara really going to run off?" Jasper inquired of Mary in a private moment.

"Not run off," Mary assured him. "But after two years at the Lydell-berg Female Academy, she did have some ideas in her head about matriculating at a college. Evidently there's one in Ohio now that takes girls and gives them degrees just like they do the men. Imagine. And after that she had some castle in the clouds dream of teaching at a girls' school, just like her history teacher she admired. Well, you can be sure Henry had words with the school about that and brought her straight home. We really did have a time of it, getting her to see sense, for a whole six months after she came back to Beaufort. She literally raved that we were crushing her and destroying her life. It was so dreadful, we had to have her live with Winnie for a spell until the nonsense she was spouting died down. Henry was ready to horsewhip the teachers at Lydellberg and still doesn't have a good word to say about the place."

Jasper noticed that Cara paid shorter and less frequent visits to Villa d'Este with Aunt Winnie in residence. Just before noon on the second day of Henry's absence, after hearing more clucking about the positively licentious behavior of the fortune telling scene, Jasper abandoned the house and went for a ride. As he headed down the sandy street, he came across Cara just as he had on his first day back in Beaufort. She was walking down the road next to Minnie again, a basket in the slave girl's hand.

He tipped his hat. "A fine day for a walk, Miss Randall. Good afternoon, Minnie."

After looking up with a disgruntled start, Minnie duly curtseyed with an irked expression on her face. Cara tipped up her parasol and looked skyward to confirm no squirrels lurked in the branches. "It's heavenly," Cara agreed.

Jasper considered her a moment from his horse. "Are you going out or returning?"

"Returning," she answered. She could have told him she'd been visiting her mother's grave, but while such an admission might move other people to praise her, she felt reluctant to mention it to him.

"Then, if you're not too tired from your excursion, would you like to ride with me?"

Cara looked more than a little surprised. "But my clothes," she said, gesturing to her linen walking dress.

"You can change them."

She clutched her parasol. "And I'd need a horse. My father doesn't keep any."

"I'll go back to Henry's stable and get you one. By the time it's saddled up, you'll be ready. Truly, Miss Randall, you'd be doing me a kindness. *Jane Eyre* is the constant topic of conversation at Villa d'Este, and I confess with Henry gone, I'm in need of sterner intellectual fare."

Though she still looked hesitant, Cara accepted his offer. Minnie just shook her head, knowing what was now in store for her.

True to their agreement, a little over thirty minutes later Cara met Jasper in front of her house outfitted in her midnight blue riding habit, white blouse and black ankle boots, with something close to a man's black cravat tied very prettily around her neck. Jasper suspected but naturally did not fully appreciate the heroic level of activity on the parts of three servants it'd taken for Cara to be dressed at the height of equestrian fashion in a mere half an hour. Though she would've graced Rotten Row in London's Hyde Park admirably, such apparel was hardly necessary for the expedition he had in mind.

"But Hock knows I ride Lysander," Cara said when she saw the horse Jasper had brought for her. She reached up to adjust her hat, a cut-down version of the black top hat that Jasper was wearing. It was feminized by a wide brim to shade a delicate complexion, a plume for decoration, and a filmy veil hanging down the back that could be pulled forward, if necessary, as a defense against dust, insects, or too intrusive stares. "Why did you bring this horse?" she said with consternation.

"Lysander's a great big dull brute with no spirit. Titania's a better fit for you."

Cara frowned as Mercury, the yard Negro, came out with a step-stool to help her mount onto her sidesaddle. "She looks . . . vigorous."

"You'll be fine," Jasper assured her cheerfully.

As soon as Mercury had helped her on and she was situated properly in her seat with the long skirt of her habit gracefully cloaking the left side of her horse, Jasper turned his horse around so as to head away from town.

"Where are we going?" she asked.

"Towards Saltwater Bridge," he said. "Get some country air." He nudged his horse with his riding crop and started off. Holding her reins tightly in her gloved hands, Cara tentatively urged her mount to follow him. She sat perched absolutely correctly in her sidesaddle, her shoulder and hips aligned forward, her right leg around the fixed pommel, her left foot in its stirrup. Her left leg just touched the leaping horn while her spine was centered exactly over the spine of her mount.

"When were you thrown?" Jasper asked casually as they made their way down the sandy street.

Cara glanced sharply at him. "Did Mary tell you that?"

"No," Jasper said. "Henry told me you used to ride a blue streak when you were a girl, and now, even though you have plenty of natural ability, you're nervous and tense. The two add up to a good throw. You were obliging to come with me given that."

It took her a moment to answer. "It was six years ago. Ever since then, Aunt Winnie hasn't wanted me to ride much."

"Aunt Winnie controls a great deal of your life, doesn't she?" Jasper observed.

"She helped raise my mother, and she doesn't have children of her own. She feels responsible for me."

"Was it hard for you, giving up your dreams of college and teaching?" Jasper asked.

Cara brushed aside a garland of moss dangling from an oak. "They were just fancies," she said. "Uncle Henry was right—my place is here, with my family and my heritage."

"Was there anything in particular you wished to study?"

"History," she answered a little forlornly. "Oriental history."

Jasper glanced at her before swatting his horse with his crop to prompt it to canter.

"What are you doing?" Cara asked anxiously.

"Come on," Jasper called behind him. "It's fun."

Gritting her teeth, Cara didn't need her small whip to increase her horse's gait. When Titania saw Oberon cantering in front of her, she was happy to indulge.

It wasn't until Jasper pulled up half a mile later that Cara finally caught up to him breathless, but smiling. She reached up to adjust her hat that had tilted askew.

"See, you did fine," Jasper said. "Titania knows what she's doing, don't you, girl?"

Titania's ears pricked at Jasper's compliment, and the snort she gave said of course she knew how to carry a lady on her back.

Cara patted the horse's neck. "She's a beautiful beast."

"If it's any consolation," Jasper said, "I think you know more about the early Chinese dynasties than any professor in Ohio does."

"There's more than just that to study," Cara murmured, reaching to her hat yet again. It was just not settling on her head the way it should.

"Why do you keep fussing with your hat?" Jasper asked with amusement.

"It isn't angled properly," Cara answered, still trying to twist it into alignment.

Jasper eyed her curiously. "Do you think I care how you look? Come on, let's go." And he was off at a canter again, forcing Cara to abandon her concern with her headgear just to keep up.

Chapter Five

J asper finished the last of his ham and grits not too long after the boys headed to school. Though the family breakfast table was lacking without Henry's spirited presence, Jasper found himself companionable with Mary, as if they'd been sitting across from each other like this every morning for years. Still, time was advancing. After conferring with his pocket watch, Jasper wiped his moustache with his napkin and rose from the table.

Mary looked up from the coffee she'd just finished pouring from a silver pot. Atop her head she wore a muslin and lace cap, as married women often did during the daytime hours. "Do you have plans this morning?" she inquired with a friendly smile. Usually Jasper dawdled with her over breakfast and didn't disappear until Aunt Winnie, who preferred to take her first meal in bed, emerged from her room late morning.

"Just going for a ride," Jasper answered.

"Oh," Mary said. Then she tilted her head. "With anyone in particular?"

Mary's eyes were far too keen. Jasper now realized he should've been more leisurely in his departure. "Miss Randall has agreed to accompany me," he admitted.

"Has she? Well, you're honored. She rarely gives up her mornings to anyone."

"Really?" Jasper said. "Why is that?"

"She says it's her time to take care of housekeeping and practice her piano without interruption. She's extremely strict about it." Mary appraised him as she sipped her coffee. "She also rarely rides."

Jasper shrugged. "She's a fine horsewoman. When she took that fall all those years ago, you should've gotten her back in the saddle, not coddled her fears."

Mary looked down. "That was Aunt Winnie's doing, I'm afraid. And shortly afterwards, Cara went away to school." She smiled warmly at Jasper. "So it's wonderful that you're getting her out again. It's kind of you."

"Not kind, selfish. Henry's away, Jim's been out in the woods and marshes gathering medicinal plants, and you're dedicated to your extensive duties here. I've done enough riding by myself for a lifetime, believe me. Miss Randall is just being obliging."

"I see," Mary said with a bland smile.

Cara wore her fashionable riding habit again that was tight enough Jasper suspected she'd been sewn into it. Still, he had to admit it suited her as they made their way down a trail that kept a rough acquaintance with the banks of the Beaufort River. The morning sun was warm, and the heady scent of gardenias from Beaufort gardens had drifted to the tidal marshes spreading out before them. It overlay even the odor of the marsh mud baking in the sun after being revealed by the low tide. It was a smell that the locals didn't mind although they were quick to admit it was an acquired taste.

"May I inquire into your opinion as to whether slavery will exist a hundred years from now?" Jasper asked Cara. "I notice you're not always allowed to express your thoughts in the family gatherings."

She reddened slightly. It was true, she was expected to hold her tongue on political subjects after expressing herself vociferously too many times in the past, and it embarrassed her that Jasper should notice. "I think eventually the South will evolve away from slavery," she said tentatively. "But gradually, and not any time soon."

"Not in your lifetime?" Jasper asked.

Cara considered. "Maybe in fifty or sixty years. But we must take care to provide the Negroes with as good a situation as they presently enjoy. Sending them back to the African continent or letting them loose on the frontier without wealth, education or resources would be a grave injustice."

Jasper rode along silently before he spoke. "Are you aware, Miss Randall, that grave injustices happen to Negroes in the South right now daily?"

The suggestion perturbed her. "I know there are tales the Northern abolitionists like to promote, but those are the exceptions, not the rule. It would be against the honor of a gentleman to ill-treat his slaves."

"I think you're overly influenced by the example of your uncle."

"Are you saying Henry's not an honorable master?"

"On the contrary. Through enlightened self-interest, he's among the very best masters you'll find in the South. Most are worse. Some are much worse. And there's essentially no regulation of their conduct, nowhere slaves can turn to for fair treatment. You must grasp, Miss Randall, that to be a slave is to be entirely at someone else's mercy."

Cara eyed him. "I believe you are an abolitionist, Mr. Wainwright."

He rode along placidly. "I still own slaves. Forty-six of them, last I heard."

"And what kind of master are you?" she asked.

"The worst," he said. "Entirely absent. Luckily my brother, who both uses their labor and oversees their welfare, is a good man and takes care of them adequately."

"So your conscience is clear," she asked.

The horses pressed forward several paces before Jasper had an answer. "In regards to slavery, Miss Randall, I've seen such things in my life to ensure my conscience will never be clear."

Cara was going to reply, but as they rounded a bend in the trail where a thicket of plum trees obscured their view, they came suddenly upon another horse and rider, a blonde man on a white stallion. Since the trail wasn't wide enough for the width of three horses, Jasper began to back his mount up to make room for the oncoming rider. Cara, however, moved forward, not even squeamish of Titania's mincing resistance. "Johnny," she exclaimed. "I didn't know you were back from Charleston. I thought your mother wasn't expecting you until tomorrow."

"I came back with Harold Rutherford and a friend of his so we could make it to the Rutherford fête tonight. Are you going?"

"Me and everyone else in Beaufort," Cara said. "It'll be a terrible crush."

"What a surprise to see you here," Johnny said, looking her over approvingly from atop his horse. "I didn't realize you were riding again. I thought you'd sworn it off forever."

Cara frowned. "I never said forever." She then had to rein in Titania, who neighed and sidestepped when a bored Oberon behind her gave her hindquarters a nip. Cara glanced over her shoulder. "Oh, Johnny, do you know Mr. Wainwright? He's a cousin of my Uncle Henry."

Johnny nodded brusquely at the older man. "We met at the Birch party in April, I believe."

"And you've been in Charleston ever since," Cara noted. "What can you have found to do there all this time?"

Johnny drew himself up in his saddle. "I've been busy enough. I've joined the Charleston Light Dragoons, if you must know. That's what's been keeping me."

"But I thought you had to live in Charleston for that," Cara said.

"I'm using my aunt's address. The Dragoons are particular, you know, but they chose me right as rain. And I'm also clerking for Coffin and Pringle. Paps wants me to get trained as a commission merchant, says it'll make me a better planter if I understand the selling half of the business. So you see, I've been applying myself, just like you always said I should." He looked at Cara as if wanting her approbation but also ready to ridicule it once given.

Cara had no such hesitation. Her answering smile was warm, her face radiant. "I'm so glad, Johnny. We in Beaufort will have to be consoled with your absence by knowing you're such a credit to us all in Charleston."

Johnny looked pleased. "Where are you headed?" he said to Cara. "I'll join you."

Cara looked back at Jasper awkwardly. "We were just—"

"We were just about to turn back," Jasper said, resigned to the intrusion. He let Johnny pass him, followed by Cara who quite naturally rode beside her childhood friend while Jasper trailed placidly behind, accepting his odd role of chaperone to the young pair. The two made an attractive couple, Jasper thought as he idly watched the black veil on Cara's hat bob softly while Titania's well-groomed hind quarters ambled along. Cara probably would end up marrying Johnny, especially if the young man was taking up a mantle of responsibility and settling down. But would she be happy with him? There was something in Johnny's eyes, some insecurity or instability that Jasper didn't altogether like.

Doing his absolute best to ignore Jasper entirely, Johnny monopolized Cara's attention with his exploits of the last five weeks. Over the trill of birdsong and the occasional snorts and headshakes of the horses that jingled the brass on their bridles, Jasper heard about uniforms and mustering and slave patrols, and much less about whatever one did as a clerk in the merchant counting houses. Johnny didn't leave them until they'd nearly arrived at the Randall house, and Cara seemed well gratified by Johnny's company the entire time.

However, as Mercury helped her down from Titania, Cara looked up inquiringly at Jasper. "Will you be coming to the Rutherford's tonight? I know Mary's invited, but she probably won't go because she expects Henry back, and she'll want to be home when he gets there."

Jasper considered. Would Winifred be more likely to be at the Rutherford party or at Villa d'Este that evening?

Cara seemed to read his mind. "I'm sure Aunt Winnie will stay with Mary until Henry gets home," she said with a small smile, "so if you could attend with father and me, we'd be very pleased."

In the end he agreed to go, a state of affairs Mary approved of whole-heartedly when she heard of it, though Winifred showed less enthusiasm. The matriarch of the family did not object too strenuously, however, in light of the pronouncement she must now make. Handing the volume back to her nephew's cousin, Winifred Pickens informed him that *Jane Eyre*, while not immoral in and of itself, was not fit reading material for Cara's tender sensibilities. "I do find some virtue in the book that Mr. Rochester's debauched behavior is so thoroughly punished," Mrs. Pickens went on. "But the actions and thoughts of the heroine would be disturbing to my great-niece's peace of mind. I hope this does not disappoint you too severely, Mr. Wainwright. I accept that your intentions in offering her the book were honorable."

Jasper's mouth twitched as he looked down at the crimson cover blocked with gold lettering in his hand. "I'm obliged to you, ma'am, for your thorough evaluation of the book's properties. I appreciate you have Miss Randall's best interests at heart."

Winifred Pickens almost softened over this response, but in the end, she held firm. Cara's desire to go north for college had been a truly harrowing episode for them all. If they weren't careful, Cara could end up like the Grimké sisters, good Charleston girls who unaccountably turned Quaker, moved north, and started writing strange tracts about the condition of women and blather about abolition. Most horrible of all, they spoke their views before audiences in public. Their father, Judge Grimké, was lucky to have died before such shame was visited upon his family. His sons, however, were less fortunate, and the names of Sarah and Angelina Grimké still could not be mentioned in polite society.

Back in his room, Jasper was about to toss the book in his trunk when Jim stopped him. "I know someone with a strong interest in that there piece of literature," Jim said.

Jasper looked over at him. "Who would that be?"

"Miss Randall's maid, Minnie. But she has something different in mind than you might expect. Will you meet with her?"

Jasper found himself behind the dependencies of Villa d'Este, out of view of the big house, in an alley off the main road that served as access to the stables. Across the way was a lot wooded with oaks and cabbage palmettos that Henry also owned and had no intention of letting anyone build on. While Jim stood to one side leaning against the back of the laundry building, Jasper held out the book to Minnie. The slave girl stood with her arms folded across her chest and a suspicious look on her face. "You wanted this?" he inquired. He was surprised by the request in a number of respects. Not by the fact that Minnie could read, because if she wrote letters for Cara, she was obviously literate. But why would she want to peruse a tale of an English orphan girl, and if she did, why hadn't she managed to sneak it when Cara was off at dinners or parties? It would've been easy enough.

Minnie didn't unfold her arms to take the book from his hand. "I gib yuh ten cent fuh ebry read. Dats my bes offuh."

"What are you talking about?" Jasper asked. It wasn't her vernacular that puzzled him. Through long practice he was well able to decipher the Gullah patois indigenous to slaves on the Sea Islands. "I'll loan it to you for nothing."

"I'z gwine lend dat book fuh hire. Twenny cent. Yuh git ten, I git ten."

"You're going to loan it for money?" Jasper was amused. "To whom?"

"All dem missus in Beefut who wantuh read dat book but who's too much stylish tuh let folks know. Dem missus git tree day wid it."

"Three days? You expect them to read this book in three days?"

"Or dey pay mo."

Jim laughed. "The audacity alone is priceless."

"My dear Minerva," Jasper said, "I do believe you are a businesswoman. Tell you what. I don't want to make a profit out of this book; it was given to me as a gift. But I'll capitalize this scheme by giving you the book outright as long as you take pains not to get me into trouble. Do we have a deal?" He held out the book again.

With a curt nod, Minnie took it. "I gwine put uh new cubbuh on de book fuh uh disguise."

"What kind of cover?" Jim asked her.

"I hab Pilgrum Puhgess bout big nuf. Mis Cara don't luk dat book no how."

Jasper and Jim both laughed aloud at the idea of upper crust Beaufort women pouring through the seventeenth century religious allegory better known as *The Pilgrim's Progress.* Minnie glared.

"Too pious, Minnie," Jim said. "Folks'll be suspicious."

"How about one of Sir Walter Scott's novels?" Jasper suggested. "That'd be more believable. Though I hate to see you ripping covers off books. Can't you just paste some fabric on it?"

"I tink bout dat," Minnie said. "Are der odduh books same like dis? Books dem missus wantuh read all in secret?"

Jasper smiled. "There are but you won't find them here in Beaufort. You'll have to write to a bookstore in Charleston and have them sent. *Mary Barton*, *Vanity Fair* and *The Tenant of Wildfell Hall* come to mind."

"Don't forget *La Dame aux camellias*," Jim reminded.

"Certainly not," Jasper agreed, "if it's out in translation." This just caused Minnie to frown even more, this time in confusion.

"I'll make you a list," Jim offered.

"Yuh sho yuh don want nuttin fuh trade?" Minnie asked Jasper suspiciously.

"How about a kind memory of me in your heart?" Jasper said.

Minnie snorted. "Money be bettuh."

And so the *Jane Eyre* lending library for profit was born. Jasper hoped that when Cara found out about it she wouldn't be too furious with him.

"How is it," Jasper asked Jim later, "that Minnie gets away with being the surliest slave in Beaufort?"

"Kinda makes you wonder about her mistress, don't it?" Jim replied. "You realize Minnie's scheme probably violates six different laws?"

Jasper shrugged. "If it goes bust, I'll pay the fine for providing reading material to a slave."

"Most white men would just accuse her of stealing the book," Jim noted.

Jasper looked askance at his former slave. "If you thought I'd do that, you'd never have let me know her plan."

"True," Jim agreed. "Just wanted to remind you how different you are from the rest of the white folk here."

Even though the Rutherford house was a mere two blocks from Villa d'Este, Mary insisted Jasper take the carriage and call for Cara and her father so they could all arrive in style. It seemed frivolous, but Beaufort was Beaufort, and Mary couldn't keep her head held high without some show of ostentation.

When Jasper arrived at the Randall residence at nine, however, at the last minute the Professor was not up to attending the party, which left Cara with Jasper inside the carriage while Hock sat in the driver's seat up front. The lantern on the carriage's exterior faintly illuminated Cara's mauve silk dress with its flounces and ruffles as well as the lacy fichu that scantly covered her exposed shoulders. In honor of the evening's festivities, a spray of rosebuds had been delicately entwined into the curls of her coiffure, no doubt by her dexterous, capitalist maid. Jasper recognized that the girl he was looking at was a pinnacle achievement of her class and time, a product both of Henry's wealth and multiple generations of rigorous female tutelage. She'd been constrained and adorned, prodded and bedecked into a form that he couldn't deny was gratifying to the eye. He didn't know whether to admire or pity her.

There was a question in her eyes as she wondered about his silence, but since the trip was only a few blocks long, they'd already arrived. Once inside, Cara soon joined the young people dancing upstairs in the ballroom. After scouting the already crowded room, Jasper went to stand by the Senator who had braved the party without his wife and seemed glad enough of Jasper's company. The Senator had industriously already found himself in possession of a generous cup of punch.

"It's Charleston Light Dragoons' Punch," Mrs. Rutherford told them as she hospitably flitted among her guests. "With just the right amount of lemon and sugar, I'm told. In honor of Johnny and Harold joining the regiment."

From the smell of it, Charleston Light Dragoons' punch was a potent brew. "Has Harold joined the Dragoons as well?" Jasper said. "I didn't realize the militia had become so popular with the young men. You must be very proud."

"Why, yes, we are," Mrs. Rutherford said with a smile that showed a flash of relief. "You know he didn't even tell us he's been signed up for a month already until he arrived home yesterday. Silly boy wanted to surprise us. And did you hear he's clerking at a factor in Charleston, just like Johnny? Johnny's been such a good influence on him. Now I wonder where those boys have gotten to. It's just like Harold to be late to his own party." And she left them to try to ascertain from her grown, married daughter just where her errant son might be.

Dancing had begun, the fiddlers beginning with a lively reel. Jasper observed Cara lining up across from a lanky, diffident, red-headed boy. Absorbed in watching the couples chassé down the floor, he didn't notice the tall, balding, portly man with a stern patrician air that had joined him and the Senator until he spoke.

"Pickens, I see you're attending the festivities without your wife," the man who sported a close-cropped beard and whiskers said stiffly, as if such small talk was bound to be pointless but must be attempted for form's sake.

"She's with her niece tonight," the Senator said. "They'll spend the evening gossiping or some such thing."

A white-gloved slave approached Jasper with a cup on a silver tray. "Yo refrushment, suh."

"Thank you," Jasper replied, taking the cup.

The new man frowned at Jasper until the Senator finally registered that he had a social duty at hand. "Congressman Rhett, let me introduce to you Jasper Wainwright, cousin of my nephew, Henry Birch."

Jasper waited for a hand to be extended. When he didn't see one, he merely bowed slightly.

Barnwell Rhett pursed his mouth. "What's that you're drinking there?"

Jasper looked down at his cup with a slight smile. "Water, sir." Having long ago lost his taste for the sweet beverages offered at parties, tonight, actually thirsty, he'd asked for plain water on first arrival. The unusual nature of the request meant it'd taken half an hour to materialize.

"You're a temperance man?" Rhett questioned.

"Let's just say liquor doesn't agree with me," Jasper replied.

Rhett scowled for a moment and then held out his hand. "Jasper Wainwright, is it? I believe I knew your father. Plantation up towards Buddenville?"

"Yes," Jasper said. "My brother runs it now."

Rhett nodded. "Glad to see a non-drinking man in Beaufort. Maybe you can balance out some of these wild boys. That brew you've got there, Senator, is going to turn this fete into a drunken bacchanal before long. Be that as it may, Pickens, I wonder if you'll oblige me with a moment of your time. I want your opinion on whether Wilmot will try to slip his wretched Proviso through again this session—has Calhoun made any noises about it to you?"

Realizing he was being dismissed, Jasper gratefully excused himself from the statesmen's company to drink his water without the machinations of Congress filling his ears. Wilmot, a young congressman from Pennsylvania, had tried three times in as many years to ban slavery in all territories acquired from Mexico. Persistent, he had introduced a proviso as a rider on two appropriations bills and then attempted to make it part of the formal treaty with Mexico. Each time the South had succeeded in defeating the ban, though not without considerable effort. Jasper didn't doubt that the entire Southern congressional delegation fretted continually about what the Pennsylvanian Free Soiler might do next.

Tad McCloskey was the son of a successful Scot merchant who had bought a plantation on Fripp Island a decade before. Shy and inclined to poetry rather than cotton, he revered the girl who had danced two dances with him and who had agreed to a stroll in the garden near the river off the front porch. In his eyes, she was the muse Calliope and the goddess Aphrodite rolled into one. That his father approved of both her family and her wealth was icing on the cake. And when she refused him, as he expected she would, he could only love her more. But what was this talk of his cousin Miriam?

"She's adores you, you know that," Cara gently admonished as they stood by a torch set in a stand that illuminated a small patch of the riverside garden.

"Well, I don't adore her," he said, a little miffed. "She's as plain as sand."

"Tad McCloskey, don't you know beauty is the most ephemeral thing in this world?"

"But beauty—" He searched for the words. "Beauty is truth. Beauty is poetry. Beauty is soul, Miss Randall."

Cara paused a moment. "I believe you're acquainted with my Aunt Winifred?" she asked.

Tad frowned. "Yes." What did that have to do with anything?

"Well in her day, she was the most beautiful girl in three counties. What does that tell you about beauty?" Tad's response was just to look at his angel doubtfully. She tried again. "What you want, Tad, is true soul, not just a vision of it, and Miriam has that. She can be your muse if you have the wisdom to look deeply. The eyes may deceive but not the heart." Tad squinted at her, his face puckered as if something were causing him pain. "She knows your poetry word for word," Cara assured him. "She's actually quoted it to me. She understands you, Tad, she truly does. Do you know how many girls in the Sea Islands like poetry? I can count them on one hand." Thoroughly perplexed now, Tad was trying to absorb this information when he and Cara were disturbed by three very loud, very drunk young men.

"What do we have here?" Harold Rutherford drawled, swigging from a flask that held a substance even more potent than Charleston Light Dragoons' punch. "Why, if it isn't Miss Cara Randall and an amorous swain—heavens, it's our scarecrow on fire, Tad McCloskey." He grabbed one of the other young men and roughly pulled him forward so he could be seen by the light of the garden torch. "Cara, this here's Bill Whitfield. He's in the Charleston Light Dragoons, too."

Cara bowed her head and curtsied slightly. "Mr. Whitfield," she said civilly. "I believe we met at the St. Cecilia ball in February."

"Not out in a dark garden we didn't," Bill said with something close to a leer. "I'd remember that."

Cara looked up at Tad. "I think we should be going in."

"Why so soon, Cara?" Johnny, the third of the party, said. "We just got here. Tell us what you and Tad were doing out here in the dark."

Tad took Cara's arm and started towards the stairs and the light streaming out the front door.

Harold grabbed him. "Where you going, loverboy? We want to know, were you proposing, Scarecrow?"

"Let go of me," Tad said, trying to shake him off.

Bill, the visitor, puckered his lips and made kissing noises. "Marry me, Miss, Miss . . ."

"Randall, you idiot," Johnny told him. "Is it true, Cara? Did you rack up another proposal? Your uncle will be so proud."

After glaring at them with contempt, Cara daintily picked up her skirts and started up the stairs. The drunken visitor from Charleston, however, got in front of her. "We say who comes and goes, and right now, you don't go."

"Get back from her," Tad said angrily.

"You gonna make me?" Bill said.

"Yeah, you gonna make him?" Harold said. "I think you're too busy proposing." He started to spin around, one hand above his head. "I love you, Cara, marry me, marry me, maaarrrrrry me."

"Stop it right now, or I'll—I'll—"

"You'll what?" Harold said, stopping his dance. "Punch me?"

"Yes," Tad said, decidedly red in the face now.

"Then I'll do it first." And Harold threw a fist and caught Tad square in the eye, sending Tad flying to the ground.

"You swine," Cara hissed at Harold. "You apologize now."

Harold and Bill thought this uproariously funny. Johnny just stood to one side, half-amused, drinking from a flask.

"You going to make me?" Harold said to her.

"I thrashed you once, Harold Rutherford," Cara said, her hand clenched in a fist at her side. "And I'll do it again. Just try me." Drunk as he was, Harold looked down bemused at the young woman threatening him whose physique was nearly a foot shorter and at least a hundred pounds lighter than his own.

Tad tried to get to his feet, but Bill put out a foot and pushed him back down with his boot. "Go for it, Harold," Bill laughed. "Take her out, too."

But a fifth man had joined them.

"Gentlemen," Jasper said calmly enough, but the look he gave the three inebriated youths conveyed his doubt that they had any acquaintance with the term. Bill and Harold stepped back, abashed as the significance of their recent actions sank in. Even Johnny had the grace to look slightly guilty. Jasper turned to Tad. "You might want to see if the kitchen has some ice for that eye." After Tad scrambled up and left with as much dignity as he could muster, Jasper offered Cara his arm. "Shall we go in, Miss Randall?" Cara nodded, not giving another glance to the three rueful young men she left in the yard.

Cara was silent on the carriage ride home.

"Are you all right?" Jasper asked. Perhaps he should've intervened earlier, before the punches started flying, but after Johnny's attentiveness on the ride that afternoon, Jasper had assumed Johnny would intercede for Cara himself.

Cara looked down at her gloved hands. "I just don't understand deriving pleasure from cruelty."

Jasper didn't have an answer for her. He didn't understand it either.

"I don't understand why Johnny didn't step in," Mary said back at Villa d'Este after Jasper finished relating why he and Cara had left the party early.

"Because he's a damn scoundrel, that's why," said Henry, who'd just arrived home after a long day's journey and was now none too happy to hear his niece had been treated in such a manner. He rose from the settee he'd been lounging tiredly against. "I'll tell you what I'm going to do—I'm going to find their fathers and raise hell."

"Henry, you just got back," Mary pleaded. "Let it rest a night and then you can—"

"Couts," Henry called out loudly, "tell Hock to saddle up Oberon for me. Demetrius is too tired to go out again." He turned back to Jasper and his wife. "If it'd been my boys doing that kind of mischief, I'd want to know as soon as possible. And that's just what I'm going to tell George Rutherford and Samuel Patterson. Now this knave, Billy, I don't know what I can do about him except report him to the Dragoons for behavior unbecoming to a gentleman. And what's all this about Johnny and Harold joining the Charleston Light Dragoons anyway? If the Beaufort Volunteer Artillery was good enough for three generations of Birch men, I can't see why it's not good enough for them. "

"Henry," Mary begged, "you're too tired. Don't go out."

Henry got his riding gloves. "Threatening Cara. The nerve. I leave for four days, and these boys get out of hand behind my back. Well, they're going to regret their Charleston Light Dragoons' punch tonight, let me tell you." He strode towards the door, but then stopped suddenly and turned. "Did Cara really threaten to thrash Harold?"

Jasper smiled. "She did."

"Well, she did give Harold a bloody nose when she was ten. Remember that, Mary? Ha! Maybe Cara could thrash Harold at that." And Henry was out the door to make the lives of three young men in Beaufort even more deservedly uncomfortable.

Mary turned to Jasper with a tired smile. "Well, I tried."

"Should I not have told him?" Jasper asked her.

"No, you did the right thing. Henry would have horsewhipped them then and there, so when it comes down to it, they're going to get off lightly."

"Should I have struck the young men myself?" Jasper asked, not a little puzzled.

"Absolutely not. Defending Cara's honor is Henry's responsibility. And you know," Mary said confidingly, "I think he enjoys it. I'm actually sorry we're going to miss the theatrics."

The next morning during a downpour Cara received an enormous bouquet of roses from the Patterson family and an equally large basket of fruit from the Rutherford's. Half an hour later she received a remorseful visit from Harold who stammered out an apology, and twenty minutes after that a somewhat less humbled Johnny showed up on her porch. Though perhaps chastened by the alternating opprobrium of Mr. Birch and his father the night before, Johnny managed to use his considerable charm to cajole Cara into forgiving him without ever exactly uttering actual words of regret.

As for Bill Whitfield, he was sent back to Charleston on the first morning steamer. (A bad influence on Harold, Mrs. Rutherford confided to the ladies during their morning calls, who all nodded their heads in sympathy.) By noon the entire town had heard of the incident and was in agreement that young Whitfield had been the instigator of the dreadful behavior that Henry Birch was entirely justified in rebuking. Good riddance to that one was the consensus, and some even asserted that the elders of Charleston should take a more active interest in the behavior of their youth. In contrast, Beaufort citizens still knew what it meant to be a gentleman and would remain the bastion of good taste and manners that it had been for its one hundred and thirty-eight years of existence.

The clouds cleared that afternoon, giving way to warm sun with a steady breeze. As Jasper sat on the piazza perusing Henry's copy of *The Southern Quarterly Review,* he glanced up with a frown at the sight of a sailboat launching from the Birch dock. During low tides, Henry's slaves kept a trench from the dock dredged clear of marsh grass and river mud in order to provide Villa d'Este access to the river. Now, with the tide high and the passageway navigable, the boat carrying a young man and woman easily made its way to through the watery periphery to join the main river. The woman held a fringed, blue silk parasol. "Is that Cara?"

Henry stood on the porch, hands on his hips, watching as the boat tacked back and forth on its way across the river. "Looks like Johnny's working hard to be the favored horse again." He glanced sideways at his cousin. "Lucky for him, he doesn't have much competition."

Jasper frowned further. "You think letting her go with him is a good idea?"

Henry shrugged. "Why not? Cara enjoys sailing, and after last night, Johnny won't dunk her. Well, at least not on purpose."

Jasper continued to frown. Little Robert, who'd been playing with a toy wagon on the porch looked up. "Do you know how to sail, Uncle Jasper? Father says he'll teach me when I'm nine."

Jasper looked down at the lisping boy with a smile. "Your father and I used to be the best sailors in Beaufort—at least we thought so. How about a lesson right now? You have a boat?"

"Sure do," Robert said with excitement. "In the shed by the dock. I'll get Hock to get it for us. Hock—HOCK—" The boy went away yelling for the easygoing Negro who could always be counted on to aid and abet his schemes.

Henry laughed. "You don't need to go out—you can watch from here. She'll be fine."

Jasper eyed Henry sourly. "And you're going to pretend you don't remember all the hiding places in the marsh grass across the way? There are a thousand places not to be seen on that river."

"That I took full advantage of with Mary, I assure you," Henry said. "That's what courting is all about. You have to give them some chance to be alone. As I remember, you used to take a certain Kitty Potts out there yourself."

Robert came running breathlessly back to the porch. "I've got it— I've got the boat. Can we sail all the way to St. Helena Sound, Uncle Jasper?"

"Not that far today, Robert. You'll have to make do with just the bend in the river here. All right, your first lesson is the rigging, if I can remember how to do it."

After some wrestling with knots and the mainsail, and after many assurances by Jasper to Mary that he would take great care with her youngest, Jasper and Robert did get the boat on the water, cutting across the gleaming stretch of river and narrowly avoiding a collision with a steamer than came at them a great deal faster than steamers had twenty-five years before. Though Cara waved merrily when she saw them, Johnny glanced at them over his shoulder with some annoyance and then ignored them. Robert thought it was one of the best afternoons of his life, especially when Uncle Jasper let him take the tiller. Being on the river turned out to be less of an advantage than Jasper hoped, however, because when Cara and Johnny did disappear into the cord grass, for the life of him he couldn't come up with a pretext to follow them in. All he could do was tack back and forth, keeping his eye on the white triangle of sail that could still be seen above the grasses. When they came out at last, Cara looked flushed and Johnny miffed, so perhaps Jasper needn't have been so concerned.

Mary stood on the porch with Henry and leaned her head on his shoulder. "You think there's progress?" she asked.

"Definitely," Henry said, watching the two boats zigzag each other across the sparkling water. "Definitely. Even if he doesn't know it yet."

The social season that year in Beaufort had gotten off to an unusually strong start, and now the Patterson's, perhaps anxious to make up for the previous week's misstep, decided to throw a party two nights before the Birch party at Silver Oaks.

"How could they," Mary said, piqued. "Of course we can't attend."

"Well, everyone else can," Henry said. "Let the Patterson's have their party—ours will be better." Jasper was recruited to stay in town and keep Billy company so that he could attend school the last three days of the week. He and Billy would take *The Beaufort Heron* with all the other guests Saturday morning. Cara had thought about traveling to Silver Oaks early with Henry and Mary, but now, not wanting to miss the Patterson party, she decided to go with her father Saturday morning on the steamer as well.

"See, Mary?" Henry said as the boys sat down for their supper. The adults had been invited to a party that evening that was likely to offer substantial refreshments, so they looked on the boys' meal without partaking. "It's all working out for the best. Even Winnie and the Senator are staying for the Patterson party. We'll get two whole blissful days at Silver Oaks all to ourselves."

Mary pursed her lips as she handed her husband a julep, a concoction so full of ice and sugar he considered it more akin to lemonade then liquor. "We get all winter at Silver Oaks to ourselves," she said with exasperation. "Sometimes I think you'd be happy to be one of those hermit fakirs living alone in a cave."

"Chanting all day, wearing nothing but a loincloth," Henry laughed. "Yes, indeed, my dream life. And here I am instead with a beautiful wife, three marvelous sons, and the finest set of plantations in the low country. Poor, pitiful me. Now, Jasper, you spent six months in a cave in China with a holy man, didn't you?"

Jasper sipped his tea at the end of the table. "It wasn't a cave; it was a monastery. Primitive, but not that primitive."

"No loincloths?" Billy said with a sly look at his mother.

"William Birch," his mother reprimanded him.

"None at all," Jasper said. "The Chinese are modest in their attire in even the hottest weather, and in the winter it got cold up in the mountains. Generally I wore as much clothing as I could manage."

"Did you chant?" Billy asked.

"Not much. Mostly just meditated."

"What's medtated?" little Robert asked.

"Meditating is sitting still with your thoughts," Jasper answered. "Being quiet in both mind and body. Emptying out."

"Why would you want to do that?" Hugh asked incredulously.

"Well, I needed it. Some people do. And it was a great privilege. I was only allowed to do it after three months of chopping wood and carrying water."

"They made you a slave, Uncle Jasper?" little Robert asked, shocked.

Jasper had to laugh. "No. I volunteered for those duties. I had a beast of a time getting them to take me on any terms. They didn't much like *fan kwei*—foreign devils. That's what they called us."

"What did they call Spit Jim?"

"Oh, he was *fan kwei*, too. Black skin or white, we were the same to the Chinamen. But Jim was clever enough to find a Chinese doctor in Macao who let him be an apprentice, so he didn't go to the temple with me. I was the stubborn one, trekking inland to the mountains to someplace I'd only heard stories about."

"But you found it, Uncle Jasper?" Billy asked.

"Well, to tell the truth," Jasper said, "I traveled with a Chinaman who showed me the way. I doubt I could've gotten there without him because the Chinese had laws forbidding *fan kwei* from traveling outside of Canton. Worse, people there had a terrible prejudice against *fan kwei* and thought it entertaining to pelt foreigners with rocks anytime they got the chance."

"Did you get pelted with rocks, Uncle Jasper?" Robert asked with concern.

"No, I didn't because—" Jasper looked around a moment, knowing this was going to shock his audience. "I disguised myself as a Chinaman."

The boys' jaws dropped. Even Mary looked startled. "You didn't, Jasper," she said with no little horror.

"What exactly did disguising yourself as a Chinaman entail?" Henry wanted to know. "You didn't shave your head and give yourself a queue, did you?"

"I did actually."

"You did?" Hugh looked like he was going to faint from incredulity.

"It was the only way," Jasper said. "Actually, my friend shaved my head, the front part anyway, from my temples up to just about the crown." He indicated the line on his scalp with his hand. "Then he dyed what was left of my hair black and sewed a queue—a thick braid of real Chinese hair—into my hair with some silk thread."

"Was that enough to disguise you?" Billy asked. "What about your moustache? And your eyes? Your eyes are blue. I thought Chinamen had dark eyes."

"Very astute," Jasper said. "I wore crystal glasses to hide my eyes, and I shaved my moustache to make it long and wispy so I looked like an old Chinese patriarch. Plus I wore completely Chinese clothes—trousers, jacket, and cloth shoes, as well as a good-sized hat to keep my poor, nearly bald head covered. And before I did any of this, I had to learn to speak Chinese passably well, or I would've been found out for sure. So as you can see, it was quite a scheme."

"You did all that just to see some stupid temple?" Hugh said, aghast.

"All that, just to get to a stone temple perched on a hillside, miles away from any village. Three monks and two novices lived there, that was it. They practiced a sect of Buddhism known as Ch'an."

"Did people come there to worship?" Billy asked.

"Sometimes," Jasper said. "But it wasn't like here, where people belong to a congregation that comes each Sunday. Sometimes people would show up, make an offering. A few people would stay longer to study with Master Wu."

"His name was Wu?" Hugh said as if this were the strangest name anyone could possibly have.

Jasper nodded. "It was Wu. I don't know how old he was, but he seemed ancient. He hardly ever spoke. The first three months I was there he wouldn't even look at me."

"And he made you into a servant?"

Jasper smiled. "Well that was actually a step up. At first they wouldn't even let me in the door. They told me to go away. And that was after I'd travelled a week by boat and another two weeks on foot to get there."

"What did you do?" Robert asked in his small voice, genuinely concerned.

"I pulled my blanket out from my pack and slept on the doorstep," Jasper said. "Even though my Chinese friend had warned me that this was likely the reception I was going to get, it was pretty bleak, to tell the truth." One of the bleaker nights of his life, in fact.

"These Chinamen sound decidedly unfriendly," Henry said. "Cara, come in and sit down. Don't lurk there in the doorway."

There were times when Cara wanted to murder her uncle. After sidling in, she gingerly sat on a chair as near to the door as possible. Jasper glanced at her briefly before giving his attention back to the boys.

"Did you have anything to eat that night, Uncle Jasper?" Robert lisped.

"Not a lot, except for a little food I carried with me. The next day one of the novices took pity on me and gave me some rice."

"Just rice?" Hugh said. "No meat?" Clearly China was a barbaric place.

"Creature comforts were spare up there on the mountain. If I was lucky, I got a few vegetables with my meals, too. I must have lost two stone in weight that year," Jasper said with a smile.

"Was that when you started drinking green tea?" Billy asked.

"It was. It was a great privilege. I think it was a reward for chopping the wood and fetching the water."

Hugh shook his head. "Just like a slave. I wouldn't do that for anything. And you did that just to be able to sit still and think?"

Jasper nodded. "I did. If I was particularly lucky, Master Wu would look at me."

"What was so lucky about that?" Hugh scoffed.

"Hugh," his mother reprimanded.

"He had an amazing way of looking," Jasper said. "Straight into your soul."

"You liked that?" Billy asked.

"I needed that," Jasper said simply. "Eventually I was allowed into the main room to meditate. I needed that, too."

"Did you become a heathen pagan?" Hugh asked. "That's what Aunt Winnie says all those Chinamen are, not good Christians."

"Hugh," his mother reprimanded again. "That's a very personal question."

"I don't mind answering it," Jasper said evenly. "Hugh, I've found what people say they believe doesn't matter all that much, it's how they live their lives that counts. In my experience, Chinamen run the gamut, just like Christians. Some are compassionate and kind to their fellow man; some are heartless, selfish, and cruel. We all have to decide where we fall on that spectrum. But to answer your question, even after spending a year in a Ch'an temple, I still consider myself a Christian. Meditating doesn't necessarily change one's faith in God. For me, it reestablished it, if that's not too shocking a thing to say."

Both Henry and Mary, who had been listening intently, relaxed slightly, now thankful their son had been impertinent enough to solicit such vital information. However much they loved Jasper, and however willing they might be to overlook his abolitionist views, there was not the remotest chance that they'd allow their niece to marry a pagan.

"Why did you leave eventually?" Billy asked. "Did they kick you out?"

"No, eventually it was time to go. I just felt it."

"Did Master Wu say good-bye?" Robert asked with his lisp.

"He didn't speak to me the entire time I was there. Of course, my knowledge of Chinese wasn't extensive, so I'm sure they thought me a stupid brute. But he did nod to me when I took my leave."

"That's it, a nod? He was that proud?" Hugh couldn't believe his Uncle Jasper hadn't challenged this Chinaman to a duel and demanded the respect he was due.

"It wasn't pride, Hugh. Things are different there. It's likely I'm the only *fan kwei* he ever even nodded to his whole life."

"So the monks knew you weren't Chinese? Did anyone else figure it out?" Billy asked.

"The monks knew because my Chinese friend who led me there told them. He was only going to stay at the temple a short while, and there was no way I could keep fooling people without his help. Plus, if I wanted to be taken on there, I really couldn't do it under false pretences. As far as others go, I don't think anyone else suspected. You see, except for the inhabitants of Canton, foreigners are completely outside of the average Chinaman's experience. They'd expect to see a ghost walking down the street before they'd expect to see a *fan kwei*. So I was accepted by most people as a funny-looking Chinese pilgrim, as long as I was careful to eat like them, sleep like them, and travel like them.

I told people I was from a province in the north, which in a pinch was a good enough explanation for my awkward manners, pale skin and funny-sounding Cantonese."

"But if the monks knew you were this *fan kwei* and didn't report you, weren't they breaking the law of the Celestial Emperor himself?" Mary asked, just as engrossed in the story as her boys were.

"They were. It was a serious risk for them. In fact, they probably could've gotten a reward for turning me in, but once they accepted me, they instead took pains to shelter me from the outside world. I'll always be grateful to them, and to Wan Li, my friend who guided me there."

The three boys looked at their uncle in wonder, still dumbfounded at the idea of him nearly bald with a Chinese braid hanging down his back, waddling around in funny Chinese shoes and trousers. Though they admired him and his travels to foreign parts, they couldn't imagine why he'd done it. Their father knew more, but not all. Only Jim had been with him through those bleakest, darkest days early in his travels when Jasper has despaired of hope, absolution, or anything approaching forgiveness.

In Cara's face, curiously, there was no trace of astonishment at the lengths Jasper had gone to just to sit on a stone floor for a year with little to eat besides rice. Instead, what Jasper saw in her face in an unguarded moment was envy so fierce she looked as if she wanted to pick up her chair and throw it at him.

Chapter Six

The day before the Patterson's party Henry and Mary left with the two younger boys who were delighted with the prospect of playing hooky from their studies and enjoying the warm weather by fishing and riding instead. As high tide neared its peak, Jasper and Billy waved them off from the Villa d'Este dock and then watched as two slaves rowed the family across the Beaufort River and then out of sight into the mouth of Broomfield Creek. Once they were on their own, Billy, studious and a reader, was quiet company, but Jasper had grown fond of the boy, and they had a number of interesting discussions about the ancient history and Latin that Billy was studying.

For the occasion of the Patterson party Professor Randall was yet again unwell, but this time Aunt Winnie insisted on being Cara's escort, leaving Jasper to find his own way the three blocks to the Patterson's mansion down the river from Villa d'Este. Since saddling a horse for such a distance seemed a waste of the servants' time, Jasper decided to walk. Immediately on leaving Villa d'Este he began to pass a long line of empty carriages and bored drivers in the street, making it apparent not many guests had made a similar choice of perambulation.

The crush at the Patterson's was fierce. Wondering why he'd come, Jasper made a mental note not to attend any more Beaufort parties unless Mary or Henry were also going, preferably both of them. Making small talk with people who either remembered him as an unruly child or, worse, a murderous young man, was painful at the best of times, but combined with overly warm rooms and copious amounts of liquor, it bordered on excruciating.

Even finding the Senator was not much relief due to the fact that his attention was monopolized by Barnwell Rhett and other fire-eaters who continually advocated secession as the most delightful solution to whatever political perils the country might face. With South Carolina clearly the most pugnacious state in the South, Beaufort was showing itself to be the most bellicose jewel in its palmetto crown. Yes, the men conceded, it was regrettable that unscrupulous slavers had brought the wretched Negro to America's fair shores so long ago, but that was history now. Hadn't the South had done its best with the circumstance, transforming the evil to the point that slavery was now a positive good? In fact, wasn't slavery now so inextricable to the social and economic well-being of everyone concerned that it couldn't be disentangled without unraveling the entire tapestry of the nation?

What the Northerners couldn't get their thick heads to understand was that the present social order had developed as it had for good reason. Why, the African's inferiority to the white man was an immutable law of nature, and therefore subordination was the Negro's normal condition. Everyone knew that the finest feats of civilization were due to slavery; in fact, it was well recognized that slavery was the crucial stepping ladder that allowed a nation to reach the highest rung of achievement. Why couldn't those Free Soilers causing commotion in Illinois and Massachusetts understand that without slavery there would've been no Cicero and no Plato; no Euripides, Aeschylus or Sophocles? There certainly would've been no Coliseum, Roman Republic or Julius Caesar. Even Jefferson himself hadn't meant the nonsense about all men being created equal. After all, he never did free his own slaves. Self-evident truths indeed.

As he listened to rationalization after rationalization, Jasper kept his own counsel though he certainly thought about leaving the party early.

Johnny kept Cara to himself as much as possible that evening, dancing, teasing, not letting her out of arm's reach even when other men wanted to claim her. Cara knew he was still trying to make up for his previous bad conduct and was pleased to see him refrain from spirits of any kind. Though Johnny received longing looks from several young ladies at the party, he had eyes only for Cara. After a succession of dances, couples spilled out onto the upstairs porch overlooking the river to cool off in the gentle evening air. With that space now too crowded for his taste, Johnny persuaded Cara to accompany him to the darker, quieter verandah below.

As he strode purposefully onto the lower piazza with a glass of lemonade, it was clear the youthful host of the party was claiming the territory for his own. The two other young men on the veranda with girls whom they'd also coaxed downstairs for tête-à-têtes got the not-so-subtle message and drifted back inside.

"You don't want anything to drink?" Cara asked as Johnny handed her the lemonade. Two lanterns hung from the ceiling above them creating golden circles on the porch floor in the calm spring night.

He shook his head, smiling slightly at her. Then he took her hand. "Cara, I'm truly sorry about the Rutherford party the other night. It was inexcusable, but I was jealous."

Cara looked down. "That's perfectly silly. You know very well what my answer was to Tad."

"Yes," Johnny said, "I know. But you were still with another man, not me."

She looked up at him, noting the change in his voice. "Cara," he continued softly, "is it finally time? Will you finally tell me yes?"

They were alone now, near the railing overlooking the dark river. Cara tried to draw her hand away. "Johnny—"

"Darling, we're meant for each other. I love you, and I'll do anything to make you happy. You know I will. Yes, I've been wild, and you were right to insist I made something of myself. But now I have, and next winter Father's going to give me Orange Hill to run all by myself. You've been good for me, Cara, you've made me see my responsibilities, and it's time to give me my reward. All of it means nothing without you. Tell me yes, and we'll announce it here and now, tonight at the party."

Cara reached her fingers to his face. "Dearest Johnny—" She stopped, unable to go on.

"Say it, Cara. Say you'll marry me."

"Oh, Johnny, I wish I could make you happy, but I can't."

Johnny pressed his lips together. "That's absurd. You'll make me happy—I guarantee it. Say you will." He pulled her close. "Say it, Cara."

"Johnny, I—" Johnny bent his head down to kiss her, but at this Cara began to struggle to free herself. In the end all his lips found to kiss was her cheek.

"Damn it, Cara, I'm tired of this."

Cara's face was white. "Then let me go. I didn't ask you to do this."

"You didn't? You didn't charm and bewitch me and keep me running to you like a pet dog? Johnny, do something with yourself," he mimicked in a tight voice, "Johnny, take your life seriously. Well, now I am serious, damn serious, and this is it, Cara, the last time I'm going to ask. Will you marry me?"

Cara looked stricken. "I meant to help, not lead you on."

"I don't want your help," he spat out. "I want you. Do you want me? Think carefully before you speak."

Cara gazed at him, pain evident on her face. "I'm so fond of you, Johnny. I admire and respect you, and I hope great things for you. But I can't marry you. That's my final answer."

For a moment Johnny looked as if he'd been punched in the stomach. Then, as a muscle flexed in his jaw, he picked up Cara's glass and threw it at a porch post where it shattered into pieces, Cara flinching at the impact. She watched him gravely, tensely, trying to anticipate what he might do next.

Johnny clenched his hands, as if it took every ounce of self-control he had to resist wringing her neck. "You are selfish and cold, Cara Randall. A siren that lures men only to drown them in despair. Maybe you want to be a nun, maybe you want to be a saint, but I think you're the evilest person I've ever known. As you age, broken and alone, you will shrivel and shrink into a pile of bitter venom, and I won't care. Because I will hate you every day for the rest of my life." With that, Johnny turned on his heel and went inside.

Cara stumbled backwards as if she'd been struck. When her legs hit a chair, she sank into it and covered her face with shaking hands. She wasn't crying, at least there were no tears, but she did find she had to gasp for breath and she couldn't seem to control her trembling. After a few inhales, her breath calmed. It was then she realized she wasn't alone.

She looked up to see Jasper in his white cravat and tailcoat, his thumbs tucked into his waistcoat pockets.

"That was a bit rough," he said gently after a moment.

Cara bent her head and turned away. She'd almost mastered it, she'd almost gotten through, but now, with his sympathy, tears sprang to her eyes. "He—he has a right to be angry."

Jasper pulled a handkerchief from an inside pocket of his tailcoat and handed it to her. "His pride's more wounded than his heart, I'd say. Not that he wouldn't have been happy to have had a different answer from you."

Cara turned to him imploringly as she wiped away tears. "Don't tell me to marry him. I see that future. It might begin well, but soon he'd resent my books, my music, all the things I care about that make me different from him. He'd drink, I'd be left alone, then he'd get angry with me for not being happy, and we'd spiral into the worse kind of misery. He needs someone who's content to raise his children and be a planter's wife."

"That's what every girl at this party has been trained for," Jasper observed. "And I'd guess most would be thrilled to have Johnny as their lord and master." He'd seen the admiring glances directed Johnny's way and had no doubt the young man was considered quite a catch. Jasper appraised the young woman in front of him. "Do you want to move to Charleston and marry a doctor or a lawyer? It'd give you more access to culture and social discourse."

Cara looked down. "I'm happy here in Beaufort. I just want to live my life according to the dictates of my nature, not someone else's."

Jasper smiled. "Well, then, stick to your guns. Somehow it'll work out."

Cara looked off at the dark river. "With Johnny hating me."

"The things he said, let them go. They're the brash words of a scorned young man. He'll be sorry for them as soon as tomorrow."

This advice didn't seem to cheer her much. "What if he's right?" she said in a quiet voice. "What if I'm destined to be bitter and alone?"

"My dear, if there's anything I know for sure in this world, it's that bitter venom is not your fate. That, at least, I can guarantee you. Come, Miss Randall, a waltz is playing. Shall we?" He held out a hand to her.

"I thought you couldn't dance, Mr. Wainwright," she said, blowing her nose one last time.

"Miss Randall, I'm a Southerner, and I have legs. Of course I can dance. Now come, or it'll be done before we get started."

Cara slowly rose as the fiddlers upstairs marked a jaunty three-four time. Tentatively she put her left hand on his shoulder and her right in his outstretched gloved one. With Jasper's hand lightly on the small of her back, they began to take small steps between the furniture in the tight space, taking care to avoid the shards of broken glass by the post. Cara held herself gracefully upright, easily following where he would lead. Gradually Jasper extricated them from the confines of the porch furniture into the more open area in the porch's center. There, their steps increased in length and velocity and the distance between them shrank as Jasper guided her in the tight turns and retrograde movements of *waltzer à deux temps*, the latest French style that had only recently been reported in *Godey's Lady's Book*. Though unused to this European fashion, Cara kept up with him as they whirled round and round in a spinning equilibrium. The music pulsed, her skirts swirled, and suddenly the night felt open and free and her troubles a thousand miles away.

"That's better," Jasper said. "You're almost smiling now." The music might never end as they swirled in the scented night air. Her heart beat faster and freer than it had in ages. The porch could have been an infinite ballroom, the river a palace of mirrors reflecting the starlight above.

"You dance well for a man who doesn't dance," Cara observed, her breasts rising and falling against her stays as her lungs claimed their need for more oxygen. Jasper looked down at the roses in her hair, the lace framing her bare shoulders, her hand delicately resting in his. Suddenly their movements slowed and stilled, became so gentle, in fact, that their steps almost stayed in one place. Though he knew he was holding her closer than Southern propriety allowed, he saw no harm in following European custom in this instance.

"I just need proper motivation," he said. "And as you can see, a damsel in distress will almost always do. Dancing, they say, can slay the most vicious of dragons."

"Cara," a vehement voice said. "Come inside this instant." In the doorway stood Aunt Winnie with several curious onlookers peering around her formidable girth.

"Well, most of them anyway," Jasper said dryly, releasing his partner. "Miss Randall, it's been too short a pleasure," he averred with a bow.

Cara had no choice but to follow her aunt's orders, although she did give Jasper a last look as she left him on the porch. Though she tried to put it out of her mind, she thought about the waltz on that dark porch as other young men asked her to dance, as Mrs. Patterson gave her a watery, disappointed look, as Johnny sulked on the far side of the room the rest of the evening. The waltz was on her mind as she saw Jasper leave on his own, it claimed her attention when Aunt Winnie informed her it was time to go, and it was even present in her thoughts as she received the requisite stern lecture on "the proper behavior becoming a young lady" during the mercifully short carriage ride home.

Saturday turned out to be a fine morning for an excursion on *The Beaufort Heron*. The captain wore a clean collar for the occasion, Mary had seen to it that refreshments were available in the cabin, and scores of excited Beaufort citizens filled the deck as the steamer pulled away from the main town dock. As the captain pulled on the boat's whistle, he sent a large puff of smoke rising into the air, signaling to all the world that an event was at hand. Children had been invited, too, and a bevy of them swarmed and played tag between the skirts and trousers of the adults. Many of the citizens had brought slaves with them who were now below deck, their masters unwilling or unable to be without their service for even a day. Jim was down there with them, not only because Jasper planned on staying an extra couple days at Silver Oaks, returning when Henry did, but because Jim had gotten word that there would be a ring shout at Lucy Point, a plantation not too far from Henry's.

"You'll be careful?" Jasper had asked back at Villa d'Este. Though attendees from off-plantation were officially forbidden at ring shouts, they were tolerated by most planters as long as the planters didn't actually have to know about it.

"As if I'd let Beaufort slave patrols catch me," Jim said with some disdain.

"Maybe I should write you a pass."

Jim shook his head. "Why bother? I won't even be going on the main road. I'll stick to the slave paths. And at the shout, we'll have lookouts, you know."

"Is it nostalgia?" Jasper asked. "Is that why you want to go?"

Jim shrugged. "Ring shouts go right down to my bones, restores them. It's as close as I ever get to where I'm truly from."

Jasper was still dreading getting close to where he was truly from.

Johnny Patterson was on *The Beaufort Heron*, but not his parents who hadn't entirely recovered from Cara refusing Johnny a third time. Johnny kept his distance from Cara, giving her the cold shoulder whenever he happened to pass her by, an event that occurred with more frequency than innocent chance could explain. Jasper and Billy helped Cara attend to her father who seemed to become more foggy and frail with each passing week. Once they'd found a seat to make the older man comfortable, Cara and Jasper stood by the boat's railing and watched the shores of the Beaufort River pass by. Henry and Mary had been lucky with the weather for their gathering. There was a scattering of cirrus clouds in the blue sky, but that was all. After Mrs. Pickens finished enjoying the celebrity of being the aunt of the hostess of the party, she found Cara, took her away from Jasper's vicinity, and then proceeded to chat cordially with Johnny Patterson while Cara stood by awkwardly, leading Jasper to wonder if the aunt was aware of Cara's most recent rejection. On the whole, Jasper thought Cara had done the right thing, though he didn't know off-hand who might be a better prospect for her. He had yet to see anyone tenable in Beaufort. Perhaps there was some educated young man in Charleston who could appreciate her and not damage her too badly in the normal course of a marriage. Preferably, he wouldn't be a member of the Charleston Light Dragoons.

It wasn't all that long before the steamer completed its passage on the Beaufort River that grew ever narrower the further north they traveled. Then, after rounding Brickyard Point, the Beaufort River suddenly opened into the broad, estuarial Coosaw River that fed into the Saint Helena Sound and, beyond that, the ocean. Well before reaching the Sound, however, they arrived at a large dock jutting into the Coosaw, a structure built with enough heft and into deep enough water to allow a steamer to put in at Silver Oaks at high tide. A dock like this meant that during the winter, for an extra fee of course, the Birch family could catch a steamer en route to Charleston rather than having to go back to town to embark.

Henry was there to greet his guests with jovial energy, complimenting the ladies, ribbing the men, encouraging the children to run and find his boys and enjoy themselves. He promised watermelon, ice cream, and a Punch and Judy show later in the day. Henry had a carriage to bring ladies the short stretch from the dock up to the house, but as it could carry only four at a time, six if they were willing to squeeze, there was a bit of a wait. The men were expected to walk the five minutes up the gentle slope. Naturally this rule didn't apply to Henry, who'd ridden the short distance and had also brought a horse for Jasper. The two mounts now stood in the shade tied to a tree by the sandy river shore. Disembarking last from the boat were the Negroes who never considered any method of transit to the house other than foot.

In all the crush of people, Cara was separated from her father and had some trouble finding him. Curiously, she discovered him next to Spit Jim, who was scrutinizing the Professor in his calm but not particularly subservient way. It was Spit Jim who helped Cara get her father a seat in the carriage with three of the oldest ladies present, and it was Spit Jim who told Cara he'd walk along with the carriage and get the Professor settled in the house until she could get there herself. Though it rarely crossed Cara's mind to thank Negroes for the actions they performed, she did this time.

As Jasper and Henry stood near the dock waiting for the crowd to make its collective journey to the house lawn, Johnny sauntered up to his host, his chin lifted. "Can I take one of your horses?" he asked, only partly joking. "I'll send a slave back with it."

"What's the matter, the Charleston Light Dragoons cripple you?" Henry asked cheerfully. "It's a quarter mile. You can walk."

"Hmpf," Johnny snorted not entirely pleasantly before sauntering away.

"What's gotten into him?" Henry said in an undertone.

Jasper gave a pointed look at Cara who stood in the shade of a tree holding her fringed parasol. It wasn't clear if she was waiting for the carriage or something else. She was studiously not looking at Johnny.

"Ah," Henry said. "Another proposal?"

Jasper nodded.

"She give him the mitten?"

Jasper nodded again.

Henry gave a low whistle. "Well, it's been a busy month. That makes nineteen. That girl is the darnedest. One of these days Johnny's going to break into her house and carry her off like they did the Sabine women."

"Keep your voice down," Jasper said. "You don't want to give him ideas."

Perhaps Johnny suspected he was the topic of conversation because he ambled back over. "Since Cara's gotten over her aversion to riding, you should put her on one of your horses. It would cut the line for the carriage."

"For that matter, Cara can walk," Henry said. "She's been over every inch of this place since she was a child."

Jasper smiled. "I bet she could outrace any of us to the house if she wanted to, long skirts and all."

Johnny turned to Jasper, his lip curled in a sneer. "What are you saying, sir?"

Jasper frowned. "Excuse me?"

"I believe you just insulted a lady."

Henry, who had been momentarily distracted by the return of the carriage, turned back to the conversation. "What are you talking about?"

"He just insulted a lady," Johnny repeated. "And I take offense at that."

"I meant no insult," Jasper assured him. "Rather a compliment."

"You compared her to a horse, a beast of burden, and you shall pay for it, sir."

Henry pointed his finger at the bristling young man. "Stop that talk right now, Johnny. I mean it."

"I demand satisfaction. You may choose the place and time as long as it's before the sun goes down today."

The boy was mad. Jasper looked to Henry for help, but Henry was gazing uncomfortably at the crowd of interested onlookers. "We'll discuss it when we get to the house," he said.

"I demand satisfaction," Johnny asserted with his jaw jutting forward and his voice rising in volume.

"Yes, yes," Henry said impatiently. He beckoned Harold Rutherford to come claim his friend. "Get him up to the house, preferably silently." And Henry gave the young man a slight push in the right direction. "Crazy coot," Henry said, watching him go. "He must've taken Cara's rejection hard."

Jasper looked over at Cara and found she was staring at him with a pinched, white face. Suddenly she began to walk towards the house.

"He sees you as a rival, you know," Henry said.

"Me?" Jasper frowned. "That's ridiculous."

"Not after a certain someone danced with a certain someone else out on the dark piazza during the Patterson party."

"How do you know about that?"

Henry laughed. "Gossip travels around the Sea Islands faster than a greased pig at butchering time. We heard it by noon yesterday."

"I was just trying to cheer her up," Jasper said. "There was nothing improper, and I am not Patterson's competitor. Besides, if he's this damn stupid, Cara was right to refuse him."

"I agree with you there," Henry said.

Since Johnny's father wasn't there to talk sense into his son, Henry pulled the Senator and George Rutherford into his conference with Johnny for reinforcement. When they were done, Henry found Jasper and shook his head. "It's not looking good. He won't budge. I always thought he was as savage as a meat axe, and this proves it." He glanced at his cousin. "Just like you were."

"Maybe if we give it some time, he'll cool off," Jasper said.

"Let's hope so."

Before the guests arrived that morning, during preparations that had diverted a score of field hands from their regular tasks, almost every table and chair in the house had been brought outside and set under the arching arms of the oaks, pines and magnolias that dotted the yard. For the two preceding days, a pair of carpenters and three less-skilled hands had worked to construct a tent out of wooden supports and untold yards of muslin. Under this airy canopy, food that had taken half a week to prepare was now piled high on serving tables with bored slave children waving palmetto fans to keep the flies at bay.

Deciding it was politic to avoid Cara for the time being, if only to let Johnny simmer down, Jasper sat with Henry and a group of planters who were immersed in the practicalities of their trade. As the afternoon progressed, they debated whether to ship their crop to counting houses in Charleston or Savannah, and whether it would be the mills of Manchester or those of Massachusetts that would offer the highest prices for Sea Island cotton this year. The young men might flirt with the crowd of gaily-dressed young ladies and boast among themselves about their racehorses and gambling winnings. This crowd of men knew they were the pillars of the South's economy and political strength. And the Curacao Rum Punch that Mary had concocted with plenty of ice made it a pleasant afternoon indeed.

Johnny neared the conclave of elders to obtain his own serving of punch from the large silver bowl, even though he easily could've sent a servant to fetch one for him. Once he poured himself the libation, he stood on the fringe of the group, appearing to listen to the conversation. His intention, however, was set on another purpose.

"Will you speak with me a moment?" he said to Jasper.

Though not anxious for an interview with the young man, Jasper consented to step away from the group with him.

"Have you decided on a time and place?" Johnny asked imperiously.

Jasper evaluated his would-be assassin. "I see no reason to fight. At worst, we have a mild misunderstanding for which I'm glad to apologize."

Johnny's brow grew darker. "That's not how I view it."

"Then," Jasper said, "we'll have to agree to see things differently. Excuse me." And Jasper went back to his seat among the older men.

Johnny swigged his punch and followed him. "You, sir," he said, his voice rising, "are a scoundrel, and I demand satisfaction."

Jasper turned, truly mystified. "I'm a scoundrel for suggesting Miss Randall is capable of running?"

"You leave her name out it," Johnny spat. "You refuse to fight me because you don't follow the code of a gentleman."

At this, all other conversation ceased. Henry rose from his chair. "You forget yourself, Johnny," he said calmly. "Go over with the other young bucks. We'll start target practice in twenty minutes, and you'll all have a chance to unloose your aggressions." Henry took his arm and started to direct him away.

"No," Johnny said, shaking off his host and turning back Jasper. "You'll fight me, Wainwright, or you're a coward." There was a collective intake of air at this, followed by several gasps as Johnny accentuated his defaming words by reaching out his hand to tweak his adversary's nose. Johnny might have succeeded if Jasper hadn't grabbed him hard by the wrist, or perhaps he did succeed for the briefest of instants, it was impossible for anyone besides the two involved to know for sure. But now the course was set. The insult was too grave to be ignored by even the most lenient of standards, and the standards for gentlemen in Beaufort, South Carolina were not lenient.

Though the consensus was that Johnny was behaving badly, he was the native son and so had a general claim to sympathy. In addition, there was a palpable sense that Johnny was entitled to Cara, and that Jasper had somehow interfered in a way that, while not exactly disreputable, had understandably upset Johnny, and indeed the whole Patterson clan. In fact, most of Beaufort was quite perturbed that Cara had refused Johnny a third time. Why torment the boy when it was obvious she would eventually succumb to his unmistakable advantages of wealth, good name, and pleasing appearance? Henry Birch should give that girl a stern talking-to as soon as possible and end this incessant dithering. As to the duel, rumors quickly spread that Johnny had already been involved in one during his time in the Charleston Light Dragoons, with the other party suffering a slight flesh wound, leading some to bet on an outcome favoring Johnny. Then again, there were tales of numerous duels in Jasper Wainwright's past that made the men shake their heads and women cluck their tongues in doubt that Johnny would leave Silver Oaks alive.

Though Mary pleaded privately with her husband to intervene, she knew as well as anyone that if Jasper tried to dodge a challenge as serious as this, he could never again show his face in Beaufort. Even so, Henry was damned if he was going to let this idiocy ruin his party. Festivities were going to happen, and everyone was going to go home that evening on *The Beaufort Heron* just as he had arranged whether they liked it or not. Johnny and Harold, his appointed second, would stay the night, and the duel would happen at dawn the next morning with Henry's set of dueling pistols. The field of honor would be by the north oak grove near the creek. The whole town of Beaufort might be on tenterhooks Sunday morning not knowing the duel's outcome, but they could jolly well find out the results whenever the information happened to get to them. Besides, Henry had one more card up his sleeve.

"Let's see if shooting practice can change our hell-raiser's mind," Henry told Jasper.

"Henry, it's not as if I'm going to intimidate him. I haven't held a gun in my hand in a decade. I doubt I can hit a post at ten feet."

Henry looked deflated for a moment but then quickly cheered up. "Jasper, by God, you were the best shot at South Carolina College. No one could touch you. It'll come back."

Though Jasper doubted this assertion profoundly, he found himself at the riverbank where Henry's slaves were setting up crude figures made from Coosaw River clay expressly for this event. A work of slave imagination, the figures possessed a flat base that rose into a cone-shaped body. At the top of each rested a round, pig-like head topped by rabbit-shaped ears. These figurines were placed on small shelves nailed onto four-foot posts with pointed bottoms that had been stuck into the riverbank mud. As men ranging in ages from sixteen to fifty pulled out the guns they'd brought with them, Jasper was more than a little surprised to find out exactly how much firepower had accompanied them on *The Beaufort Heron* that morning. Single shot pistols were the most popular, but there were a number of revolvers in the crowd, and one man even brought his rifle that Henry promptly vetoed. A rifle had far too much advantage over even the best pistol, and they'd have to set the target halfway across the river to give him any challenge.

After shedding their frock coats in the warm afternoon sun, the men began to take practice shots in their shirts sleeves and waistcoats. Henry loaned Jasper his favorite pistol as well as the bullets, percussion caps and powder for it. As host of the party, Henry declined to participate himself but instead directed activities, deciding, in a spurt of spontaneity, to organize the whole thing into a competition. The first round of four targets was set up ten feet from the shooters. After a period of practice shots, each man had two opportunities to either shatter the clay figurine or knock it off its perch. Failure to do so meant not advancing in the competition.

The womenfolk, interested in the men's goings-on, had slaves set up chairs for them halfway down the rise above the river so they could watch the proceedings from a safe and less noisy distance. The younger ladies stood in clusters under their fine parasols, chattering and laughing together like decorative birds as they picked out their favorites among the young men. From time to time they moved around for a better view. It was far too exciting an event to be confined to a seat, and, besides, standing showed off their figures to better advantage. Not far away, half-grown boys took practice shots using sticks as pretend guns while the even younger children scampered about like rabbits, oblivious to the hazard at hand. Henry was obliged to assign three slaves to do nothing but keep the wayward imps at a safe interval from being mowed down.

Stepping up to be first in the competition, Johnny sent his figure cleanly into pieces with his first shot and looked pleased with himself. For his efforts, he received a smattering of applause from several skirted admirers in the distance. Declining to take any practice shots, Jasper could hardly bring himself to even put the heavy but well-balanced piece of wood and metal in his hand. It was a deadly specimen of human ingenuity that he knew far too well. After everyone else had proceeded, Jasper resigned himself to taking a turn. He aimed, fired, and was a little surprised at the strength of the recoil after all these years. Who knew where the bullet went, but it certainly didn't disturb the rough figurine waiting mockingly for his shot. Jasper reloaded. "Aim, man," Henry hissed to him as he passed by on his way to joke and banter with the other participants. Jasper fired again. This time he nicked the edge of the figure just enough to send it scooting to the edge of its platform where it tipped for a moment, as if undecided what it wanted to do. Finally it fell into the mud with an undignified plop. He received no applause. All twenty-nine men participating had made it to round two.

Harold and Johnny sniggered together, no doubt already sizing up the coffin Jasper would soon find himself in.

The targets were set out five feet further, still more in the mud than water since the tide had just started to return. Two men missed their target, then another one, but Johnny again smashed his figure cleanly on the first shot. Harold took aim, and on his second shot his target wavered but stubbornly remained on its perch. Harold was out. Jasper again missed on his first shot, but the feel of the gun was coming back to him, and he broke the figurine on his second try.

Sixteen men moved to round three. The slaves had to wade into ankle deep water this time, and the targets were wont to move slightly as the river lapped against their supporting posts. Johnny took out his target again with ease. This time Jasper got his with his first shot.

"Excellent, excellent," Henry called out. "Henderson, no, that doesn't count if a bird knocks over your target. You're out. All right, on to round four."

Only seven men lined up for their marks this round after the slaves in shin-deep water set up the posts. Johnny took his aim as a slave was setting his figurine on the shelf and fired just as the slave moved out of range, prompting the Negro to duck and cover his head. The stunt, while amusing to the younger men in the crowd, caused Johnny to miss his target.

"Cut that out," Henry shouted. "I've half a mind to disqualify you for that, Johnny Patterson."

"Oh, come on, I didn't touch him," Johnny said.

"Henry may disqualify you," Jasper said to the younger man quietly, "but if you do that again, I'll shoot you here and now."

Johnny looked over his shoulder at him. "You won't be putting any holes through me, old man, don't worry." Johnny reloaded and fired again, this time taking out his target cleanly. Four of the other men missed, all of them grumbling about the posts moving in the river current. One of them, Lydell Roberts, an older man with whiskers outlining his entire jaw, got his target on the second try. Then came Jasper's turn. He watched the figurine on its swaying shelf for a few moments, his arm hanging at his side. People began to look at him oddly and a murmur went through the crowd. Then, raising his arm up, he swiftly fired. The target went flying. There was no applause, just a hum of conversation that rose from the spectators like a swarm of bees on the move.

For round five, the slaves went into knee high water with mallets in order to hammer the posts securely into the river bottom. The three men left lined up—Johnny, Lydell and Jasper. Only Johnny and Jasper prevailed.

Henry informed Johnny and Jasper that the posts would stay where they were: the gentlemen would now move back five feet instead of the target moving forward. Johnny waited with annoyance while Henry measured out the distance and then set himself up at the new spot. Raising his arm, he quickly fired and missed, causing a girl or two up the hill to moan with disappointment. While Johnny reloaded, Jasper repeated his procedure of gazing absently at his figurine for half a minute before firing and hitting it. Johnny glanced at his rival with a first glimmer of discomfort. This time he aimed carefully for quite a while before firing. His figure went skidding sideways off the perch and fell into the water without shattering. The competition had gone beyond applause. The entire crowd of a hundred or more watched in taut silence, except for the occasional yelp of a boisterous child.

After Henry moved them back five more feet, Jasper indicated Johnny should go first. "No, you," Johnny said sulkily.

They were now a substantial distance from the figurines that looked rather diminutive as they swayed on their river perches. Jasper again watched his figurine as if idly curious about its small ballet of movement. Casually picking up his arm, he fired without even seeming to aim. The figurine shattered.

Johnny pursed his lips and aimed his pistol. Glancing behind him, he saw Cara among the crowd of watching ladies. He ran his finger around the neck of his cravat as if it'd grown tight and commenced to aim again. After a long moment of concentration, he fired and missed. The crowd was hushed as he reloaded. Sweating now around his hairline, Johnny carefully aimed and fired again. The figurine stayed where it was.

There was a collective sigh of disappointment.

"Would you like another try?" Jasper asked.

Johnny glared at him. "No." And he strode away. Being second best in such a company of men would normally have been cause for celebration for Johnny. But not today.

Henry slapped Jasper on the shoulder in congratulations as the crowd began to disperse and whisper quietly among themselves. Obviously a sizeable portion of the guests were less than keen about the victor of this match.

"I knew you could do it," Henry said. "Twenty years, and you haven't lost your touch." Jasper looked down at the weapon that fit so comfortably in his hand. The attraction it held for him was almost equal to his revulsion. He handed it to his cousin. "I'd hoped to God never to fire one of these again."

"It was just target practice, Jasper," Henry reminded him.

"Practice to be a better killer," Jasper said. He felt a hand on his arm and turned to see Cara, her face white and drawn.

"Mr. Wainwright, don't do it," she said anxiously. "He's so young; he didn't know what he was saying. Don't kill him, I beg of you. Promise me you won't."

"Cara," Henry said severely, "you can't ask that of Jasper. The duel is going to happen."

"Please," Cara pleaded, ignoring her uncle. "I'm not saying not to do the duel. Just don't kill him."

Jasper looked at her, pained. "I can't promise that. The way a duel works, I can try for his arm, but if he moves at all, I'll get his chest. It's not within my control." He wasn't speaking theoretically. It was what had happened with his brother-in-law. He had not wanted to kill that boy.

"So don't shoot at his body," she urged. "I know you're not permitted to fire into the air, but you're such a good marksman, you can miss him on purpose and no one will ever know."

Jasper looked at her with an expression somewhere between perplexed and outraged. "You expect me to just stand there and get shot at?"

"He's young. He'll get distracted and miss. You won't. Please don't shoot him. Please. Promise me."

"He absolutely cannot make that promise," Henry said. "I forbid it. Cara, go back to the house with Mary right now. I mean it." After a last silent appeal to Jasper, Cara sadly turned and obeyed her uncle. "Don't listen to her," Henry said, watching his niece walk slowly with a bowed head. "You have to aim for his body."

"You want me to kill him?" Jasper asked. "He's twenty-two. He has his whole life ahead of him."

"Yes, yes, it'll be a tragedy, but I'd rather him dead than you. Look, in his addled mind he wins either way. Either he kills you and gets rid of his rival, or he dies making a noble last gesture to his beloved. Now come, I believe there's ice cream to eat."

There was indeed ice cream that clusters of children had patiently cranked all through the afternoon. In addition, there was barbecue, there was lemonade and ice, and there was more punch that even the ladies found refreshing in moderation. The duel was the talk of the day, women discussing it behind fans, men discussing it in twos and threes along the river. The children didn't discuss, they just played at shooting each other continuously, and many a mock victim was felled. One boy managed to get a hold of his father's pistol and brandish it at his friends, but this was quickly stopped and a slap upside the head applied. Even given the volume of conversation, everyone fell silent on the subject whenever Jasper drew near. In fact no one wanted to talk much when he was around at all. Jasper thought the day would never end.

Henry had brought Hock from Villa d'Este to play his fiddle, and in the early evening much of the tension was dispelled when all the children lined up for a reel on the grass while the adults approvingly clapped in time to the music. When it got dark, there was even a pretty little fireworks display that started a small fire and burnt a few slave fingers but overall it could've been much worse. Duel or no duel, the party was a success.

As the evening and the party wound down, Henry brooked no entreaties and loaded every last guest onto *The Beaufort Heron* no matter how creatively they came up with excuses to stay until morning. Silver Oaks would be full up as it was because Cara and her father had already planned to stay another day, as had Jasper. Of course the Senator and Mrs. Pickens couldn't be denied a room, even if they'd brought no change of clothes with them. To rectify the situation, two slaves were dispatched to take *The Beaufort Heron* back to town, collect the Pickens' clothes, and row back to Silver Oaks first thing in the morning.

As to Johnny and Harold, it was decided that Smullen Point, half a mile away, was best for them. To be sure, Henry and Mary consulted Cara and her father for permission to house their guests, but since neither Randall spent any time there to speak of, it was natural that the Birches would consider it an extension of their property. While Smullen Point wasn't as luxurious as Silver Oaks, the young men were given two servants to wait on them and horses for transport, so they were content enough with their accommodations.

As the party guests were loaded on the boat, Jasper retired to his room to find Jim with a whale-oil lamp lit and a magazine on the table in front of him. "I hear you've landed yourself in some trouble," Jim said, barely glancing up when Jasper entered.

Jasper shook his head. "I hate the South. I really, really hate it."

Jim shrugged. "Then let's leave. Tonight."

"If I did," Jasper said, "it would disgrace Henry until the end of his days."

"As near as I can tell, he's not the one doing the dying," Jim pointed out. He eyed Jasper critically. "You know, you left the South but it didn't leave you. If your white man's honor is more important to you than your life, so be it. But don't pretend you're doing it for Henry. You're doing it for yourself."

Jasper sat down heavily in a chair. Of course Jim was right. After Johnny's challenge, it was his own honor at stake, his own social acceptance in Beaufort, as marginal as it was, that now hung by a thread. The honor of a gentleman might be just a matter of custom and values but it was as real as a set of manacles. He either had to leave tonight with his tail between his legs or fight tomorrow. And he just wasn't ready to leave.

"Will you come to the duel?" Jasper asked at last. "Put me back together if any pieces fly off?"

Jim nodded with resignation. "So long as he doesn't get you in the heart or the head, I can probably patch you up. Funny how you managed to avoid French husbands calling you out when you deserved it, and now, when you don't deserve it, you wind up with this. I told you that petticoat would cause you trouble. Admit it, I was right."

Jasper had to smile. "You're always right, damn you."

"And I'm also right about you wasting your time trying to change something that'll never change."

Jasper considered the assertion. "When you weigh it against all the potential suffering, it's got to be worth a try." Jim shook his head as he stood up. "You really have to go?" Jasper said.

"You need me to hold your hand?" Jim asked.

"If I only have seven hours left to live, I could use some company."

Jim snorted. "Now that I've seen the world, I can truly say what I've always believed: southern white men are the biggest idiots on earth. I don't know why we worry about freeing the slaves. A few more years of you all shooting holes in each other, and there won't be any of you left to be masters."

"Have a nice ring shout," Jasper said sourly to Jim's back as he left. Of course Jim was right: he was an idiot to be caught up in what was essentially a lover's quarrel. Though he might recognize in Cara an unusual sensibility being squashed by the South's parochial culture, being maimed or killed by her rejected lover was hardly doing her a service. Yes, the whole farce was absurd. Unfortunately, there was no way out except through.

Glancing at the table, Jasper picked up Jim's reading material and idly examined it. It was the maiden volume of a magazine called *Æsthetic Papers,* and the essay it was opened to was titled, "Resistance to Civil Government," by some New England transcendentalist named

Thoreau. Wondering where Jim had gotten it, Jasper pulled his reading glasses out of his waistcoat and sat down to read about the moral imperative not to cooperate with an immoral government.

Half an hour after midnight, Jasper was sitting on the porch, looking out at the river that was just a glint of protean black in the gentle night air. He drank his green tea in shirtsleeves and waistcoat, the ends of his loosened cravat hanging down his chest. Beside him a whale oil lamp was shining softly, keeping him company in his vigil.

Henry joined him on the porch. Jasper noted that he came from the direction of the slave cabins. "Why aren't you in bed," Henry said, pulling up a chair next to him, "sleeping the sleep of the just?"

"If I only have six more hours to live, I hardly want to spend them unconscious," Jasper replied.

Henry waved a hand dismissively. "I don't know why you're worried. You're the better shot; plus, Johnny and Harold, the young fools, are spending the evening putting away the bottle of whiskey I gave them. They'll be good for nothing in the morning."

Jasper glanced sideways at Henry. "Is your middle name Machiavelli by any chance?"

"Look, I didn't tell Johnny to challenge you to a duel. He gets what he gets now." Henry yawned and stretched out his arms. "Well, I'd like to keep you company but I'd better get to bed. Mary'll wake up, wonder where I am, and start fretting. She always does, and Lord knows she's worried sick about this duel already. Really, I could strangle Patterson for challenging you with all the women around. Women should learn about duels after they happen, not before. And who knows what's going on in my boys' heads. I certainly don't want them lurking around the field tomorrow morning. Maybe I'll lock them in their room before I go." He pointed a finger at Jasper. "What they don't need is their favorite uncle dying at dawn. Mary will never forgive you if you get yourself killed—just remember that."

"I'll take it into consideration," Jasper said dryly. "Are your dueling pistols any good?"

"They are," Henry said. "The Senator and I inspected them, and they're spending the night in the room with him and Winnie. No one would accuse the two of them of favoritism, not to you, anyway. Now go to bed. It'll be dawn soon enough."

"Maybe in a little while," Jasper said. "You go up. I'll need my second awake and alert tomorrow."

"I was awake and alert the other six times," Henry said, patting Jasper on the shoulder before heading inside.

The night was calm, and the saline river languid as the tide ebbed once again toward the sea. Jasper must have dozed off in his chair, because all of the sudden an apparition in white appeared before him. It was Cara in a lace-adorned nightgown, candle in her hand, her hair falling down around her shoulders. At first Jasper wasn't sure he wasn't dreaming.

"Mr. Wainwright," she said nervously.

"Miss Randall," he answered with surprise. "You should be in bed."

"I can't sleep. Oh, Mr. Wainwright, please promise me you won't shoot Johnny in the morning."

Jasper looked at her bemused. "If you love him that much, why don't you marry him?"

"You don't understand. I'm not in love with him, but if he dies, it'll be my fault. I'm not a man, I can't fight, I can't vote, I can't stand up in the U.S. Senate and try to direct the fate of nations. All I can do is influence those around me, and even then so very indirectly. I tried to get Johnny to be sober and serious and become the best man he can be. And—and—look what I've done. It's all such a mess." She put a hand to her face. "It would be better if I'd never been borne."

"Cara," Jasper said softly. "Sit down a moment." With an uncertain frown she complied, perching on a chair across from him. He leaned forward towards her, his bent arms resting on his knees. "Listen to me. None of us can truly know all the repercussions of our actions, ever. We make the best choices we can. Ultimately, even not to act is to act—we can never stay impartial, immobile. Life pushes us on, and we can't know the ultimate outcome. But if we make our choices with as much kindness and genuine good intent as we can muster, well then, what more can life ask from us? Our failures are not solely personal; they're derived from our time and place and the knowledge available to us." He pointed at the stars sparkling above the river. "The universe is infinite in its wisdom, not us. Whatever happens tomorrow, you must know that you and I and Johnny are just threads entwined together for a time in life's immense fabric. Johnny's doing what he's doing for his own reasons. If it hadn't been you, he may well have wanted some other girl he couldn't attain so that he could experience frustration and learn to rise above it. It truly isn't your fault."

Cara looked at him, her eyes wide and lovely in the lamplight. "How did you learn to be so kind?" she asked.

The question startled him. "By having to grieve for my sins of being so very unkind," he answered.

She bowed her head. "Mr. Wainwright," she began.

"Yes?"

She looked up full into his eyes. "Don't shoot him. Please don't shoot him. He'll get distracted and miss. Don't shoot him."

Jasper didn't know what to say. She wanted a promise he just couldn't make. Given the situation, he was willing to take a risk, yes, but not face certain death. He actually thought it a bit unfeeling of her to reveal so clearly that she valued Johnny's life above his own.

Realizing she could argue no further, Cara rose with her candle and quietly went inside, her nightgown trailing on the floor behind her.

Chapter Seven

Henry was right. Dawn arrived soon enough. As the dark eastern horizon began to glow like an iron rod in a blacksmith's fire, Jasper stood with Henry in a small meadow bounded by oaks near the bank of Broomfield Creek. In the dim light it could be seen that he wore only a loose shirt and trousers, the traditional garb donned by duelists to prove they hadn't resorted to padding or additional protection. The light clothing also made it easier to attend to wounds in the event any occurred. The Senator, who had elected to oversee matters, was conferring with Johnny and his second, Harold. Progress was moving slowly because the Senator had brought with him a copy of Governor Wilson's *The Code of Honor, or Rules for the Governing of Principals and Seconds in Dueling* to ensure all rules of honor were followed meticulously. He insisted on consulting the manual by the light of a lantern with infuriating regularity.

While they waited for the Senator to properly commune with the rules and the sky above turned the palest of robin's-egg blues, three young men from Beaufort came galloping up on horseback. Though they'd indeed gone home on *The Beaufort Heron* the night before, they'd evidently bribed the ferryman to make his first trip of the day across the Beaufort River before dawn. Now, combined with a hard, reckless ride across Lady's Island, they'd arrived at the field of honor just in time. After dismounting, they made merry with Johnny and Harold while Henry and Jasper stood glumly off to one side. Jim sat by himself under an oak tree, his head bent into arms as if he were sleeping in the half-light. Wisps of ground fog lay over the meadow and extended to the creek bed, creating an otherworldly backdrop for the drama at hand.

"Don't look so damn nervous," Henry said finally to Jasper. "You've done this six times before, remember?"

Jasper looked around him uncomfortably. "Never sober."

Henry nodded at Jasper's opponent. "Look at that boy. What'd I tell you? After his spree with the whiskey last night, he's got a katzenjammer I wouldn't wish on a dog."

Johnny did look worse for wear, his eyes wincing against the fingers of sunlight as they filtered through the mist, but it didn't stop him from sauntering insolently over. "I hear Cara begged you not to shoot me," he said to Jasper. "Well, if you let a woman's tears sway you, you're a fool. After all, she didn't ask me not to shoot you. I intend to take you out."

Jasper made no response, just dourly eyed the bloodthirsty miscreant that was causing him so much trouble.

At length, the Senator opened the polished mahogany box that held two identical smoothbore pistols. Constructed of gleaming rosewood and engraved steel, the polished weapons looked resplendent nestled in their silken purple lining. Jasper allowed Johnny to choose his weapon first; then both men handed their guns to their seconds for loading. The seconds also had the duty of marking off the distance. When Harold and Henry had completed their tasks, Jasper and Johnny stood twenty paces from each other, a span they'd both easily managed with accuracy the day before. Neither of them, however, was familiar with the heavy matching pistols they now held in their hands.

The Senator ensured that both he and the seconds stood well off to one side, out the way of danger—too far for Harold's taste. Henry stood tensely at the edge of the meadow, his hands clasped behind his back, while Harold lounged against a tree, one leg carelessly crossed over the other. Their merriment toned down several notches, the other young Beaufort men stood next to their horses under the moss-hung oaks, ready to quiet their steeds when the shots came. Looking like he wasn't paying much attention, Jim was crouched fairly close to Jasper, though he'd been careful to place a good-sized tree between himself and Johnny's aim. In the near distance behind Jasper the creek flowed six feet or so lower than its bank so that from their vantage point, the gurgle of the water could be heard but not seen.

Both Jasper and Johnny turned so that their right sides were facing each other, each man presenting the narrowest possible target to his adversary. At this stage in proceedings, the pistol in each man's hand pointed down.

"Gentlemen," the Senator intoned, "on the count of three. One . . . Two . . . Three."

But even after the word had been given, neither Jasper nor Johnny raised his weapon. Both were waiting to see what the other would do.

"Gentlemen," the Senator said again.

Feeling a familiar nausea, Jasper gazed at Johnny absently, as if the boy were no more than a clay figurine of the day before. He studied the scene in a kind of meditation, as if he were going to paint the fragile mist, the golden sunlight, the surrounding arching trees. With a deep inhale, he raised his arm and fired.

The bullet whistled past Johnny's ear, ruffling a blond curl but nothing else.

"Damn it, Jasper," Henry hissed.

Johnny's lip curled in a sneer. As the young man raised his own arm above the early morning mist, Jasper drew a long, measured breath and thought about the stone temple, its serenity, its silence. Though he couldn't be sure he'd atoned enough, he had some sense that the after-life was not a place he need fear. In a kind of slow motion he watched Johnny aim and then felt more than saw the muscles in his hand contract as he began to pull the trigger.

Unaccountably Johnny's eyes twitched. Something behind Jasper had caught the younger man's attention. As Jasper turned his head to see what it was, Johnny's gun went off, the report echoing in the trees. After a quick glance to make sure no crimson was pouring from his body, Jasper threw down his gun and tore off on a run.

"It was Cara," Johnny said in a daze. "I swear I saw her. She was like . . . an angel, a vision all in white. She was floating, I swear she was."

Though Jasper ran fast, Jim got to the creek's bank first. There, down at the edge of the water, was Cara, in a light blue dress smeared with large splotches of mud, tangled up in some sort of fine white netting. Jasper jumped down the bank to where Jim was lifting her up and looking her over. She could hardly move, so caught up was she in the long piece of wispy fabric around her.

"Is she hit?" Jasper asked anxiously.

Jim shook his head. "Doesn't look like it."

"She's holding her arm oddly," Jasper said. "Is it broken?"

"I'm not hit," Cara said, trying to brush the fabric away from her. "I just lost my footing and banged into a rock."

Henry arrived at the top of the bank. "Is she hit?" he asked breathlessly.

Jasper shook his head. Then, as was his custom, Henry took charge.

"Spit Jim, get her behind that bush. As soon as we're gone, take her back to the house. Jasper, stomp around on those footprints."

"If you'll just get this fabric off me, I can—"

"Hush, girl," Henry ordered.

Jim speedily picked Cara up and got her out of sight just as the others arrived at the bank.

"Nothing here," Henry said.

"I swear I saw her," Johnny said, still dazed.

"I thought I saw something, too," Jasper said from the muddy water's edge. "But there's nothing. I've checked up and down."

"I did spy an egret spreading its wings just a moment ago," Henry said. "Took off over the creek. I bet that's what you both saw." Henry reached out a hand to pull Jasper up the bank and then turned to Johnny. "Well, neither of you managed to murder the other yet. Another round, Patterson?"

"She was like a vision," Johnny said. "Floating, ethereal. An angel come down from heaven for me."

The Senator frowned at the young man. "Are you satisfied, man? Or do you want to go on?"

Johnny appeared not to hear the questions. He turned to Jasper. "What did it mean?"

Jasper evaluated the younger man who was so like the reckless, trigger-happy youth he'd been twenty years ago. After a long moment, he held out his hand. With a distracted frown Johnny shook it.

"It was a vision," Johnny told Harold as they walked back to where horses and guns had been left. "Did you see her?"

"Didn't see nothing," Harold grumbled. "I can't believe both you and Wainwright missed at that distance. You were both hitting every dang thing like clockwork yesterday."

"Come, come, Harold, the pistols were fired, honor was preserved," Henry cajoled, clapping him on the back. "You can't expect blood every time. Let's go have breakfast."

Spit Jim was moving quickly along an overgrown path that was a shortcut to the house. Cara was still caught up in the twists of fabric but had managed to free one hand to protect herself from the branches that glanced her face. She didn't know what to make of the Negro carrying her. That he had obeyed her uncle's orders even though he was no longer a slave didn't surprise her. That he was strong enough to carry her with so much speed did, especially since she could see small amounts of grizzled gray in his short hair. He smelled unlike any Negro she'd ever known, and his gaze and mannerisms were far closer to a white man's than any Negro in Beaufort had ever dared. She did know people were saying that if it weren't for the fact that Jasper Wainwright was the cousin of Henry Birch, this full-of-himself freed Negro wouldn't last long in the Sea Islands.

Spit Jim glanced down with some annoyance at the squirming young woman in his arms. "Don't toy with him," he said in a low voice. "You've got to let him go."

Cara batted away yet another branch. "What are you talking about?" she said crossly.

"I've been watching you, and one thing I know for sure is you're not stupid, so listen up. If you keep him here, he'll end up dead. Is that what you want?"

"You mean Mr. Wainwright? I'm not keeping him here."

"Yes, you are. He's like a moth to a flame."

"We have an understanding," Cara said indignantly. "He specifically told me he doesn't want to marry anyone."

"Who said anything about marriage?" Spit Jim said. "You keep him here, it'll be drink or duels, but I guarantee you he'll be dead."

"He's not been drinking at all," Cara objected, her face flushed by Spit Jim's reference to Jasper's lack of matrimonial intent.

"Not yet, but this place is taking its toll. Just remember, Calypso kept Odysseus on her island with her for seven years, she even offered him immortality. In the end she had to let him go."

Pursing her lips, Cara couldn't believe she was speaking of these things with a Negro. "I'm not trying to keep him," she insisted. "And it's not for you to tell me how I feel about anyone." Truly, it was hard to be dignified when she was being carried about like a sack of onions.

Spit Jim glanced at her with even more disdain. "You're nothing but trouble, you know that? By the way, your father. He takes too much laudanum. It's going to kill him faster."

Cara looked up with alarm at the man carrying her. "Dr. Goode gave him the laudanum for his stomach pains."

"It's more than just pains. My guess is it's tumors, but now he's addicted to the opium in the solution and needs to take more and more. You can see it—it's dulling his mind."

Cara was quiet, startled by this analysis as Spit Jim hustled her along. "What can be done?" she asked finally. "If his needs are escalating, maybe without the laudanum the pain would be unbearable."

"Let me examine him," Spit Jim said. "If it is tumors, I might be able to shrink them. If nothing else, I can reduce the pain and wean him away from the laudanum."

They were at the house already, Spit Jim taking her in through the side yard door, Mary crying out at the sight of her niece injured or worse. "I'll think about it," Cara told Spit Jim hurriedly before reassuring Mary she was fine.

Spit Jim had been swift, and Cara was back in her bedroom before any of the men reached the front lawn. Mercifully, he even got her hidden away a full thirty seconds before Mrs. Pickens emerged from her room late because she had to wait for her change of clothes to be delivered from Beaufort. When the men approached, Mary ran out of the house with tears streaming down her face, so relieved was she to see Jasper unharmed. The boys all whooped and hollered with glee that their uncle wasn't dead, and somehow both Jasper and Johnny were the men of the hour. With the exception of Henry, everyone agreed that the dueling pistols were a wee bit old fashioned and didn't have the accuracy of the newer models. Harold declared any duel he fought in the future would use the most lethal firepower available, even if he had to send to Charleston and wait a week for it to be delivered.

After breakfast was underway on a table outdoors set gaily with linens and china under the oaks, Henry conferred with Mary privately and debated the wisdom of sending for Doctor Goode to attend to Cara. They ultimately decided it would just incur gossip, which must be avoided at all costs. Besides Spit Jim was looking after her, and didn't Jasper have complete confidence in him? The guests were all told that Miss Randall had a slight headache and wouldn't be down until later in the morning.

Jasper, however, found his way to Cara's room where she looked pale and small against a wealth of embroidered white pillowcases behind her head. Her sleeve had been rolled up to expose a raw, scraped arm into which had been inserted six thin steel needles. On top of each needle burned a small wad of dried mugwort that emitted an odor not entirely pleasant but definitely familiar. Jasper looked at Jim.

"It's not even a sprain," Jim said, "but she hit a rock pretty good. It'll be sore, and she'll have a nice bruise." He looked down at his patient. "You were lucky. You could have had a hole clean through you."

"I was out of range," Cara said indignantly. "His shot went way above me."

Jim shook his head. "You weren't out of range. It was sheer luck he didn't hit you or Jasper. Now me, I was behind a tree where any sensible person would be."

"Why did you risk your life?" Jasper asked her, incredulous.

"You risked yours," she said. "I saw you. You didn't aim at him. Thank you."

Jasper gazed at her in bewildered disbelief. "That was no reason to put yourself in front of his gun. Jim's right; you weren't out of range. If you'd been hurt—" The image of her falling backwards into the creek as the gun went off kept flashing before his eyes.

"If you were of an age to be spanked," Henry said, coming into the room, "I'd do it right now. Cara Livinia Randall, what were you thinking?"

"No one was killed, Uncle Henry," she defended herself. "Isn't that what we all wanted?"

"Maybe, but not at the risk of your death, and scandal to boot. Men are allowed to throw away their lives on silly things. If you'd been injured, don't you know how devastated Mary would've been? It would've nearly killed her. Young lady, you will never ever cut a shine like that again. Do I make myself clear?"

Cara looked down at her bedclothes. "Yes, sir."

Henry glared at her, hands on his hips. Then he relented. "All right, you saved the day, you little goon, even if it was pure fluke. Now get some rest, you look tuckered out. Great God Almighty, what in Sam Hill is that in your arm? And what's that awful smell?"

Since Cara really did need to rest, having been up all the previous night, Jasper took Henry out of the room and did his best to explain the odd but powerful intricacies of the Chinese way of medicine.

That afternoon Cara, her father, the Senator and Mrs. Pickens set off in the Birch carriage to the ferry and the short trip across the Beaufort River. Wearing elaborate undersleeves attached to the regular sleeves of her dress, Cara held her arm a little tenderly against her side, but other than that Jasper could detect no evidence that anything untoward had occurred to her. Jasper stayed on at Silver Oaks, planning to return with Henry and his family the next day.

"You see what I'm up against," Henry said that evening as they sat on the porch after supper enjoying the sunset. "That girl has a mind of her own, and she concocts all sorts of schemes. Not a man in a thousand would be able to keep her out of trouble. The good Lord knows I barely can, and I've got the willpower of ten mules."

Mary smiled at her husband. "More like twenty, but you exaggerate, dear. Besides playing her music every morning and wanting to go north for more schooling, what has she done that's all that headstrong?"

"Well, today was enough to turn my hair gray," Henry said. "It's my fault, I suppose, for not being stricter, but I didn't want to crush her spirit."

"You and Mary have done a fine job with her," Jasper assured him. He was always struck by how they gave absolutely no credit to Professor Randall for Cara's upbringing. "Having both mind and spirit isn't a liability in a woman, as nineteen marriage proposals more than testify."

"She needs someone who'll appreciate but not coddle her," Henry said, looking sideways at Jasper. "Johnny, that belligerent cur, would've been a disaster. If he married Cara, six months later he and I would've ended up taking shots at each other some miserable dawn for one reason or another. I hope he's off to Charleston before we get back."

On that point they could all agree.

The outcome of the duel spread through Beaufort before nightfall. It was quickly agreed that Henry's pistols were more to blame for the bloodless result than any failure of nerve on the part of the participants. Everyone expressed relief that satisfaction was achieved without loss of life, and all the women made a mental note to insist on Henry's pistols if a duel ever came the way of their men.

Curiously, the duel seemed to strengthen Jasper's reputation in Beaufort, especially when the details of the two previous men he'd dispatched decades earlier circulated the town. On arriving back in Beaufort, Winifred Pickens immediately sent off letters, and was rewarded with detailed accounts from the wife of a longtime faculty member at South Carolina College and from a good friend who had a cousin who lived within shouting distance of Sleety Pines who knew Jasper Wainwright's sister-in-law in person. Winifred only regretted she had not inquired more extensively earlier and had relied so heavily on her cousin Verbena's account of Jasper Wainwright's wife's tragic death. Maybe she would have let Cara read *Jane Eyre* after all.

"The first death was what prompted his expulsion from South Carolina College," Winifred informed Mrs. Rutherford and Mrs. Patterson during their morning calls. Mrs. Patterson blanched slightly to think of her son at this sharpshooter's mercy. "By spring of his first year, he'd been in four duels already—all over silly matters, college boy things. Each of the first four duels ended without grave injury, though there were some minor wounds. None to Mr. Wainwright, naturally."

Naturally, the women nodded.

"They say he only made the first challenge himself, but that once he had a reputation, all the boys were eager to fight him for any reason, as boys are wont to do. They say he was such an expert marksman he could shoot an acorn from a tree at fifty paces. They also say there would've been more duels had not Henry, who was at school with him, not smoothed over half of the demands for satisfaction. Henry always was so genial and persuasive, even then. It's a pity he never went into politics, like the Senator."

The other women concurred. Winnie's niece and nephew-in-law could never be complemented too often to please her.

"Well, this was all well and good until . . ." Winifred gazed around her audience for dramatic effect. "Until the son of the President of the college challenged Wainwright. That's the one he killed. All according to the rules, to be sure, but he was expelled just the same. Or at least he was invited not to return, on no uncertain terms."

"I think I remember that," Mrs. Rutherford said. "Didn't he come back to Beaufort with Henry that summer? It was the year my Victoria was born, summer of '27."

Winifred nodded with authority. "And my niece, Annabelle Smullen, was married that spring to Professor Randall. Well then, since South Carolina College wouldn't have Jasper, what else could he do but go to school in the north? Howard Birch was so fond of the boy, treated him like a son really, and arranged it all quickly with some connections he had. You'll remember Howard Birch always doted on his sister, Sarah, and my understanding is that when she died he took pity on the boy because he was so like his mother. I remember Sarah Birch." Winifred looked off dreamily for a moment. "She was only two years older than me. Her father, William Birch, Henry's grandfather, spent so much time in Columbia after the war, he didn't realize his overseer was cheating him, so when it came time for Sarah to marry, there wasn't much money for a dowry. Still, George Wainwright took a fancy to her, and off to Buddenville she went. She was such a gentle, cultured creature." Winifred recalled herself. "Anyway, after the duel, even the

University of Virginia, which had only just opened and was begging for students, wouldn't take Jasper because the dead boy was the nephew of a dean there. So off to Boston he went and made the best of that Yankee school. I'm sure he'd have rather have stayed in South Carolina."

"It must have been cold there in the North," Mrs. Patterson observed with a shudder.

"Appallingly," Winifred agreed. "Maybe the cool weather chilled his temper, or maybe Yankees aren't concerned much with honor, because he wasn't in a single duel up north."

"Not one?" The idea was shocking.

"Then, just as he was finishing up his studies, his father died. His older brother, Walter, took care of things, evidently he's upstanding and responsible and was even then. The father had left the older boy two-thirds of the property and Jasper one-third. There was some talk of favoritism, but maybe it was because Walter stayed in Sleety Pines with his father, while Jasper spent so much time here in Beaufort and then up North. Anyway, Jasper went home, claimed his property, and married Elizabeth Bateson—you remember, the goddaughter of Honoria Stimble, who is the second cousin of my cousin, Verbena? He had a lovely house built for her, but poor Elizabeth was sickly and died with her first baby. Jasper was distraught, naturally—"

Naturally, the women nodded.

"And went out of his mind with liquor. At the funeral, Elizabeth's brother, Thomas, said some things he oughtn't to have, Jasper said some things back, and unfortunately it escalated into a duel. Jasper's brother, Walter, tried to stop it, he even postponed it long enough to send for our Henry to see if he could iron things out. Jasper was ready to back down, but Thomas wouldn't budge. He was only nineteen, the poor thing."

"He died?" Mrs. Rutherford asked weakly. Winnie nodded. The poor boy, they all agreed. Why had he been so stubborn? It hadn't brought Elizabeth back. His poor mother—two children dead in a month.

"And that's what set Jasper off on his travels," Winnie concluded. "He sold his land to his brother, took that slave, Spit Jim, with him, and went to China. They say he put his money from the land sale into northern mills and railroads and has a substantial fortune now. To be sure, he still owns the forty-six slaves he left with his brother in Sleety Pines."

The women all sighed. If Jasper could've seen it, he would have been astonished that any part of his story, however stretched and shaped, could evoke that kind of sympathy in the middle-aged female breast.

"His brother and sister-in-law are looking forward to a visit from him," Winnie said. "They're wondering why he's staying in Beaufort so very long." She gave the other women an arch look. The look didn't please Mrs. Patterson, for whom Cara was still a sore point, but the implication was conveyed just the same. Absolutely everyone knew the details of the waltz on the veranda.

"But will she accept him?" Mrs. Rutherford almost whispered. "She's turned down nineteen."

"Henry's got to talk sense into her," Winnie said authoritatively. "It's up to him."

"Has Mr. Wainwright actually asked her?" Mrs. Patterson inquired sharply.

"Not yet," Winnie admitted. "But why else is he still here? It's been almost eight weeks."

Why else, indeed.

Professor Randall consented to Jim's treatments, amenable to experiencing the application of Chinese medicine he'd so often read about during his scholarly pursuits. The result was remarkable. Gradually, through two weeks of daily treatments, the Professor's laudanum dose was reduced until, by the middle of June, he had emerged from his morphine haze back to his normally inquisitive, if still fairly passive mode of consciousness. Once he felt better, the Professor invited Jasper to a series of suppers so as to plumb the depths of Jasper's Chinese erudition. Cara said little during these meals, attending to her father's needs with solicitous care but otherwise just listening quietly. Professor Randall often appeared to forget about his daughter entirely, so interested was he in the surface composition of Chinese roads, the intricate network of Chinese canals, or the exploits of the mythic warriors of the Shaolin Temple. Jasper, however, never quiet forgot about Cara, his eyes finding her as she adjusted the wick of the lamp or gave directions to servants, or played piano quietly inside while he and the Professor enjoyed the mild evening breeze on the porch. He would drink his green tea, listen to Chopin, and wonder which was worse, wanting to leave Beaufort, or not wanting to.

"Well, well," Henry said, scanning *The Charleston Courier* late one afternoon on the piazza. "Eustace Woods has written in condemning the evils of dueling. I wonder if this is in response to any particular duel, one that happened last week, for instance. Who knows? Maybe unbeknownst to us, the illustrious Eustace was at our party at Silver Oaks."

"What does he say?" Jasper asked, somewhat distracted as he watched Cara play a game of boules with her cousins. Jasper had brought the boys a set from France, and it'd already become popular with the children of the neighborhood. After many requests, Cara had succumbed to her cousins' entreaties to play it with them. Now cries of "No, you cheated," and "I win, I win," as well as much laughter rang out from the yard as they rolled wooden balls at a smaller, target ball.

Henry noted which of the gamboling figures Jasper's eyes were following. "Woods is declaring there ought to be a law requiring at least a week's delay between the challenge and the duel itself. To allow the passions to cool and phlegmatic reflection to prevail. As if your average hothead in these parts can't keep a rage up for a week without problem. Some can keep it going a lifetime."

"Still, the law wouldn't be unreasonable, and it's probably a good idea," Jasper said, his eyes still on the yard. "With duels entirely extra-legal, they're basically a way to murder without penalty. As least this would give the practice some small oversight."

"Well, I'll say this for Mr. Woods—he's reasonable and level-headed as usual, and thoroughly persuasive. The scheme will please the ladies, the venerable elders, and anyone with any sense actually, although I doubt this includes our exalted legislature in Columbia. I keep pondering who the estimable Eustace could be. He's certainly a reformer, not a revolutionary, but every time I come up with a possible candidate, I meet up with the fellow in person and have to cross him off my list."

Jasper finally turned his attention from the boules game to give Henry an evaluative look. "Whoever it is, he should know that his opinions would carry more weight if they weren't anonymous."

Henry smiled. "I'll tell Eustace just that when I meet him."

Henry had to make another excursion to Three Reeds to deal with yet another failed sluice gate. "My fault," he said, "for not inspecting the place better when I bought it from that blackguard, Turner. What I saw at high tide looked sound enough—that's why he showed it to me then. I should've known every mechanism below the high water mark would be rotten and fail as soon as you could say jiminy cricket. Rice is a devil's crop, that's what it is. I have half a mind to hunt down the cur in whatever backwater he absconded to in Mississippi and demand my money back."

"The miasma at Three Reeds—you'll be careful?" Mary asked weakly. Though she knew there was no way to restrain her husband from overseeing the particulars of his investment, she was truly beginning to hate rice and the demanding nature of its cultivation. Henry, actually, wasn't far behind her.

After Henry set off on his horse early in the morning, things were fine with the family for a day or two. Though Winnie was over too often for Jasper's taste, she was being unaccountably cordial to him, rendering Jasper's life a degree more pleasant. During the next night, however, Robert, the baby of the family, acquired a sore throat that hurt each time he swallowed. Mary kept him home from school the following day, feeding him broth and applying carrot poultices to his neck. He didn't improve.

"Why does Dr. Goode have to be in Charleston just now," Mary fretted.

"Do you want me to send for him?" Jasper offered. "Or Henry?"

"No," Mary sighed. "I'd feel silly calling them back to Beaufort for just a sore throat." Still, because Jasper could see her forehead was lined with worry, he sent word to Cara who promptly came to spell Mary in her nursing tasks. Aunt Winnie soon arrived as well with prescriptive advice on protocols and remedies, though she didn't stay long. Winnie didn't like illness and preferred not to be around it, a state of affairs just as well for everyone concerned. After sending her regrets to the Rutherford's that she couldn't attend their latest party, Cara remained in the sick room with Mary and Robert throughout the evening, applying poultices and reading her cousin a collection of Danish fairy tales to distract him, not leaving until nearly eleven. All the tender ministrations proved to no avail when just after midnight Robert developed a severe fever and could hardly swallow at all. Certain now it was quinsy, Mary stayed up all night with her sick son. The next morning, Jasper found her in the boys' room nearly in tears as she applied more compresses, linseed now, servants coming and going at her bidding. At last she gave her assent to send for both Henry and Dr. Goode, though she knew once summoned Dr. Goode couldn't be expected to return for another twenty-four hours.

"Let Jim have a look at him," Jasper urged Mary.

The recommendation only caused alarm. "I don't dare, Jasper. Not without Henry's permission."

"Well, how about that other doctor in town then? Braddock?"

"Oh, I couldn't. Henry hates the man. Besides," Mary lowered her voice and nearly whispered, "he drinks."

"I see," Jasper said evenly.

"Oh, Jasper, I didn't mean—"

Jasper raised a hand. "No need to apologize, Mary. I know better than anyone what liquor does to a man."

By the time Cara came to spell Mary and allow her an hour's rest, Mary's anxiety had heightened further because little Robert seemed to be growing steadily worse. Still, because she was exhausted, she accepted Cara's insistence that she lie down for a spell. While she slept, Jasper ushered Jim in to see the child. Cara neither assented to nor prevented the visit, just looked back and forth between the former slave and master. After reading the boy's pulses and palpating his swollen neck, Jim determined that the illness, while severe, wasn't yet life-threatening. Together he and Jasper decided not to antagonize his hosts with unsanctioned ministrations but that Jim would gather the necessary herbs and instruments so as to be ready if the situation took a turn for the worse.

It turned out Henry was already on his way home when Hock, posthaste on horseback, intercepted him. With Mary's message in his coat pocket, Henry doubled his pace and arrived by suppertime. Without even doffing his riding boots, he went straight upstairs to see little Robert. After feeling the boy's forehead and hearing his feeble moans, he turned around to see Mary, Cara, and Jasper in the doorway.

"Why isn't Spit Jim in here?" Henry demanded.

"Wouldn't you rather have Dr. Braddock?" Mary asked tremulously.

"Braddock's a charlatan," Henry spat out. "I wouldn't trust my worst horse with him. Why is it this town has only one decent doctor who can't resist visiting his blasted grandchildren in Charleston?" Henry leaned his head out the door. "Couts," he shouted. "Get Spit Jim up here on the double." He turned back to his wife. "Why didn't you send for me earlier? I leave for a day and you nearly kill my children."

Mary shrank back, tears now falling down her face.

"Henry," Jasper remonstrated. Cara, however, caught his sleeve. With a slight shake of her head, she pulled him out the door with her.

"Why did you leave me here alone?" Mary sobbed back. "Why do you always leave me alone?"

"Come," Cara whispered to Jasper. "They'll work it out better on their own."

Jim arrived at the top of the stairs just as Jasper and Cara were ready to descend them. Hearing the raised voices coming from the sick room, he looked at Jasper questioningly. "Good luck," Jasper said.

"Wonderful," Jim replied dourly, but not lacking for courage, he entered the room with his herbs and box of needles.

Jasper and Cara went out to the piazza to cool down in the evening breeze that rustled the camellia bushes and gently stirred the live oaks. In the fading twilight all was in semidarkness under the overhang of the porch.

"Are they often this way?" Jasper asked, looking off at the river that had turned silver in the dusk.

"Only when one of the boys is ill," Cara said. "Once, when Hugh had scarlet fever, Henry even cussed out Dr. Goode. But it's because he loves his children so much. Afterwards he always apologizes."

There was a sound behind them. Through the window they saw it was Mary, sitting in the parlor next to a lamp one of the servants had lit, weeping into her handkerchief. Jasper frowned, unsure what to do.

"Go tell her it's not her fault," Cara said. "She might believe you."

From the window, Cara watched as Jasper sat down next to Mary, as he spoke his words of consolation, as Mary turned to him with eyes of hope, as Jasper smiled with reassurance, as Mary began to sob even harder, as Jasper put an arm around her to comfort her distress, as Mary put her head on his shoulder. Cara gave a start when she realized there was another set of eyes watching the scene. Her uncle stood in the room's doorway scrutinizing his wife and cousin together. Cara must have made an involuntary movement because Henry glanced up to see her in the shadow of the porch. He quietly backed away from the door and joined Cara on the piazza.

"Uncle Henry," Cara said quietly but anxiously. "It's not what you think."

"You don't know what I think, Cara," Henry said slowly, tiredly.

"I'm the one who told him to go comfort her. It's my fault."

"It's no one's fault," Henry said, gazing out at the bats swooping over the water to catch their evening repast of insects.

"It's not—there's nothing—"

He turned to her. "I know that. You think I'd leave him alone with her for days at a time if I didn't trust both of them?"

"So you're not going to call him out?"

Henry frowned in the faint light. "Of course not. It'd be like shooting myself."

Cara's shoulders sank in relief. "You don't know what Mary's gone through these past two days."

"And I just exacerbated it," Henry said quietly. "Spit Jim says the quinsy isn't so bad, that Robert should be fine in a few days. So this will pass. And no one will be the worse for it."

Mary must have heard Henry's voice because she tentatively stepped out on the porch, candle in hand, and looked questioningly at her husband. "He's going to be fine," Henry said.

Smiling through her tears, Mary took a step towards Henry. But just as she reached him, she seemed to lose her balance and tilt to one side, her candle dropping to the floor. Then she fainted dead away.

Henry caught her as she pitched forward. "Spit Jim," he roared as he carried his unconscious wife up the stairs. Now Jim had two patients to look after.

It was late evening before Henry finally returned downstairs to the piazza for a nightcap. Once Cara had helped see to Mary's comfort as best she could, Henry had insisted Jasper take her home since she looked bone-tired and Spit Jim didn't need a third invalid on his hands. Jim was indeed busy, passing back and forth between the master bedroom and the boys' room keeping both patients under surveillance while doing his best to calm Henry down and get him out of the way. Jasper had largely stayed downstairs so as not to aggravate the situation.

Henry's face looked unusually lined as he joined Jasper on the dark porch in the sighing evening breeze. "Well, I've been a greater fool than usual this time," he said as he sat down and sipped the whiskey Couts had waiting for him.

"I'm sure Mary'll be fine," Jasper assured him. "It's just fatigue."

"It's more than that." Henry stared dully off into the dark distance. "She's with child."

Jasper gave his friend a sharp look. "You don't seem to welcome the news."

"Of course I don't," Henry snapped. "Five pregnancies are plenty. You think I enjoy spending nine months fearing for my wife's life? Mary's my heart and soul. I want her with me for the rest of my days." Henry swigged his drink glumly. "In the future I'll just have to practice more self-control."

Jasper was silent a long moment. "In Europe, there are methods people use to prevent pregnancy."

Henry looked askance at his friend. "And I'm sure you're acquainted with every one of them. We're not so backward here, cousin, as you like to think. In fact, ever since Robert, keeping track of days has worked well for us. It's all a matter of timing and abstinence."

Jasper raised an eyebrow. "Abstinence? On whose part?"

With a shrug of his shoulder Henry admitted to his concubine at Silver Oaks. "I'm weak. I freely admit it. But it was always to protect Mary's health."

"I see," Jasper said.

A glance at his cousin told Henry that Jasper wasn't buying the line he was selling. "You know," Henry said, changing tack, "when we were boys, and Mary followed us around all the time, you were the one she was sweet on."

Jasper gave half a laugh. "Hardly."

"It's true. The looks she used to give you. The hopeless sighs. Lucky for me you got kicked out of college and had to go north for such a long spell. Gave me a clear field to woo her."

Jasper shook his head. "You say the most idiotic things. Mary has always been desperately in love with you."

"Not always." There was something dark and odd in Henry's expression. "Not until I decided I wanted her. She loves me now, though, I've no doubt about that." He upended his drink and finished it. "Well the bright side is, we get one more chance."

"Chance at what?"

"At having a girl," Henry said. "Cara's too old for Mary to dress and coddle and pet anymore. A daughter. Yes, Mary would love that."

The next afternoon, after checking on his two patients who were so far on the mend he hardly needed to have rushed back from Charleston, Dr. Goode asked for a moment of Jasper's time. With a certain amount of foreboding Jasper received him in Mary's elegant front parlor.

Sporting a head full of white hair, Dr. Goode had been the mainstay of Beaufort medicine for two score years and didn't have many more left in him. A much younger man, Dr. Braddock, had recently started a practice in Beaufort with the expectation that he would gradually take on the older doctor's clientele. So far, the townsfolk were resisting the exchange.

"I'd like to talk to you about Jim," Dr. Goode said, sitting down on a settee and resting two hands on the walking stick that he had declined to give up to Couts on entering the house.

"Certainly," Jasper said politely. He suspected that in short order Jim's burgeoning medical practice was likely to be condemned if not absolutely forbidden. Well, he had encouraged Jim to take this path and now must help shoulder the repercussions. In many respects, it was fortunate that Dr. Goode had not yet retired since the doctor had a long acquaintance with Jim. Twenty-five years before, when George Wainwright had agreed to send Jim to Beaufort to counter his son's rambunctiousness, he had stipulated that since the Negro couldn't be used in the fields of Sleety Pines he be hired out in Beaufort with the wages earned used to pay for Jasper's educational expenses. Howard Birch had complied and found Jim work with townsfolk, one of them Dr. Goode. It was through wrapping bandages and assisting Dr. Goode on patient visits that Jim had gained a substantial background in the Western version of medicine, not to mention paid for youthful Jasper's clothes, books and tuition. Howard Birch had readily supplied his nephew with room and board. At the time Jasper had considered his father the biggest skinflint alive.

"I speak to you as one educated man to another," the doctor began. Jasper nodded noncommittally. "With Jim's return to Beaufort, I find myself faced with a situation that is fraught with . . . complications."

Jasper nodded again even more cautiously. He appreciated that, with the exception of himself, Dr. Goode was the only white man in South Carolina to call Jim by his given name.

"I was always fond of him, you know," Dr. Goode said. "Even when he first came to Beaufort with you as a youth, he was reliable and smart as a whip, if I do say. Though my view is not widely shared, it is my belief that Negro intelligence, in certain cases, can be wholly comparable to Caucasian."

Jasper nodded yet again, a little more sympathetically this time.

Dr. Goode cleared his throat. "It came to my attention a number of weeks back that Jim has been attending to various slaves with the use of Chinese herbs and needles. When only slaves were involved and no one was made worse by treatment, the matter could remain quiet enough. But now . . ."

"Doctor, you must see that Jim has done wonders for anyone he's helped. Professor Randall has regained the use of his faculties without the recurrence of pain; little Robert can swallow and his fever's subsided. Though this medicine may be strange to our eyes, the Chinese have three thousand years of tradition that has made it effective. I don't dispute that—"

Dr. Goode raised a hand, interrupting him. "I'm not here to condemn, Jasper. I've lived long enough and am close enough to my own end that I have no false pride to defend."

Jasper frowned. "Then why are you here?"

Dr. Goode's hands repositioned themselves on the cane. "While I appreciate Jim's expertise, it's my suspicion that as a free, well-educated, well-traveled Negro he won't last long in Beaufort, or anywhere else in the South for that matter. He's far too much of a threat. But before he leaves, I want to encourage him to do what good he can. I know there are things I can't treat or cure, so let him try his Chinese ways, I say. If a crippled leg is healed, if one less baby dies of whooping cough, I'll be glad to see it. To that end, I propose to officially make Jim my assistant so that he may use my name where possible to deflect censure or suspicion. I believe he'll find it an asset, and I hope the town of Beaufort may find itself in better health as a result."

For a moment Jasper was speechless. "I must express both surprise and gratification, sir, as well as apologize for misconstruing you. However, Jim's the one who should consent to your proposal. Would you mind waiting while I fetch him?"

As might be expected, it was Couts who did the fetching via the garden boy who found Jim in the stable, but in any event, Jim soon stood in the parlor in front of the seated doctor. He was not invited to sit, as that act would be more revolutionary than even broad-minded Villa d'Este could stomach, but Jasper remained standing to keep him company.

Jim was evaluating the doctor skeptically. "You expect me to only treat Negroes? How about the Professor? I can't keep the tumors small and the pain away without needles twice a week."

The doctor spoke carefully. "I've no objection to your attending white patients if your services have been specifically requested by the parties in question. But I urge you to be discreet."

Jim frowned as if not entirely convinced.

"With my name as a shield," the doctor said, "you'll last twice as long and do twice as much good as you otherwise might. That's all I want, Jim."

Jim looked the doctor over. "How about you? Can I help you last a little longer in exchange?"

Dr. Goode smiled. "If you'll come to my home at nine tomorrow morning, I'd be glad to see what it is these Chinese call medicine." With some difficulty, the old man got to his feet and leaned on his stick. He now turned to Jasper. "I perceive that your travels have changed you, son, broadened you. I wonder if you're ready to shoulder the mantle of your citizenship? I'm old enough to remember the ratification of our Constitution, how exciting it was, how we were creating our future. As a boy I saw George Washington ride down the street while crowds cheered. As a young man I attended Jefferson's inauguration. Difficult times lie ahead for our country, but as for me, I won't be around to see it. It is your generation that must take stock and prepare. People like Barnwell Rhett are leading us off a cliff to disunion and we seem to follow willingly, not caring for our history or even our future, just our wounded pride of the present. It will take courage and determination to find another way."

Jasper gave the doctor a long look. "Perhaps there are some in Beaufort who possess these qualities."

"I hope so, young man." The doctor gave a friendly shake to Jasper's hand. "I will do what I can in support of whoever might lead in another direction."

Jasper nodded and threw a quick glance at Jim, who was looking on gravely but skeptically.

"So are you still so pessimistic about the South being able to change?" Jasper asked Jim later that day in his room.

Jim, who was occupied carefully brushing one of Jasper's frock coats, shook his head with a snort. "Tell you what. You get Henry to voluntarily give up slavery, of his own volition release what he believes is his hard-earned property, and then I'll believe the South can change. In fact, I'll make it easy on you. Just get him to agree to end slavery during his lifetime—to not pass his slaves on to his sons. Doesn't have to do it today, tomorrow or next year, just agree to the concept. I don't think you can."

"If I succeed, will you let me stay another month?"

Jim just snorted again.

Chapter Eight

Henry wouldn't let Mary get out of bed the next day, even though she insisted to everyone within hearing that she was perfectly well and didn't need to be coddled. Still, because Henry's word was law, she had to content herself with books and magazines and visitors. Cara came by to oversee the older boys going off to school and to try to amuse little Robert, who was also finding life in the sick room dull. Jasper read the boy some of *Last of the Mohicans*, which was probably more bloodthirsty than Mary would've liked had she known about it, but Henry was fine with it. Henry was less satisfied with the book he found by his wife's bedside when he offered to read to her to allay her restlessness at the enforced idleness.

He frowned at the book. "Why does it have cloth pasted on the cover? Are you ashamed to be reading it?"

When the occasion called for it, Mary could think as fast as her husband. "No, dear. It's from a reading library some of the ladies in town have joined. We thought it would be nice if the books had special covers."

Henry squinted at the title page. "*Wuthering Heights*. What kind of title is that? Wuthering? Highly unappetizing, if you want my opinion. And the author—Ellis Bell. Is he the same idiot that wrote that other book, *Jane Earwig*, or whatever it was? I seem to recall that author's name was Bell, too."

"No, dear, that was Currer Bell. Different man. After all, Bell is a common name. Now stop being so argumentative and just read to me while darling Cara, here, rubs eau de cologne on my temples. Cara, have I ever told you that you are the best niece in all the world?"

"You have Aunt Mary," Cara said, giving her aunt's forehead a kiss. "Many times."

Henry settled back in a chair with the book and crossed his legs. "So what've we got here, some blasted English moor again, I suppose. Don't the English live anywhere but moors?"

"Henry, just read."

He sighed. " 'Chapter one. 1801. I have just returned from a visit to my landlord—' Well, they all have landlords, because no one owns anything in that country. Completely inegalitarian."

"Henry."

" '—the solitary neighbor that I shall be troubled with. This is certainly a beautiful country.' Hmph. They haven't seen Beaufort, or they wouldn't be calling some English moor beautiful, that's for sure." His wife gave him a look, and he continued on with the story. After a few pages, however, he fell silent.

"Henry, we're waiting," Mary said.

Henry looked up with a start. "You don't like how I'm reading?"

Cara smiled from the corner of the bed she was sitting on. "You've been reading silently to yourself, Uncle Henry. We'd like to hear the story, too."

"Yes, Papa, let us hear the story." Little Robert, too restless to remain confined to his own room, had climbed into bed with his mother for the hour's entertainment. Even Jasper, who'd followed the boy after failing to contain him, was in a chair in the corner of the room, amused by the novelty of Henry's recitation.

Henry continued on, but the main character was eminently not to his liking. "What an annoying fellow this Heathcliff is," he muttered, turning a page. "Only thinks of himself. Just going to make himself miserable, that's what he's going to do." And a while later, "Bitter and vindictive, that's all he is, but no doubt you ladies find him romantic and attractive. Before you can snap your fingers, our whole town'll be sighing and swooning over this cad. Isn't that always the way." And later still, "Well of course, Cathy can't marry him—he's as poor as a church mouse and he hasn't proven himself. The whingeing this Heathcliff does is disgraceful."

"Papa, read the story," Robert implored.

Henry obliged until finally he could bear it no longer. "That's it. Enough of English moors for today."

"But Papa, you read so well," Robert said. "Billy and Hugh are going to be mad they missed it."

Henry shook the book at his son. "No more *Wuthering Heights* for you, my boy. It'll give you the wrong idea of how to grow up to be a gentleman. This book's only good for the ladies to sob and sigh over. No sense any man wasting time with it."

Half an hour later, while Mary was napping in her darkened room, Jasper had to laugh when he caught Henry with the book in the front parlor, frowning and muttering under his breath as he turned pages.

"What are you looking at?" Henry said crossly. "So I want to know what happens. Is that so wrong?"

"Not at all," Jasper assured him. "I could tell you, but then I'd deprive you the pleasure of hating the main character so thoroughly."

"You mean you've read it? Just tell me he comes to a bad end. I couldn't bear it if it turns out well."

"He comes to a bad end," Jasper assured him.

"Good," Henry said and kept on reading.

"Ha," he said, closing the book shut at nine that evening. "I am done with Mr. Heathcliff forever. A more worthless individual I can't imagine. This book should be burned and its ashes scattered to the winds, that's my opinion. It's too hot indoors for a fire—I'll have to toss it into the kitchen stove tomorrow morning, pasted fabric and all."

"I think Aunt Mary really wants to read it," Cara said from the piano where she was quietly playing a sonata. "And the book's not hers anyway."

"Maybe I should buy a copy so I could have the satisfaction of seeing it in flames," Henry muttered.

Jasper just smiled at his cousin, his eyes soon slipping over to piano and to the young woman who sat before it. An hour later, when Henry suggested he take her home in the buggy, he did, and they had a very pleasant conversation about the use of ghosts as metaphor in current literature which continued for at least twenty minutes on the Randolph porch in the warm, moonlit night until Cara excused herself and went inside with a face rather warm and flushed.

The breeze the next evening was extraordinarily pleasant. Henry and Jasper sat on the porch with their usual drinks—whiskey for the master of the house and green tea for the guest. Both men had decided to forgo the Winterspoon's party, though since Mary was feeling entirely herself again, Henry had allowed her to make a brief appearance there with Winnie and Cara, for form's sake. The air was warm and scented as a heron took wing towards Lady's Island against a sky lit pink and gold by the setting summer sun. The sounds of laughter and gay fiddle music could be heard wafting from the party a few blocks away.

"It's perfect here," Henry said with a contented sigh. "Truly perfect. I ask you, who in their right mind would fool around on some frigid English moor if they could have this? People call me too driven, too zealous, but at least I know my life is blessed. If I'm ardent rather than indolent, if I don't have the usual languor of a Southern gentleman, it's only in order to provide my sons with the same as bounty as I have now."

"So that's what you're preparing three plantations for? To be divided among three sons?"

Henry nodded. "They'll all be getting much more than my father left me."

"You did well enough with what you had," Jasper observed.

"With a bit of luck and a lot of hard work," Henry said.

Jasper nodded. He couldn't deny that this bend of the Beaufort River was a paradise . . . if you were a rich, white planter. After all, it was a town created expressly for that purpose. With its beauty, culture and wealth, Beaufort seemed suspended in a timeless, immutable bubble that the harsh reality of the outer world could never touch. "From here you'd never know it," Jasper said casually, "but times are changing."

"Not in South Carolina," Henry countered affably. "Europe may have its civil turmoil, the North may be forging ahead in its sooty industrial glory, but here the eternal pastoral reigns supreme. It's a way of life that has lasted a thousand generations. It'll last a few more."

Jasper looked at his cousin more intently. "Times really are changing, Henry. They will catch up to Beaufort—it's just a question of when."

Henry frowned. "In what way?"

"The telegraph will reach here, railroads will arrive. Farming will become mechanized; even the market for cotton will change someday. And one way or another, slavery will eventually be gone."

Henry took a large swig of his drink. "I knew this was coming. Well, let's have it then. Jasper Wainwright, you've turned into an abolitionist. You believe slavery is morally repugnant, it should be eradicated from the earth, and everyone who participates in it is an evil villain. Go on. Give me an earful. I can take it."

"My personal view on the morality of slavery has nothing to do with it," Jasper said evenly, matching Henry's conversational tone. "I don't think you and Mary are evil; I think you treat your slaves for the most part very well. However, slavery as a practice is on its way to extinction, especially among civilized nations."

Henry shook his head with annoyance. "That's just abolitionist prattle."

"England ended slavery at a considerable expense because public sentiment there is vehemently against it. That sentiment will spread."

"To the point they'll refuse to buy our cotton for their mills and put their population out of work?" Henry said. "I don't think so."

Jasper sat up in his chair a little. "When I travelled in India, you know what I saw?"

"Yes, fields and fields of cotton, all short staple, I'm sure. Still, Britain prefers to buy from us rather than them. In fact they turn around and force the Indians to buy British cloth so they can take the few pennies those poor people have and turn them into profits for themselves. Britain is as rapacious and unscrupulous as any country in existence."

"Maybe," Jasper conceded. "After India, I travelled west. Do you know what I saw in Egypt?"

Henry looked down into his glass. "Do tell. I suppose it wasn't pyramids?"

"More fields of cotton, irrigated by the Nile. Except this cotton was experimental, and the experiment was going well. It was long staple cotton."

This made Henry sit up a little straighter. "As good as Sea Island?"

Jasper shook his head. "But almost. Close. And Egypt is much more accessible to Europe. The British are developing alternative markets, Henry, which they should. They're at risk being so dependent on you."

"But if they're just starting out, it'll be years before they have the volumes they need. They have to buy from us for now."

"Maybe," Jasper said. "Maybe it'll take a decade, if they're not given a reason to rush it."

"And just what would that reason be?" Henry said.

"You know as well as I do what would push them to replace your cotton. If the South secedes. If a war develops between the two halves of the United States."

Henry snorted. "That would be suicide. Jasper, you've got to remember, just because we have a few lunatic fire-eaters trying to stir up trouble doesn't mean the majority of us belong in a lunatic asylum. I love my country. I don't want it destroyed."

"You say so now, but the pressure will build. As the territories we acquired from Mexico—well, stole from Mexico—are made into states, as the great plains fill up, every admission to the Union will have to be slave or non-slave. Every single time it'll be a fight that'll threaten to rip any compromise between North and South right apart. The North has huge immigration to settle the land, Henry. The South can't keep up. Eventually, the North will dwarf the South in terms of population, in terms of industry, in terms of any kind of wealth beyond slave wealth. If you don't adapt, when slavery does go away, you'll have nothing left."

"What do you mean 'adapt'?" Henry asked irritably. "My slaves are two-thirds of my assets. Without them, there's nothing. There's no 'adapt.' The North wants us to snap our fingers and 'poof' the slaves are free—of course who's going to clothe and feed them, that's what I'd like to know. They don't care that then we'd all instantly be paupers; they don't care that the productivity of the entire South would plunge to nothing and we'd all starve. You know, it's not like I'm asking Cornelius Vanderbilt to give away all his money to the poor and go around dressed in a barrel, but that's what they want of us. How are we supposed to plant our fields? Where is the labor to come from?"

Jasper paused a moment. "It's called paying wages, Henry."

Henry waved a hand. "You'd put us under the yoke of a factory economy where the hapless underclass are worked until they die of hunger and exhaustion. My slaves are better off than mill workers in the North and in Britain, that's all there is to it. They eat better, they work less, they're better clothed, and they're happier."

"Mill workers' children are not sold away from them," Jasper said quietly.

"And seeing them go to an early grave from consumption, that's better?" Henry asked sharply. "You tell me of the great happiness of Indian and Egyptian peasants, Jasper. Tell me the rights they have, how stuffed their bellies are, how grand their mud and stick hovels, how extensive their political freedoms under their rajahs or nabobs or whatever."

"Our country was founded on the right to life, liberty and the pursuit of happiness," Jasper said evenly. "Slaves in America are denied them all. As an institution, slavery can't be justified on the basis that the poorest, most backward nations in the world treat their citizens worse than we treat ours. Henry, right now the large planters in the South essentially control the economy and politics of the entire region. That's three thousand men dominating eleven states and seven million people. It's not exactly how democracy is supposed to work."

"It's not so different than the early Roman Republic," Henry countered. "And you can't tell me the North doesn't have its own set of controlling oligarchs in its bankers and mill owners and railroad magnates." When his cousin didn't answer, Henry was silent a long moment. "Jasper, in regards to slavery, I fear you and I are unlikely ever to agree."

Jasper leaned forward in his chair. "If there were an alternative to slavery, an alternative that wouldn't impoverish you or substantially diminish the future for your sons, would you consider it?"

Though Henry looked extremely doubtful, Jasper knew he loved him enough to hear him out. He pressed on, painting a picture of a slowly changing economy of freed Negro wage laborers in South Carolina who would work most of the year upland in water-powered mills at the fall line, and then travel to the low country for the cotton harvest. The journey could be accomplished by rail in less than a day.

Planting in the fields could be mechanized to require minimal amounts of labor—why the North was already doing it in some areas. "Henry, you know you only really need lots of hands during the last six weeks of the harvest. The rest of the time you keep your slaves busy doing things to provide for them—growing vegetables, weaving cloth, repairing cabins, building furniture, tanning hides. If they were wage laborers, they would do all that for themselves or pay someone else to do it. And they would buy the cloth produced at the mills, creating an instant market for it. Everyone would benefit."

Henry frowned. "But if the Negroes didn't belong to someone, some of them might up and go who knows where."

"That would be fine," Jasper said gently. "If there were more jobs than hands, the South would attract immigrants from Europe, just like the North."

"You mean we'd have Irish running around here instead, drinking and brawling? I'm not sure that'd be better."

"If the freed Negroes felt secure and prosperous, most wouldn't have reason to move on." The numbers could start out small and gradually increase as more mills were opened and more plantations were willing to participate.

Henry frowned some more. "So the federal government would put up the capital for the mills in trade for the slaves' freedom, the planters would be owners of the mills as well as their plantations and would get the profits from both, and South Carolina would benefit from the increased volume of trade and a whole new class of people who would be buying things. You don't think some of the slaves would want to farm themselves?"

"Maybe some," Jasper said. "You know in Upper Saint Peter's Parish there are a fair number of free Negro farmers who make a go of it. From what I hear they do no worse than the yeoman white farmers."

Henry snorted. "All of them, black and white, just squeak by. On that small scale, none of them have the discipline to keep up their soil. They eat up their land until there's nothing left." Henry reflected a moment. "So would you have overseers at all these mill towns in the upcountry? There'd go some of your profits."

"You'd have factory managers to oversee the workings of the mill," Jasper said. "But not overseers. The Negroes would be free. As long they didn't break laws, they could do as they liked, just like white people."

"You mean congregate together and travel after dark? They'd be up every night at ring shouts and then sleeping all day. What if they refused to work?"

"First of all, congregating and travel after dark are only problems when you're afraid there's a Denmark Vesey out there plotting an uprising to murder you in your bed." Denmark Vesey had been a free Negro in Charleston twenty-seven years earlier accused of organizing slaves to slay their white owners and take over the town. Though the scheme was leaked before the uprising could begin, white reaction to the episode had been extreme. "If the slaves were free, the reason for that fear would go away. As far as not working, it's simple. The factory manager would fire anyone who didn't work, they'd lose their job, and they'd stop getting paid, just like every other worker in America. Most people work out of a desire for a reward, not out of fear of getting whipped. Weekly pay is generally incentive enough. That and hope for a better future for their children."

Henry took a moment to digest this. "I suppose you think Negro children should go to school?"

"Literacy is an important part of citizenship."

Henry looked alarmed. "Are you saying the Negroes should be able to vote? Good God almighty, there are more Negroes than whites in the Sea Islands, seven to one. We'd be sending black men to Congress. I'd rather send Mary."

Jasper smiled patiently. "Remember, the transition would happen gradually, not all at once, but yes, the freed slaves should eventually, over the course of a generation, be citizens with rights equal to whites in every respect. Some day there'll be black politicians and judges, black lawyers and doctors. It's all a matter of education and letting them develop to their potential."

"You're not just talking school—you're talking college. You mean Negro children would be going to college with my children?" He was obviously aghast at the idea.

"You may not be able to imagine it, but to your grandchildren it won't seem so odd at all. We're talking long, slow change here, Henry. Nothing overnight. Give everyone lots of time to get used to it. You and I, we'll be long gone by the time much of what we're talking about ever occurs."

"Long slow change," Jim said casting a dour look at Jasper in his room later that evening. "Don't think I didn't hear what you said to that planter king. You were promising him change so slow you could hardly tell it was happening."

"I got him to consider it, didn't I?" Jasper said. "Look, slow change is good. People can agree to almost anything if they think it's far enough out in the future. If the South digs in its heels and refuses to change at all, what will happen? I'll tell you—there'll be cataclysmic change. It'll happen all at once, it'll be painful, and do you think the Negroes will benefit? Maybe they'll be free, but they'll have nothing. No jobs, no food, no clothes, no education, no property, no prospects. Even if the North gives them the vote, whites here will figure out a way to trick them or terrorize them into keeping whites in power. And if the cataclysm happens through war, then God help everyone because the South will collapse and there won't be a pot to piss in for anyone, black or white, for three generations. Twenty years of gradual change is better that a hundred years of suffering, Jim. Really, it is."

"You and your migrant cotton mill, cotton planting economy. What about Alabama and Mississippi? What about Texas and Louisiana? What kind of post-slave economy is going to work there?"

"Just let me work on South Carolina," Jasper said. "It's a big enough problem. Please?"

A few rooms over a servant helped Mary undress while Henry, already in his nightshirt, watched.

"Cara was awfully quiet at the party tonight," Mary said as her dress came off over her head, revealing her chemise and corset. "I think she was disappointed Jasper wasn't there. And she hasn't received any new proposals since Johnny. I asked her specifically after we dropped off the Senator and Winnie."

"Of course, she hasn't," Henry said. "After Jasper's duel with Patterson, none of the young bucks want to end up on the wrong side of his gun. They're waiting to see if he'll claim her."

"Then why didn't you and Jasper come with us tonight?" Mary said crossly. "Cara looked lovely. It was a wasted opportunity."

"Not wasted at all," Henry said. "Jasper and I had a good talk. He wants me to embrace abolitionism; I want him to embrace slavery. We're bound to find common ground somewhere, don't you think? Anyway, we have to be careful about dangling Cara too much in front of him, or the man's going to snap. I don't think he's had a woman in months."

The maid unloosening Mary's corset darted her eyes towards her master for the briefest of seconds, but she knew her attention had better seem to be on her task. Though there were some subjects Mary and Henry took pains not to talk about in front of the servants, in general they didn't bother since the Negroes knew everything and anything regarding every aspect of their lives. Mary and Henry could only rely on the pride their house staff took in belonging to the Birch family and Villa d'Este to prevent them from damaging the family reputation. In general, their faith was justified.

"Henry, you shouldn't say such things about your own cousin, not when we love him so." Mary was taking pins out of her hair while her maid unbuttoned the three layers of petticoats that had made the skirt of her dress so full and flattering. Henry had no idea how women could stand the weight and insulating properties of their undergarments in the summer heat. He thought it'd be fine if they all went around in their chemises and pantaloon drawers. It'd certainly be entertaining.

"Why not?" he said. "It's the truth. It must be nearly killing him. It would if it were me."

After the maid helped Mary on with her robe, she was dismissed from the room with a wave of her mistress's hand. "Maybe he doesn't have your insatiable desires, Mr. Birch," she said, her long hair flowing down her back as she stood before him, the curve of her pregnancy just showing.

Henry caught her hand and pulled her down to him in his chair. "Maybe he wasn't clever enough to fall in love with a healthy, beautiful woman who could always be right at his side to prevent long months of monastic torment." Though Mary eyed him sharply, wondering when in his life he'd ever been monastic, in the next moment he was kissing her and soon he was profiting from the estimable benefits of the marriage bed so long denied his cousin.

Early the next evening Jasper went out back to the slave quarters. Late in the day he'd received a note from an acquaintance in Boston with an enclosed message for Jim, and knowing Jim would be pleased, he wanted to deliver it sooner rather than later. When he found Jim at the stable, he was surprised to see Hock there with half a dozen slave children around him sitting in the straw and listening as Hock told stories with colorful voices and gestures.

Jim caught sight of Jasper and stepped outside. He was indeed pleased by the note.

"Good news?" Jasper asked.

"He's got lodgings all lined up, mostly in the same neighborhood."

"Reverend Brently is a good man," Jasper observed.

Jim nodded, folding the letter and putting it into his waistcoat pocket. "He's also expeditious. Gets things done quickly."

"I know what expeditious means," Jasper drawled. "You're implying a contrast with my lack of haste, I take it?"

"Not me," Jim said. "I never criticize."

"By the way, people have been offering me money as payment for your medical services. Should I refuse and have them pay you directly, or just take it?"

Jim's shoulders sank and the lines on his face deepened. "Once a slave, always a slave. In Beaufort's eyes, I'm still Spit Jim and you're still the master." Jasper said nothing, just waited quietly. "Take the money," Jim said with some bitterness. "I can use it."

"At least they value you," Jasper said. Then he nodded at the stable. "What's going on in there?"

Jim waved a hand. "Just Hock, telling the children stories. Keeps them out from underfoot while their mothers get supper."

"What kind of stories," Jasper wanted to know. "Buh Rabbit?" He smiled a little, thinking back fondly to tales he'd heard as he'd loitered in slave cabins in his youth.

"Sometimes. Tonight, it's the Bible, I believe."

"Can I listen?"

Jim shrugged. "Why not?" He and Jasper went and stood by the open stable door.

"De fust man," Hock was telling the children as he squatted down before them, "Adum, bin uh black man. Hiz lawful lady, Ebe, bin a ginguh cake colluh, wid long black hair down tuh her ankles. Dat Adum hab just one ting boddrin him in dat gahden Eden, an dat bin his kinky hair. Ebe hate tuh see him sad, cause her lub her man just like all wife outtuh do.

"Well, Adum play wid Ebe's hair, run his fingers tru it and sigh." Hock exhaled sadly for emphasis. The children nodded with melancholy commiseration, as if Adam's obsession with hair was a completely understandable affliction. "Ebe couldn't do dat wid his kinky hair. Now, de debbil, he set up in de plum bush and take notice uh de trouble gwine on. Ebry day Ebe hair grow longuh and longuh, while Adum git sadduh and sadduh, and de debbil in de plum bush git gladduh an gladduh."

Hock raised a finger. "Dere come a day dat Adum excused hisself from promenadin among de flowuh bed wid his arms round Ebe, a holdin up her hair. Dat day, de debbil take de shape uh de suhpent." The children started back with gasps and wide eyes as Hock wriggled his arm towards them to show the sinuous motion of this wily character. "He glide aftuh Ebe, an stole up and twist hisself up into det hair far nuff de whispuh in one uh her pooty ears: 'Sumbody got sumptin tuh tell you, Ebe, sumptin dat'll make Adum glad an luk hisself agin! Keep yo ears open all day long.'"

"Lawd a muhcy," said one of the little girls, her hands clasped to her cheeks.

"Lawd a muhcy, dats right," said Hock. "Den de suhpent distangled hisself, dropped tuh de ground, an skedaddle tuh de red apple tree, nigh by de beeuhful fountain. He know dat Ebe gwine dere fuh tuh bathe. He git der before her, cuz she was perusin' sorta slow, griebbin bout Adum and tinkin bout how cheer him up.

"When she git der, dat ol debbil done changed frum de snake tuh uh angel uh light." Hock extended his hands over his head and waved his fingers, projecting a radiance that understandably would have dazzled the first woman. "Dis angel bin uh man angel, I reckon. He tek off his silk beavuh hat, wave his gold cane, an say: 'Mawning! Lubby day! What uh beeful apple, just in yo reach, too, ahem!'" Hock placed his hand on his chest and raised the pitch of his voice. "Ebe say: 'I's not bin intr'duced.' 'Well,' say de debbil, 'Muh subjects call me Prince, cause I's de Prince uh light. My givin name iz Lucifuh. I's at your suhvice, dear lady.'" Hock put a finger to his temple. "Ebe tink: 'Uh prince, he be king some day.' Den de debbil say: 'Course, I expect one uh yo beety one day be uh queen. I see sadness on yo lubby face as you come long. What bin botherin you, lady?' Ebe tellum, an he say: 'Jis get Adum take one bite out dat apple 'bove yo head, an tuhnight his hair grow long, an black, an straight as you'own.'"

Hock put prim fingers to his chest. "She say: 'No suh. Us not low'd eat de fruit uh de tree in de middle de gahden. Us dare not touch it, lest us die.'" Hock bent down closer to the children. "Den dat slippery Satan, know what he do? He step dis way, an he step dat way, an den he come back an say: 'Gracious lady! Dis tree not in de middle uh de garden. De one in de middle bin dat crabapple tree yanduh. Course de good Lawd don wanyuh eat no crabapple.' De debbil, so slippery and clevuh, done git her all mix up. De apple look so good, she reach up, an quick as yo kin say 'Jack Robisuh,' she bite de apple." Hock pretended to chomp into the benighted piece of fruit.

"Den she run tuh Adum wid de rest an say: 'Husbin, eat quick, an in de mawnin yo hair be long, black, an straight luk my'own.' Adum eat de apple, an while he take de last swallow, he membuh hiz disobeyin an choke two time. Ever since den, all man hab de 'Adum Apple' in der troat tuh remembuh de sin uh disobeyin. Twasn't long before de Lawd come alookin fuh dem. Adum git so scared, hiz face turn white right der an den. An de next mawnin he bin uh white man wid long hair but worse off den when he bin uh nigguh."

With his audience gazing up at him in absolute horror, Hock broke off as he caught sight of Jasper and Jim outside the stable door. In the distance Henry's voice could be heard from the house bellowing, "Hock, Hock, where are you?"

"Marse Henry's calling old Hock, chillun. Be off witcha now." Hock glanced again at Jasper, unsure how much he'd heard and how much trouble he was going to get for it. Hock was inclined to try and explain away this slave version of Genesis that would certainly make Miz Mary angry, but since Marse Jasper looked amused rather than outraged, he instead took off at a trot towards the direction of his master's impatient voice.

"I don't know whether to be charmed or horrified," Jim said as he and Jasper headed back toward the house at a slower pace. "Of all the theories I've heard about skin color, this is a brand spanking new one."

Jasper gave him a sideways look. "You ever loose sleep over kinky hair?"

"Not a wink," Jim assured him. "You know, it's funny how in any version of Genesis you like, it's Eve that the devil takes so much trouble to persuade. He knows Adam will run and do whatever she tells him to like a big dumb dog."

"And then he gets scared white before he's cast out of Eden," Jasper said. "Loses his color along with his innocence. You have to admit it's a nice touch."

A few days later, Henry and Jasper were leisurely walking with the ladies towards town to while away the hour before Sunday supper. "Well, the latest Eustace Woods letter has knocked everyone into a cocked hat," Henry remarked. "I haven't heard such discussion in a coon's age. He's got people actually considering a mother-child unison law seriously. I'm impressed."

"So you'd support such a law?" Jasper asked. "You'd stand up and speak for it?"

"You know I'd never sell a child under twelve away from his mother, nor would most reputable planters. More and more I think Woods is right, we'd all benefit from codifying the practices of the best planters rather than protecting the disgraces of the worst."

Jasper glanced curiously at Henry. If Henry were anonymously Woods, why had he come out with this mother-child proposition rather than the economic reforms they'd been speaking of? Not that the mother-child law wasn't a good thing. Maybe Henry was just trying to advance the notion of step-by-step reform?

"So this new economic system you're proposing," Henry said casually. "If you think it's such a good idea, why don't you convince folks to give it a try?"

"I'm no politician," Jasper said, twirling his walking cane slowly. "Besides, I'm an outsider. No one here's going to listen to what I have to say. But they'd listen to you, Henry. You have credibility."

"They'd listen to Eustace Woods, that's who they'd listen to. It's his ear you need to bend. Remember, I'm no politician either. I've spent the last two decades avoiding any whiff of the stuff. But Jasper, you could have credibility, you could be an insider. Become a planter again. Get a mill started, have your migrant workforce. Show folks it can work."

Jasper looked off at the river. "What I'm proposing would require approval by both Congress and the South Carolina legislature, which would take time. Two, three years, maybe more. And then it'd be at least another year before a mill got built and the machinery put in place."

"So what's three or four years? It's not like you have one foot in the grave."

"It'd mean I'd have to own slaves and run a plantation," Jasper said quietly. "And I can't do that."

Henry was going to contradict him, but they'd met up with Winifred and the Senator who were also out taking the early evening air. Even though they'd just seen them a couple hours before at dinner, Mary and her aunt never failed to find something to talk about. This time the subject was Cathy and Heathcliff, discussed in tones low enough to prevent Cara from hearing.

Cara, who'd finished the book some weeks ago, amused herself watching the dolphins splash in the water that was turning a mercurial silver blue as the sun began to lower towards the western horizon. Hearing a noise, she looked eastward where the river made a bend around the Point. "That's odd. There's a steamer coming. But there aren't any steamers Sunday evenings."

Henry scanned the boat rounding the river's curve. "I'd say that's not one of the regular runs. It's smaller and fancier. Maybe it's a private steamer."

"Private?" said Winnie. "You mean someone has a personal steamer all for themselves? That would be decadent."

"I've heard some of those rich bankers do, up in New York," Henry said. "Shows there's more money in money than in farming, even if you're farming Sea Island cotton."

"Mary, you shouldn't let Henry call himself a farmer," Winnie said crossly. "It's not becoming."

The party watched with curiosity as the steamer pulled up to the dock. A number of other townsfolk had stopped as well, interested in this new arrival.

"Who can it be?" Mary asked. "It must be someone terribly rich, but I haven't heard of anyone expecting exotic guests, have you, Winnie?"

"Maybe they're tourists and want to see the attractions of Beaufort," the Senator suggested.

"What a ridiculous idea," Winnie said. "It's not as if we have ruins or cathedrals to gawk at."

"Look, a lady's getting off the boat," Cara said.

"My, my," Mary said. "Isn't she fashionable." The women all gazed avidly at the elegant blonde woman who was being handed down the plank to the dock.

"Would you look at that dress," Winnie said almost in awe. "I declare, an exact likeness of it was in Godey's magazine just last week. The tucks, the folds, the cascade of lace. And that delicate shade of mauve. I've never seen anything like it. And how elegantly she wears it. She must be French. There's no other explanation." In the course of her life Winnie had seen a dozen gowns actually sewn by Parisian dressmakers. She remembered each in loving detail.

"The lady may be a beauty," Henry said in an undertone to Jasper, "but who's the clown with her? I've never seen such a preening, conceited haut monde type in all my life. I'd bet my house he's some failed European aristocrat."

"Good call," Jasper said. "He's the Count Torlini, and quite failed, though that would imply he'd ever been a success."

"Wait," Henry said, "you actually know this joker?"

The lady and the gentleman were coming up the dock, followed by a dour old woman dressed entirely in black. Bringing up the rear of the party were a male and a female servant laden with hatboxes and other forms of luggage deemed too fragile to leave to the rough handling of Negroes at the dock.

"She's an angel," the Senator said in awe. "An angel has come to us in Beaufort."

Although disinclined to agree with her great-uncle's sentiment, Cara noticed Jasper wasn't taking his eyes off this blonde arrival.

On reaching the end of the dock, the woman took a few dainty steps into the street. She stopped in front of their party. "*Bonjour, Jasper. Es-tu heureux de me voir?*"

"Aurore," Jasper said, "what on earth are you doing here?"

The woman just smiled a smile that could melt even her ill, elderly, rich husband's heart.

Henry took his wife's arm and pulled her aside. Though his voice was low, Cara could still hear the urgency in it. "Mary, we've got trouble, serious trouble."

"What do you mean?" Mary said. "She's obviously a friend of Jasper's here to pay a visit."

"You don't come all the way from Paris for a friendly Sunday call," Henry observed grimly. "She means to take him back."

Madame de Saintonge and Count Torlini, as well as wizened Madame Verneil, were quickly introduced by Jasper to his relations in Beaufort. Jasper correctly placed Madame Verneil as the cousin of Madame de Saintonge, but Madame was obliged to explain that the Count was her brother-in-law since this fact appeared to be news to Jasper. Evidently Madame's sister, the Count's wife, was visiting friends in New York. Since she had young twins, the trip south to see Madame's dear friend, Monsieur Wainwright, had been too fatiguing for her. The Count, however, had kindly agreed to accompany Madame as he had wanted to see the glories of the south of Carolina, too.

While his wife couldn't take her eyes off Madame's dress, the Senator appeared nearly ecstatic to make the French woman's acquaintance, bowing low when presented. "Madame, you do Beaufort an honor not equaled since we had the visit of another of your countrymen, General Lafayette. Oh, that was a grand day."

Madame de Saintonge paused, taking in this information in the gathering twilight. "You cannot mean," she said with her pretty French accent, "ze Marquis de La Fayette?"

"Yes, ma'am," the Senator beamed. "He was here in 1825. Stood right on the steps of the house you see behind me and addressed the town. We had a candlelight parade in his honor. In fact, this here dwelling is still known far and wide as the Lafayette House because the General stood right here."

Madame de Saintonge looked at the rather ordinary steps—ordinary, at least, by Parisian standards—that the Senator so proudly gestured to. "*Charmant.*" She turned to Jasper. "How come you never told me *mon grand-pere* was here in your delightful city?"

Jasper raised an eyebrow but didn't answer.

"Are you—" The Senator could hardly get it out. "Are you related to the General, Madame?"

"Why, he is—how do you say it?—my great uncle," Madame de Saintonge said. "I used to call him grandfather, and as a child he would tell us of his great battles and adventures in *Amerique.* It's such a co-incidence, *n'est-ce pas,* zat I should come to ze same town he visited?"

The Senator nearly choked. "Great Uncle." He bowed even lower than he had the first time. "Madame, forgive my presumption, I don't know your plans, but I wonder if you would give my wife and myself the remarkable honor of staying at our home during your time in Beaufort."

Winnie stepped forward a little anxiously. "And your cousin and your maid, of course. But I'm afraid—" She glanced nervously at the male members of the foreign party. "I'm afraid we don't have room for Count Torlini and his manservant." Since the servants were white, they couldn't very well be accommodated in the slave quarters and must have rooms of their own in the house.

"You are too kind," Madame de Saintonge said, "but I'm sure we can stay at ze hotel."

"There's no hotel here," Jasper observed. "Only a boarding house. Of course, if you'd written, I could've told you that."

Henry eyed the Count with a sigh. Yes, he had to do it. For the South's sake. "Count Torlini and his servant are welcome to stay with us at Villa d'Este. We have room for them both."

The Count cocked his head. Villa d'Este?

"Zen it is settled," Madame de Saintonge said happily. "You are all so *sympathique*. So kind. I know we have arrived without warning, but I wanted for Jasper it to be a surprise." She smiled prettily at him as she conveyed her charming grammatical errors. She was a woman who was obviously not twenty and obviously not forty, but other than that it was impossible to tell her age. Her skin had the translucent luminosity of Greek sculpture, the Senator would later say while Henry rolled his eyes; her eyes were the green of limpid mountain pools. That she had wealth and beauty and aristocratic grace was clear to everyone in town and would soon be known to everyone in the county. That she also had a deep intimacy with Jasper was evident to every member of the Birch clan who watched the two of them together closely.

"I think I hate her already," Mary said as they made their way home. Jasper had stayed behind at the Senator's house to converse with Madame, at Madame's request. Madame de Saintonge had many requests for Monsieur Wainwright. "Jas-pere" she called him, with the first syllable like the flower jasmine, and the second syllable like the fruit. It made Mary want to slap her.

Count Torlini remained at the dock overseeing his servant who was overseeing the removal of their luggage from the steamer. This primarily involved the Count, a tall, handsome, fastidious man, taking snuff and looking morosely at the confines of the provincial backwater he had been talked into visiting, while a number of black slaves lugged trunks up the wooden pier and his servant berated them in Italian to absolutely no effect whatsoever. The Count already longed to be back in New York where the gambling and the women had been oh so agreeable.

"Thank goodness she's staying with Winnie," Mary said as they ambled home. "Or I might be inclined to scratch her big green eyes out."

"Yes, but we're stuck with Count Tortufutti," Henry said. "I think he's going to be worse."

Cara said nothing, but she did look a little ill. Madame was so very beautiful.

The private steamer was the talk of the town. So grand. So luxurious. It'd been hired along with its captain in Philadelphia and had been used before by Russian as well as Dutch nobility when they'd visited the continent of democracy. Everyone wanted a chance to see it up close. Since, as a practical matter, it couldn't stay at the dock with all the other steamer traffic coming and going, the sumptuous ship was anchored in the middle of the river, in clear view from every inch of Bay Street. Jasper, naturally, was the first to be invited to witness its magnificence. The very next day, in fact.

"Ze captain and my maid will serve us dinner on board, giving us a chance to talk of old times zat would—how do you say—be boredom to everyone else," Madame de Saintonge said with a special look at Jasper as they sat in Winnie's front parlor. "Oh, and Madame Verneil will dine with us, too." She turned to Winnie. "In France, it would never do not to have a chaperone. Do you have a custom similar here?" Winnie nodded, taking in the splendors of Madame's lemon-yellow day dress that made her heart ache, it complemented Madame's blonde hair so perfectly.

And so Jasper was rowed with Madame de Saintonge and Madame Verneil to the anchored boat. Once on board he found it to be a veritable floating palace, with a plush parlor, a mirrored dining room, captain's and crew quarters, and three small rooms for the less important members of the travelling entourage. Last but not least, it possessed two resplendent staterooms. The Count's room reeked of cigar smoke and whiskey when Jasper poked his head in on Madame's insistence before he was ushered in to see Madame's boudoir. His curiosity about the private steamer was quite low, but that was not why he was there.

On boarding the boat, Madame Verneil promptly ensconced herself in her favorite chair in the parlor and settled in for a snooze. She had clear instructions on her role as a chaperone, and since she spoke no English, she was unlikely to communicate these directives to others.

In the aft stateroom, Jasper looked down at the beautiful woman who had travelled half a world to see him. "When did you become such an accomplished liar?"

"It was just a few small . . . exaggerations," she said in French. Their private conversations were often a blend of both languages. *"And if they make these simple people happy, what harm is in it?"*

"How is it an 'exaggeration' to say Torlini's your brother-in-law? You don't even have a sister. And you're no more Lafayette's great niece than I'm Washington's horse."

She pursed her lips. *"I can hardly travel with the Count if I'm not related to him, and I can hardly travel alone. I needed someone, and he was available. Are you jealous, my dear?"*

"Of him? Not at all."

She raised her chin. *"And my grandfather knew the Marquis, he even came to our house once. It's almost as good as family. Really, Jas-pere, accusing me of crimes like I'm the lowest of peasants. I begin to think you're not glad to see me when I've taken ever so much trouble to arrange things to please us both."* She took a step to him, and then another. *"Well,"* she said with a tilt of her charming head. *"Is this how you welcome me after such a long time apart?"*

"Aurore, when I said good bye, I said *adieu*."

This time she spoke in English. "And when I said good bye, I said *au revoir*. And now you see which of us was right."

"You're so damn beautiful," Jasper said with a shake of his head, "of course I'm glad to see you. I just wish you hadn't come."

Before she could take offense, his arms were around her pulling her close, his mouth was on hers, and it was as if it were again last winter in Paris, snowflakes swirling across a grey sky outside the windows of his rooms in the Marais, instead of a sultry day in Beaufort on a boat gently swaying in a tidal river. Though there was a great deal of clothing to remove without the aid of servants, *ce n'etait pas un problem.* Through long practice, both of them were good at it.

Chapter Nine

While Beaufort was normally festive during the summer months, the arrival of the European visitors launched the town into a near carnival of parties and balls. Henry and Mary had to rush to host a soiree the very next night in order to introduce the Europeans properly into Beaufort society. As usual, even though hurried, the Birch arrangements came off without a hitch, and Madame de Saintonge seemed duly impressed with the splendors of Villa d'Este under the flicker of a luxurious profusion of candles. Though the Count had been disappointed to find that the Birch residence boasted nowhere near the grandeur of its Renaissance namesake, (after all, there wasn't a fountain or fresco in sight), he deemed it pleasing enough for a backcountry sojourn. At the soiree he found a card table removed from the main party with a number of young men and accepted their offer to teach him the nuances of poker, a game he professed he'd not yet run across, not even in the casinos of Monte Carlo. Since he didn't seem to mind losing, he was heartily embraced by this contingent of gambling enthusiasts.

Punch was flowing, fiddles were playing, and Winnie was introducing Madame to everyone in sight. The entire town already knew of the Frenchwoman's relationship to the venerated general since during the previous thirty-six hours the Senator had personally spread the news to half the adult population.

Jasper and Henry watched the events and the dancing from one corner of the room, both of them noting that Cara seemed less animated than usual. She did not lack for partners, but all the attention in the room was directed elsewhere, an unusual state of affairs for her. It was Madame who held everyone's gaze as she laughed and smiled and complimented the citizens of Beaufort until she was a popular new arrival indeed. Yes, all eyes were on Madame except for one particular pair that still tended to land with regularity on Cara. As usual, Henry took notice.

"Madame de Saintonge's introduction to Beaufort seems quite a triumph," he commented.

"Does it?" Jasper asked, glancing only briefly at the party in question before again seeking a particular figure on the dance floor. "Well, she always does land on her feet, wherever she goes. That's the benefit of charm, I suppose."

Across the floor, circumstance offered Madame a welcome break in her round of introductions. She used the time to locate Monsieur Wainwright, only to find that the focus of his attention was, to her dismay, not her. When she perceived the object of his interest, a small frown creased her elegant forehead. Then her scrutiny was diverted by yet another benighted citizen of Beaufort that she took pains to greet and flatter and win over. Like her grandfather before her who had commanded troops under Napoleon, she knew well the value of surveying the terrain and establishing one's position at the outset of any campaign.

Henry was not without his own set of stratagems and tactical maneuvers as he took a drink off a silver platter held out to him by one of his white-gloved slaves. "I hear you dined with Madame on board her steamer *de luxe* this afternoon."

Jasper glanced sideways at his cousin. "Does all of Beaufort know?"

"Land's sake, where do you think you are, some anonymous city like New York? You could've fired six cannons and not provoked more attention. Did you actually consume any food?"

It took Jasper a moment to answer. "I do believe a bite or two were involved."

Henry laughed. "I thought so. Trust you to have a beautiful woman show up with her own floating chateau for trysts. Was that what it was like in Europe, women constantly throwing themselves at your feet?"

Jasper eyed his cousin dourly. "I'm not profligate, as you well know. In fact, I'm rather particular."

"Oh, I see that you're selective, Jasper. And that you select well."

Earlier that day, when Mary told Henry about the mid-river dinner, he'd guffawed and wondered how Winnie had allowed it. When he'd been assured that Madame Verneil had chaperoned, he pointed out that Madame Verneil was a poor relation who was there precisely because she was paid to see and hear nothing. Though Mary had been shocked, she accepted her husband's pronouncement as truth because Henry was always right about these things. "What can we do?" she whispered, not wanting even the servants to hear this time.

"Nothing," Henry said. "If it got out, it'd only humiliate Winnie and the Senator, seeing as how she's staying with them. So since we can't stop it, I say we let it take its course and hope it shipwrecks itself along the way."

"But she's a . . . loose woman," Mary said, still blinking with surprise.

"You're so innocent, my dear," Henry said. "In the old world, respectable people behave in ways that would make you blush if you knew the sordid truth. Here let me do that." And he took from her hands the diamond and topaz necklace he'd given her last year and fastened the clasp around her neck himself. "There, you look lovely. Too lovely for the dratted Count, I think. I don't like the way he eyes you one bit."

Mary's cheeks turned pink and she waved a hand. "Now you're just being silly."

But Henry was rarely silly. He'd expected the married Count to set his sights on Cara, given that she was the prettiest girl in town. But instead, this wolf was proving to be interested in prey closer at hand, prey that might be tired of her husband and might be amenable to a dalliance with a cunning suave fraud with no morals or anything else to recommend him other than a great deal of linen that the Birch laundress, Reesa, was obliged to spend an inordinate amount of time keeping clean. The Count had bent over and kissed Mary's hand twice that day, and paid her numerous small compliments that had set Henry's teeth on edge. When Cara had arrived for the party, on the other hand, the Casanova had been indifferent to her slim neck, fine features and rosebuds entwined in her hair. Henry thought he'd successfully diverted the Count to cards for the evening, but now, glory be, the Italian had rejoined festivities and seemed to be confiding something very particular to Mrs. Birch, Mrs. Birch laughing and leaning slightly towards him so she could hear what he was saying.

Jasper thought Henry might burst a blood vessel in his forehead.

"That dang-blasted cur," Henry growled. "He accepts my hospitality, and then in front of my very nose he does this."

"He's just trifling," Jasper said. "It's what he does. He probably can't help himself."

"He can damn well help it with my wife." Abruptly Henry pushed himself off from the wall he was slouching against and went to ask his wife to dance. It was an action almost without precedence, and yet soon the host and hostess of the party were leading a reel down the room.

Jasper's eyes reverted to Cara, who stood off to one side watching her aunt and uncle with an affectionate smile. Her hair shone in the candlelight, and her eyes seemed sad somehow, yet so still, so quiet. A peaceful center inside a whirling vortex . . . She should marry a doctor in Charleston, Jasper told himself. A sensible, sober man of science. That's what would make her happy. He should ask Dr. Goode about possible candidates.

Madame de Saintonge was at Jasper's side. "Will you teach me zis Virginia re-ell, *mon cher*?" With a quick smile, he agreed, and then he and Madame were joining hands like all the others to create a long archway that Mary and Henry passed under at a lively pace.

The next night the Patterson's hosted a party, and the night after that the Witherspoon's threw one. The following evening there was a merciful break in festivities before an onslaught of nearly a week's worth of dances, soirees and fetes. After all, since the inhabitants of Beaufort were left to their own devices on their plantations all winter, there was no reason to waste a single moment of the summer in solitude or reflection.

With a night "dark" for parties, Mary did what any good Beaufort hostess would do and invited a crowd to supper to entertain the out-of-town guests. Nearly twenty people ended up in attendance, a score that barely fit down both sides of Mary's grand mahogany dining table. And, to be sure, this supper wasn't a light, inconsequential affair. It was a seven-course meal, the kind Europeans were used to in the evenings. There were roasted quail and broiled fish, eel and oysters, ham and turtle, as well as half a garden plot's worth of vegetables cooked in good Southern fashion. Henry pulled out a score of bottles of French wine from his cellar that had cost him a pretty penny in Charleston. It meant he'd have to send for resupply before half the summer was out, but he'd had a good crop last year and he'd have no one doubt his hospitality—certainly not these imported guests, even if he'd like to smack one of them over the head with one of the heavy French bottles.

Jasper escorted Madame de Saintonge into dinner, but when they went to be seated, he found he'd been placed not next to her at the table, but next to Cara. He hadn't spoken much to Cara since the arrival of the Europeans, and she was initially quiet as the meal began, answering in monosyllables any lines of conversation he proffered. As the meal progressed and he coaxed a little more, she became willing to talk about the extraordinary response to the Eustace Woods's mother-child unison proposal. Reaction seemed to be evenly split, with most letters in *The Charleston Courier* cautiously in favor, and most letters in *The Charleston Mercury*, controlled by the Rhett family, vehemently opposed. It'd become a tempest in a teapot, and there was some speculation that the Governor might weigh in on one side of the debate or the other.

"So I take it you favor such a law?" Cara asked, not quite looking at him as she delicately cut up her quail.

"I think it would be an excellent start at reform," Jasper said. "I confess I'm surprised to see it proposed in a Carolina paper."

"Maybe there's more scope for change here than you think," Cara said quietly.

Jasper smiled. "Nothing is ever hopeless. Perhaps the storm clouds I see ahead can be avoided after all."

Cara looked at him seriously. "These clouds, are they so ominous, Mr. Wainwright?"

Jasper glanced around to see if anyone might be paying enough attention to overhear what he was going to say. As far as he could tell, his near neighbors were occupied. "Miss Randall, I know I sound like a veritable Cassandra, but yes, I foresee wholesale destruction if the South can't figure out a way to end its practice of slavery. It's that dire and that likely."

After scrutinizing him in her tranquil but serious way, Cara turned back to her plate. "Does my Uncle Henry agree with you?"

Jasper swirled the green tea in his cup. "It's my job to get him to agree with me. He has a great deal of influence, if only he'd use it."

"As do you," Cara noted.

Jasper smiled. "Not really. Not any more. And even back in the day . . ." Cara waited for him to finish. "Even when I was a planter," he finally continued, "I wasn't a good one. Not like Henry. Anyway, I made my choice to travel and leave it all behind, so that's what I'll always be, a visitor, just passing through. I'd like to do some good for this place before I leave though."

"You have done good, Mr. Wainwright. You lead by example more than you know."

Jasper smiled again. "You're kind, Miss Randall, but I'm well aware of my shortcomings."

She looked at him intently. "History is full of men with shortcomings who did extraordinary things despite their flaws. Despite their histories. The first half of one's life does not dictate the second."

Her vehemence took Jasper aback. "Miss Randall, I'll be glad to get your opinion on the matter again when you reach my age and are facing that second half of life."

Cara looked back down at her plate, her face and neck flushed.

"Come," he said gently. "I don't mean to quarrel. Especially not with you."

As Cara looked up, her heart more than mollified by Jasper's conciliatory tone, she happened to notice Madame de Saintonge. The French beauty was sitting across and down the table, in a place of honor between her Uncle and the Senator. Madame had been gazing her way but now quickly smiled at the man across from her. Cara, however, was startled. Though she well knew that other girls her age could be jealous, spiteful and vindictive, as they had, on occasion, been so to her, she'd never encountered such a projection of pure venom as she'd fleetingly seen the moment before on Madame de Saintonge's beautiful face.

When the gentlemen rejoined the ladies after their brandies and cigars, or, in Jasper's case, more green tea, Cara was invited to play the piano for the guests' entertainment. Henry and Mary were, of course, incredibly proud of her, beaming as she took her place before the piano in their large front parlor, even more so than her father who sat amiably enough to hear a continuation of what he already heard in his house two or three hours a day. Though Cara seemed uneasy in front of such a large audience, she rose to the occasion and played with spirit and finesse. Jasper was especially pleased that she included the waltz by Chopin that she'd been working on since the spring. It had such a wistful quality, evoking the fleetingness of life, of joy, of beauty. The piece was like a sylph running through the forest, a hunter following in pursuit, trying to catch her, keep her with him permanent and forever. But even as he circles his arms around her, she becomes mist, and his embrace is empty. And there she is again, dancing and leaping ahead, never to be captured, barely even to be savored by anything but memory. Ah, but beautiful. Beautiful enough to tear the world and all its meaning apart forever.

"Mademoiselle Randall is quite pretty, is she not?" Madame de Saintonge said, leaning conspiratorially towards Jasper. "Isn't 'pretty' what one says about *une jeune fille* in zis country?"

Jasper nodded, hoping to hear more of Cara's playing, but the third song had passed, the usual length of attention at a soiree such as this, and people were beginning to murmur softly.

Madame de Saintonge began again, this time purely in French. *"I expect that her family is quite protective of her. I've told the Count as much, that honor in America is apt to be defended with a great deal more primitive violence than on the continent. I think he took the lesson to heart. See, he doesn't even notice her."*

"He notices my cousin's wife," Jasper said dryly, also in French. *"You should tell him that's just as dangerous a pastime."*

Madame smiled. *"But I think Madame Birch does not object. After all, it's only natural. All women like some spice, some variety after so many years of marriage."*

"Still, Count Torlini might not like a bullet through his chest," Jasper observed.

"*The pretty niece, I suppose her family wants to marry her off to some worthy young man,*" Madame said, adjusting the folds of her dress.

"*I suppose they do,*" Jasper said.

"*She is certainly a treasure—so talented. She and I will have to become good friends.*"

Jasper gave the blonde women an amused look indicating his skepticism, but soon Madame de Saintonge had invited the precious *jeune fille* to sit down beside her. She proceeded to breezily complement Cara on her musical facility while appealing to Jasper did he remember when Chopin had played that exact waltz—was it in C sharp minor? Yes, that was the one!—in Madame Lotille's salon? Ah, that had been an evening to remember! And now Chopin was enamored with dear Jenny Lind whom Madame had befriended last winter when she'd performed in Paris. Charming girl. Mademoiselle had never heard her sing? *Quelle domage.* She'd never heard Maestro Chopin play? *Quelle tragédie!* Mademoiselle must come to Paris immediately, and Madame de Saintonge would introduce her to ever so many interesting people, including dear Monsieur Chopin, and take her to ever so many charming places. Life in the south of Carolina, while pleasant, must lack for variety, must it not? Paris, now there was the center of civilization, the veritable heart of the world. Didn't Jasper think so?

Cara meekly absorbed Madame de Saintonge's chatter, admitting, yes, she would like to visit Paris someday; yes, she would like to hear Monsieur Chopin play. With eyes cast down, she acknowledged she'd never been further than Virginia and even conceded that most Southerners lived their whole lives without ever traveling abroad, however astonishing a fact this might be. While Madame did not out and out state that Beaufort was a dreary backwater that cultured people would limit their time in, she most certainly implied it and looked to Jasper every few sentences to see if he concurred with her sentiments. Remarkably, he found a way to acknowledge her opinions without ever quite agreeing with them.

"This Madame's got her hooks into him but good," Henry told his wife from across the room. "She practically has a big sign written across his chest saying, 'Taken.'"

"Cara doesn't look too happy with the conversation," Mary observed. "Maybe I should rescue her."

Henry put out a hand, stopping her. "That would involve you passing by the Count."

"Oh, Henry, don't be absurd," Mary said lightly. "Don't you know all men are that way? I can manage him."

"If all men are that way," Henry muttered as he watched the Count indeed intercept his wife and make some witty, intimate comment to her, "then I'm going to have to stock up on bullets."

Madame invited Winnie, Mrs. Patterson and Mrs. Rutherford to tea on the steamer, quite a coup for her hostess and necessary to assuage Beaufort's overwhelming thirst for information. The magnificence of the private ship did not disappoint, and afterwards other townsfolk also pressed for invitations aboard. Luckily Madame was unstinting with her hospitality, so soon a sizeable portion of the local population had boarded and scrutinized in detail the luxurious vessel. Jasper was the most favored company, sometimes accompanied by others, sometimes singly, although Madame Verneil was always along at all times, as was only proper. Curiously, some circumstance or another always prevented Cara from being invited—not the right mix of company, or the party already too full, although it would happen soon because Madame was longing for an intimate *tête-à-tête* with her. Cara did her best not to take offense, telling herself that the steamer was that last place she wanted to go, especially in such hot weather. The Count himself had not stepped foot on the boat since disembarking the week before. With his needs attended to with such great assiduity at Villa d'Este, what was the point? The Count was beginning to win at his nightly poker games, losing just often enough to retain the impression that he was a cordial, good-natured fellow with a deep purse.

As June turned to July the weather grew hot indeed. The breezes still arose in the evenings, but with the exception of a few brief showers that passed through all too quickly, the days were dreadfully still, keeping most Beaufort residents in the interior of their houses, or on their piazzas, if they were lucky enough to have houses on the river. The Senator and Winnie's house did not front the river. The Senator and Winnie's house tended, in fact, to be quite warm the entire month of July. While Beaufort residents were used to heat waves and bore them without much complaint or real discomfort, for the Count and Madame de Saintonge the high temperatures required concerted adaptive measures. They took to staking out a section of Villa d'Este's porch and spending much of the day there in limp submission, the Count asking not infrequently how much longer they would have to remain in this dreadful place and Madame de Saintonge regularly shushing him up.

But all was not misery. A few summer's previously Henry had contracted an engineer passing through from Connecticut to rig a set of large, woven, palmetto fans suspended from the ceiling of the porch. The fans were operated with a pulley and cord, allowing the entire series to be waved in unison at a distance. With the Count and Madame nearly prostrate with the humidity, slaves were assigned to operate the cord almost ceaselessly from noon to sunset, as well as serve an unending stream of drinks. Henry checked his ice block covered with straw in the icehouse out back regularly. Since the unabated temperatures were made tolerable to the Europeans only with vast quantities of ices, lemonades and juleps, he gloomily recognized that what in April had been a chunk of frozen water nearly the size of Plymouth Rock was now unlikely to last the summer. Another, quite expensive block would have to be ordered, and God knew where it would come from, he pondered morosely. Nova Scotia, probably.

With the basement being the coolest spot in the house, many of the servants took refuge there, coming up with tasks that would give them some excuse for their presence. Even the Count's manservant suddenly found reasons to occupy himself in the nether quarters. He was too haughty to speak to, or even acknowledge the Negro servants he shared the space with, but still shoes were polished, coats brushed, even cravats and shirtfronts ironed in the partially subterranean space so as to keep the Count looking his best. The short, balding, middle-aged manservant would've been pleased enough to consign these tasks to the house staff, but his master had specifically insisted that he perform them since African slaves could hardly be trusted with the finer points of gentlemanly couture.

In the heat, Beaufort turned nocturnal with parties lasting until three or four in the morning and inhabitants not rising until midday. Not the Birch family, however, and this included Cara. Constitutionally incapable of sleeping past six, Henry could barely stand for his family to sleep until eight, so they rarely stayed out much beyond midnight. Having to tolerate the Count sleeping until noon after a night of cards was almost more than Henry could humanly bear. He certainly wasn't going to keep the boys quiet for the benefit of some indolent aristocratic snoozer. Jasper had long ago adjusted his ways to please his host and was at breakfast each morning in time to keep the Birch family company.

"I think we should send the ladies to the Rutherford party by themselves tomorrow evening," Henry told Jasper over a generous helping of grits topped with salt, pepper, bacon, and a fine sprinkling of cayenne, just the way Henry liked them. "I've invited the Senator and Josiah Walford for supper. It's time someone else heard your theories besides me."

Jasper was surprised. "Should I prepare to be roasted alive?"

"The Senator may bluster, but he's a unionist, through and through. Neither of these men like Rhett; both of them hate his calls for secession. They're in no way against slavery, but I think they'll at least hear you out. With respect, I might add. I'll see to that. After that, well, let's see how persuasive you are."

Jasper evaluated his cousin. What Henry was arranging was not without risk to himself. "Are you doing this as a favor, or because you believe it's right?"

Henry smiled whimsically. "Does it matter?"

The sun was just hitting the treetops the next morning when Henry found Spit Jim in the laundry dependency in the backyard off the kitchen. The laundry was the realm of Reesa who, with a waist three feet in diameter and a head wrapped in a blue kerchief, had already started a kettle to boil for the wash while little Sam busied himself bringing in the water for the rinsing and the bluing. She intended to get the hottest part of laundering out of the way early, before the heat set in. Jim, who had risen with the sun with the same idea of doing hot work in the morning cool, was on one side of the room, using an iron to press one of Jasper's shirts. The light was still too dim in the basement to do the job properly there. When Marse Henry entered, Reesa gave a start and then thanked the good Lord that he wasn't looking for her. Surreptitiously she glanced at Spit Jim who looked unperturbed at the appearance of the master. Nerves tough as tabby that one had. Reesa waddled out of the laundry as fast as she could without it looking like she was running away. As little Sam came back, she caught him and pushed him out the door with her. Heat or no, the laundry could wait.

"So, Spit Jim," Henry said, folding his arms once the two were alone in the rough brick room. "You've been around. Tell me what you know about this here Count I've got staying with me."

The corners of Jim's mouth curved in amusement as he pressed a sleeve flat. "What do you want to know?"

It took Henry a few seconds to broach the subject most pressing on him. "Does he have designs on my wife?"

With a shrug Jim turned the shirt over. "Probably. He has designs on all women, near as I can tell."

Henry kicked at a bit of kindling that had fallen onto the hewn plank floor. "And this doesn't upset the Countess waiting for him in New York?"

"Which Countess would that be?" Jim asked raising an eyebrow.

Henry squinted. "He's got more than one?"

"He's got none, as far as I know. He's certainly not married to any relation of any Madame in town."

"I see," Henry said slowly, his mind busy reevaluating the entire situation. "So I take it he's not the father of doting twins, then, either. In fact, in all probability he's on the de Saintonge payroll. Just how much money does that wretched husband have?"

"More than you can count," Jim said. "You think she'd marry a man that old if he didn't pots of gold and one foot in the grave?"

"Once the old geezer kicks off, is Jasper supposed to marry her or just hang around in perpetuity?"

"I'd say marry," Jim said, pressing flat the other sleeve.

"I'd say you're right," Henry agreed. "So any other tidbits about the Count? How about something even Jasper doesn't know?"

Spit Jim tilted his head to one side. "He cheats at cards?"

"He does? Excellent. That might actually get him killed. How does he do it?"

"Check his sock garters, that's my advice. And just so you know, you might want to keep your wife's jewels locked up while he's in residence."

Henry looked surprised. "He's a thief as well?"

"Let's say I wouldn't put anything past him."

"My, my. We have a complete bounder on our hands." Henry put his thumbs in his waistcoat pockets as he considered the possibilities with a certain amount of relish. "So what do you think, Spit Jim, will Madame succeed in her quest to lure our fair boy back to the City of Light?"

Jim twisted his mouth, his attention on the shirtsleeve in front of him. "What do you think?"

Henry raised an eyebrow. "I'd lay money she doesn't."

"I'd lay money you're right," Jim said.

Henry appeared satisfied with this pronouncement. Then he looked the Negro over. "Why are you still ironing his shirts? You're free; you could go anywhere."

"I've been almost everywhere," Jim said with a shrug.

"So you're too devoted to leave him? It's touching, really."

Jim set the iron down and looked Henry square in the face. "Let him go. You don't know the shape he was in when I took him away from here."

"You took him away from Sleety Pines, not Beaufort. That place would kill anyone."

"It wasn't Sleety Pines, it was the South. He had a month left, maybe two. That's how close he was."

"And you saved him. How noble. That's why he freed you?"

Jim shook his head. "You're not likely to understand."

Henry was silent a moment, his eyes narrow. "Spit Jim, how is it I talk to you like you're a white man? Are you the exception that proves the rule, or are you the exception that proves us all criminals?"

Jim looked at the man whom he'd known as a boy, a boy who been largely fair and kind to him, a boy who had grown into a man powerful beyond measure. "Let him go."

"I can't," Henry said. "I won't." The two men stared each other down. Curiously, it was Henry who looked away first. "But since you've done my family a number of services, Spit Jim, I'm grateful to you, and I'll find a way to repay you. I truly will." Henry started to go, but when he reached the door, he turned back. "Is she really the great-niece of Lafayette?"

Jim just laughed as he picked up the iron again. "You white people are so damn stupid."

Senator Pickens and Josiah Walford listened skeptically, as Jasper had expected. Interestingly, they gave him less trouble over the concept of a free migrant workforce vacillating between mills and farm work than over the assertion that a war with the North would necessarily spell disaster.

"Not that I want one, mind you," the Senator said. "My father fought the British alongside Henry's grandfather to get us where we are today, and I'm proud of what we've achieved as a nation. Our Constitution is a wonder of the modern age and will lead the whole world to prosperity and right action. But if it were really to come to it, I think the South could put up a good fight against the North. We have better men, better skill—why, all they have is a bunch of immigrants."

"The South would put up a good fight," Jasper agreed, diplomatically not pointing out that they were all descended from immigrants. "That's the problem. If you lost quickly, the North would forgive, things would be restructured, and you'd all move on."

Josiah Walford drew on his cigar. "Without slavery. That's what you mean by 'restructured.' "

"That's a given," Jasper said. "But you're right, the South does have some military advantages. You'd be defending your own territory, your men have more experience with arms, and in this last war with Mexico, the majority of officers were from the South, so you'd probably end up with more seasoned commanders. So, yes, you'd put up a damn good fight. So good, that you'd cause the North to lose thousands upon thousands of men. And as the war dragged on, the North would realize for its own security it'd have to crush you so severely that you could never, ever threaten them again."

"But surely," the Senator said, "we could hold them off just like our forefathers held off the Redcoats. Wear them down, wear them out. Eventually they'd get tired and go away."

"Remember, when the British were here, they didn't have all that many men, and Washington just basically led them on a merry chase for seven years. Most of the battles the Continental Army fought, they lost. The war was expensive and annoying to the British, especially when the whole point of the colonies from their point of view was to make money for the mother country. And most importantly, we had the French on our side. If the French navy hadn't come in and bottled up Cornwallis with their fleet—well, maybe we'd all be singing 'God Save the Queen' like they do in Canada."

"But now both Britain and France are sympathetic to the South," the Senator said. "And Britain needs our cotton, so they have every reason to support us—even actively intervene on our side."

"Don't count on it," Jasper said. "For one thing, public sentiment towards slavery in Britain is square against you. For another, with the repeal of the Corn Laws, Britain now imports wheat from the North's Middle West hand over fist. So they'll be left with a choice—do they want food or do they want work? It's a devil's conundrum, but in the end cotton'll be easier to replace than wheat."

Henry drummed his fingertips on the table. "Jasper says they're growing long staple cotton in Egypt."

"They are?" Josiah Walford said with alarm. "You have proof?"

"Here," Jasper said, tossing them a copy of the winter 1849 edition of *The Quarterly Bulletin of Colonial Plant and Animal Products*. "Look on page 27."

With a grimace, Henry picked the journal up and scanned it quickly, his expression souring further as he read. He shook his head before handing the periodical on to Walford. "It's enough to make one ill. Damn British, always meddling. Why don't they let well enough alone?"

"They only have a couple thousand acres in production," Walford commented, dropping ash from his cigar on the journal as he flipped through its pages. "And their yields vary extremely. Some fields they hardly got a boll out."

"But some fields aren't bad," Jasper observed. "They'll take the lessons from those and apply them to the others."

"What you're saying is that it's just a matter of time before Britain doesn't need us," the Senator said heavily. "So if war's a necessity, it should happen sooner rather than later."

"Well, that would help," Jasper agreed. "Every year that goes by, the North builds more foundries, more railroads, and more warships. All things that the South lacks and isn't in any hurry to acquire. The disparity will only worsen with time, not improve."

The Senator downed the rest of his brandy in a swallow. Henry refilled his glass.

"Another conundrum the South will have," Jasper continued, "is at the core of your situation—state's rights. The South's antipathy towards centralized government will play havoc when you go to form your own country to fight a war. A weak central government will paralyze you."

"But that's just the point," said the Senator. "We want decisions to be made at the state level because each state knows what's best for it."

"To fight a war takes money, or at least credit," Jasper suggested gently. "Somehow, funds will have to be raised, but how, given Southerners' aversion to taxes? Yes, at first people will loyally buy war bonds, but once your men go off to war, your fields will produce less, and you'll have to dedicate a large portion of your crops to feed and clothe your army. Worse, once your harbors are blockaded—and don't fool yourself, they will be because the South doesn't have and never will have a navy—you won't be able to get much cotton to market. So where's the money to come from to buy ammunition, cannons, and medicine? What will happen is the little gold you have will be sent overseas to pay for munitions, and then money and more money will be printed until it all becomes worthless. Your currency will be destroyed. And then when the North comes through to loot and pillage, your economy will be smashed flat to match it."

Walford flicked ash into a tray. "Could you be any more pessimistic? You sound like Cassandra of Troy predicting havoc and ruin."

"Gentlemen, remember," Henry said, "Cassandra was right."

"But not believed," Jasper said with a slight smile.

"And Troy destroyed," the Senator observed, swigging another drink. "But Jasper, why on earth do you think the North would loot and pillage us? We're their brothers, for heaven's sake. We fought and suffered and shed blood together. We sweat and worked in unison to create this country and our government. Yes, we have our differences, but I can't believe even the worst Yankee would treat us like what you're proposing, even with the passions of war."

"Senator," Jasper said sadly, "you don't go to war against your friends. And that's why the war won't happen soon, and why we have some time to avoid it. First the North and the South will become estranged, like a quarreling husband and wife. Then they'll become bitter, and in a very emotional way. I expect this war to be much more about emotion than anything else. Then, at last, the two halves of our great country will become enemies, able to kill each other without mercy. Maybe with some regret, some pangs of conscience, but they'll still do it. Burning crops, ripping up railroads, killing livestock so as to make it more difficult for your enemy to wage war—well, that's a whole lot easier than taking tens of thousands of lives on the battlefield, but that'll happen as well."

"Tens of thousands," Henry repeated. "The scale·you're talking about—we've never seen it. How can you be so sure?"

"Europe's seen that scale," Jasper said. "Napoleon was a master at slaughter. In Russia, he lost 95,000 men in a single week. And remember, the North will have hundreds of thousands of immigrants to build their army with, and thousands more flooding in every year to replenish it. The South will only have the number they begin with, a number that will shrink with every battle and with every epidemic of measles and dysentery. There'll be no reinforcements for the South beyond drummer boys and old men. If you do go to war, win it in the first twelve months. If you fail that, then sue for peace and get the best terms you can. That's my advice."

Walford closed his eyes in frustration. "The picture you paint is in no way a certainty. You want us to give up concrete wealth now in order to avoid some ephemeral possibility later. It just isn't worth it."

"If it truly was a choice," Jasper said, "between losing a fifth of what you have now or losing everything in ten years, if you knew beyond a doubt the outcome, which would you choose?"

Henry tilted his glass and stared into it. "You're more fun than a trunk full of meat axes, Jasper. You could depress the devil himself."

"Nothing's ever that certain," the Senator said. "What's most likely is that our present circumstances will continue, just as they have for the last fifty years."

'The world is changing, sir. The industrial age has unleashed powers I don't think you can imagine, transfiguring the North in a fashion few could have guessed only a decade ago. Anti-slavery sentiment there gets stronger each year, as we can see by Congress's repeated attempts to ban slavery in the Mexican territories. The march to war is unrelenting, and if you can't hear its footsteps yet, you will. The only method of avoiding it is to reshape your slaves into citizens who earn wages, and to do it before the North makes you do it by force. We have the opportunity, gentlemen to transform the South in a way that preserves her culture, her honor, and her beauty. Down the other path lie ashes and a hundred years of bitterness. Be wise, gentlemen, be wise."

The three other men around the table were silent, each assessing for himself risks and probable futures. And not liking the answer being returned.

Fourth of July turned stormy, the first few drops of rain hitting just as the political speeches were set to begin. Old Glory flags with thirty stars, issued the year before to replace the twenty-nine star version of 1847, were tucked under frock coats to protect them from water spots while the copious amounts of red, white and blue bunting generously draped on stair railings and balconies along Bay Street were quickly brought inside. Some of the crowd hastily moved on to St. Helena's Church to hear the planned celebratory orations, but most went home because a good drenching with high winds was in store. After scanning the horizon Henry invited the Senator, Winnie and their French guests to his house for the afternoon as well as Cara and her father. Though it was a pity they couldn't show their European guests the usual high-spirited celebration of the birth of American democracy, at least they could entertain themselves with games and cards during the storm, amusements that, with any luck, might keep the Count occupied and not constantly at Mary's side.

The wind was blowing in strong gusts as the guests arrived via the Senator's carriage. Madame de Saintonge's fashionable Parisian hat with its wide brim nearly blew away, and all parties became more than a little damp just getting inside the front door. But the heat had eased, which was much to be thankful for. The wind picked up strength and pitch to become a howl, rattling doors and shutters as the rain beat down in sheets. With all the shutters drawn it grew dark enough that Mary instructed the servants to light the whale oil lamps. Professor Randall began a round of chess with Billy, the oldest Birch son who was quite fond of the game. A quartet of adults settled down to a game of whist, the Count one of them as long as Mary played as well. But Mary also had to attend to her younger boys to prevent their stored up energy and antics from disturbing her guests as well as calm her entire retinue of slaves who had moved en masse into the basement for the tempest's duration. But this storm, for all its crashing wind and rainy fury, this storm was nothing, Henry informed his foreign guests. Barely a little squall. Why two summers ago, such a storm had blasted the coast that the Beaufort River had jumped its banks and poured straight into the basement. Animals that normally wouldn't be found in the salty Beaufort River had washed down from freshwater creeks, and it'd taken weeks to catch all the baby alligators and clear them out. Thankfully their mother hadn't made the storm journey with them. ("All-i-gators?" Madame asked weakly.) Oh, and don't forget the stinging sea nettles high and dry in the front garden. That'd been a regular frolic. Yes, this storm was nothing, all the Beaufort residents nodded in agreement.

After discussion of the storm waned, the recent occurrence of virulent ague on the outer islands became the subject at hand. Slaves were laid up with fevers and chills; a number had even died. It was dreadful. By some accounts the miasma's force was so pestilent, a grown, able man could be fine at breakfast and dead by the next morning. Even an overseer had succumbed.

"When Jim and I were in Asia," Jasper commented, "we heard speculation that the culprit for marsh fever might actually be the lowly mosquito."

"Mosquitoes?" Winnie said. "Utter nonsense. Diseases aren't transmitted by insects. Everyone knows marsh fever comes from bad air. People just need to stay in healthy climes appropriate to the season and they'll be fine."

"It's only a theory at this point," Jasper said "No one knows the mechanism of how an insect might transmit such a disease."

"They don't know," Winnie said severely, "because there is no mechanism. Fevers caused by insects—is that the gibberish these Orientals prattle about while they lounge in their silk pajamas smoking their hookahs?"

The Senator wasn't part of this discussion. Instead he sat on a settee with Madame trying to instruct her on the proper way to say his town's name. "Madam, it's Be-yew-fert. That's us here in South Carolina. Bow-fort is a town up in North Carolina. Entirely different place. Nice enough, I'm sure, but nothing like here."

"You mean zere are two Bow-fors in ze Carolina? Don't ze people get confused?"

"Charming woman," the Senator said later that week to Josiah Walford. "Can't say our town's name properly to save her life, but charming woman."

When Mrs. Pickens inquired of the Count as to the health of his daughters, he'd looked at her as if puzzled before catching himself.

"Ah, yes, they're well," he replied quickly. "My wife writes that they've taken to riding ponies in the park."

"Ponies?" Winnie said. "I thought they were only a year old."

Madame de Saintonge glanced with some annoyance at the ignorant father. "*Bien sûr*, he means zey took pony and cart rides in ze Washington Square. What charming recreations you have for ze little ones in zis country."

"Tell me, Count, are Giselle and Arielle identical?" Mrs. Pickens asked. He stared back blankly.

"Yes, zey are," Madame quickly asserted. "Absolutely indistinguishable. *C'est extraordinaire.* And I must say, zey favor zeir father. Zey are so very dear." She glanced sharply at the Count. He sat up a little in his chair.

"Yes, little Genelle and Aimee," he said. "Quite dear."

"Giselle and Arielle," Madame corrected. "*Naturellement*, doting papa will have his little—how do you say?—nicknames for his sweet babies."

After that, each time the Count was asked about his daughters, he came up with entirely new names that were accepted under the guise of endearment. Ginnia and Sardinia and Arles and Astral were all monikers that passed his lips.

Soon the Senator decided that, in keeping with the day, it was time to read the Declaration of Independence aloud. To the eternal regret of the non-American's in the room, Hugh resourcefully managed to supply the Senator with a copy of the seventy-three year old proclamation from his father's study. When he finished, the Senator would've moved on to a recitation of the Constitution and its amendments if Henry hadn't mercifully redirected him outside with a cigar and brandy on the west-facing porch that wasn't getting hit as hard by the storm as the rest of the house. In fact, it provided an engrossing view of palmettos nearly bending over against the force of the wind.

With the help of Couts, Henry kept the guests supplied with liquor, which did much to preserve the men's amiability even as Hugh and Robert raced through the living room chasing an escaped frog. Madame, already jumpy with the tension of the storm and the prospect of baby alligators, was not amused. Dourly she pondered if she'd descended yet a further rung into the hell popularly known as "the South." Though Jasper was worth much to her, especially when she thought about him at her side in the salons of Paris where his drawling accent and nonchalant demeanor had made him irresistibly exotic, at some point torture was torture. And some of his little mannerisms that had been endearing in the sixth arrondissement, like insisting on green tea and being courteous to servants, were beginning to grate on her here.

Pulling herself together, she decided she simply needed to turn the circumstance to her advantage. With dexterous charm, she firmly caught Jasper's arm as he stood near the piano while Cara played softly and settled him into a chair next to her for a duration intended to span as long as the storm. He, of course, was obliging, he was kind, he even smiled at her in his old way, but he was always . . . distracted. Madame was about ready to throw that piano out the window if that girl couldn't stop playing it.

At one point Mary joined their duo for conversation.

"Your niece," Madame observed, "is such a pretty girl, she must have a special young man with whom zer is an understanding?"

With enormous self-discipline Mary managed not to glance at Jasper at all.

"No, there's no one," Henry said from behind his wife, his hand on the back of her chair. "She's quite fancy-free right now. As you might expect, we're in no rush to see her parted from us."

As Mary and Henry both smiled blandly at Madame and she smiled blandly back, she realized at that instant exactly what the two of them had in mind. "*It's a conspiracy,*" she told Madame Verneil bitterly later. "*A Bow-for conspiracy against me. I don't know why I didn't see it before.*" Madame Verneil nodded and said nothing since that was what she was paid to do. The fact was, Madame de Saintonge hadn't needed to deduce the conspiracy because she expected Jasper's visits to the private steamer to be absolutely guaranteed to work. After all, how could that *jeune fille*, so cloistered, so pure, so closely guarded by her family, hope to compete with the *boudoir* of a *femme du monde*? Jasper certainly seemed to appreciate his shipboard visits with a fervor appropriate to the munificence granted him.

While the storm pounded and Madame monopolized Jasper, the Count found his way back to Mary's side at the card table as Henry glowered from across the room. Catching his companion's attention, Jasper nodded at her supposed brother-in-law. "You've got to stop him, Aurore. There's only so much Henry's going to take."

"Why doesn't Madame Birch stop him?" she answered crossly.

Jasper smiled. "It's difficult for her—she's his hostess. All you'd have to do is snap your fingers, and you know it."

She gave the slightest of Gallic shrugs. "I have him on a short leash as it is. He's a man—he has to entertain himself somehow. Let him have his amusement. Besides, Monsieur Birch shouldn't be such a despot with his wife. You'd think he was a medieval baron, ready to lock her in a tower."

Jasper looked at his scowling cousin again. "It's not going to end well. Mark my words."

After an early supper consisting mostly of cold leftovers from dinner, the wind and rain died down enough to allow the boys to set off some fairly dangerous but highly entertaining fireworks by the seawall along the swollen river. Jasper had brought the fireworks from Boston where he had purchased them from the famous purveyor of pyrotechnics, Mr. James G. Hovey. Mr. Hovey's reputation appeared to be deserved because the Illuminated Stars, Bengola Lights and Chinese Flyers did not disappoint, even with Henry continually barking out instructions to his sons and Mary constantly urging them to take care. Firecrackers could be heard going off throughout the town, indicating the Birch boys weren't the only ones bent on incendiary pursuits. As the last firework fizzled ash to the ground, Henry put his hands on the railing of the damp piazza, surveyed the fast moving clouds overhead, and breathed in the storm-fresh air deeply with satisfaction. "Well," he said heartily, "the good news is it'll be much cooler tomorrow. A good day for me to travel and check over Silver Oaks. Mary, I'll leave first thing in the morning. Should be home by nightfall."

The Count darted a glance at Henry and then at Mary. Mary studiously did not look at either of them. "If you must, dear," was all she said.

The storm having abated, the guests prepared to return home. With Madame engaged in her good-byes to her hostess, Jasper was able to catch Cara at the door and finally speak with her alone.

"Miss Randall, as Henry said, tomorrow looks especially pleasant for a ride. Would you be so good as to accompany me?"

She looked up at him cautiously. "What time?"

"How about before the town's up—eight-thirty? I'll bring Titania for you."

She smiled her assent. But before she turned to go, she had a question for him in return. "Mr. Wainwright, you once told me about a Chinese text you translated for your own edification. I'm wondering, would you allow me to read that translation? I'd be most grateful."

The request caught Jasper by surprise. "It will no doubt expose my lack of linguistic prowess, but for you, Miss Randall, I'll lay bare my ineptitude. Yes, you may read it."

She glanced down, her face flushed. "You underestimate yourself, Mr. Wainwright. Reading it is a pleasure I anticipate." As Cara departed through the front door, neither she nor Jasper were aware that pretty Madame de Saintonge had watched the exchange about horse rides and Chinese texts from across the room with extremely narrowed eyes.

Cara was once again in her form-fitting habit riding sidesaddle as they made their way along the river still dilated from the storm. This time her cut-down top hat with its veil was perched at the correct angle atop her head. Jasper had not brought his translation for her, and Cara hadn't liked to remind him of his promise. Still, any disappointment she might have felt was quickly forgotten as they rode together side by side, their horses' hooves sinking softly into the wet earth. The delicate grasses along the trail, still beaded with droplets of water from the storm, were luminescent in the sunlight. Even if it would be fleeting, the coolness of the morning was delicious.

"So you believe an argument based on utility might persuade planters to gradually end slavery?" Cara asked as Titania carried her along.

Jasper lifted a low-hanging branch to allow Cara to pass underneath. "Insisting that slavery is sinful, like the North likes to do, won't ever work in the South. They'll dismiss that argument out of hand. Telling them that slavery is finite, and that they can dictate how it ends or let someone else do it—yes, I think that's the way to get through. Or at least it has a chance."

The brass on Titania's reins jingled as the horse shook her head, impatient with their slow pace. "But you think slavery is immoral," Cara ventured tentatively.

"Yes," Jasper answered evenly, "yes, I do. Unequivocally."

"And yet you still own them," she observed more forcefully.

Jasper glanced at her. "It does seem inconsistent." He gave his horse a good prod with his heels. "Come on, Oberon, let's go." And he was off ahead, Cara not having to do much to coax Titania to a canter to catch up.

Chapter Ten

The same morning, while pouring over housekeeping accounts in her back parlor, Mary looked up with surprise to see the Count. It was unusually early for him to make his appearance for the day. With Henry departed for Silver Oaks, the boys already off at school, and Jasper out for a ride, she was alone in the house—well, alone as a woman with a dozen slaves could be.

"Count, let me have one of the servants bring you breakfast."

He stopped her. "Dear madam, I have no need. Just a cup of your delicious coffee," he said, gesturing to the pot on the side table. But when she hospitably rose to pour him one, the Count, stealthy as a panther, immediately came up behind her.

"Count," she said with surprise as he caught her hand that would have picked up the pot. He turned it up and brought it to his mouth.

"Signora, I can no longer contain myself," he said as he kissed her palm, the inside of her wrist, even the inside of her elbow. "After these weeks in your company, my passion for you cannot be subdued." He was kissing her neck, her ear. "Your beauty, your charm . . . they defeat my reason. I must submit."

"Count," Mary said, shocked, but since she was yielding to him as much as resisting, the Count knew he had momentum, and he was certainly the man to take advantage of it. He turned her around for a full embrace, his arms encircling her, his mouth seeking hers, bending her backwards . . .

There was a crack sharp as a rifle report as a door hit a wall. "Step away, Count." Henry Birch stood in the doorway, his hair mussed, his eyes wild, a pistol in his hand.

Mary gasped, her hand to her throat. "Henry, no. It wasn't—"

"I know just what it was," Henry said. He pointed jerkily with the gun. "Get away from him."

But, lifting her chin, Mary stepped in front of the Count. "I won't let you shoot him, Henry. Not here, not now. Think of the scandal," she pleaded. "I'll be banned from church. We'll never be able to hold our heads up in town again. Call him out if you must, but do it by the rules, and for some other reason. No one must guess what has happened. Please, Henry, think of our boys, and the terrible, terrible shame."

The Count was silent, his eyes darting between his possible murderer and the body that stood as his sole protection at the moment.

With a look of disgust, Henry lowered his arm. "Damn you, woman," he snarled, "where was your worry about shame and scandal two minutes ago? You're going to pay for this the rest of your life. All right, Count, since you're my 'guest,' I'm going to be hospitable and give you a choice. You're either on your way to Charleston on your precious steamer by nightfall, or tomorrow at dawn you'll meet me at the field by Salt Water Bridge. We'll say you insulted my wife. And should you fail to meet me, you can bet some fellows in town will hear about your curious predilection for scratching your ankle during card games. Oh, and when you go, I expect you to take the French contingent with you. Don't be leaving them here, or certain matrimonial 'facts' will make their way around town."

The Count pulled his heels together and bowed with as much dignity as he could muster. "As you wish," he said, and then stalked out of the room with head held high.

Henry watched Mary closely. They both stayed absolutely still, listening as the Count's steps climbed the stairs to his room. When the door was shut upstairs, Henry came over and took his wife tightly by the waist, pressing her close. "Well, well. You're a much more cunning actress than I thought. You had me half-convinced I was going to shoot him myself."

Mary smiled and looked down. "You took your time coming in."

"I wanted him in a compromising position he couldn't talk himself out of. Believe me, my dear, it was painful to see anyone touching you, especially that blackguard knave. But this has killed two scoundrels with one stone—now Beaufort will be rid of them both."

"You're sure he'll leave and not meet you at Salt Water Bridge?"

"Oh, I'm sure."

"You never have actually called anyone out, have you?" she teased. "In fact you go to lengths to avoid it."

Henry put his fingers under her chin. "Duels are for idiots. But I'd kill for you, my darling. Don't doubt I would."

"You'll never have a reason to," she assured him.

"I know," he said. "That's why I married you."

She looked taken aback. "That's the only reason?"

Henry tilted his head as he reflected. "As I recall, there was also the fact that I could hardly keep my hands off you, and that your father would've visited me with a threatening amount of weaponry if I hadn't proposed."

"As I recall," Mary said, "you didn't keep your hands off me, and my father had nothing to do with it."

"Far be it from me to contradict a lady. And since seventeen years later I still can't keep my hands off you, how about we go upstairs? The boys aren't home, and the Count's going to be occupied for a while, I should think."

There was a hurried conference in two languages in the Pickens's front parlor.

"*You idiot. You imbecile,*" Madame de Saintonge spat out in French.

"*He knows we're no relation. Wainwright must have told him,*" the Count said in Italian without too much concern.

"*Monsieur Wainwright did no such thing. He would never compromise me in any way.*" Madame de Saintonge took a deep breath and recaptured both her composure and her mastery of the situation. "*This just means we'll put things in motion earlier than planned, that's all.*"

"*This afternoon you mean?*" The Count had no intention of sticking around to let himself get shot at in the morning.

Madame pressed her lips together as she made her calculations. *"Be on the boat and ready to go at four. I'll return to shore at a quarter past and then you can depart."*

"You're not worried Signor Birch will defame you with accusations if you stay?"

Pretty Madame's gaze was steely. *"He'll be far too distraught to bother with me."*

"As you wish," the Count said with a slight bow.

Cara received a charming invitation from Madame de Saintonge to have late-afternoon tea with her on her steamship. She was so sorry this visit had been so often postponed, but with the cooler weather, the visit would now be even more pleasant. After reading the invitation with curiosity, Cara sent a reply with the same messenger.

The Count found his servant in the basement where he was polishing his boots to the impeccable sheen they were known for. He gave him instructions to pack his belongings and board the boat with them by a quarter of four.

"Will the Signora be coming as well?" the manservant asked.

"No, it'll be the young signorina," the Count said off-handedly. *"She'll be with us as far as Havana, I should say. The Signora wants her competition discredited and out of the way."*

The manservant glanced at Spit Jim, who was ironing a pair of pants over in one corner and paying them no attention. *"Should we be talking in front of him, sir?"*

The Count gave a derisive snort. *"Surely you don't think any of these great apes know the language of Dante? I'll be glad to see the last of this wretched abyss of culture. At least I'll have a luscious souvenir to console me."*

The manservant shrugged. *"Without an older woman along, a girl like that'll have no reputation afterwards."*

"Indeed," the Count said. *"I intend to make sure there's nothing left of her good name by midnight. After the way I've been treated, it'll be most satisfying."*

Cara stood with Madame at the dock under the shade of her fringed blue parasol, a small frown on her face. "Why is there smoke rising from the steamer?" she asked as they waited for the Negro with the rowboat Madame had arranged to pick them up and transport them.

"Oh, ze captain heats ze engine now and again to—to—keep up its power," Madame answered brightly. Her parasol was pale green. It matched her eyes well. "He'll stop soon."

"The crew seems to be moving about, too," Cara observed.

"Zere is much to do to maintain a ship, I suppose," Madame said carelessly. "You will see when we get zere."

Isaiah, a grizzled, old, free Negro with a lined and careworn face, approached with his boat. "At last," Madame said a bit peevishly. He jumped out, lashed the boat to the dock and helped Madame step carefully in. Then he turned to assist Cara.

"Whatever you do, Cara, don't get into that boat," a voice behind her said quietly.

She spun around. "Mr. Wainwright," she exclaimed in surprise.

"Jas-pere," Madame de Saintonge said from the boat with a charming smile beneath her silk parasol. "What are you doing here? Miss Randall is coming to have tea with me, you see, and we don't want any men to bother us."

"Isaiah, these are the two others you want to take, not Miss Randall, here," Jasper said, indicating Madame Verneil and the French maid who were trundling down the dock with bundles in their arms.

Madame de Saintonge frowned. "No, no. They're not coming."

"Yes, they are," Jasper said. He pointed to a cart at the top of the dock with trunks in it. "We'll send those with Isaiah when he returns."

Madame turned her head slightly. "Jas-pere, I don't understand. Why are you doing this?"

"Oh, you understand, Aurore. You and the Count are leaving Beaufort now. And not coming back."

"But Jas-pere, no. You must come with me. I won't leave without you."

"You'll leave, and you'll leave now. I know what the Count's plans were for Miss Randall."

"Whatever you've heard, I'm sure you're mistaken—" She looked up to see that Jim now stood behind Jasper. The expressions on both men's faces were not encouraging. She turned back to Jasper. "*What did this wretched place do to you so long ago? Whatever it was, it broke you, and you never recovered. I loved you with my heart, and in return you—you were just amused. It meant nothing. You don't feel, Jas-pere. You don't love. However pleasing and handsome you are on the surface, on the inside, you're a fraud, defective, like a jewel movement watch that can't keep time.*" When Jasper, who listened silently to this tirade, didn't answer, she turned once more to Cara. "Miss Randall, are you sure you won't come take a look before we leave? It would be such a pity if you were never able to visit our little ship."

"You are too kind, but I believe I must say no," Cara said quietly. "*I suppose I should wish you bon voyage?*" she finished in French.

Madame pursed her lips under her green parasol. "Row," she ordered Isaiah. As the oarsman pulled away from the dock, Madame's face grew wistful. "*Au revoir*, Jas-pere," she called out.

"No, Aurore," Jasper replied. "Farewell."

As the boat went further from shore, the figures inside it grew smaller and smaller, the green parasol forming a pretty halo above the blonde woman's head. Jasper turned to Cara. "Miss Randall, may I escort you home?" She nodded her assent.

"You want me to watch until they go?" Jim asked as Jasper made ready to leave.

"I surely do," Jasper replied. "And don't let anyone swim back to shore, either."

"Are many Italians like the Count?" Cara questioned as they strolled to her house under the gentle shade of Beaufort's fern-encrusted oaks. Maestro Pavini, a wiry, intense man with a short temper and boundless enthusiasm, was the only other Italian she'd ever met.

"Heaven's no," Jasper laughed. "The Apennine Peninsula would crumble into dust if it were populated by bloodsuckers like him."

Cara glanced at him from under her parasol. "I hear Henry didn't go to Silver Oaks after all this morning. Mary said with the storm surge, he mistimed the tides. Will you tell him what has passed?"

"And have him spend the rest of the summer hunting the Count down to murder him? I'd rather not. How about you, are going to tell him?"

"Not if you're not," she said.

Jasper nodded and they continued on. She hadn't thanked him for rescuing her, and he hadn't apologized for putting her at risk with his unsavory friends in the first place. Indeed, the understanding between them went well beyond that.

"I believe one of the twins developed a severe illness," Cara said. "So naturally the Count and Madame de Saintonge had to leave immediately. They were terribly sorry they couldn't say their good-byes properly."

"One of the dear twins," Jasper agreed. "We hope to hear she's better soon. Which one was it, little Aspic or little Garlic?"

"We can't be sure," Cara said with a small smile. "They're both so indistinguishable."

Henry really did need to go visit Silver Oaks and also Birch Hill, so he left for four days, squelching with nary a qualm Mary's objections about the epidemic of ague circulating St. Helena Island. When he invited Jasper to accompany him, Jasper declined, mentioning correspondence he wanted to catch up with. Detecting an ulterior motive that didn't include fear of fever, Henry didn't press him. And indeed, Jasper went riding with Cara twice more in the brief spell of warm rather than relentlessly hot weather that had oppressed Beaufort earlier. But the third afternoon, when the mercury in the thermometer rose again, he paid a different type of call. This was after he'd read the previous day's *Charleston Courier*.

"Mr. Wainwright," Cara said, greeting him in her front parlor that was still cool because the curtains had been drawn all morning against the sun. "My father's napping just now but I know he'd be glad to visit with you in an hour."

"I didn't come to see him," Jasper said, choosing to remain standing rather than sit down on the settee she had gestured to. "I came to see you, for two reasons. The first is you were interested in the Chinese text I translated. Here it is, deficient as it may be." He handed her a leather-bound journal that she'd actually despaired of ever seeing since it'd been nearly a week since she'd requested it. As she leafed through it, she saw that the left-hand pages held calligraphic Chinese characters, and the right hand ones their hand-written English translations. On the final page there was a line of writing that looked Western in nature. No, on further inspection, it wasn't words, just lines and circles, nonsensical. Perhaps it was some sort of decorative pattern he'd copied. "Thank you, Mr. Wainwright. May I keep it for a week? I promise to take good care of it. And would you mind if I made a copy of your translation for my personal use?"

"You may keep it as long as you like," Jasper said, "and copy it if you wish." He was then silent, as if debating what to say.

Still standing since her guest refused to be seated, Cara waited, perplexed. "You said there was a second matter?"

"Yes," he agreed but seemed to have trouble finding the words to introduce it. He began at last. "Miss Randall, I have reason to believe you are acquainted with the man known in the newspaper as Eustace Woods." He held up a hand as she tried to interrupt him. "Hear me out. I don't want to unmask him; I wish to make contact and ask for his assistance. As you well know, his ability to sway and shape public opinion could be a tremendous asset in our endeavor."

Finally she was allowed to speak. "Mr. Wainwright, what has brought you to this faulty conviction that I've met Mr. Woods? I assure you, I haven't."

"The letter in yesterday's *Courier*. He doesn't mention eliminating slavery per se, just that the South needs to adapt to a constantly changing world or that change will be forced upon it. It was well-expressed, but so identical to my own thoughts as to nearly mirror them. Deny it though you might, it was no coincidence, Miss Randall. You talked to him about it, didn't you?"

She looked off towards her piano. "Couldn't he have heard it from one of the other gentleman from the other night?"

"They're all still wrestling with the necessity of change. Not one of them is ready to defend it, including Henry. No, you're the one with the connection. It was through you." Cara walked to the front window and looked out on the quiet street. "Miss Randall," he said gently to her back, "I know half the unmarried men in Beaufort have thrown their hearts at your feet at one time or another. It wouldn't surprise me at all if a well-educated man whom you had kindly refused still enjoyed conversing and exchanging ideas with you, and you with him. You have enough freedom here," he gestured to the empty room, "that it wouldn't be difficult for someone to come and go unnoticed."

She looked back at him sharply. "Mr. Wainwright, are you suggest-ing—"

"Forgive me, I'm not suggesting anything but the best intentions. Certainly nothing improper. Again, I don't ask to know his true iden-tity, I just want to communicate with him."

"Through me," Cara said, bowing her head.

"If you would be so good as to consent," Jasper said. "Utilizing Mr. Woods' persuasive power is the best opportunity I have. I would ap-preciate your opinion, Miss Randall—you would know best—do you think he's persuadable to the eventual cessation of slavery?"

Cara pressed her lips together. "Oh, Mr. Wainwright," she said in distress. He just looked at her steadily. "Yes," she said finally, miserably. "Yes, he's persuadable."

"Will he help us?"

"How much 'us' is there?" Cara asked forlornly. "You really mean, will he help you?"

"For now, but Miss Randall you must see that these ideas are like kindling, ready to ignite. Henry's arranging an even larger meeting when he gets back with nine or ten men. If Woods were to write some-thing supportive, he could be the match that sets the bonfire alight."

"I'll see what I can do," she said reluctantly. "But I can't promise you anything. Anything at all."

"That's enough for me," Jasper said.

The next day Cara sent word via Minnie to Jim that she'd like to see Mr. Wainwright. When he arrived in her parlor, she stood tensely by her piano.

"Mr. Wainwright," she said. "Please summarize for me the main message you wish to have conveyed before your next meeting."

"He's willing?"

"This one time. I can't say more."

Delighted by Woods' proffer of assistance, Jasper launched into his ideas. "Have him bring in the theme of gradual change again, but this time economic change that accommodates new inventions and new ideas," he said, spelling out a strategy that he and Jim had mulled extensively the night before. "We can study the North and take the best of what it has to offer and leave behind the worst. Have him bring up the railroads as an example. Most South Carolinians are proud of the lines from Charleston to Hamburg and Camden. Bring in the telegraph, remind the readers of the revolutionary benefits of the cotton gin, and then talk about mechanized plowing and harvesting. He can then suggest that the future lies in a wise adaptation of machinery to farming. No need to talk about slavery at this point."

Cara listened patiently, impassively.

"You're sure you don't want me to write any of this down?"

She assured him she didn't.

"Are you going to the Bonner's party tonight?" he asked.

She shook her head. She was a little tired. She thought she would sit this one out and have an early bed.

"Miss Randall, my demands are fatiguing you. It's inexcusable. You mustn't let me impose on you like this. When I'm unable to restrain my enthusiasm for my project, you must send me away."

She smiled wanly at him. "I'll be fine."

On Henry's return, when Mary reported that Jasper had ridden with and visited Cara frequently during his absence, Henry was more than pleased. However, since it was now the middle of July, he began to wonder how to prompt Jasper to speed up the pace of his courtship. In many respects Henry was in a fine mood. The cotton crop on both plantations was shaping up well, and it looked like an excellent harvest was in store. And there was talk of the price per bale going up by almost four dollars this fall. The rice yield was another matter, but even so, there was much to be optimistic about. If only he didn't have Jasper's doom and gloom predictions creating dark clouds around all this plenty and prosperity. Who in their right mind wanted to get off a horse that was in the lead down the straightaway?

Though Henry had set up the initial discursive supper in order to humor his cousin, the arguments presented had been niggling at him no small amount. He wanted no war, he was sure of that, and while he saw nothing wrong with slavery, at least how he practiced it, if it could be replaced with something better that didn't destroy the Arcadian nature of life of the South, he was willing to consider it. He viewed his slaves as simple creatures, similar to children in their need of guidance, protection, and sometimes punishment. Spit Jim—Spit Jim was troubling. Though he was loath to admit it—and wouldn't to anyone, not even his wife—Henry had a certain amount of grudging respect for the former slave who had traveled the world learning medicine and languages at will. And respect wasn't a commodity that Henry bestowed lightly. In the innermost recesses of his thoughts Henry had to ask himself whether it was possible that the form and nature of slavery suppressed Negroes from achieving their true capability. No answer was forthcoming.

The next day the drover arrived in town. He rode on horseback with a rifle at his side while a dozen slaves chained together trudged down the road on foot to be sold or traded for the best bargain available or marched on to the next town. Some drovers walked their goods all the way south to Alabama. This one, Hubert Holloway, had been expected. When he arrived, a number of planters brought out slaves to where the drover set up shop on Bay Street so that the surplus stock of human beings they were interested in trading or selling could be evaluated. Jasper and Jim looked on from across the street. The slaves, six men, five women and a boy, were filthy from road dust and had sores on their wrists and ankles where their skin contacted the metal cuffs. They were given water and then instructed to sit down at the side of the shell-lined road while planters looked them over. A more dispirited group Jasper had rarely seen.

"You know, you forget," Jim said hollowly as he surveyed the shackled troop. "You forget just how bad it can be."

"I don't," Jasper said, watching an aging Negress endure having her teeth inspected by a potential buyer. "I don't forget a day of it."

"That was always your problem," Jim said, glancing at his former master with a mixture of tenderness and sadness that no one, not even Jasper, saw. "Sometimes forgetting can be a good thing."

Mary asked Henry if he was still going to get rid of Run Charlie who'd developed an uncooperative attitude since he'd been sent to Three Reeds last year.

"You want me to sell a slave right under Jasper's nose? It'd be a disaster," Henry told his wife in the privacy of their bedroom. "I'll wait until Holloway passes through again."

Jasper and Henry were on the piazza, watching Cara help Robert build a teepee he was wildly excited about after she read him a magazine story describing the customs of the Plains Indians. The teepee was being constructed from sticks, twine, and an old sheet. Good-natured Hock provided more actual assistance than Cara in the assembly, but she was consulting the illustration in the magazine and making suggestions. Jasper's eyes never left the figure with wide petticoats.

"Jasper," Henry said, watching his cousin watch his niece, "this whole new model of agriculture—why do you care so much? I mean, if you're just passing through, why not leave us to our fate? The way you frame it, there'll be a war, we'll lose, the slaves will be freed, and you'll get what you want, right? Why all this passion for us to change?"

It took Jasper a long moment to answer. "Because I love you and Mary and the boys, Henry. You mean the world to me." Setting down his cup of tea, Jasper gazed out at the river, the gently swaying marsh grass, the shady banks of Lady's Island across the way. A fishing boat was passing just in front of Villa d'Este, her crew trimming sails as the craft made the last leg of its journey to the city dock. "And though you may not believe it, in my own way, I love Beaufort. God help me, I even love the South. I care. I can't stop myself."

Henry smiled. "That's what I thought. That's why I listen to you at all, you know." In companionable silence they watched as the teepee progressed, Hock winding more rope to entwine the top of the poles while Cara plucked at the sheet so that it draped without puckers. Robert helped matters by doing his version of an Indian war dance.

"Speaking of loving the South," Henry said to Jasper conversationally while he sipped his whiskey, "Cara's a good Southern girl."

Jasper frowned as Robert jumped under the sheet's flaps prematurely and the structure teetered. "What's that supposed to mean?"

"It means she won't end up in any man's bed without marriage."

Jasper sipped his tea, not willing to favor this remark with even an answer.

"And if she did lose her head," Henry continued on as if discussing the weather, "one of her family members would have to shoot the rascal. Heavens," he said, pressing a hand against his chest, "I should have to shoot the rascal."

Giving his cousin an annoyed sideways glance, Jasper wondered if he should've sicked him on the Count after all. "You're not going to have to shoot me, Henry."

"Glad to hear it," Henry said. "I'll sleep much easier at night."

Jasper glanced at Henry's drink. With an inaudible sigh, he took another sip of green tea and stared off at the ebbing tidal river whose direction was determined not by the lie of the land but by the will of the ocean.

Before Jasper went to bed, he sought out Jim in the room he shared with Hock in the dependencies back of Villa d'Este. Hock was away as he often was, spending the night with his wife, Therese, who was a slave at the Witherspoon house. Jim was there, measuring out herbs by the light of a candle.

"Think you could give me some of those needles in my ear?" Jasper asked.

Jim's expression was concerned. "The cravings getting bad again?"

Jasper just looked away.

"You've got to get out of the South," Jim told him as he got out his kit. "If you can leave Paris behind, you can leave Beaufort."

Jasper lay on Jim's sagging bed with its straw mattress and rope springs. Staring up at patterns that the flickering candle created on the rough ceiling, he mentally prepared for the not entirely comfortable procedure ahead of him. "I just need a little more time," he said.

Though the abrupt departures of Madame and the Count were startling to Beaufort, after only an afternoon of discussion it was decided it was for the best since the pair had become a tiny bit tiresome anyway. Jasper's star, however, was still in ascension. Beaufort appreciated his ability to attract such illustrious guests, and applauded further still that he had stayed behind when the flighty Europeans left. It was generally accepted that Jasper Wainwright had as good as proposed to Cara Randall, with the result that the town now claimed Jasper as one of its own. To some people's surprise, Beaufort even found itself able to accommodate his green tea and rumored abolitionist eccentricities. After all, such things proved Beaufort to be both cosmopolitan and broad-minded, and tales of Jasper's travels through Europe and Asia were mentioned in a number of letters to correspondents in far-flung counties as an example of what made Beaufort such a stimulating place to live. When Jasper married Cara and settled down again with all the concerns and cares of any planter, he would see the light. Until then, during that summer of 1849, with flourishing crops in the field and high cotton prices in the offing, Beaufort was inclined to be indulgent.

When Henry saw the letter in *The Courier*, he was so impressed, he whistled in admiration. "My, my, Jasper. This dispatch from Woods about taking the best of what the North has to offer and leaving behind the worst—it's as if you've got him eating out of your hand." Jasper's vague reply to this assertion caused Henry to look at him sharply. "There's something you're not telling me. You've joined up with him somehow, haven't you?"

"I've made a connection," Jasper admitted. "He seems tentatively willing to help."

"Who is he? Come on, this is too delicious not to know."

Jasper shook his head. "I don't know his identity. And I can't tell you my conduit to him. It's confidential and so tenuous it might fall apart at any moment."

Henry appraised his cousin. "Well, well. It does ratchet everything up a notch."

As might be expected, *The Mercury* increased the volume of its bellicosity to match the new ideas in *The Courier*. Barnwell Rhett himself published a signed editorial stressing the false promise of any path other than secession. To conciliate with the North, to compromise, to bend at all was the direct route to ruin. In fact, he turned the North's argument of abolitionism on its head and claimed the North wanted to enslave the South. The North became Britain and the South the plucky colonists in resistance.

"*To continue under this government,*" he wrote, "*I would be a slave— a fearful slave, ruled despotically by those who do not represent me, and whose sectional interests are not mine, with every base and destructive passion of man bearing upon my shieldless destiny. Once indeed, my pulse beat high for this Union, but the American flag no longer waves in triumph and glory for me. A greater theme calls: Revolution! Sir, I feel no chilling fears, no appalling terrors come over me at the sound: on the contrary, I feel my mind elate, and my spirits rise. What, sir has the people gained but by Revolution? What have Tyrants ever conceded, but by Revolution? From the beginning of time, Liberty has been acquired but at the price of blood, and that bloodshed is Revolution. What, sir, has Carolina ever obtained, but by Revolution? An oppressed people who dare not resist tyranny face one evil, worse, far worse in its existence and consequences than Revolution—Slavery.*"

As Jim read the diatribe in Jasper's room, he looked like he wanted to stuff the newspaper right down Rhett's throat. "To accuse the North of tyranny and oppression in order to justify his own civilization's tyranny and oppression is outrageous hypocrisy. By his own logic, the Negroes should revolt all across the South tomorrow and murder their masters. The South suffers from tyranny! What a load of sanctimonious rot. The South wrote the damn book on the subject."

"Irony isn't Rhett's strong suit," Jasper observed. "What he's good at is riling people up. Not unlike what Thomas Paine did seventy years ago, really. Use anger and resentment to inflate a common grievance against a perceived oppressor."

"If he's trying to frame a Southern Revolution like it's the American Revolution all over again, he's more than a fool, he's a criminal."

Jasper shrugged. "Jim, if he gets us mad, he wins. We've got to appeal to reason, not get caught up in histrionics."

Jim shook his head as he folded the reviled *Mercury*. "I don't know, Jasper. So often appealing to the lowest instinct works. This lunatic may actually get what he wants and start a war. Maybe it's for the best."

Jasper's shoulders sank at this loss of faith. "Hundreds of thousands of men dead, that's what you want? And afterwards, an end to slavery, yes, but no equality, no justice. No education, no opportunities. Just the dregs of war and defeat that will mean bitter, grinding poverty for a hundred years for black and white alike. We can do better. This battle's worth fighting, Jim. Don't give up on me now."

Though Jim shook his head with pessimism, he didn't argue, and Jasper knew he'd back him as long as there was at least a chance.

When Mary heard about the large gathering Henry was organizing she began to grow concerned. After all, if it went badly, it could reflect on the Birch name, and hotheaded secessionists had been known to viciously attack the character of those opposed to them and make their lives uncomfortable. Unafraid of Rhett and his minions, Henry played down his wife's worries, assuring her they had powerful allies on their side, too. In fact, just that day, Henry had learned that Governor Aiken was in town and would be joining them for the men's supper. It was quite a coup. Though Governor Aiken had been out of power for three years, he was a pillar of politics and society not only in Charleston but the entire state. His participation would lend credence to whatever cause he supported. Now, remarkably, he was here to listen to Jasper Wainwright, a Southerner whose ideas about avoiding secession were at least worth considering.

The evening of the supper Mary was busy directing affairs behind the scenes, ensuring every course of the dinner was appetizing and served in a timely manner. The boys were fed early and then kept in the back parlor with their studies and explicit directions to be quiet. On no uncertain terms, all scampering, leaping, and slithering fauna were to remain outside where they belonged. When she had the chance, Mary had a bite or two of supper herself.

Cara had offered her assistance to keep the boys entertained during the gentlemen's supper, and she was helpful while the men were eating, but then she was in as much of a hurry as Mary to get the boys off to an early bed. It wasn't until nearly ten that the two women succeeded in their task and were able to creep back downstairs. After cautiously padding into the living room, even quiet as they were, they could hear little of what the men in the dining room with their brandy and cigars were saying. So they tiptoed out to the dark porch where the dining room windows that gave onto the piazza were open and would allow for better eavesdropping. And found Spit Jim already out there, his arms folded across his chest, his head cocked as he concentrated on the voices coming from the candlelit interior. Though Mary looked at him sharply, she didn't send him away. For the next two hours the three of them sat or stood silently in the dark listening to the portentous discussion inside to which their voices might not be lent.

Couts had kindly kept Jasper as generously supplied with green tea as the other ten men were furnished with brandy under the flickering chandelier.

"You're asking for the entire fabric of Southern society to be transformed," Governor Aiken said with a shake of his head. "It's too much."

"The fabric will be transformed one way or another," Jasper said. "The question is in what fashion and by whom?"

Dr. Goode let out a long breath. "As much as I'd like to think the human intellect is capable of foresight, I fear few would actively sacrifice to avoid future harm for their children. Present harm, yes—most would give their lives in a heartbeat. But look down the road a few years, and then complacency and the lure of immediate gratification take hold. Slavery means wealth, it means ease, it means our entire agrarian way of life. Yes, I know, Jasper, you've shown us another possibility, but in my opinion, the South will not give up slavery without a fight, even if that fight destroys us utterly."

"Even worse, many look forward to a war with the North," George Forster, a planter on Fripp Island, said. "War for them isn't about disease and death and destruction, it's about glory and honor and silly excitement. The threat of war doesn't deter secessionists, it positively leads them on."

"But you gentlemen don't want war," Jasper countered. "You see the folly. That's why you're here."

Henry gestured with a sweep of his hand. "You're looking at the only rational men in the Sea Islands, Jasper. This is it, right here around this table."

Benjamin Heywood, a planter in St. Peter's parish, leaned back in his chair and puffed on his cigar. "It's just like that attorney, Petigru, says, 'South Carolina is too small for a republic and too large for an insane asylum.'"

"Be that as it may," Jasper said, "does it mean you'll all just lie down and play possum while Rhett goads your fellows down a path you know to be disaster?"

"It's worse than you know," Governor Aiken said quietly. "The compromise being worked out to bring California into the Union as a free state will likely involve a law that forces Northern states to return fugitive slaves."

"Why?" Henry said incredulously. "Only a thousand or so slaves go north a year, and everyone knows they'll just cause trouble if they stay. I say, if they want to go that badly, let 'em."

"That's an easy sentiment for us here in South Carolina," the Governor said. "The border states are less forbearing and are insisting on it."

Jasper shook his head. "It's the worst possible thing they could do. It'll infuriate the North; it'll make them collaborators with slavery. You think there's abolitionist sentiment up there now—this will quadruple it. If you want war, gentlemen, a strong fugitive slave law is guaranteed to muster armies on the battlefield."

"You don't understand the forces in motion," Governor Aiken said sadly. "Calhoun used to be interested in compromise and preservation. Not any more. He used to hate Rhett. Now Rhett's his apparent successor in the Senate."

"You must be jesting," Josiah Walford said. "Is Calhoun that ill?"

Governor Aiken nodded. "The politics in Columbia get more and more radical. Partly because the men with sense," he nodded at his companions in the room, "let others less sensible set the course. Not you, of course, Senator," the Governor added in recognition of the Senator's service.

Henry could barely restrain himself from rolling his eyes. "None of us are willing to spend our precious time arguing inanities in Columbia. The Senator here has the patience of a saint. But you're right—at a minimum we should support a more prudent representative from Beaufort."

"If we could get someone like that elected," George Forster said. "There are more rabid secessionists in Beaufort County than anywhere in the state. We're surrounded by crazy castles-in-the-air dreams of a Southern nation. There's no talking these fellows down."

"Talk up the other side," Jasper said. "Show them an alternative that has just as much promise, promise that's realistic. Men such as you need to state publicly that you favor gradual, intelligent change for the South, and that secession would spell disaster."

The men around the table fell grimly silent.

"Well, there is the Beaufort Agricultural Society meeting coming up the first of August," Dr. Goode said at last. "There should be a good attendance of planters, and we could bring up the idea of new agricultural methods then."

"Who would speak for us?" asked Benjamin Heywood. "Wainwright here's persuasive, but the fact is, he's a newcomer, he won't have credibility with the hotheads. They'd eat him alive. We need someone with stature."

Everyone looked at the Governor. He waved a dismissive hand. "Unfortunately, I can't be here that week. I promise I'll do what I can to support you on a state level, but I'm afraid for the time being it has to be behind the scenes. If even a word slipped out that I might support the cessation of slavery, I'd lose whatever influence I have."

Eyes looked around the table again. They settled on Henry. He shook his head. "You've got the wrong man. I'm not an orator, and I hate politics. I'm here because the prospect of war and disunion horrifies me, not because I have the slightest enthusiasm for abolition."

"Then you'll be starting from the same place everyone else is," Jasper said. "You're not arguing to end slavery per se. You're advocating the reform of Southern agriculture and the expansion of Southern industry. Phasing out slavery so as to terminate hostility with the North is just a useful by-product."

Henry continued to look slightly ill. "What about Eustace Woods," he said suddenly. "Will Woods support us? Publicly, I mean."

All the men turned to Jasper, curious. "You've got Woods on your side?" Josiah Walford said. "That's quite an ace up your sleeve." Even the Governor was interested in the identity and disposition of Eustace Woods.

"I believe he'll support our new agricultural-industrial model," Jasper said with more confidence than he felt.

"Will he speak at the meeting?" Henry asked sharply.

"And reveal his identity?" Jasper drew in a breath. "I can ask."

Cara sat primly in her parlor resisting all of Jasper's considerable attempts at persuasion.

"He has told me unequivocally no, he won't speak at the meeting," she said. "He's willing to write in support of you. That must be enough."

"If you'd just let me talk to him, I'm sure I could convince him," Jasper said.

"I'm instructed to say that's not possible."

With a grimace, Jasper got up and paced the room.

Cara's hands twisted in her lap. "This is just what I feared would happen, Mr. Wainwright, once I agreed to act as your go-between. Now you're angry with me for what Mr. Woods will or won't do."

He turned to her. "I'm not angry, Miss Randall. I'm just . . . frustrated. Surely you must see how important this is."

"No, I don't see," Cara said peevishly. "Mary's right—you men think the world revolves around you when it doesn't at all. Have your meetings if you wish, just don't make me miserable over them."

From his standing position, Jasper looked down at her sitting so prettily on the settee, the lace around her neckline setting off her collarbones, the silk flounces on her dress cascading to the floor like a rococo waterfall. With a sigh he tried again. "Dear Miss Randall. If I've made you miserable, I abjectly apologize."

She looked back sternly, but he continued to gaze down at her with a gentle, quizzical smile. At last she relented. "I'll ask him again. But the answer will be no."

"Do you want me to give you the points to cover in his next letter?"

"No," she said with a sigh. "He told me he already has something in mind."

Jasper couldn't stop himself from frowning. Just what was her relationship with Woods that the man was content to hide behind a mere girl? It was a question he'd pondered not for the first time.

Later that evening, under the cover of darkness, Jasper returned to the Randall house but he didn't knock at the door. Instead he stood partway down the street in the shadow of a tree and gave Sam, the Birch stable boy, the dime he'd promised him for watching the house from earlier in the afternoon until now. He'd also had to pay Hock a dime in order to free up the boy for this duty. When asked, Sam recited all the persons who had come and gone from the house, but no names were remarkable. To a person they were all slaves with deliveries or messages. Perhaps Cara had sent a message herself. Was it possible she might receive Woods late in the evening? Jasper watched and waited. In the course of an hour, he saw nothing more than an opossum creep along the road. What he heard was music—sonatas, impromptus and preludes played with energy and passion. Even, he could have sworn, with ferocity and fury. And then the Chopin waltz drifted out the window, down the street, through his mind and into his soul, creating a sense of loss so acute that he momentarily forgot about Woods, about the South, even about slavery. He forgot about everything but his aching heart.

Woods certainly did have something in mind. His next missive in *The Charleston Courier* three days before the Beaufort Agricultural Society meeting was a blistering attack against the secessionist movement. It recounted South Carolina's great role in the American Revolution and as founders of the nation. It summarized the tremendous achievements the country had made as the flimsy fabric of separate colonies hardened into the steel of nationhood. It argued for the strength of the American people when they stood undivided against the other powers of the world, the benefits that accrued in trade and security and prosperity. It reminded of the shared brotherhood between all the states in matters of blood and custom and lineage. It finished with a rousing defense of patriotism—American patriotism that could be found deep in the heart of every true Southerner, his pride, his birthright, his future. The South and the North must find ways to embrace their common fate, not quarrel like children who couldn't take turns at a game. It was natural that a new nation would face growing pains in the course of its maturation. To respond to these troubles with calls for secession was unprincipled and even criminal. Never forget that secession meant treason, both to their forefathers' memories and to their children's patrimony. Those who advocated it wanted to destroy the South under the pretense of saving it. They were traitors, nothing less.

Henry slapped the paper with satisfaction when he finished reading it. "Well done, Eustace, well done. That should put Rhett in his place."

Jasper smiled. "It is quite good."

"You're sure Woods won't unmask himself?" Henry asked. "Have you asked him in person?"

Jasper shook his head. "I'm not allowed to see him." Jasper had employed Sam to watch the house for two more days with no result. He'd considered bribing Minnie for information but couldn't bring himself to stoop that low.

"Who's your contact?" Henry said. "You can tell me. It might give me an idea about Woods' identity."

"I can't say," Jasper said. "I gave my word." He was beginning to regret having done so.

Jasper went to visit Cara yet again to see if he could coax Woods' identity out of her, but she was resolute in her refusal. Besides, she had a different matter she wished to discuss.

When Cara handed him back the leather-bound journal that held his translation, Jasper looked down at it ambivalently. It represented such a dark, difficult time for him that he actually hadn't looked through it himself in years. In Macao while receiving treatment so many months from a Chinese doctor, he'd hired a tutor to teach him and Jim Chinese language and calligraphy. It'd been something to occupy the hours, since drinking, the most popular pastime of visitors to Macao, was not possible if he placed any value on his life at all. After six months, he'd gone on to Canton seeking further treatment by a

Chinese doctor who specialized in liver ailments, leaving Jim behind with the gruff first doctor who had agreed, without ever actually acknowledging it in words, to take Jim on as an apprentice.

In Canton, Jasper had hired another tutor, an ex-Buddhist monk, who had assigned him the classic Chinese text as an exercise. Lonely and aimless, Jasper had been at loose ends those months in Canton, but the text had intrigued him and he had decided to make a copy for himself. It was as he was finishing it that he set his sights on the monastery in the forbidden inland province with the failed Buddhist monk as his traveling companion.

"I hope you found it adequate," Jasper said now, a decade later, to the pretty young woman who was so inexplicably interested in Oriental esoterica. "As you may know, classical Chinese has no punctuation, so I'm afraid much of it was guesswork on my part. But there's a bookstore in Boston that sometimes carries translations of Chinese texts, and if you were write to them, they might be able to help you find a better version."

"Mr. Wainwright, I assure you, your translation was more than satisfactory; it was illuminating," Cara said. "I'm grateful to have been allowed to read it." She paused. "I'm also glad that you survived that period of your life. You may find this impertinent, but *desperatio fortitudinem veritam nostram manifestat.*"

Jasper looked at her oddly. "You know what that means?"

She nodded. " 'Times of despair reveal our true strength.' "

Jasper looked out the window, his hands clasped behind his back. "Of course you know Latin. Of course." He remained at the window, facing away from her. "I suppose you read the last page then."

"Yes," she said.

It'd been one line, written backwards in mirror writing. Roughly translated, it said, "All is darkness. Death would be welcome." He'd needed to put those words down somewhere so that they were no longer inside him. He'd thought in that language and in that form they'd be safe from Jim ever reading them since Latin was the one academic subject Jim had never attempted. Indeed, Jasper had thought that those few words, written in the back of an old journal locked away in his trunk, were safe from everyone.

"I see now that I wasn't meant to decipher it," she said quietly.

"No," Jasper concurred. He turned to her. "Those words were written long ago, Miss Randall, and while I appreciate your sympathy, I don't require it. But the error was mine in underestimating you. Can we forget this?"

Cara looked down, her expression dimming. "Of course," she said.

Chapter Eleven

The trouble with Hock started early in the morning when Henry called for him, impatiently as usual, and received no response. Sam the stable boy was then sent to find him, but Hock wasn't in the stable, his cabin or any of the dependencies. Though Henry frowned at this news, he was soon distracted by other matters requiring his attention, and it wasn't until noon that he thought to investigate again. When Spit Jim came through the back gate after spending the morning treating a slave with an injured arm, Sam, a lively, industrious lad, nearly pounced on him for information. Looking down at the boy in amusement, Spit Jim pointed out that Hock would likely be found at the Witherspoon house where his wife lived since that was where he'd spent the night. On receiving this news from Sam, Henry then recalled having written Hock a pass as he'd done so many times before, but all the other times Hock had been back by dawn. So Sam was sent posthaste to the Witherspoon house to remind Hock he had a job he was actually expected to perform and to return home on the double. An hour later, the enterprising lad returned alone with all sorts of news. Spit Jim joined Henry behind the house to hear what the boy had discovered.

"Marse Henry, suh," Sam said, a little out of breath. "Hock not at Witspoon house, suh. He wife say he be uh no'count usbin. He wife say he hab nodduh woman. He wife sho be vex, Marse Henry. Da Witspoon stable boy, suh, he say Hock hab feber. He say Hock not right in he mind. Tuhrese, she say she gwine kill Hock ovuh dat odduh gal. De stable boy say Hock take offuh."

Henry shook his head. "The Lord preserve me from my adulterous slaves and their murderous wives. Damn that Hock—he cut this shine once before when Therese was ready to kill him. Took off for the swamps until she cooled off. Well, I guess we won't see him for a week, blast his hide. Good thing we don't have any parties coming up where we need music."

Spit Jim was frowning. "Did Hock have a fever," he asked Sam, "or chills and fevers?"

"Dunno, suh," Sam answered Jim. Though Henry looked at the boy sharply at this use of the honorific "sir," he didn't interrupt. Like every Negro in Beaufort, Sam was in awe of this free black man who had lived up North, traveled the world, and learned more languages than you could count on one hand, not to mention knew the mysterious medicine of the Chinaman. "He say Hock take uh blanket wi'dum round he shoulduh, an last night bin mighty hot."

Henry looked at Spit Jim. "You think it's the ague? Where would he have gotten it? He's been in Beaufort all summer."

"I don't know. But I have a good idea where he went. You want me to go get him?"

Henry sighed. "If he's sick, you probably should. Otherwise he might wade into a creek and serve himself up as breakfast to an alligator. So you know his swamp hiding place?"

"I have a vague idea."

"Sure you do," Henry said.

Of course Jim knew the swamp hideout. And it wasn't just Hock's. It was a place seven miles from town often frequented by slaves during cooling off periods. Sometimes it was a place that served as a precursor to running north periods. Wet, accessible only by foot or horseback, it was a hidey-hole even hounds with the best noses couldn't find. And so far, the slave patrols hadn't ferreted it out either.

"Can you bring him back before nightfall?" Henry asked.

Jim shook his head. "Not if he's sick. I'll be lucky to get him back here before midnight."

"Let me write you a pass then," Henry said and went into his study for the purpose. "I'll write one for both of you."

Jim was going to object—only slaves needed passes—but he decided it wasn't worth the trouble. He got some herbs and quinine together to take on his trip, a flask of water, some food from the kitchen, a lantern and matches. Henry had Sam saddle up Oberon for him and he was off.

But Hock wasn't at the hidey-hole. It'd been so many years since Jim had been there, he had some trouble finding the spot but did eventually reach it just before nightfall. A blanket lay on the ground, and it looked recent. After tying Oberon up to a tree, Jim lit his lantern and searched by foot. It wasn't until two hours later that he found the errant fiddler and storyteller, lying unconscious under a bush half in a pool of water. Jim half-dragged, half-carried him back to the hideout and gave him herbs to clear the heat and expel the pathogen. At first Hock was delirious and so thirsty he nearly emptied the flask of water. When he had settled and calmed, Jim helped him up on Oberon and then got on behind him.

They couldn't travel fast since Jim had to hold on to Hock as well as hold up the lantern to see the road. They were perhaps a mile from town when the sky began to vaguely lighten with dawn not far off. Hock was asleep and extremely heavy to keep upright, but they would be back soon. Jim clicked to Oberon to keep up the pace. He rounded a corner right into two white men on horseback with their own lantern.

"What have we here?" said a tall, thin man smoking a clay pipe. Jim knew him to be Winslow Dotter, a poor white farmer who eked out a living with the help of six children and two slaves on thirty acres. "Looks like Jasper Wainwright's nigger is out cavorting around after curfew. I reckon that constitutes a breaking of the law, don't you, Finnegan?"

Tom Finnegan was a young man not yet twenty years old, still living with his parents on a modest farm in St. Peter's parish. He looked nervous. "It's almost day, Winslow, and he's got one of Henry Birch's best horses. I seen Birch on it in town last month. Better let them go."

"How do we know they didn't steal that there horse to stir up trouble?" Winslow asked. "That what the slave patrol's for, isn't it, to prevent trouble?"

"Win—let's go." Tom seemed ready to turn his horse around.

Winslow pulled a pistol from a saddlebag. "You," he pointed at Jim with it. "You git down."

"I have a pass from Henry Birch," Jim said. "This man's sick. I need to get him home."

"He looks sick," Tom whispered. "He's Birch's best fiddler. Better let them go."

"What's Henry Birch to me?" Winslow drawled. "Just another highfalutin planter too rich for his britches who thinks he owns the world and the rest of us in it. I said git down," Winslow repeated emphatically to Jim, gun still pointed.

After a moment, Jim slid down off the horse. Hock remained upright, slumped in the saddle. Reaching into his waistcoat pocket, Jim pulled out the pass Henry had given him and handed it to Dotter. Winslow glanced at it for the briefest of seconds.

"I think you might've written this here pass," Winslow said. "That's what comes of educatin' slaves. Dangerous, dangerous, dangerous. And illegal."

"How do you know the pass isn't from Birch?" Tom said. "Win, you're going nutty."

Winslow held the pass up to the bowl of his pipe and drew in, causing the smoldering tobacco to ignite the paper. After a few brief seconds of flame there was nothing but ash for him to drop to the ground. "I don't think this nigger ever had a pass, Tom. We never seen it."

Jim said nothing, but now Hock began to stir. "Slabe patrol can't stop Spit Jim," Hock said groggily. "He uh free man."

"Shut your stupid clam," Winslow snapped. Swinging his leg over his saddle, he dismounted his horse. "Tom, funny thing about freedom in South Carolina. I did myself some talking to a lawyer in town. Did you know in South Carolina freeing a slave takes an act of legislature? The South Carolina State Legislature. And my lawyer friend assures me there ain't never been no act of legislature for this here nigger. Even if his master says he's free, it's a lie. He's still a slave."

Dawn was near. The lanterns were losing their glow as a grey light filtered through the trees. Tom convulsively swallowed. "This is gonna be trouble, Win. Come on. Leave it be."

Winslow pulled down a whip attached to his saddlebag. "And since he's a slave at night without a pass, it's our job, Tom, to mete out punishment. That's why the grand planters pay us to keep watch all the dark night. To keep law and order at hand and rebellion at bay. And this slave, he's uppity. He don't look at white men right. He don't look with respect. He don't hop out of the way fast when he meets one on the street. He thinks why should I? I'm just as good. He just don't know how to be a slave anymore, Tom, but we can fix that. Nigger, git over here."

In the hushed gloom that served as shoulder between night and morning, Jim sized up the situation—the scared boy, the crazed Cracker with the gun and the whip, the sick man on the tired horse. He could create a diversion and make a run for it, Dotter would probably miss with the pistol, but that would mean leaving Hock to Dotter's possible vengeance. In his state, Hock couldn't withstand much abuse. No, there was no help for it. He would have to take the whipping.

"No," Hock said hoarsely. "You can't. He uh free man."

"Shut up," Winslow said over his shoulder, "or you're next."

Hock swung his leg over to get down off the horse. "No," Jim said. "Hock stay there." Hock dropped to the ground anyway.

"Win, are you out of your mind?" Tom pleaded. "Come away. Come away now."

"Take off your waistcoat and shirt and turn round," Winslow directed with the gun. Slowly Jim did as directed. With a crack Winslow brought the whip viciously down across Jim's back cutting through the skin. Jim smelled the whip and its familiar acrid tang before he felt it, but he felt it as fiercely here as he had in the fields of Sleety Pines twenty years before.

"NO," Hock shouted thickly. Hock, who was always genial, good-natured. Hock, who could be counted on to be docile, patient, subservient. "NO. YOU CAN'T. HE UH FREE MAN."

"Calm down, Hock," Jim said over his shoulder. "It doesn't matter."

Winslow brought the whip down again. Jim flinched against the impact.

"NO." And Hock was coming for Winslow. It all happened fast. Winslow spun around; Jim shouted for Hock to get back; the gun went off. Hock fell to the ground. A split second later, Winslow also fell to the ground because Jim had hit him hard on the back of the neck, rendering him unconscious. Jim rushed to Hock who'd received a bullet in the chest. Using the shirt he'd already taken off, he applied it as a bandage to staunch the bleeding.

"I – I – I," Tom stuttered in shock.

There was little time. Hock needed to be treated immediately with the herbs and poultices that were back in the dependency behind Villa d'Este. Jim picked up the whip and gun, put the whip in Winslow's saddlebag and the gun in his own. He then heaved the unconscious Winslow up and draped him over the back of his horse. With even more difficulty he got Hock back onto his own horse, mounted behind him, and then grabbed the reins of Winslow's horse so as to tow it along, all while attempting to hold the shirt-bandage firmly against Hock's chest.

"Go," he told Tom. "Nice and steady to Villa d'Este."

Henry met them two minutes later, galloping up to them.

"I thought I heard gunfire. What happened? My god, Hock—"

Tom looked scared to death of Henry, as well he should be. After hearing Jim's brief account of what had transpired, Henry squinted for a moment up at the sky that was turning powder blue beyond the shadowy treetops. The situation was thornier than a bramble mattress. Henry was acutely aware that if he didn't think fast, Spit Jim would surely hang.

Henry sent Spit Jim ahead with Hock, then took over towing the unconscious Dotter and rode his horse up alongside the young slave patrol. "Tom—your name's Tom, isn't it?—you showed extraordinary courage. After Winslow, here, shot Hock, you knew it was wrong, and you knocked him out. You're a hero, Tom, a true hero, and I'm going to see you're rewarded. You understand, Tom?"

Tom nodded though he seemed so scared out of his wits it wasn't clear he understood anything. At Villa d'Este, Jim rushed Hock inside his room to tend to him while Henry dealt with Winslow who was coming round. When Jasper came outside to see what the commotion was about, Winslow was tied up and awaiting authorities. Tom had already slunk home.

"I was doing my job," Winslow said. "That nigger attacked me. He deserves what he got."

"Your job was not to shoot my sick slave who was too weak to rassle a one-eyed flea," Henry said. "Now shut up, or I'll gag you."

Henry was an important man. The sitting judge at the Beaufort County courthouse was woken early to come listen to Henry's complaint. Winslow was taken away and bail set for the attempted destruction of Henry's property. The trial would likely be in several weeks. Winslow's accusation that Spit Jim had assaulted him was paid no attention because Henry insisted Tom had knocked Winslow out, and Henry made sure his word carried the day. In South Carolina, no matter the provocation, any black man who attacked a white man was automatically put to death.

"How does it look?" Jasper asked in the quarters where Hock lay motionless on a bed.

Jim was nearly frantic trying to stop Hock's bleeding while applying herbs to the wound. His hands were covered in Hock's blood; his bare back showed two stripes of his own. "I don't know," he said despairingly. "The fever, the ride. He's lost so much blood. I don't know."

Henry came up jauntily as Jasper emerged from the dependency. "Spit Jim got Hock fixed up right as rain yet?"

Jasper shook his head. "It's bad, Henry."

"What do you mean? Spit Jim's a magician. He can cure anything."

"A point-blank gunshot wound is beyond magic," Jasper said. "Even Jim has his limits."

"Should I send for Dr. Goode?" And Sam was sent running off.

Just then, Jim emerged from the doorway of the dependency. With his hands against the small of his back, he closed his eyes against the morning sun. When he opened them again and saw Jasper and Henry looking at him inquiringly, he just shook his head. Then he wearily walked out the back gate, his bloody hands on his hips, the raw slashes on his back cutting across the rippled scars of other whip marks received long ago.

"I'm going to see that bastard Dotter hanged," Henry said through gritted teeth. "Hock was the best fiddler in three counties."

Dr. Goode arrived. After viewing the body, he patted Jim on the shoulder and told Henry he seriously doubted he could have saved

Hock either. In fact, with a wound like that, it was a miracle Hock had made it back to Villa d'Este alive.

Missives were quickly sent to Columbia via steamer and telegraph and as quickly were returned. By the next day, Beaufort learned that the Governor would not endorse a hanging penalty for Dotter. Every time a white man hung for a black man's death, riots nearly ensued, and he just wasn't going to do it, no matter how good a fiddler the Negro had been. The best he could manage was to run Dotter out of the state, and Henry would just have to accept it. Tom had received a hundred dollars for his bravery from Henry Birch the day of the shooting, infuriating Dotter who still insisted Spit Jim had assaulted him and deserved hanging. By the next day, Tom had cleared out of town—off to California, his parents said, to seek his fortune. Henry was livid.

Jasper tried to calm him down. "Look, if my testimony were all that stood in a feud between Henry Birch and Winslow Dotter, I'd clear out of town, too. I bet Dotter threatened him within an inch of his life to turn sides."

So Henry had to make do with the consolation that no charges were filed against Jim, even though Dotter was now accusing Spit Jim of being the one who shot Hock. But Henry still had to absorb the loss of a slave that he had considered an extended member of his family, and his boys grieved, especially little Robert to whom Hock had a been a special friend. Mary, try as she might, just couldn't explain to him what had happened in a way he was able to grasp.

For his part, Jasper felt unbearably guilty about the two red welts on Jim's back. His keeping Jim in South Carolina, his obsession with trying to change what very possibly couldn't be changed, had made Jim for a brief moment a slave again. Jasper knew it was inexcusable. When he attempted to apologize, Jim just looked away.

"The meeting's tonight, Jim. We'll go to Sleety Pines right after."

Jim looked skeptical. "But then there'll be another meeting, another pathetic hope, another straw to grasp."

"You really think I'm just spitting in the wind?"

Jim glared back at him. "Jasper, right now, I'm so disgusted with this place I don't care if the whole damn state goes up in flames and blood runs in the streets."

Hock's funeral would be that evening, after chore time when masters allowed their slaves to attend such events. Even if he'd been welcome, Jasper couldn't attend. He would be at the Beaufort Agricultural Society meeting. It was originally scheduled to be held in the main hall of Beaufort College on Craven Street, but word had been given out just that day that the venue had changed to St. Helena's Church.

Henry was nervous. Why had the venue been changed? How many people were they expecting? He wasn't fond of church as a rule, attending only at Easter and other times when Mary wouldn't take no for an answer. He'd been able to picture himself speaking to thirty or so of his fellow planters in a familiar Beaufort College classroom. The echoing grand interior of the Episcopal Church—that was another thing entirely. When he and Jasper entered the hall, there were already a hundred men in the pews and more streaming in with a low rumble of conversation filling the grand space.

"What is this?" Henry said to Jasper. "People are here from all over the county. Something's up. I don't know what, but something."

Jasper tried to calm him down, but after looking around at the faces, he had to agree. This was supposed to be a normal, fairly dull meeting of planters with agricultural interests in common, yet the atmosphere in the church crackled like the air during an electrical storm. And men were still coming in, probably over two hundred in the room now, though there was space for all on the main floor. The upstairs galleries, where the Negroes sat on Sundays, would not have to be used.

A low murmur rippled through the crowd as two particular men came in the door. The first to enter was Barnwell Rhett who wore a small, smug smile on his face. Next through the door was John Calhoun, the seventh Vice-President of the United States, the sixteenth Secretary of State, and the senator from South Carolina for the previous eighteen years.

Henry slunk in his seat. "We're in the wrong place at the wrong time, Jasper. Rhett's dealt this hand, and he's going to play us tonight for fools."

"Don't give up yet," Jasper said. "Wait and see. It may still work out."

With the exception of the governor, the others from the meeting at Villa d'Este were all there to give Henry support, but to a man they looked decidedly uncomfortable.

George Patterson, president of the Society this year, rose to officially open the meeting. "We have a full agenda tonight with a number of speakers who wish to address our community. First off, I'd like to welcome Reverend Richard Fuller who is a native of Beaufort and was the minister of the Baptist Church here in town for fifteen years. As most of you know, he left two years ago to serve as pastor of the Seventh Baptist Church of Baltimore, and we're sure he's done a world of good for our brethren in the North." There was laughter among the crowd. George Patterson consulted his prepared remarks. "In addition to his pastoral accomplishments, Reverend Fuller was the author of the well-known public correspondence with Francis Wayland, published as *Domestic Slavery Considered as a Scriptural Institution.* In it he famously proved beyond a doubt that the Bible nowhere prohibits slavery. He even offered to free his slaves to Mr. Wayland or any other reader who could give him bond and security that their condition would be improved. Not one person took him up on this offer, proving indeed that the Negro's situation as a slave in the South is superior to that of freedom anywhere else." Jasper began to tap a finger against his knee. There was only so much of this he could bear. He was glad Jim wasn't there as he would probably throttle the complacent Patterson around the neck.

Fuller rose to applause. He was a self-assured, good-looking man with a handsome Roman nose and a full head of hair, but Jasper thought he looked anxious. Wary. Why would that be when he was preaching to his own slavery choir?

Fuller opened with a prayer, annoying Henry no small amount, and then brought matters to the secular realm by mentioning it was good to be back in Beaufort, land of his birth. His sojourn in Baltimore, while rewarding, did not offer the consolation of scented Beaufort breezes or good Southern cooking. He assured his audience tolerable grits were impossible to find north of the Virginia state line. Then, after a slight cough, he changed his subject.

"Gentlemen, as Jefferson so aptly said about our predicament with slavery, 'We have the wolf by the ear and feel the danger of holding or letting loose.' " People in the audience began to stir uncomfortably. The Reverend coughed into his hand and raised his voice. "The clouds of war between the states are gathering, and this violence we must avoid at all costs. As you all know, I have long owned slaves that I treasure like my own family. But I have come to the conclusion that our country needs radical change. We must repatriate slaves from America back to Africa on a massive scale, emancipating all who would participate and compensating the owners for their losses." The jaws of many in the audience, including those of Henry and Jasper, dropped in complete surprise. A great murmuring began to grow throughout the church. "Gentlemen, the path we are presently on will surely lead to ruin. We must alter our course."

Voices of dissension began to rise in cacophony.

"Traitor!" someone shouted.

"You let those Yankees addle your mind," another called out.

The Reverend raised his hands. "I know this is difficult to hear. I own slaves just like you do. But the time has come to consider—"

One man rose and pointed at him. "The time has come for you to sit down and stop your Yankee preaching. The South will never give in. Never! Live free or die!"

There were many calls in support of this sentiment, all of them emphasizing the inalienable Southern right to own slaves rather than its logical corollary that the Negro might have a right not to be one. The babble of noise grew even louder. The Reverend looked like he didn't know whether to continue or attempt to leave gracefully.

"Go back North," someone called out.

"Yeah, git out of town now. We don't want you."

"Maybe we can help you along by riding you out on a rail."

The roar of talk grew even louder, most men standing now and yelling various insults and even threats.

The Reverend began to look alarmed, as well he might. George Patterson appeared frozen, obligated to defend the guest but not wanting to face the audience's fury. With a small smile, Barnwell Rhett strode forward and courteously asked Revered Fuller to stand aside.

"Gentlemen, gentlemen," he said over and over, his hands held up until the crowd quieted down. At last all had retaken their seats. "We must—we must—remember our manners. Reverend Fuller is both our brother and our guest." A rumble rose again. Rhett quieted it down. "We do not have to be impolite in order to firmly disagree. His sentiments are misguided, yes, impractical, yes, would lead us to ruin, yes. But let us be sensible, rational and reasonable in our disagreements."

With a sour look, Reverend Fuller realized his turn on the floor was quite over, and that in fact it might be more than politic to return to his brother's home without further fanfare. He quietly went to stand at the back of the church.

Although Henry was slated to speak next, now that Rhett had the floor he was not going to relinquish it for any purpose but his own. "We know in wise and sagacious Beaufort that there has been a call to remember our glorious forefathers and their patriotism. It has even been asserted that those of us who hate Northern interference and aggression are treasonous." A whisper went around the room. "I say those who make such claims should not hide behind anonymity. I say those who make such claims should stand up before us all and assert them to our face." The mumbling undertones grew louder. Rhett waited a moment, looking around with satisfaction. "Well, Mr. Eustace Woods, if one has convictions, one must be willing to speak for them like a man among other men. If you cannot do that, I suggest you speak in print no more." There was applause at this, though not a wide ripple.

"That sanctimonious prig," Henry muttered. "I'd like to horsewhip him to an inch of his life."

Rhett's eyes narrowed, expecting more enthusiasm than this, but he wasn't done. He had another, singularly powerful act at the ready, and like a showman he lost no time in unveiling it. He begged the gentleman to allow him to introduce a true patriot who had served his country for thirty years. He offered them not a turncoat, not moral chider, but a true defender of the South who for decades had constantly done his best to prevent Northern avarice and cupidity from overpowering Southern magnanimity and good nature. With immense gratitude for his service and awe of his towering achievements, Barnwell Rhett presented Senator John C. Calhoun.

Furious applause erupted. Calhoun was as close to a saint as South Carolina might ever have. Even if Henry had a mind to insist on the scheduled order of the agenda, there was no way he was going to toss the Palmetto state's savior from the lectern. Jasper was now ready to write the evening off as a total loss.

When the ovation finally subsided, a pin could be heard to drop in the room. Calhoun was tall, spindly, ill. His white hair, long and bushy, stuck out from his head. His eyes that burned with intensity at the best of times now seemed positively feverish and glared at the audience like a hawk hunting for prey.

"As I'm certain everyone here knows," Calhoun began in a voice that was surprisingly strong and piercing despite his infirmity, "I have long believed slavery to be a positive good, both for the South and for the entire human race. Though some may shift their opinions," he glanced just slightly at Reverend Fuller, "I have not and will not. In fact, I may say with truth that in few countries beyond the South is so much left to the share of the laborer, and so little exacted from him, or where there is more kind attention paid to him in sickness or infirmities of age. Compare our slaves' condition with the tenants of the poor houses in the more civilized portions of Europe—look at the sick, or the old and infirm slave, on one hand, in the midst of his family and friends, under the kind superintending care of his master and mistress. Compare that one's lot with the forlorn and wretched condition of the pauper in the poorhouse. The conclusion is clear: the condition of the slave in the South is superior in every way to the malnourished peasants in Europe and to the sickly, anemic wage earners in mills and foundries in the North."

There were many voices calling out, "here, here," and other indications of concurrence. Jasper began to tap his finger against his knee again.

"This isn't going well," Henry muttered. Jasper could only nod in agreement. It was hard to imagine it going worse.

Calhoun coughed the deep, wet cough of a consumptive and passed a handkerchief in front of his mouth before continuing on. "There are forces at work to deny us the liberty of our property and our way of life. Because these forces must be resisted at all costs, the time is coming when your united energies will be demanded for the struggle. Our way of life is not negotiable. We must defend it, or perish in the attempt. As such, I am drafting a Southern Address where I call all Southern states to join South Carolina to stand united in defiance of Northern aggression. Unless the South stands united, the North will not believe that we are in earnest in opposition to their encroachments, and such encroachments will continue to follow, one after another, until the work of abolition is finished. To convince them that we will not be moved in our adherence to our liberty, we must prove by our acts that we hold all other questions subordinate to it. Among other items, we must insist upon a law that requires the Northern states to return to us our property when it absconds from our reach. If we unite and prove ourselves in earnest, the North may be brought to a pause, and to a calculation of consequences. If it should not, nothing would remain for us but to stand up immovably in defense of rights involving our all that is most dear to us—our property, prosperity, equality, liberty, and safety. To do any less is cowardice, and in that case, gentlemen, we would deserve the consequences that would result. There are circumstances worse than war, and there are predicaments worse than revolution."

All the men around Jasper and Henry jumped to their feet, hooting and clapping. "This is madness," Henry said as he looked around him. "Pure and utter madness. It's not just Rhett anymore, Calhoun himself is threatening war. I never thought I'd see the day." When Jasper gave Henry a questioning look, Henry raised an eyebrow in return. "Jasper, you know I'd do almost anything for you, but if I went in front of this crowd right now, I'd end up tarred and feathered. The only one who might have any effect is Woods, but where is he?" Henry looked around. "Is he here, in the crowd? Why didn't he take Rhett on when he had the chance? Why didn't he speak?"

Jasper didn't have an answer to give. Calhoun, coughing, was making his way down the aisle toward the door. Unable to stomach anymore of Rhett who'd retaken the lectern, Jasper followed the senator out of the church, past the silent graves, catching up to him at the front gate as he waited for his carriage to be brought around.

"Senator," Jasper said. Calhoun turned to look at him with his feverish eyes. "This path, this course. It'll most likely lead to the utter destruction of everything we hold dear, not its preservation."

Calhoun looked at Jasper intently. "It's a risk I believe we must take."

"Other paths still are possible," Jasper said urgently. "Don't push for the return of fugitive slaves. It'll enrage the North beyond reason or compromise."

Calhoun's eyes grew distant. "Son, these past thirty years, I've done my absolute best to keep the Union together. I've compromised, I've cajoled, I've tricked, I've threatened, I've promised. I've even begged. Now the forces I tried so hard to keep at bay have been unleashed. How they will be resolved is beyond my scope and time. I leave it to you." His carriage pulled up, and Calhoun climbed inside. Leaning back, he shut his eyes with exhaustion as the pair of horses pulled him away.

Shouting and cheering emanated from the church behind Jasper. He couldn't bear to return. Instead, vacillating between rage and despair in the deepening dusk he wandered back in the direction of the Point and Villa d'Este. On reaching Carteret Street, he had to stop, his way blocked by a procession. Four Negro men, Jim one of them, carried on their shoulders a plain wooden coffin fashioned out of pine. It was well-built—Henry had seen to that. He would also later see to a small headstone. Behind the pallbearers, a hundred Negroes followed, singing a low, sad spiritual. Some of them held torches to light the way; others carried bits of broken pottery and mirrors to decorate the grave and ward off evil spirits. Some of them were children. None of them looked at him as they passed, not even Jim. Jasper was white. He was a master. He was responsible for this death just as much as every white man who tolerated a culture where patrols roamed the dark nights to ensure that the enslaved four-fifths of the population did not rise up and slaughter the other fifth. The procession would continue another mile to the slave graveyard in a boggy area off a tidal inlet. Though damp, there were trees there. It was peaceful. Hock would have rest, Jasper thought, and perhaps the angel Gabriel would enjoy his story about Adam and Eve. The slave spiritual echoed mournfully as the procession progressed further down the road, leaving Jasper behind in the dark, alone with his culpability and remorse.

He found himself at Cara's door.

"Mr. Wainwright, it's late," Cara said with surprise when he came into her parlor. She sat alone, reading by the light of a whale oil lamp. She frowned. "The meeting—wasn't it tonight?"

"It was," Jasper said.

"And the outcome?" she asked tentatively.

"An utter debacle. Woods should've been there. Perhaps he was, but he didn't speak up. Who is he, Cara? I've got to talk to him. He's our only hope now."

Cara rose and walked towards the front window near the piano, her hands clasped tightly behind her back. "I'm so sorry, Mr. Wainwright. I can't help you."

"You mean you choose not to help me. Who is he, Cara? Men respect him and would be willing to listen to him. With his erudition, he must be a gentleman of education and standing. Why does he shrink from assuming a mantle of leadership? So much is at stake here, I can hardly describe it."

Cara closed her eyes. "I knew this would happen. I can't do anything more for you. Please trust me when I say this."

He caught her arm and turned her towards him in the lamplight. "Why are you protecting him? What is he to you?"

"I can't tell you anything more," she said miserably.

"Is he married? Is that it?" He wanted to shake her. "Cara, is Eustace Woods your lover?"

She paled and drew back from him. "Is that what you think of me? How dare you."

He was too angry to apologize. "What other explanation is there?"

She winced and seemed to grow smaller. Her mouth opened slightly as if she wanted to speak but was somehow paralyzed. She gazed at him helplessly. "He doesn't exist," she said quietly at last.

"Cara, the entire future of the South is at risk. Your future. Your uncle's and aunt's and cousins' future. If we don't stop Barnwell Rhett, war and violence, bloodshed and ruin will be your lot."

"He doesn't exist," Cara said quietly again.

"Woods is the only one with the stature to take on Rhett. Hell, as of tonight, he has to take on Calhoun. No wonder the Governor avoided this meeting. Cara, if you say there's nothing between you and him, then I believe you, but we need Woods. Desperately. Let me persuade him."

"Eustace Woods does not exist," she said quietly once more.

This time, he heard her. He gazed back appalled, dumbfounded, uncomprehending. Finally, he tilted his head. "You wrote those letters?"

She nodded, her skin tight, her muscles tense. "I wanted to broaden people's vision, to help them see what was possible, how their lives, their livelihood, and their government could be better. I wanted my voice to matter. It was the only way."

"But it was a man's hand, nothing like yours. We saw one of the letters."

"I trained Minnie to write in my hand and in a hand very like Uncle Henry's," Cara admitted sadly. "She's clever that way." She raised her palms in a supplicating gesture. "I believed in you. I wanted to help you."

Jasper could only stare in perfect, horrific shock. Though all was quiet, he could hear the future of the South crashing around him in pieces.

Finally he spoke. "Jim was right all along. I've been wasting my time here in Beaufort." And he left.

Cara sank down on her settee slowly. Then, even more slowly, she put her pretty head in her lovely white hands and wished she'd never been born.

It was Winnie who was actively furious with Jasper for leaving Beaufort. Henry and Mary refused to disparage him, and Cara just changed the subject whenever he was brought up. But Winnie could tell Cara's heart was broken. She was so quiet, so peaked, so unlike herself. Why, she'd heard from Ceres that Cara was hardly even playing the piano. She was thinner, there were shadows under her eyes, she must not be eating or sleeping. Winnie had half a mind to bring her great-niece to her house to make sure some food got into the child, but Henry vetoed the idea.

"She'll be fine," he assured Winnie. To Mary, who had wept when they saw Jasper off on the early morning steamer after the disastrous Agricultural Society meeting, Henry promised his cousin would return, even though Jasper had told him no such thing. As Mary leaned her head onto her husband's shoulder for consolation, she felt a tad better. Henry was always right about these things.

How Cara felt, no one exactly knew, not even Mary. Cara would say nothing other than once, when asked point blank if Jasper had offered her marriage or any understanding of it, she stated unequivocally that at no time had he promised or alluded to anything, that his actions towards her, while friendly, had been entirely disinterested and honorable. And that was that. But Mary could she see her precious niece was miserable and couldn't help agree with her aunt that Jasper Wainwright had broken Cara Randall's heart.

"Hearts recover," Henry said if not buoyantly, then at least with imperturbability. "Besides, he's coming back." He didn't mention his certitude to his niece.

Beaufort itself mourned along with Cara, and was inclined to be more than a touch resentful at the hasty departure. The words "too good for Beaufort and too good for the South," were bandied about. His green tea and clandestine meetings at the Birch house were now remembered with irritability. And with Spit Jim suddenly gone, a source of medical care for the slaves they'd just grown comfortable with had disappeared as well. Good riddance to both, the consensus was. If they didn't want to stay, they weren't needed. Curiously, it seemed as if Eustace Woods was mourning Wainwright as well. At least no letters from him were printed in *The Charleston Courier*.

Weeks passed with no word from Sleety Pines, Jasper's next destination, but as Henry said, Jasper always was a terrible correspondent. Cara continued to say nothing. Henry continued to be confident of his return. Nearly woebegone, Mary wrote to Jasper's sister-in-law and received a polite, if guarded reply. Henry then received a three-sentence letter from Jasper indicating the fair health of his brother's family and himself.

Henry shook his head as he read it.

"What is it dear?" Mary asked over breakfast.

"He's fighting himself like all get out. But he'll come back. He will. Just wait and see."

Mary hoped Henry was right. The harvest was beginning, and he was now often away seeing to the puffy white bolls that meant new dresses and school tuitions and perhaps a trip to Europe for the family some day in the future.

As mid-September neared and Cara was about to turn twenty-one, it was Henry who suggested throwing a party for her. Cara did her best to demur her way out of it, but when Mary and Winnie took up the tack, she gave up and let them plan away. All she would need to do was attend, and she thought she could bear it. Her father was still taking the herbs Spit Jim had left behind, but without the treatment of needles, the pain was returning. On Dr. Goode's advice, he recommenced with laudanum. As the doses slowly grew larger, Cara watched with sadness while her father once again began to retreat from her. Dr. Goode patted her hand and didn't need to tell her the hours and days were now numbered, that the last decline had set in.

The sun cut a different path through the sky and the shadows grew longer as Cara took her walks to her mother's grave in St. Helena's churchyard. Minnie carried the basket without complaint but she was pressing on Cara. Her time was coming, too.

On the night of the party celebrating her birth, Cara dutifully let Minnie dress her in the pale blue silk frock Aunt Winnie had chosen. She patiently allowed her hair to be curled and pinned into place; she obediently put on the lovely new necklace Aunt Mary and Uncle Henry had given her as a birthday present. When the carriage came, she allowed herself to be handed into it, and at the party she accepted well wishes and even danced until she just couldn't stand it anymore. During a break in the music she escaped and went downstairs into the garden to gaze at the dark river. As she stood alone near the seawall hugging her arms in the cool evening air, a steamer went past, quite tardy in its arrival from Charleston. Boats were always coming and going but she would remain in Beaufort. It was as if this land that had loved her, raised her, nurtured her—and that she undeniably loved in return—had also placed an invisible manacle around her ankle, keeping her bound to it whatever her desires and wishes. The outside world was not for her.

Mary and Henry stood on the second floor of the covered piazza looking down at their niece in the dark garden, the light of the nearly full moon reflecting off the water in a shimmering line. The curves and folds of Cara's pale blue silk dress glowed ethereally in the night scene.

"Poor dear," Mary said. "When will she get over this?"

"She'll be all right," Henry assured her. "She's young. Next February in Charleston she'll find a young man, just wait and see."

So now even Henry thought Jasper wasn't coming back. This was the first time her husband's faith in his own prognosis had ever been shaken. Mary leaned her head against his shoulder sadly. She was in the middle of her pregnancy now, and though her health was good, she felt, well, just tired sometimes. It'd been an eventful, sometimes difficult summer, and Jasper's departure had glazed Beaufort with a varnish of melancholy that wouldn't wash off however many parties and fetes they threw. "That's odd," she said, looking off into the distance. "Is that the last steamer from Charleston? It's getting in awfully late."

The steamer sailed by like a lit palace floating on the dark river. Henry checked his pocket watch by the light of a candle protected in a hurricane glass. "Three hours late. Must've gotten stuck on one of the shoals. I keep telling Bunter they need to dredge the route more often."

The music started back up, prompting Henry and Mary to drift inside to attend to their guests. All was merry as the dancing began again. Henry had found a replacement for Hock who wasn't nearly as good but acceptable enough. As the two fiddlers finished a reel and then began a waltz, Mary got the start of her life when she looked up to see Jasper suddenly in front of her. He wore travelling clothes—a dark plum waistcoat, houndstooth checked pants and a brown frock coat—a contrast to the other men's white cravats and black tailcoats.

"Where's Cara?" he asked.

Mary vaguely gestured. "Out in the garden. Jasper, when did you—"

But he was already gone, leading Mary to wonder if she'd dreamt him, or if pregnancy made one prone to hallucinations.

"Mr. Wainwright," Cara said, more than startled to see him beside her. "When did you get into town?"

"Just now," he said, staring intently. No, he seemed to be glaring, Cara thought—as if he were angry with her. Had he come to berate her further over Eustace Woods? She began to shrink back, but he caught her arm. "I tried to stay away. God knows I tried." A muscle flexed in his jaw as if he were irritated.

"Why did you return?" she asked hesitantly.

"For you," he said.

And then she was in arms and he was kissing her, holding her tightly, asking without speech things of her no one had ever asked before. She couldn't breathe, she couldn't think, the intensity was overwhelming, narcotic, elating. He wanted her. She hadn't known, she hadn't known . . . But as the embrace continued, though his passion was clear, something niggled at her. There were words that hadn't been said, words she needed to hear before she could continue. Even with him. She pulled away, breathing hard as she faced him in the moonlight, hopeful yet wary.

"What's the matter?" he said. "Have I been gone so long? Is there someone else?"

"Of course not," she answered, startled.

"Well, then—" He took her in his arms once more, ignoring her efforts to wrestle free. "Cara, I'm not one of your county boys you need to be coy with." And he was kissing her again, she was out of breath, her heart pounding, her body responding to his beyond her will until she was nearly delirious. But when his hand reached to her breast, she again remembered what hadn't been said, remembered it sharply, and before Jasper knew what had happened, she'd wrenched away, gathered her skirts and was running up the stairs to the front porch.

He blinked without comprehension. "Cara?"

Why had she left? He followed her up to the ballroom. When he arrived, he saw that she had stationed herself next to the greatest dragon in Southdom: Winifred Pickens. It was then that Jasper realized just how badly he had miscalculated the difference between a Madame in France and a Miss in South Carolina.

Cara hadn't told Winnie of Jasper's return, she hadn't said anything, just sat down next to her aunt in an obvious state of perturbation. But now that, as she fixed her evil eye on him, Winifred knew the source of Cara's distress, she would ensure Jasper Wainwright would no more get near her grandniece than he would jump over the moon with the aid of little white mice.

Henry was extremely pleased to see his cousin, clapping him on the back. "You devil, you, sneaking up on us like this. But we're delighted to have you any way we can get you." He noticed the direction of Jasper's attention. "Does Cara know you're here?"

"She does."

"Why is she sitting over there by Winnie? She should be dancing."

"It appears she's upset with me," Jasper said.

"What did you do? You just got here."

"I think," Jasper said slowly, "I think for women actions don't always speak louder than words."

Henry started laughing. "Well, you fool, go apologize. She'll forgive you with enough abasement and humble pie."

Jasper eyed the formidable Aunt, a Gorgon more fearsome than the guardians of the Chinese underworld, Ox-Head and Horse-Face. "I don't think I'm going to be allowed anywhere near her."

"There's more than one way to skin a catfish." Henry nodded at Professor Randall who was dozing in a wingback chair in a corner. He was present at the festivity, however feebly, to help celebrate his daughter reaching her majority. "Have him invite you to dinner tomorrow."

The advice was good. Cara was mortified when she heard the next morning who their guest would be that afternoon. "Oh, Father, you didn't."

"What?" Professor Randall said hazily. "I thought you liked Mr. Wainwright. Should I cancel, dear?"

Cara bit her lip. "No," she said with a sigh. She would just have to manage it.

Chapter Twelve

When Jasper arrived the next afternoon, Cara made sure her father was in the parlor to receive his guest. The long-retired professor had purposefully not taken his dose of laudanum so he could enjoy Jasper's company but was experiencing some pain because of it. Still, over dinner they had a lively discussion about the latest British maneuvers to develop their recently occupied territory of Hong Kong into a trading center and the reaction of the Qing government to this incursion on its sovereignty. Though such a subject would normally have engrossed Cara, she maintained an arctic silence that conveyed her indifference to her guest and his sentiments. Glancing at her from time to time, Jasper received barely an acknowledgement of his presence in the room and so had to content himself with the attentions of his host.

As the meal came to a close, the Professor had to apologize and excuse himself. Concerned, Cara accompanied him upstairs, leaving Jasper on his own in the dining room. After a time, Ceres, whose graying head showed she was getting on in years, shuffled in to clear the table. As she took his plate, she gave Jasper an odd glance that prompted him to wander off into the parlor. He inspected a book on a side table, leafed through the music on the piano, and then stood looking out the front window at the house across the street that had gone empty all summer when there were families in the boarding house who would have paid to let it. The minutes ticked by on the longcase clock in the corner of the room. Still Jasper was alone. As the shadows cast by the waning sun began to slant emphatically, he noticed a drawer open in the desk along one wall. Curious, he went over and pulled it out an inch further, revealing a stack of postal cards tied with a ribbon. Picking the stack up, he saw that the cards were all from him. Every one he had sent her from across the continents and across the years.

Cara appeared in the parlor doorway. He spun away from the desk. "Oh," she said unenthusiastically. "You're still here."

"Miss Randall," he said, pushing the desk drawer shut behind him. "Will you grant me the favor of allowing me to apologize?"

Cara pressed her lips together as she crossed the room to pick up a vase of flowers on the mantle. "I see no reason to discuss anything," she said lifting her chin while contemplating a different spot for the late summer roses.

"As I said, I request it as a courtesy. You must permit me. I won't desist until you do."

Clearly annoyed, Cara sat down stiffly on one end of the settee. "As you wish. Speak."

He gestured to the other end of the settee. "May I?"

Cara eyed the ceiling. "If you must."

Jasper sat down, remembering just how good she'd been at freezing him out when he'd first met her. "Cara—"

She gave him an extremely cross look.

"I mean, Miss Randall. I abjectly apologize for my behavior last night. I'm afraid I was overcome with emotion."

"Emotion," Cara repeated with severe disbelief.

"Emotion," Jasper confirmed. "You see, yesterday I wasn't supposed to come to Beaufort at all. I was supposed to be in New York."

"New York?"

"Two days ago I was in Philadelphia. I took a train to Washington, then one to Richmond, another one to Raleigh, and then another to Charleston."

"You traveled all night?"

"And then I caught the last steamer to Beaufort. See these clothes? They're the same ones I wore last night. I don't think my trunk made it past Richmond. I forgot to get a porter."

"Spit Jim couldn't do it?"

Jasper shook his head. "He stayed north. He's on his way to Boston right now."

Cara decided to be less interested in what he was telling her. Clasping her hands together, she looked decidedly out the window.

"Miss Randall," he began again. When she looked back over at him, she was startled to see that he was no longer on the settee but down on one knee before her. "I've not stopped thinking about you for one moment since I left six weeks ago. I know I was horrible beyond words to you that night, and I profoundly hope you can forgive my ignorance and stupidity. You are the most extraordinary creature I've ever met, and I am drawn to you by an agency I've long tried to deny. No more. I am here to request the considerable honor of your hand in marriage. I adore you and lay my heart, very humbly, at your feet." He didn't say like nineteen others have done before me, but he certainly thought it and was quite in doubt of the outcome of his own suit.

She looked as if she couldn't believe what she was hearing.

"Miss Randall?" She still seemed too perplexed to speak. "May I get up?"

"Of—of course," she said.

With relief Jasper sat himself back on the settee, but he wasn't comforted by her gaze that was both stern and incredulous, as if he'd just told her he was planning on redecorating a church with the aid of blasting powder. "Before you give me an answer," he continued, "there is more I must say." Her expression inscrutable, she nodded for him to go on. "My history is a long and difficult one. There are many particulars, but three items you must know in depth. The first is that I cannot live in the South. If you were to marry me, we would go many places, we would, perhaps, see and live in much of the world, but this is the one place I cannot stay. So I would take you away from everything and everyone you've ever known and loved. Everything. We could visit, but only for short periods. While alteration of one's life is a usual requirement of marriage, I'm aware that change of this magnitude is difficult to expect of anybody."

Cara absorbed the information impassively. "I see, Mr. Wainwright. That is item number one. You may continue to number two."

Jasper wasn't at all sure how well this was going. "The second matter is that I also can no longer participate in the system of slavery. I can't, and I won't. So if you were to marry me, when your father's slaves came into your possession, they would have to be freed."

"Would the lands and houses have to be sold as well?" she asked dispassionately, as if property settlement were all she had in mind.

"Not necessarily," Jasper said, "but of course we wouldn't live in them."

Cara nodded slightly. "And condition number three?"

Jasper winced. Condition? "The third item, or condition, if you will, is of a more personal nature. Perhaps you remember Madame de Saintonge's parting words to me—that though I looked satisfactory on the outside, on the inside I was broken like a watch that couldn't keep time? Well, she was right, though in a different respect than she intended. I believe I am capable of love and great attachment. However, as a young man, I had egregious difficulties with liquor. I drank so much, in fact, that I nearly destroyed my liver as well as my life. I now cannot drink. I now must not drink. But every day it calls to me, and every day I want to drink. Every day it's a choice and a struggle. As my wife, you'd necessarily be party to that struggle, though I'd hope to shield you from it as much as I could. But there's a risk that one day I might fail to persevere in my efforts. In fact, it's one of the reasons I must leave the South—the call here is stronger than anywhere and hardest to resist. So it's only fair that you know what you'd be letting yourself in for. I'm afraid it's what destroyed my first wife."

"Mr. Wainwright," Cara said sharply, "she died in childbirth."

"There are reasons, and there are reasons," Jasper said heavily. "I was there. I know what I did. I've suffered much for it, and, I hope, learned something in the process. So you now know the risks and provisos attached to this proposal. My heart is yours, and so is the decision of whether our fates are to be entwined. I can't promise that we'd live as grandly as Sea Island planters. You'd likely have a few less dresses, definitely fewer servants, and while I'd make sure you'd always have a piano, it might not be as grand as the instrument in this room. Still, with some care we'd be comfortable enough."

He fell into silence looking at her, wondering. He couldn't glean her disposition in the least, though he did deduce she was likely to spurn any physical advances he might be inclined to offer. She sat calmly, her hands in her lap, gazing off attentively towards the window as if an invisible symphony played outside that only she could hear.

At last she spoke. "Mr. Wainwright," she said with the briefest of glances at him, "I am conscious of the honor you do with me your proposal. I ask you to give me time to consider it."

Jasper blinked. "Of course. Take all the time you need."

"You may return tomorrow at noon," she said primly.

Jasper rose from the couch to collect his hat and gloves. "All right. I . . . I look forward to it."

When Jasper returned to Villa d'Este, Henry was waiting on the front porch trying to judge from his cousin's posture what his niece's answer had been. He couldn't tell. Jasper seemed . . . perplexed? "So, how'd it go?"

"I'm not sure."

"Did she accept?"

"She told me she'd tell me tomorrow."

Henry blinked, disconcerted. "But she didn't refuse you, anyway. Let's take it as a good sign. She turned all the others down at the starting gate."

Jasper sat down beside his cousin and looked out at the late afternoon river. When Couts brought him a cup of green tea, Jasper thanked him and leaned his head on his fist. "Women . . . women are confusing, Henry."

"Aren't they," Henry agreed. He wanted to go throttle Cara's little neck, that's what he wanted to do. Here, Jasper had finally proposed—it'd taken the whole damn summer—and now she couldn't give the man an answer. That evening, up in their bedroom, Mary couldn't explain it either. Her belly round beneath her nightgown, she cuddled next to Henry in bed, his arm around her as moonlight shone through the gaps in the curtains. The air was finally cooler at night. Lovely sleeping weather.

"I know she adores him," Mary said sleepily. "But she's so stubborn. Who knows what she might get into her head—that he'd be better off without her, or some such thing."

Henry shook his head. "We gave her too much freedom growing up. There's never been such a headstrong cuss in six counties."

"But you were right," Mary said with a drowsy smile. "He came back." Henry was always right about these things.

At noon, Cara told Jasper she didn't have an answer yet and could he please return at eleven? She clarified that yes, she did mean that evening, not the next morning.

"Aren't you going to the Witherspoon party?" he asked.

Cara shook her head. "I'll be staying home. You'll slip away. Unnoticed."

"Cara—"

"Miss Randall," she corrected him.

"Miss Randall, this makes no sense."

"It does to me. If you want an answer, come at eleven."

Henry frowned. "What do you mean, she didn't tell you? When's she going to?"

"I don't know," Jasper said. "Maybe never." Maybe this was her way of getting revenge over Eustace Woods, he thought. It was possible. And definitely an effective torment. It was killing him not to know. He certainly couldn't tell Henry he'd agreed to visit her at eleven in the evening. Henry would shoot him.

Henry squinted at the river a long moment. "If she doesn't tell you by tomorrow night, I'll give her a piece of my mind. But this is delicate. Sensitive. And not entirely unpromising. She's leading you on for a reason, we just don't know what the reason is. She's a tricky business, that girl." Henry glanced sideways at Jasper. "You can see why I want her married. Then she'll be your problem and not mine. Think you can handle her?"

Jasper laughed. "To be honest, I have no idea."

Jasper left the party with little regret since social functions had become remarkably tedious without Cara. In addition, all of Beaufort seemed intent on snubbing him for various offenses he'd no doubt committed, were impossible to apologize for, and about which he cared little.

When he reached Cara's house on her dark street, no lights shone from the windows. Before he even knocked she opened the door, a candle in her hand. Her hair was down, and she wore a shawl wrapped around the shoulders of her muslin nightgown. She looked strange, beautiful, a creature of the night. Putting her finger to her lips, she shushed him when he tried to speak, then closed the door gently and indicated silently that he should take off his shoes. He did but he had a bad feeling about this. A very bad feeling. With her own feet bare, she led him up the dark stairs that creaked slightly under their weight. What did she want to show him so late at night? He couldn't guess. It was incomprehensible. As she ascended the stairs ahead of him, she was smaller, more delicate than he remembered, almost diaphanous in the glow of the candle flame. And so entirely perfect. Her rich, auburn hair cascaded in waves down her back to her waist.

After she led him into a room and closed the door, she set her candle down on a table. The room opened to the double story piazza in the front of the house, but the windows were shut and the curtains drawn. He saw a bed against one wall of the room as well as a dressing table that held a looking glass and various other feminine accoutrements.

"Cara, what are we doing in your bedroom?" he said quietly but urgently. "You absolutely know I shouldn't be here."

"You're here because I invited you, Mr. Wainwright."

"Will you give me your answer and free me from this torment?"

"After, Mr. Wainwright. After."

"After what?"

She seemed nervous. She took a breath and reached up to kiss him. He succumbed, but just for a moment. "Cara, are you going to marry me?"

"There's only one way to find out." She reached up to him again.

It was even harder resisting her this time, and he kissed her for at least minute in a kind of hungry anguish before pushing her away by the shoulders. "Do you delight in torture? Give me your answer and let me go."

"After," she said.

With a glance at the bed, Jasper began to have an idea of what she was talking about. "What are you saying? Cara, do you even know what happens between a man and a woman?"

She took a shaky breath, but her gaze was unwavering. "I expect you can show me."

Jasper shut his eyes. "I know I haven't treated you like I should have, but this is more than I can bear." He started for the door.

"Mr. Wainwright—"

Jasper turned and was instantly paralyzed. Cara had taken off her nightgown to reveal her bare body underneath. He was rooted to the floor at the sight. She walked towards him, reached her arms around his neck, and began to kiss him again. "Oh Cara," he whispered, taking her to him and kissing her ear, her neck, her mouth, pulling her closer and closer, wanting every inch of her, just as he had every second of every day since he'd first seen her with that ridiculous squirrel. "You *are* going to marry me, aren't you?"

She began to unknot his cravat. "I'll give you my answer afterwards, Mr. Wainwright."

After putting on his shoes at the bottom of the stairs, Jasper let himself out the front door and closed it softly behind him. He was part way down the dark street when a shadow separated itself from a tree trunk.

"Just what do you think you're doing?" It was Henry. Pistol in hand.

"Shoot me if you want, Henry," Jasper said, "but she just agreed to marry me."

"She did?" Henry nearly hooted with glee and slapped Jasper on the back with his free hand. "Well done. So that's what took you an hour? More pleading entreaties? Why were you in her bedroom?"

Jasper glanced at Henry. He'd never in his life uttered a lie to Henry that Henry hadn't seen through, so there was no use starting now, even if he wasn't going to like the truth. "It was more than just entreaties."

"What do you mean 'more'?" Henry said suspiciously.

"Just what you're thinking," Jasper said walking along. "That's what happened."

"You . . . you low-down, despicable, two-faced, son of a—"

"She wouldn't give me an answer otherwise. She honestly wouldn't."

"Oh, that's supposed to justify it? I am so tempted to put a bullet through you I can barely control myself."

Jasper shrugged. "All right."

Henry was furious. "All my threats, all my warnings. Did they mean nothing?"

Jasper lifted a hand. "Henry, she got me to the point where I just didn't care if you shot me. That's all I can say."

This took him aback. "That little cuss." Henry stopped aiming his gun in Jasper's direction, an improvement from Jasper's point of view.

He frowned as his thoughts veered off on a tangent. "You don't think she's done this before—I mean, with anyone else?"

"If it makes you feel better," Jasper said, "I can assure you with certainty she has not."

Henry glared at him. "My finger is so hankering to pull this trigger."

"As you wish," Jasper said, but he was far too happy for Henry to be angry with him for long.

Mary was shocked. "She invited him into her bedroom? What was she thinking? You mean they . . ."

"Well," Henry said fondly, "as I remember the two of us didn't wait for our wedding day either."

"Yes, but it wasn't the same night I agreed to marry you. What could've gotten into her?"

"Jasper said she wanted to be sure there was no going back."

"But she knows Jasper's honorable. He'd never break a betrothal."

"The second thoughts she was worried about were hers. This way she can't entertain any."

"Certainly not," Mary agreed. "Those two are going to the altar now if it kills them."

The short-lived snubbing of Jasper Wainwright was over. With a bona fide engagement to Cara Randall, his star scaled the airy heights of Beaufort once more. Not that Jasper particularly cared, but it did make the town more ready to cast a blind eye to his somewhat frequent visits to Miss Randall's house at startlingly improper hours. After so many proposals and so many years of anxiety on the parts of her aunts, Miss Randall was now settled and so happy and so exceedingly in love that no one in town could help but smile when the affianced couple were seen together devoted as two Carolina turtledoves, not even Johnny Patterson's mother. Besides, Johnny had become engaged to a nice girl in Charleston, daughter of a factor, a rich one. He was doing quite well for himself, thank you for asking.

The wedding was set for the end of October. Jasper had wanted it earlier, but men always did. Naturally Cara's trousseau couldn't be completed in any shorter time, so the date of October 30th was set. Since Cara would need at least two trips to Charleston for fittings, it would all be rushed as it was. The couple planned a wedding journey up north and then on to Europe. It all sounded terribly romantic. There was only one dark spot on the horizon, and that was the health of Cara's father which seemed to decline each week.

After one of Dr. Goode's visits, Cara anxiously consulted Jasper in her parlor. Her father would probably not last until the New Year, she said in a quiet voice. Was it possible to delay their wedding journey until things were, well, settled with him?

"Of course," Jasper said, pulling her close. "Of course we won't leave while your father's ill. Should we delay the wedding?"

"No," she said, shaking her head with her forehead against his chest. "I want him to be there for it. I don't think he'll last long afterwards though." She looked up at him, her eyes tearful. "Thank you for understanding."

Jasper smiled fondly back but now realized with some unease he was stuck in the South for another four months. Still, the time spent with Cara was so idyllic and his contentment so nearly perfect, he was confident he could soldier on with his green tea for the duration. Though staving off cravings might be harder without Jim and his needles around, he would just have to endure.

"Where is Spit Jim, anyway?" Henry said one evening after supper when he was both home from supervising harvests and able to obtain a fraction of Jasper's attention. Mary and Cara were in the parlor with Winnie, conferring about wedding plans like generals strategizing battlefield maneuvers.

"Boston," Jasper said. He glanced sideways at Henry as he readied himself to launch a conversation long dreaded but necessary. "With his family."

"What do you mean, with his family? His family is all in Sleety Pines."

Jasper looked down at his cup. "Not any more. I freed them."

"You what?" Henry's voice rose alarmingly.

"I freed all of my slaves, Henry," Jasper said quietly. "All who would go. That's what I was doing the six weeks I was away. Nineteen are in Philadelphia now; twenty-two are in Boston. For the rest, I transferred ownership to my brother."

"Why?" Henry said incredulously. "That's forty thousand dollars up in smoke when you could've used them here at Smullen Point."

"I promised Jim years ago I'd free his family. It's why I came back to South Carolina. Henry, you should know this wedding trip Cara and I are planning—it's not a trip at all. It's meant to be permanent. I don't intend to ever live here again."

Henry's face turned wooden as he took in the news. Slowly he drew in a long breath, his nostrils flaring as he inhaled. "Did Cara agree to this?" he asked.

After assuring him she had, Jasper could almost see the great construct of his cousin's mind absorbing, thinking, switching mental gears. If brains had been made out of wheels and cogs, the machinery of Henry's would've filled the basilica of St. Peter's in Rome.

"You're not planning on selling anything, are you?" Henry finally asked casually.

"Not right away," Jasper answered. "But eventually. Naturally if we sell any land, it'd be to you."

Henry nodded. "Good. For now, then, let's just leave all the arrangements as they are. I'll continue to run Smullen Point and pay for the Professor's living expenses. By the way, you might not want to spread the news around about freeing your slaves. It wouldn't be too popular, not to mention someone might contradict the legality of it."

Jasper had told no one but Cara. His brother knew, to be sure, and had been less than pleased, but since he'd been told in advance of Jasper's intentions, he hadn't argued much either. In general, Jasper thought Henry took the news of him and Cara leaving rather well. He'd half expected remonstrances and emotional blackmail to get him to stay. At a minimum, he thought Henry would reprise his tune of Jasper reforming the South from the inside out as a planter, one of their own. Since the disastrous meeting in August, all efforts towards agricultural reform had been suspended, and Jasper didn't have the heart to rekindle them. It was clear that Beaufort and South Carolina were too far gone for him to have any real chance of affecting, even if he had the stamina to argue, cajole and persuade year after year, and even if he were confident he could resist the pull of the bottle. He resigned himself to watching the South's future unfold, however painfully, from afar. Henry and some of the other men did comment that they regretted the loss of Eustace Woods in print, concurring among themselves that

Rhett must have scared him off with his challenge at the Agricultural Society meeting. It was a pity, Henry sighed. With Wood's absence, *The Charleston Courier* held little sense anymore.

A week later, Mary and Winnie were at Cara's house supervising while Minnie, a competent seamstress, was fitting Cara for some nightgowns and undergarments. Jasper and Henry were companionably on the porch again in the same chairs, Jasper taking looks now and again at Henry's whiskey and wishing the smell of liquor wasn't so penetrating.

"Isn't it remarkable how Cara is the spit and image of her mother?" Henry asked conversationally. "It's too bad there was never a portrait painted of Annabelle so everyone could see the resemblance. Of course, that was back in the day before daguerreotypes."

Jasper smiled. "Cara's the best kind of portrait—a living one."

"Yes, our children are our true legacy, aren't they?" Henry commented. He glanced at Jasper, remembering too late that this might be a sore subject. Jasper just waved a hand. Henry went on. "Cara was Annabelle's pride and joy. She doted on her that first year before she got ill." He squinted at the river. "Annabelle wasn't entirely happy with the Professor."

"Why do you say that?" Jasper said. He'd never heard that rumor.

"They had trouble having children. Not unlike Winnie and the Senator."

"Well, they had Cara, didn't they? And that was only a few years after they married as I recall. So it worked out. It's a shame she died so young."

Henry sipped his whiskey. "There was a cholera scare at college the year after you left. It turned out to be nothing, but they still sent us all away for three weeks. Most of the lads went to Charleston, but I decided to come home. It was winter and hardly anyone was in town. As you know, Annabelle and the Professor stayed year around. I was going to spend a night at our house on Craven Street and then head off to see my father at Birch Hill in the morning when Annabelle saw me at a shop and invited me to dinner. The professor was away in Richmond at some scholastic gathering, and she hadn't wanted to accompany him."

Jasper frowned. "Henry, does this story have a point?"

"I hardly knew her really. I remembered that you'd been sweet on her when we were boys and that was all. I was eighteen, full grown, handsome enough, I suppose. Virile, if I say so myself."

"Henry, you're not saying—"

"I came for dinner; I stayed two days. Two exceptionally pleasant days, I can assure you. Then I left for Birch Hill. When I saw her again, she acted as if it'd never happened. Ceres knows, though; she was there. But even twenty years later, she wouldn't sully her mistress's good name for the world."

"Are you implying that—"

"I don't think Annabelle really wanted to be unfaithful; what she wanted was a child. I was available and the lowest risk she could find. After all, if she used one of her servants, she'd end up with a mulatto."

"You're telling me," Jasper said with incredulity, "that you're Cara's father?"

"I'm ninety-nine percent certain I am," Henry said. "The timing fits. And she's like me in so many ways. Anyway, I thought you should know."

Jasper sat silently, stunned by the news. "So Cara's my cousin?"

"Once removed, I suppose," Henry agreed. Then he turned to Jasper with some energy. "Mary must never find out. It all happened before I started courting her, but she wouldn't understand, to say the least. If you want to tell Cara, wait until I'm dead."

"How can you be sure I'll outlive you? Well, it does explain it. Everyone always puts your overseeing of Cara down to doing your duty by Mary's family, but that's not it at all. You love her to bits, just like your sons."

"Yes," Henry said. "I love her to bits. But she'll never know why."

The autumn days were some of the pleasantest Jasper could remember. Parties were held for them, and he didn't mind attending because he and Cara could dance together almost the entire evening with everyone around them wishing them joy and happiness. During the days he would listen to her play for hours at a stretch, and then they would talk, Cara seemingly determined to know of every nook and cranny of his life. And then there were the evenings when Cara invited him to visit quite late . . .

"Henry says your father was a monster," Cara whispered as she lay in his arms in her bed, her hair undulating over the pillow while the moonlight shone on her ivory skin. Jasper couldn't gaze enough, couldn't drink enough of her in. In the hushed midnight hours, there was an intimacy between them so perfect, it was as if they created their own Eden outside all space and time. Perhaps these stolen hours were risky, but Professor Randall was too insensible from laudanum to know what went on in his house at night. Ceres was undoubtedly aware of Jasper's nocturnal visits and gave him some interesting looks when she served him meals when he dined there. Still, she didn't interfere. Neither did Henry, who knew just as well as Ceres what was going on when Jasper returned to Villa d'Este at two in the morning.

"Not a monster," Jasper said. "He was a sick man. That's what the drinking is, you know. A sickness."

"But you control your drinking through your will," Cara said. "Your father could have, too."

"He did, to some extent, until my mother died. That's when everything fell apart." She'd been a graceful, cultured woman, and however difficult her husband had been, she'd manage to shelter Jasper, his older brother, and his younger sister from any ill effects. In fact, Jasper had few memories of his father while his mother had been alive. "I think he must've been in his study or travelling much of the time," Jasper mused. "Or maybe she kept us in the nursery and the school room, out of harm's way. But when she died not long after my sister—well, I was an out-of-control eight-years-old boy, missing my mother, scaring up trouble however I could, and my father couldn't stand it. I'm told I favor my mother, which probably made it worse because I reminded him of her. My brother was sent away to school. I don't know why my father didn't send me away as well. Maybe he wanted a victim close at hand."

"He beat you?" Cara said quietly.

"Beat, hit, kicked, punched. He had a variety of options." Jasper paused, remembering. "He even got ready to whip me once, until our overseer, Bill Chisholm, reminded him that a gentleman couldn't have such scars. Bill was a good man, a smart man. He used the one argument that worked with my father, because no matter how much my father hated me, he couldn't bear me not to be considered a gentleman." Bill had rescued Jasper a time or two when George Wainwright had been drunk to madness, but it was the Negro servants who had protected him the most, kept him out of the way, even positively hiding him at times in their cabins. Jasper began to feel more at home on the slave street than his own house. Jim's mother had been especially kind to him in her brooding, impassive way, seeing he had food, tending to his bruises, mending his clothes. He would spend the night curled up in front of the fire in her small cabin with her other children, a flimsy slave blanket over his shoulders. And he'd developed a friendship with her eldest son. "Jim felt sorry for me, I think. He sort of adopted me. Let me tag along while he fished and did chores. It's funny. When I was ten years old, I told him I'd free him some day. Didn't I have nerve."

"And he held you to it?" she asked.

Jasper shook his head. "I owe Jim my life six times over. His labor paid for my education; he was the one who dragged me out of Sleety Pines and put me on a boat for Asia. He was the one who got the liquor out of my system—I can't even tell you how ill I was—and he was the one who found a Chinese doctor in Macao who restored my liver, or at least got it half-working again. He's the one who nursed me through the Dengue fever in Mombasa; he's the one that gave me years of treatments that repaired my liver so I can function like a normal person. Freeing Jim wasn't an obligation. I could no more have kept him a slave than I could keep you from thinking with that clever, inventive mind of yours." He leaned over to kiss her.

She traced her fingers along his moustache. "What made your father finally send you to Beaufort?"

"My uncle always had a tender heart for my mother. In her memory, he came to visit, saw I was getting no education, and played the 'gentleman' card with my father. He took me back with him to Beaufort, and I repaid him by getting into more trouble than Henry ever thought of on his worst day. My uncle was beside himself, but he was smart enough to write to Bill Chisholm for advice, not my father. Chisholm somehow arranged for Jim to come to Beaufort. Once Jim got here, he told me I was a fool, didn't I know he'd give his right arm for what I was busy pissing away? After that, I was conscientious with my studies and did my best to teach Jim everything I knew at night after he'd finished work for the day. I think at first it was to rebel against my father, but then—I don't know—we were just companionable. And it seemed so reasonable he would want to know everything I was learning. My uncle knew what was going on. He didn't seem to mind."

"How about Uncle Henry?" Cara asked.

"Henry?" Jasper smiled, remembering. "From the very first day I got to Beaufort, even with all my crazy, outrageous behavior, we were inseparable, fishing and sailing, swimming and hunting, coming home tired and filthy from our adventures. It was a boy's paradise, except that the mischief I was constantly getting into made the townsfolk of Beaufort threaten to send me packing. Henry was always a good talker and did his darnedest to coax me out of my stunts, but I had such a passion for recklessness, even he couldn't control it. He knew in order for me to stay in Beaufort I had to behave better. Once he saw that Jim's influence on me would do the trick, he accepted him getting an education as a fair trade. Most evenings all three of us were in the same room, studying together. Even as a boy, Henry was pragmatic and understood the intricacies of human behavior better than anyone I've ever known."

"But Jim didn't go with you to South Carolina College," she observed.

"No, my father demanded him back for the fields of Sleety Pines." Jasper shook his head. "I shouldn't have let him go. I shouldn't have gone back either." Jasper had returned home the summer before his first term at college. His brother was finished with his education but was in Columbia, studying law for some unknown reason, and courting his future wife. Chisholm had passed away, and the new man, Pinter, was fond of the whip in the fields. The slaves hated him, their misery palpable. Henry's father went on binges of drinking so furious Jasper would find him passed out on the staircase. "You'd think he would've done us all a favor and broken his neck, but he never did," Jasper said. The house was in disrepair and unkempt; his father barely spoke to him. Indirectly Jasper learned he'd fallen into debt. It was basically living hell. The only grace was he was too big to beat anymore. But the slaves, that was another matter.

There'd been one slave, Possum, who'd been born with a club foot and couldn't work as fast or as hard as the others. Chisholm had always given him half-tasks, but Pinter had been inclined to single him out, blame him when work hadn't been completed as promised. In this way, Possum had been called to Jasper's father's attention. That summer George Wainwright grew obsessed with Possum's deformity, declaring it was the mark of the devil, and after a night of hard drinking and contemplating his hatred of the world, he would whip the poor slave with the justification of driving sin out. After the whipping, he ordered that Possum be left tied to the whipping post until the sun went down. No one was supposed to give him food or drink, but of course they did, while his father slept off his spirits, and Possum survived to be beaten another day. It was an appalling spectacle that Jasper couldn't bear to witness. Finally he challenged his father over it after dinner while his father started a new bottle of brandy. His father responded by hurling empty bottles, which were plentiful, at him. In the process, a candle fell catching the tablecloth on fire along with his father's shirt. George Wainwright received a nasty burn on his arm before Jasper put the fire out, but he refused to have salve applied, preferring liquor as his medicine of choice. After drinking much of the night, George Wainwright got Possum out of his cabin, tied him to the whipping post at four in the morning, and whipped him until the blood ran. Then he sat in a chair under a tree with a pistol and a bottle of whiskey and didn't move. No one could help Possum as the sun beat down, everyone praying the master would pass out. Even Pinter had enough humanity to object. When Jasper's father responded by pointing his gun at him, the overseer slunk away.

"Why would he be that cruel?" Cara asked.

"It was madness," Jasper said simply. "And there was no one to stop him." Not Jim, he was out in the fields, driven by the whip. By noon, Possum had collapsed and hung limp and unconscious from the ropes binding his arms. Only sixteen years old, Jasper walked up behind his father and knocked him out with a bottle. It was too late for Possum; he died within the hour. Jasper got his things together and left for South Carolina College before his father regained consciousness.

"I never saw him again. While I was at college, behaving badly, drinking and dueling, my brother went home and took control of things. My father never recovered from that summer. He carried on with his drinking but his health was broken, and he kept to his room. My brother was smart enough to get a different overseer, and things improved at Sleety Pines. When I was expelled from South Carolina College, my brother even talked my father into accepting my uncle's arrangements to send me north. He managed to send Jim off to be with me, God bless him. To be sure, my father insisted Jim's wages in Boston went towards my tuition, but at least it gave Jim a chance for an education again. Only this time, I can't say I taught him anything, he just devoured every book I got for every class and anything else I could find for him."

Although Jasper had steered clear of duels at Harvard, he'd still spent the bulk of his first year drinking interspersed with interludes of classes and studying. His saving grace was the food at his dormitory. "Truly vile," he told Cara with a smile. It convinced him, his second year, to room and board with a Unitarian couple Jim found in Cambridge, the Wilsons, whose children were grown and left home. Priding themselves on being broad-minded, the Wilsons also allowed Jim a rough room over their carriage house with his meals to be taken in the kitchen. They never quite cottoned on to the fact that Jim was technically a slave and not a servant and would have been mortified if they'd known. Most importantly, the Wilson husband and wife disdained liquor and disapproved severely when Jasper came home after a night at the tavern. Jasper could've found a new place to live, but the two were kindly, affectionate, and, for some unknown reason, fond of him. Jasper's drinking diminished instead, and his studying increased. By the close of his time in Boston, he found himself relatively sober and graduating near the top of his class.

In the middle of his last term, his father died. With his brother's blessing, Jasper didn't return home until he completed his studies, and when he did, he found Sleety Pines transformed. His brother's wife and first baby enlivened the big house now, while the plantation, well managed, had actually become profitable. And Jasper had inherited his own piece of land and slaves to do with what he willed. Jim returned with him to Sleety Pines. "I knew at the time I should've freed him. I made him a driver instead. My overseer, really. I didn't have another." Jim accepted the duty and did what he could to make a tolerable environment for Jasper's slaves, many of whom Jim was related to since his mother had gone on to bear seven children after him. For his part, Jasper gloried in his coming of age, thrilled to be considered a man of the county, a planter, someone important and in charge of his own destiny. He courted a girl in Walterboro, a daughter of a lawyer. She was pretty, shy, but refined, like his mother. He built her a house. For a year or two, with Jim's management, he prospered. And he drank. And drank. And listened to Jim less and his wife less, and drank more, first in the company of other young men, then later alone, in his room. Like his father.

"I turned into him," Jasper said simply. "Looking back on it, it was appalling, but I couldn't see it. I couldn't affix blame to myself for my wife's tears and growing health problems. I couldn't see myself responsible for our lower yields when I overruled Jim's advice and realigned our tasks to make the slaves work harder. I was arrogant and foolish and destructive of everything, including myself. I drank truly phenomenal amounts of liquor. Needless to say, growing up the way I did, I'd had practice." He averaged a bottle of whiskey a night. Sometimes he put away half of another. He would catch Jim and his wife talking together, talking about him, and he'd be furious. His brother tried to intervene to no avail. Elizabeth grew unhappier and unhappier. She was going to have a child while her husband was lost in a liquor-fueled world of his own. "I was never violent like my father, well other than the duels," Jasper said. "But those never arose out of violence, they were more out of sheer stupidity. I never struck a slave in any fashion. I never even raised my voice to Elizabeth. But when I was drunk, I could be cruel, so cruel with words. I started caring more for drink than I did about the people I was responsible for, who looked to me for survival. Something took me over."

The baby, a son, lived only a day before he died. His wife lived a week longer. Barricaded in his room, Jasper had seen her only once between his son's death and her own. "Her brother was right to call me out," Jasper said. "He loved his sister, and her death was my fault. I should've let him kill me."

Cara closed her eyes. "Please don't say that."

"There actually wasn't much left of me to kill at that point. My face was bloated; I had spidery veins and terrible bouts of nosebleeds. Much of my body was wasted. My clothes hung off me like they belonged to another man. The oddest thing was watching my skin and eyes turn yellow. It was clear I was killing myself, and maybe that was what I wanted."

After the duel with Elizabeth's brother, Jim had faced Jasper down, asking him if he wanted to kill himself, why didn't he just put a bullet through his brain? He was squandering his life, him, a rich white man who had everything.

"I told him I had nothing to live for. Then the crazy coot started talking to me about China. I couldn't have been less interested, but he kept talking and talking and he wouldn't let me be. I was twenty-six.

There was reason to live, he kept saying. I could see the world. I began to realize he wanted to see the world, and somewhere deep down I had an inkling I owed him that. My brother was supportive. He agreed to buy my land from me over several years to let me raise cash, and he took over running my part of the plantation. He was probably glad to see me gone. I would've been."

"He probably wanted to do anything to see you survive," Cara said.

Jasper smiled a little. "Perhaps. People in my life have always loved me more than I deserved."

"How can you say that?" Cara said. "You deserved both a mother and father who loved and cherished you until you grew into a man. You didn't experience anything close to that."

"But I had Jim, Uncle Howard, Henry, and my brother who all accommodated themselves over and over to my poor behavior."

"They were just trying to make up for the loss of your mother. You see that, don't you?" Cara asked softly.

"You lost your mother," Jasper noted. "At a younger age than I did."

"But I had a kindly father, and Henry and Mary and Ceres to love me," Cara said. "Even Aunt Winnie did her part, however strangely she expresses her affection." She looked up at him earnestly in the room's faint light. "What you did, choosing to live and recover, choosing to face your sins and repent them, makes you deserving of love. Makes you worthy of love. You've earned your redemption so fully."

Jasper looked at the young woman in his arms a long moment. "So you're saying I had to nearly kill myself with drink; travel to the other side of the world; have needles stuck into me nearly every day for six months; shave my head, sit on a stone floor, and eat rice for a year; nearly die of fever in Africa; fritter a few years away in Europe; come back, get in a dither over Eustace Woods and spectacularly fail to change the course of Beaufort's history; then free my slaves while realizing I'd made the biggest mistake of all time in leaving you behind. And because of all that, I deserve you. Well, if that's the case—" He paused.

She looked at him questioningly. "If that's the case . . . ?"

He smiled. "Then it was entirely worth it."

Chapter Thirteen

Cara sat in her parlor looking prim and annoyed. In the room with her stood Minnie, her short arms folded determinedly across her chest. By way of her yard boy Cara had sent a note to Villa d'Este for Jasper, and they were waiting for him to arrive. Though Cara would've rather waited alone, it was clear Minnie intended to remain right where she was until Marse Wainwright appeared.

Jasper both smiled and frowned when he saw the scene, wondering why he'd been sent for with such urgency.

Minnie spoke first. "Yuz gwine make huh keep huh word, Marse Jaspuh. She prommus. She prommus, and she be sorry, see if she don't, if she don't keep it."

Jasper raised an eyebrow at Cara. She pursed her lips. "I plan to keep my promise. It's just that now is not the right time."

"Yuz twenny-one, ain't yuh?" Minnie said. "Sound like uh good time tuh me since dats what yuh prommus."

"Why don't you tell me what this is about?" Jasper said to Cara.

Cara glanced briefly at Minnie. Though she might have preferred privacy with Jasper for her explanation, she yielded to the circumstances at hand. "Minnie says if I don't free her, she'll acquaint the world with the truth about Eustace Woods."

"No," Minnie said, pointing. "Yuh promise tuh free me if I write all yo Eustuz lettuh and don't tell nobody. Yuh say yuh free me when yuh turn twenny-one. Well, yuz twenny-one now, an I write dose lettuhs and din't tell nobody. Uh deal iz uh deal."

"Well," Jasper said, looking between the two women. "I tend to think a deal is a deal, too."

"I knew you'd take her side," Cara said. "The trouble is, Jasper, I can't spare Minnie right now. I need her to do my hair, at least through the wedding."

"You could pay her wages. Minnie, how about if Cara pays you two dollars a week, starting from the week she turned twenty-one until we leave for Europe. Unless you'd like to come with us to Europe."

"Huh," Minnie said. "Luk I wannuh do dat. I wannuh be uh dress-makuh in Chaastun. Dats what I gwine do. An huh," she pointed at her mistress, "ain't gwine stop me."

Cara looked up at him. "I'll need some kind of maid after the wedding, Jasper."

He nodded. "We'll work it out. Maybe Henry has someone you can train." He addressed Minnie again. "You can be a dressmaker, Minnie, but not in Charleston. At least you can't be free in Charleston without the state legislature approving it, and I can tell you right now that's unlikely. If you really want to be free, you'll have to go north, to Philadelphia, New York or Boston."

Minnie frowned, wondering if she was being lied to. She'd been to Charleston. She knew the shop she wanted to work at, the free black neighborhood she wanted to live in. What good was being free if she couldn't do as she wanted? Eventually, Jasper brokered a compromise that Minnie would stay until the wedding, train a new maid for Cara, and then go to Charleston. While she wouldn't be officially free, no one would take her wages from her, and she could do as she pleased, so long as she kept out of trouble and took care not to get herself noticed. Minnie left satisfied. She'd heard enough from Spit Jim to believe that Marse Jasper was one of the few white men who would actually keep his word to a Negro. That was why she'd insisted he be brought into the matter.

Cara was nettled by the outcome. "What I don't understand is why Minnie doesn't love me," she said. "She never has, even when we were girls. Her clothes are some of the nicest of any slave in Beaufort; she's never been whipped or hit or had to work in the fields a day in her life.

I even educated her, taught her to read and write years ago so she could copy out the plays I used to make up. And what do I get for all this? She acts like she hates me."

Jasper shrugged. "She's a slave, Cara. You keep her from living her life as she wants. If it were me, I wouldn't like you either."

"But all Mary's slaves love her. They would never, ever talk to her the way Minnie does to me."

"Well, Henry wouldn't let them for one, and two, Mary hasn't entrusted them with a secret that could not only ruin her reputation for all time, but probably cause a significant cleavage in South Carolina politics. My dear, you left yourself extremely vulnerable."

Cara shrugged a shoulder. "I knew the risk when I took it, I just had no idea it would turn my maid insolent. Do you have any idea the work it took to train her?"

Jasper smiled. "I can't even imagine."

"When you educated Jim, he was grateful and wanted more. Minnie always acted like I was pulling out her teeth. The howling she did. She never once opened a book because she wanted to read it herself."

"I educated Jim for his purposes. You educated Minnie for yours. There's a difference," Jasper pointed out gently.

The telegraph was coming to Beaufort. A line from Charleston would follow the existing set of poles that ran along the railroad line to Savannah, and then at Yemassee it would divert and drop down to the Sea Islands. There'd been an electromagnetic line from Columbia to Charleston for over two years now, and the citizens of Beaufort, while looking down their noses on such flighty apparatus, had secretly been anxious about Charleston's leap ahead of them. Combined with the impending wedding of Cara Randall to Jasper Wainwright, Beaufort was astir with excitement. The wedding would take place at St. Helena's Church, naturally, with a wedding dinner to follow at Villa d'Este. And then there would be a party that would last much of the night because even Henry Birch couldn't deny the town a proper celebration at the marriage of his precious niece to his beloved cousin. It would be the last event of the season in Beaufort, before everyone packed up and returned to the quieter, calmer climes of their plantations, the workings of which, after all, they must attend to some time or another.

The first fittings of the new dresses for Cara's trousseau had taken place in Charleston, and a return trip was scheduled. The pace of parties and preparations was actually quite strenuous, and Cara looked a little pale to Mary up in Mary's bedroom as she sorted through her lace collars for one she just knew would work with Cara's new dark plum dress.

Mary put her hand to Cara's forehead. "Are you well, child? You looked peaked."

"Oh, Aunt Mary," Cara said, her eyes brimming with tears.

"What, dear? What is it?"

"I'm . . . I'm . . . with child," she blurted out, and the tears started falling copiously.

Mary had to smile as she hugged her niece close. "My dear girl, what did you expect? But there's no need to be upset. The wedding's in three weeks. It'll work out just fine."

Cara took the handkerchief Mary offered her. "I know, it's just that I feel so . . . strange. Not like myself. I wanted time, just Jasper and me together . . ." She left off, faltering.

"Ah dear, don't we all," Mary said, patting her hand. "But it's nature's way. And it'll be fine. You'll see. Are you going to tell Jasper?"

Cara looked up at her aunt with distress. "His first wife died in childbirth. Why did it have to happen so quickly?"

When Henry heard the news, he wasn't disturbed. In fact, he didn't have to think about it for more than five seconds before he decided to divulge the information to the father-to-be.

"Why didn't she tell me herself?" Jasper asked, frowning as he rode with Henry on horseback towards Port Royal in the cool October morning air.

Henry shrugged, eyeing his cousin. "Can I congratulate you?" Jasper looked over at him questioningly. "Are you happy?" Henry asked him.

"Yes," Jasper said. "Of course."

"So you're not morbidly fearful."

"Because of Elizabeth? No, Cara's stronger than Elizabeth ever was."

Henry nodded. "I entirely agree. She's going to be fine."

But when Jasper gently asked Cara about it, she wept in his arms. "I'm so sorry."

"How on earth is it your fault?" Jasper asked with a smile. "Come now, come. I'm delighted. Truly."

She looked up at him. "I know it's silly to be melancholy, but I feel so peculiar these days. Not like myself. Jasper, if we go away, I can't have this baby without Aunt Mary. I just can't."

"All right," he said. "We'll come back for your confinement. We can wait to travel to Europe until the baby's a few month's old."

"We can?" Cara asked. "We can still travel with a baby?"

"People do," Jasper reassured her. But now, with a certain amount of trepidation, he realized he'd likely be spending a large part of the next year in South Carolina.

The whole town was gathered outside Ensler's Dry Goods where a small storeroom had been turned into Beaufort's first telegraph office. A young man had been brought in from Charleston to operate the instrument, as well as transfer his skills of deciphering and sending code to a store clerk whose wages were a great deal less costly.

The crowd was in a twitter, the ladies all wearing wool walking dresses wrapped with their best India shawls because even though the fair weather held, the cooler temperatures of autumn had set in. At this point the harvest had been completely shorn from the fields, and since Mother Nature had cooperated this year, raining at just the right time and not raining at others, then baking the fields with a substantial amount of heat but not too much, yields had been excellent. Cotton was being ginned and bagged (baling was too rough for the silky, long-staple fibers) and shipped to factors in Savannah or Charleston. Britain couldn't seem to get enough of Sea Island cotton this year, raising prices to a level unseen in over a decade. Profits were so good, in fact, that a number of planters who'd bought lots in town previous years but had been obliged to leave them unimproved were now drawing up plans and might have the framework of their structures in place by spring. A new Beaufort College was in the works; the Armory, decimated from fire two years previously, would soon be rebuilt. Beaufort was positively set for a building boom. Its citizens could look forward to more families in town, more parties, more balls, more social prominence in the state. It was all exceedingly pleasant.

The faces under bonnets and top hats gathered outside the store looked expectant. Just what was this newest marvel of the nineteenth century going to impart to them? News of some sort was likely. Ensler was talking of posting a twice-daily sheet of the latest telegraph reports, though the timing wasn't the best with everyone set to leave town in just two weeks.

Cara and Jasper stood near Henry and Mary, waiting for the first dispatch while the Birch boys milled around with the other children. The event was momentous enough that all the students in the town had been let out of school for the afternoon. There was a whisper in the crowd that something was happening. Then, yes, they could all hear clicks coming from the open window of the storeroom. Something was coming across on the wire, the technician furiously scribbling as he interpreted the noise. Here, at this very moment, Beaufort was in instant connection with Charleston, and, via that connection, the rest of the country. It was miraculous. News that a decade ago took days to travel could reach them in minutes. Charleston could be contacted in seconds. It was too phenomenal to truly comprehend. The buzz of the crowd rose to a crescendo when Samuel Ensler himself came out to read the missive that had mysteriously and invisibly hurled itself ninety miles down the electromagnetic wire like a message from the hand of God himself.

Ensler, new to such importance, cleared his throat. "Thirteen generals in Arad, Hungary were executed last week for fomenting rebellion in those parts." The crowd murmured its horror. "There is still no word on how the writer, Edgar Poe, who died October 7th, conveyed himself from Washington to Baltimore where he was found in a disoriented condition in clothes not his own. He is now believed to have met his end due to cerebral inflammation."

"He was a drunkard," Henry muttered to Mary. "That's the end he met." Mary elbowed him slightly. After glancing at Jasper who had done his best not to hear, Henry said no more.

"And our last item is that the European pianist, Frederic Chopin, passed from this world on the 17th of October in Paris at the age of thirty-nine. Of consumption."

How tragic, everyone agreed. Wasn't that the composer Miss Randall admired so much? Some people offered her their condolences as the crowd began to disperse. The excitement of being instantly attached to the rest of the world was over. Beaufort was changed, and, yet, still exactly the same. After all, how important could rebellious generals, drunken writers, and consumptive pianists really be?

"Are you all right?" Jasper said with concern. Cara looked so odd. Of course, the pianist, Chopin, had been important to her.

"It's too late," she said. "It's already too late."

"Darling, I'm sorry about Maestro Chopin. He was a great man. I wish you'd been able to hear him play."

Cara looked up at him. "Do you believe in premonitions?"

Jasper looked her over. "Not usually. Come, you look cold. Your shawl's not warm enough. Walk with me back to the house."

Cara was quiet; Jasper was out of sorts. The brief connection with the outside world had been troubling. He'd received a letter from Jim, telling him his various siblings and mother were settling in well in Boston. Most had found jobs through a church that was sponsoring them. Jim was doing a little doctoring in the free Negro community and had obtained work editing articles for an academic journal through a connection Jasper had given him. As he read the letter over again in his room at Villa d'Este, Jasper smiled. Then he looked out his window that faced the piazza and the river beyond. The light had changed, the days were shorter, but though the golden hours were waning, the sunlight glinting on the mercurial water held its beauty in the autumn haze. The sky was often filled now with great vees of migratory birds heading from the northern latitudes towards warmer climes. Mary and Henry would be off to Silver Oaks soon. Jasper expected he would move into the Randall house. And wait as patiently as possible for his opportunity to go north.

Cara had encouraged Jasper to invite Jim to the wedding. Naturally not in the same sense as the white guests, but he could sit upstairs in the gallery with the other Negroes, including all the servants from both her house and Villa d'Este. And they would have a party for the Negroes to celebrate and make merry, though it'd be the day after the white folks' festivities, when there was time for it. Jasper, however, had demurred, unwilling to put Jim at risk by bringing him back to South Carolina.

"Jasper, you know everyone feels terribly about Hock," Cara said. "I even heard one of the Rhett brothers admit it was a shame. And they've run Winslow Dotter out of the state, just like Henry insisted on." Dotter, his six barefoot children, his hollow-eyed wife, and his toothless, pipe-smoking mother-in-law had passed through town in a wagon the previous Tuesday, his two ragged slaves trailing behind on foot. Last anyone heard, they were headed west, possibly to Mississippi where, according to hearsay, land was still fertile and cheap. Not that anyone much cared what happened to a poor Cracker like him. "No one is going to harm Jim while he's here. Truly. Send for him," she urged.

But Jasper had not written the letter. What he didn't confide to Cara was his doubt that Jim would want to come. After all, Jim hated South Carolina, he'd discouraged Jasper from Cara, and when they'd parted in Philadelphia, he'd frankly told Jasper he was out of his mind to return to the South. Further feeding Jasper's misgivings was the realization that after a dozen years, Jim was now at last truly free with even his family members no longer under Jasper's dominion. The only bond left between them was that of affection, and though Jasper felt that tie strongly, he couldn't blame Jim if other affiliations pulled at him with more force. He'd rather not put it to a test.

A little over a week before the wedding, after the ginning had begun and Henry had confidence that it would continue in an orderly fashion, he agreed to accompany Cara, Mary, and Jasper to Charleston for a few days for Cara's final fittings. Though it was painful, Winnie had generously consented to stay with the Birch boys so that their final days of study would not be interrupted. Besides, the dressmaker had acquired a newfangled lockstitch machine that made a dreadful racket, and Winnie could no longer stand to spend her usual hours in the shop ensuring the seamstresses did their work properly.

The trip on the steamer was pleasant enough, and Charleston was its familiar gay self. Intrigued by the daguerreotype studio, Henry had a portrait of himself and Mary made despite his wife's embarrassment in having her "condition" documented. After that, he cajoled Jasper into sitting for a likeness with Cara. When they saw the proofs the next day, Henry laughed at the image of himself and told Mary she looked far too stern, a portrayal that completely misrepresented her. He thought Jasper had an unfair advantage with his elegant Parisian fashions and was delighted that Cara looked as lovely in tones of black, grey and silver as she did in real life. Copies were ordered that would be shipped to Beaufort the following week.

For the women there was still a great deal of shopping to do, fittings at the dressmaker, and Cara even squeezed in a piano lesson with Maestro Pavini. Henry visited the wine merchants to restock his cellar as well as his favorite tobacconist to replenish his inventory of cigars. Jasper took advantage of Charleston's greater availability of merchandise to do some shopping of his own.

They stayed at the newest, most elegant hotel on the Battery. Though Henry expected the affianced couple to be circumspect on this trip, he booked a room for Jasper on the third floor and a room for Cara next to his and Mary's room on the second, just to be sure. Their social calendar was prodigiously full, and if they'd so chosen, they could have dined and supped every meal with friends of Henry and Mary who were delighted to welcome the engaged couple into their circle. Henry insisted they take a break, however, to try out a newly opened restaurant. "Just like New York City and Paris, don't you think, Jasper?" Henry said glancing around with obvious pride at the sophistication that the South had achieved. With a gentle smile, Jasper concurred.

The third day of the trip the weather had been especially fine, and by nightfall the upper floors of the hotel had heated up substantially. Due to tides that required an early morning departure, Henry decided they would skip that evening's party in order to return to the hotel at a reasonable hour. Before preparing for bed, Cara opened her windows and went out to sit on the piazza leading off from her room. With the weather so mild, it was pleasant to look out over the gardens of Charleston and the moon reflecting on the harbor beyond as she allowed her chamber to cool off. In the moonlight she thought she could just make out the shadowy outline of Fort Sumter still unfinished on its man-made island in the distance.

"Henry, Cara told me today that after the baby's born, they'll be leaving the South." Mary's worried voice came through a window that was ajar next to Cara's elbow. Though Cara knew she shouldn't, she couldn't resist listening.

"Jasper told me the same thing," Henry said. "Don't worry about it, dear."

"How can I not worry?" she said. "I'm ready to cry my eyes out."

"Because I know Cara. They'll come back."

"What makes you so sure? You know Jasper is chomping at the bit to be gone. If it weren't for the Professor, they'd leave the day after the wedding."

"They'll leave for a while and come back for the baby's birth. Then they'll leave again, but they'll be back. You'll see. You can't raise children flitting around the world like Jasper's been doing. Once she has her own brood, this is where Cara will want to be, with her family, her people, her roots. Deep in her core, her attachment to this place is not something she can change."

"But she promised they wouldn't live here."

"She'll renege on that promise. Yes, right now she's desperately in love with Jasper and would do anything to please him. But you know how women change when they have a baby. Cara will be a fierce, devoted mother. Sacrificing her own prerogatives is all very noble, but once she has sons, she'll realize she's denying them their birthright—their wealth, their power, their position in society. Her children's future will eat away at her until what the South has to offer them will pull her back here like an invisible cord. And Jasper, well, he loves her enough, he'll go along to make her happy."

"But Henry—" Mary's voice was low, almost a whisper. "Will he be happy? He's started again. You could smell it on him tonight."

There was a pause. "I know. He must have a bottle in his room. But Mary, between you and me and Cara, we can manage it. Living here, he may not be ecstatic, but he'll have Cara and a family. He'll be happy enough."

"How much do you think he's been drinking?" Mary asked.

"Hard to say," Henry said. "You could never tell with Jasper, even in the old days. He never showed it. It just destroyed him from the inside out."

"You really think they'll come back?" Mary said.

"Absolutely," Henry said. "They'll last three, maybe four years in Europe. Five, at the outmost. Look, darling, she's already insisting this baby be born in South Carolina. It's an excellent sign."

Mary was silent a moment. "If you really think so, then I'll do my best not to worry. After all, you're always right about these things."

Cara's heart was beating hard as she sat back in her chair. She'd smelled the liquor on Jasper tonight, too. It was the first time he had smelled like other men. How could her uncle say such things about her—that she would break the most heartfelt pledge she had ever made? That she would knowingly sacrifice the happiness and health of the man she loved beyond any other? She couldn't. She wouldn't. Deep in her heart, she must know she wasn't capable of such a betrayal.

In the hush of the quiet darkness Cara felt something on her arm. The moonlight allowed her to see that a mosquito had landed just above her wrist. Ordinarily she would've brushed it away before it could bite, but instead she watched as it protruded its delicate proboscis into her skin. With intense, focused effort, the insect drew a tiny droplet of her blood into its minuscule body before flying away. It didn't take long, and it didn't really hurt. The itching would come later.

One floor above, Jasper Wainwright summoned the night attendant for his floor.

"Suh?" the uniformed Negro asked.

Jasper handed him a bottle. "Take this. I don't care what you do with it. Drink it, sell it, whatever you wish. I don't want it." Jasper dropped twenty-five cents into his gloved hand for his trouble. The attendant later sold the bottle for another fifty cents to a sailor. Seventy-five cents that wasn't part of his wages and didn't have to be given to his master made a good night for him indeed.

Back inside his room, Jasper sat down at his writing desk and put his head in his hands. After some time, he straightened and wrote out a telegram. "Am marrying Miss Randall October Thirtieth stop Please come stop Will pay all expenses stop Regards Jasper." He wrote in the name and address of the recipient and then gave it to the night attendant, along with money to cover the fee and another tip to see that it got sent out from the telegraph office first thing in the morning.

Anxious for an answer, Jasper was considerably relieved when a day later back in Beaufort he received a brief telegram telling him Jim was on his way. Since his single drink in Charleston Jasper had adhered to his green tea with perseverance, though he'd observed that Henry, Mary and Cara were watching him with more care than usual. So they had noticed, he thought with a stab of shame and self-loathing, the like of which he'd hoped never to feel again. Well, the only person to blame for that was himself.

Still, Jim was coming. Jasper waited each day for Jim to follow his telegram, but he didn't arrive. Jasper even hoped he would show up on the morning steamer before the ceremony, but although he sent Sam, the stable boy, to check, Jim did not get off that boat. Jasper's brother, his wife, and their three children had come for the occasion, however, and were staying at Villa d'Este, causing general merry chaos as the two sets of children intermixed.

The wedding day was cool and faintly sunny, the sky pale blue beyond the changing red and golden leaves of the Sweetgum trees. The live oaks wouldn't drop any foliage, nor would the orange trees, but Beaufort definitely grew plainer and less lush as the year made its journey through the seasons. Winter in Beaufort was a time of quiet, of hibernation. A time as close to asceticism as the Sea Islands were likely to come. Clothes were packed, ballrooms shuttered, paintings and furniture covered. Most everyone would leave the day following the Randall-Wainwright wedding.

St. Helena's Church was festive with flowers that Winnie had over-seen, some specially shipped in by steamer from the south of Georgia via Savannah the day before. And Cara—Cara looked lovely. She wore a long-sleeved pale blue silk dress with flounces and lace and velvet banding at the hem. Keeping her part of her bargain, Minnie had ex-pertly arranged her mistress's luxuriant auburn hair with orange blossoms and the lightest of veils. Cara's color was high, and her eyes shone. She seemed so happy. It wasn't surprising that the prettiest girl in the county should make the most beautiful bride since—since—well, since her mother, most guests proclaimed after some reflection.

Mr. Wainwright, though reserved as he was prone to be, was cordial and relaxed. That he so clearly adored his intended was touching. That he regarded her as the most lovely and desirable of all women he had encountered in his extensive travels Beaufort took as a complement to itself, and returned the favor by holding him in esteem far higher than anyone acquainted with him as a boy would ever have thought possible.

Everyone settled into the pews knowing this would be the last wedding, the last party, the last social event of the season. After so many proposals and so much suspense, the town was delighted to witness Miss Randall becoming Mrs. Wainwright. For those who had unmarried daughters who could now have their turn center stage, it was a downright relief. Smullen Point would be renovated, and perhaps the Randall house would be enlarged. Even better, Jasper Wainwright might decide to build a newer, finer house altogether, one that was closer to the river. The couple would be an estimable addition to the town. Though rumor had it that their wedding journey would be extensive, it didn't matter. Beaufort would be waiting for them when they returned.

As Cara walked down the aisle, Jasper was fleetingly reminded of how she had looked that morning of the duel. Her dress had been pale blue then as well, with the ethereal white netting all around her. For a bizarre moment, he saw her falling backwards, silently and forever falling away from him. But no, here she was, walking towards him on the frail arm of Professor Randall. Then she was standing next to him while Father Tomlinson intoned the words of the Episcopalian liturgy. Jasper hardly heard the prayers, the hymns, the passages from the Scriptures that proceeded at a slow but steady pace that would not be rushed for even the most impatient of grooms. Finally they were repeating their vows. Finally the ring was on her finger. They were wed. They exited the church in a splash of sunlight and received the hearty congratulations of the town while overhead the pealing bells in the steeple reflected their joy. At last they were in Henry's carriage that would take them to the Randall house before it returned to the church to pick up the Birch family and Professor Randall. After a short repose, Jasper and Cara would head to Villa d'Este for the grandest wedding dinner the town had seen in some time.

Jasper handed Cara into the carriage and then climbed in himself. As she leaned her cheek against his shoulder, he kissed the top of her head. "Are you tired, Mrs. Wainwright? I fear we have a great deal of socializing ahead before we retire tonight. But we'll have peace and quiet enough in the months to come."

"I feel . . . I feel odd," she said. It was then Jasper noticed she was shivering.

He sat up straighter. "Darling, are you ill?" He put his hand on her forehead.

"My head hurts," she said, folding her arms around her as she began to shake severely. "And I'm cold. It's all so curious."

Jasper took a blanket folded on the opposite seat and put it around her. "Let's get you home." But with such a short distance to travel, they were already there.

Jasper instructed Barstow, Henry's new coachmen, to go get Dr. Goode with some urgency. He might still be at the church, but if not, to scour the town to find him. Jasper helped Cara up the porch stairs. Once inside the front door, she was so weak he had to carry her up to her bedroom.

Henry arrived before Dr. Goode and scrutinized Cara, shivering in the bed under her blankets. "It's the ague?"

Jasper nodded. "When Dr. Goode gets here with the quinine we should be able to manage it."

"I'm s-s-sorry, Uncle Henry," Cara said. "A-b-b-bout the party."

Henry went over to her and took her hand. "Darling girl. Don't think about it for a minute. I'll take care of everything. You just get well."

And then Henry left the house to see what was taking Dr. Goode so long to get there.

Professor Randall was told his daughter wasn't feeling well and was resting. Professor Randall wasn't feeling well either, but it was some time before a servant checked on him and found him collapsed on the floor of his room. Now Dr. Goode had two patients to attend to. For Professor Randall there was little but palliative doses of laudanum to ease the pain and a nurse to see to his comfort. Minnie was given this task as Ceres was needed for the more strenuous care of Cara.

The disease was progressing rapidly, and the quinine wasn't having the desired effect of controlling Cara's fever which was now raging. Cool baths and even ice were used. Mary sent over one of her maids to help Ceres with the tasks while Jasper hardly left Cara's side.

"It's just the ague," Jasper said to Dr. Goode in the hallway outside her room. "I've seen plenty of men survive it. Why isn't the quinine working?"

"There's more than one kind of ague, Jasper," Dr. Goode said. "Some forms of malaria are extremely virulent."

"It's a damn shame Spit Jim's not here." Henry had joined them, worried, irritable, pacing.

"He should be," Jasper said. "He said he was coming to the wedding. I don't know where he could be."

"So you did invite him?" Henry said.

"Where's Aunt Mary?" Cara asked when she saw her uncle.

Henry took her hand. "She's with the guests. She'll come soon." But this wasn't true. Henry had forbidden Mary to see Cara. "I can't risk you," he told her as tears streamed down her face. "You know the ague hits pregnant women the hardest."

"The air in Beaufort's good," Mary pleaded. "It was Charleston that did it, you know it was. They said on the telegraph report that there's been an outbreak there."

But Henry was implacable in his terror. "We don't know what caused it, the air or something else. I can't let you near her."

The guests gathered at Villa d'Este were somewhat surprised by the absence of the newlyweds and their hosts but were reassured that the bride had a headache, was resting, and would probably join them later. In any event the meal should not wait, or the food that had taken days to prepare would go to waste. Winnie and the Senator presided over the affair as guests seated themselves at Mary's great dining table, at tables borrowed from Winnie set up in the front parlor, and at tables borrowed from Mrs. Patterson set up in the ballroom, all beautifully decorated with flowers and linens and lain with fine china and silver. A score of slaves had been imported from Silver Oaks to cook and serve and clean for the event. As the meal progressed, information circulated that Dr. Goode now thought the bride's illness quite serious, subduing the laughter and conversation at the finely laid tables. As soon as the

Beaufort elite had finished their food and drunk their wine, they departed in their finery in a parade of carriages that stretched for blocks. There would be no evening party, no great celebration. All the candles that had been bought would remain untouched and unlit. The citizens of Beaufort would be isolated on their plantations until February, when they might make the trek to Charleston for the Jockey Club races and St. Cecilia's Ball. Beaufort would not see mint juleps on its piazzas or hear fiddles in its ballrooms again until April. The townsfolk all hoped to find Cara well and dancing in their fair city when the warm weather returned.

Mary was wild to see Cara and with collusion from Jasper managed to steal into the sickroom while Henry was distracted sending urgent telegrams to various contacts in Charleston to see if Spit Jim had made it that far. Mary, so pregnant and heavy now, spent fifteen minutes at the side of her precious darling, holding her hand and trying not to cry as she left. Winnie visited, too, but only for a short time as she hated illness and was confident in the efficacy of Dr. Goode. Afternoon faded into evening with doses of quinine and Henry appearing intermittently.

"I should've her let her go to that college in the north," Henry said brooding in the dimly lit room as the clock ticked towards midnight. "I should have listened to her. Why didn't I?"

Dr. Goode put a hand on his shoulder. "How would that have made a difference? Don't reproach yourself, Henry. It won't help, and it'll only cause you grief."

Henry left shortly after midnight because he had to arrange for Mary and the boys to be off to Silver Oaks first thing in the morning, as far away from disease and the ague as he could get them. Jasper and Dr. Goode sat all night in Cara's room dozing in chairs while she periodically stirred and muttered incoherently. It was aging, grey-haired Ceres whose eyes never closed, who wiped her darling girl's brow, who changed her nightgown and sheets when they were wet from sweat, who regularly lifted her head to help her sip water.

Jasper was in India again, gazing down at the pit. The tiger, ferocious and enormous, was hurling itself up, trying to grasp him, pull him down with it. And there was Cara, falling backwards into the hole, eternally falling, him reaching for her and missing, always just missing . . .

Jasper woke with a start to see Cara awake. Dawn was breaking, suffusing the room with pallid, grey light. Still in his wedding clothes, he rose and went to her. She smiled faintly. "This is for the best. You'll see. I would've tied you to the South, destroyed you. This way you'll be safe. You'll survive."

"Cara, what are you saying? As soon as you're better, we'll travel and see the world. Focus on getting well, darling. Promise to think only of that."

She shook her head. "I wouldn't have been content in Europe. I would've brought you back here to raise our children. Henry said so, and he's always right about these things."

"No, he's not always right," Jasper said through gritted teeth. "And I'll march him up here and have him admit it. Cara, you don't know if you'd like Europe—you've never been there. There's so much you've never experienced. We'll go to symphonies, operas, ballets. We'll tour the antiquities in Rome; I'll take you to see the genius of Giotto, Michelangelo, da Vinci. And if you don't like Europe, we'll go someplace else. It doesn't matter. Just get well, darling. That's all I care about. Just get well."

She gazed up at him, her eyes huge and burning. "I love you with all my soul. Remember me."

Her fever returned, and she grew less lucid. Dr. Goode grew more worried. And then Minnie came in to whisper in his ear. Professor Randall had left this earth a few moments before, never knowing his daughter's predicament.

Henry came through the door, furious. "They had him in a jail in Charleston. Accused him of being a free black sailor, pretending they had a right to lock him up. Someone's going to pay for this, believe me. She any better?" Dr. Goode could only shake his head.

"Just hang on," Henry whispered to his niece who was barely responsive. "Spit Jim will be here soon, darling, so soon. Hang on."

Mary and the boys were being rowed to Silver Oaks. Cara's liver was swelling. As the sun rose overhead she slipped into a coma.

"How can this be happening?" Jasper said desperately. "Yesterday she was strong and healthy. It's just the ague. I've seen plenty of men live through it. Plenty."

With Cara unconscious, it was difficult to dose her with quinine, but her fever didn't seem to be the trouble any more. A little after noon, she took in a rasping breath and then let it out, her exhale like the wind sighing on a frozen morning. It was clear what it meant. After feeling for her pulse, Dr. Goode laid the limp hand down on the bed.

Jim came into the room. He noted Ceres in the corner, weeping into her apron. He saw how Jasper, Henry and Dr. Goode stared down at the motionless patient. As he came toward them, they looked up with vacant eyes, parting from the bed to give him room. He picked up Cara's wrist, still warm, and felt for her pulses. The creases on his face deepened. Then, for his own information, he looked into her mouth to see her tongue and palpated her liver. At last he straightened.

"I'm sorry," he said to Jasper. "So very sorry. Is there anything I can do?"

Jim had never seen Jasper in such pain, and he'd seen the man in pain before that would break most men in two. "Bring her back?" Jasper said. And the three white men in the room looked at him hopefully, as if this were actually an act he could perform.

Jim put his arm around Jasper. "Come. Come." And he walked Jasper out of the room. Dr. Goode followed. Left behind with his beloved daughter, Henry put his hand over his face and began to weep as uncontrollably as Ceres.

Jasper was in St. Helena's graveyard, leaning against an old grave while gazing at a new one. He wore a black top hat and black overcoat against the cold fingers of November wind. The sky was grey. It would rain soon. Cara was buried beside her mother's grave that she had so scrupulously tended, her father's new one adjacent. There was no headstone yet, but Henry would see to that. Cara Wainwright, it would say. 1828 – 1849. Beloved wife and daughter.

Jim came up behind him. "Steamer's ready to leave. Time to go."

"Did I fail her, Jim?" Jasper asked. "Did I not deserve her? How can life be this cruel?"

Jim put his hand on his shoulder. "Jasper, this is the South. There ain't going to be any happy endings here for a long time to come. Now come with me. Come. It's time to go." And Jim physically helped Jasper to his feet and propelled him to the dock.

Epilogue

At breakfast, Jasper handed Robert Birch a copy of *The New York Times* dated December 12, 1861. It'd taken four days to cross the Atlantic Ocean to reach London. After picking it up with distaste, Robert began to read the article Jasper had indicated.

Looking Toward Charleston
Beaufort Occupied.

The intelligence which we publish to-day from Hilton Head warrants an outlook for coming business in South Carolina. Gen. Thomas Sherman has at length determined to occupy Beaufort; and at the sailing of the latest steamer had dispatched an advance guard of one thousand men to hold that point. From private advices we are able to announce that half of Sherman's whole division is now or soon will be concentrated at Beaufort.

It is at least something to know that this advance carries the Stars and Stripes twenty miles nearer Charleston. The whole country has fixed its eyes on that spot, and can never more rest content unless things are making toward its capture. The mode in which this is to be effected it is willing to leave in the fitting hands—so be, only, that, in someway, it is being brought about. Gen. Sherman's way, if not

Napoleonic exactly, is, at least, sure and safe. Those who have felt impatience that the month's possession of Port Royal has not brought forth all the fruit they had expected should, at least, put it to the credit side that our forces have so fortified their position on Hilton Head Island as to render it practicably impregnable. This, thoroughly secured as it now is, can be held by five thousand men against all the force the rebels can bring against them.

Robert's attention was broken from the article as an eight-year-old girl with flame-red hair put her arms around his neck and kissed his cheek.

"Ginnie," Jasper chided gently, "let Robert be until he's finished reading the paper."

"It's all right," Robert said with a smile at the child. "I like her morning hugs. I'll miss them more than anything when I go."

Ginnie stomped her foot. "You're not going, Robert. I won't allow it."

Her father, whose dark hair and moustache were graying, and who wore his spectacles with increasing frequency these days, chided her again. "Let him finish reading the paper, child. Here, come have your breakfast, there's a girl."

Meanwhile, reinforcements such as those that have gone down under Butler's command, and others speedily to follow, will afford opportunity for new blows to be struck into the heart of the enemy's country. It is in this sense that we look upon the new move on Beaufort: it is part of a general plan, comprehending several distinct acts, one of the first which will be the seizure or destruction of the Charleston and Savannah Railroad, and all of which will be directly in the line of On to Charleston. If need be, Gen. Sherman can take the whole of South Carolina's brief Winter to do the business. But the vernal months must bring us to Charleston. That Spring bouquet the nation must have.

Robert's perusal of the horrendous account was interrupted once more, this time by the arrival of Caroline Wainwright, a slim, red-headed woman in her late thirties, who brought with her a fresh pot of tea. She joined them at the table. "Are you really thinking of going, Robert? Is it wise?"

Jasper nodded at the paper. "Let him finish the article, dear." With an understanding smile Caroline squeezed Jasper's hand. She knew he was anxious about his beloved town. He took her hand and didn't let it go, keeping it warm within his own. Their forearms rested in parallel on the tablecloth as they watched Robert read the newspaper.

> *It is easy to underrate the importance of the foot-hold we already have in South Carolina. The true measure of it is not how it affects us, but how it affects them. The thunder of cannon on their coasts awakens echoes in their souls more terrible than such sounds are wont to arouse; and the mere holding of a portion of their soil confounds them—for that hot-brained race hardly believed sacred Palmetto soil could be held. Those rebellious aristocrats know that the world knows their boasted strength is a hideous sham—that the major part of the white element of the State is not with them, and that the whole of the black elements gravitates from them by irresistible law. And while the iron front of advancing justice is hereafter to be always in sight of them, the mere Judgment we now have on their soil—and from which they despair to drive us—is a barbed arrow rankling in the side of that haughty, high-blown State.*

Robert folded the paper and placed it out of view. "What's most sickening is how they rejoice in our suffering." He stared out the window at the lifeless winter limbs of trees. "They took Beaufort first. Of all places. They took us first."

"It makes a strong foothold," Jasper observed.

"I should've been there," Robert said. "I should've helped defend it."

"It doesn't sound like the Confederates put up much of a fight," Jasper pointed out gently. "Without a navy or real fortifications, how could they? Your being there wouldn't have changed anything."

"But I've got to go back, don't you see? The war will start in earnest now. I can't stay here studying books while my brothers are fighting."

"Your father was so thrilled with you being up at Oxford," Caroline reminded him. "I thought he was going to burst with pride when he brought you here your first term. He wanted you to take your degree more than anything."

Robert looked down at his plate. "In a way, I'm glad that steamer killed him last year. This war would've broken his heart." It'd been a boiler explosion on the passage from Beaufort to Charleston. Henry had been en route to visit his son, Hugh, who was studying law. All aboard had died. "This evacuation was so hard on Mother. Billy said she didn't care about the silver, but she wanted to disinter father and Cara's coffins right out of St. Helena's churchyard and take them with her. It tore her up, leaving them to the Yankees." Robert glanced uneasily at Jasper, realizing he might have said the wrong thing.

The remark appeared to have no impact on the older man. "I'm going to write to your mother," Jasper said, "and ask her to come to us with your sister. She's already had to endure so much; there's no reason she should suffer through a civil war, too." With the Northern blockade ineffective so far, mail was still reliably getting through to the South. For the time being. With a naval base now in Port Royal, the Yankee blockade would strengthen quickly.

"You think it's going to get worse?" Robert said.

"I think it's going to get much worse," Jasper replied.

"Well, you can try," Robert said. "Her letter last week said she's staying in Charleston for the next few months anyway. But I doubt she'll leave the South as long as Billy, Hugh and I are there."

Jasper evaluated the young man who looked so much like his father. "Robert, remember, after this war's over, whatever circumstances you and your brothers are in, whatever condition Villa d'Este and Silver Oaks are in, contact me, and I'll help you get back on your feet." For the last decade Henry had sent a portion of his cotton profits to Jasper to invest in British and European stocks. The money was for his family alone. He'd absolutely forbidden any of it to be used to finance a Southern war against the North. The stock certificates would stay in Jasper's hands for the time being so no one would be tempted. Henry had even allocated funds for his mulatto children and slave concubine. Jasper hoped he would be able to track them down when hostilities ceased.

"We'll miss you, Robert," little Virginia said as she stood next to him, curling wisps of red hair falling across her forehead, "so terribly much. You will come back to us, won't you?"

"When the war's over," Robert said, "I'll come back. I promise. I could never stay away from my adorable Ginnie." And he gave her an affectionate squeeze.

Later, in his study that also served as his second office for the small publishing company he ran, many of its works abolitionist in nature, Jasper glanced at a quartet of gleaming silver frames on his desk. One held a daguerreotype of a proud Jim surrounded by his mother, brothers, sisters, and various nieces and nephews, taken in a studio in Boston. Jim had recently written that two of his nephews were doing their best to join the Union army, though they had not found this task easy going. The second frame showed a daguerreotype of Henry and Mary with the three Birch boys and their daughter, Emily, still nearly a baby, taken when Henry had brought the family to do a grand tour of Europe. Jasper had accompanied them for most of it. The third offered a photographic portrait of the Birch family, all slightly older, along with Jasper and Caroline, taken on the occasion of their wedding after Henry had brought the family across the Atlantic one more time to celebrate the event. Jim had been there, too. It'd been a fine day. The fourth held the most recent likeness, an ambrotype of Caroline and Virginia, his English roses.

There was another daguerreotype, taken long ago in Charleston and put away in a trunk that Jasper had not looked at in many years. The fragile image it held was too painful. But he'd always had a poor ability to forget, and some dreams still haunted him. Dreams of tigers and falling figures in pale blue, from which he would wake in a cold sweat with his arms stretched achingly into empty space. And there was Chopin's waltz in C-sharp minor with its ever-beckoning, ever-receding refrain. It'd played in his mind every day the last twelve years, and would, every day, for the rest of his life.

The days were short this far north in December, and though Jasper lived in a pleasant part of London, the winter fog could be grimy and close. He would soon need to light the lamp on his desk. As dusk gathered in the waning afternoon, Jasper sipped his green tea and began his letter to Mary, while Beaufort, four thousand miles away in her Yankee embrace, silently wept.

Historical note: *On November 7, 1861, when the success of the Yankee attack at Port Royal and the imminent enemy invasion was reported in Beaufort, the citizens of the town hurriedly packed and fled en masse in a period of twenty-four hours. Food was left on the tables, and the only possessions not parted with were those that could be packed into carriages or onto waiting steamers that whisked the residents to Charleston. Most property, including the vast majority of slaves, was left behind. When General Sherman's army arrived a month later, the town had been looted by Negroes finally free from their long history of captivity. Only one white man remained. The Union Army turned the grand homes of the town into headquarters and hospitals, preserving the structures while many other Southern towns were burnt to the ground. Beaufort's library collection was confiscated and shipped to New York, where it was prepared for sale and later, in a federal warehouse in Washington, destroyed in an accidental fire. After the war, most planter families, their sons dead, their plantations burnt, their Beaufort homes sold in government auctions for back taxes, never returned. Like Pompeii, the civilization of Beaufort had disappeared overnight.*

Discussion Questions

1. At South Carolina College a duel once arose when two young men grabbed a bread plate simultaneously and both refused to let go. How might the masculine code of honor in the South have increased the probability of the Civil War?

2. How did the shift from the Romantic Era to the Industrial Revolution influence both Beaufort and the onset of the Civil War?

3. Mary, Cara and Jim all stand outside on the dark porch listening to the white men inside discuss the future of the South. Compare the social, economic, and political disempowerment of white women in the antebellum South to that of African Americans.

4. Not all Southerners endorsed secession. Many, like Governor Aiken, were unionists and only reluctantly supported going to war against the North. What impulses towards secession still exist today? Did the founding fathers make a mistake by not giving states a way to withdraw from the contract of the Constitution as freely as they entered into it? What would life be like today if the South had seceded permanently from the United States?

5. Change and resistance to change are two of the main themes of the novel. Which characters change the most during the course of the story? When is it wise to hold true to one's values and convictions? When is it even wiser to flex and adapt and reconsider?

6. If Beaufort was the Garden of Eden, who were Adam and Eve, who was the Devil, and what was the apple?

7. Many languages and dialects find their way into *Beaufort 1849*, including Gullah, the Creole language of the slaves of the area, and most characters comprehend more than one, even if they don't speak it. How does the interplay of languages and bilingualism function in the story, and what does each language or dialect represent?

8. What role does the character of the freed slave, Jim, play in the novel? What role does the slave patrol play?

9. Every society has its dark and its light. What is the antebellum South's shadow? What is its light? In what way does the predicament of the South in *Beaufort 1849* correspond to issues we face in the twenty-first century?

Appreciations

Many people, many books, and many websites helped with the research and writing of *Beaufort 1849*. Some of my favorite references were first person accounts from the time period such as *A Diary From Dixie* by Mary Boykin Chesnut, *A Glance at the Interior of China* by Walter H. Medhurst, *The Cotton Kingdom, a Traveller's Observations on Cotton and Slavery in the American Slave States* by Frederick Law Olmstead, and *Born in Slavery: Slave Narratives from the Federal Writers' Project, 1936-1938*. *The History of Beaufort County, South Carolina 1514-1861* by Lawrence Sanders Rowland, Alexander Moore, and George C. Rogers was also essential. I would like to thank Kim Gundler for reading *Beaufort 1849* in manuscript form and giving me invaluable naturalist insight into the lowcountry area. (Sorry about the alligators.) Shamsi Creps, Christie Winn, and Byron Hollinshead also reviewed the manuscript with an eye to acupuncture, music, and history, respectively. Anne Stamats assisted me with the cover. Many other friends and family members gave me feedback and suggestions and patiently supported me through both writing and publishing. (Melinda Adams, and my husband, Peter Stamats, were especially forbearing.) A heartfelt thank you to you all.

For more on *Beaufort 1849*, including web links and historical resources, go to www.cabbage-king.com. Did you enjoy *Beaufort 1849*? Refer it to a friend!

CPSIA information can be obtained at www.ICGtesting.com
Printed in the USA

239488LV00001B/106/P

9 780967 178417